CONVENIENT LIES

ROBIN PATCHEN

JDO PUBLISHING

To Eddie
For the constant support and encouragement.
I couldn't do this without you.

ACKNOWLEDGMENTS

Thank you to my critique partners, Normandie Fischer, Kara Hunt, Jericha Kingston, Candice Sue Patterson, Sharon Srock, Pegg Thomas, and Terri Weldon. These ladies make me look good.

Thank you to my editor, Ray Rhamey.

Thank you to Lacy Williams for all your publishing help.

Thank you to my husband and children for supporting me in this venture.

Finally and most importantly, thank you, Lord, for the story idea and the ability to bring it together.

ONE

There were only two people Rachel Adams trusted. One was twelve days old, and the other had mysteriously quit answering her phone. At least Gram could be counted on to stand by her side, assuming Rae could get in touch with her. And Jean-Louis? The baby didn't know any better.

The betrayers were too many to count. Julien, though. His betrayal was the most recent, and the most brutal.

Rae pretended to sleep as his lips brushed her forehead, leaving behind the scent of his cologne. She didn't move as she listened to the snap of the lock, kept still while she imagined Julien making his way down the staircase to the first floor and across the black and white tiles in the foyer. The heavy carved door slammed one story below.

Hector would fall in step beside him. Rae had asked Julien once why he didn't have his guard pick him up in the car outside their building.

"And miss the morning walk through my favorite city? Never."

She could almost hear his teasing tone. Always with a smile. Always with that look in his eyes that made her feel so loved.

Would he nod to the men he left behind to guard her and Jean-Louis? Or did they stay in the shadows the way they did when she left the building? For her protection, or so he'd said.

Julien would stride down the street past the patisserie, which would just be opening for business, the scent of freshly baked croissants and yeasty loaves wafting around him.

A few minutes ticked by. Surely Julien was in his car, out of the parking garage, and on his way to his early morning meeting by now. And yet she waited. Last week, he'd left for a meeting only to return ten minutes later for one last kiss on his infant son's forehead. She couldn't chance that happening again, especially when he'd told her he might not make it home tonight. When fifteen minutes had passed and he hadn't returned, she flipped back the covers and jumped out of bed.

After a quick shower, she dressed and pulled her hair into a bun. She grabbed the clothes she'd need and shoved them into her suitcase. She spared one fleeting thought for the wardrobe filled with designer clothes back in Tunis, but she shook it off. What use would she have for those things now?

When she finished, she tiptoed into Jean-Louis's room and grabbed a handful of outfits for him. Not too many. He'd grow out of them in a few weeks, anyway.

The messenger bag she'd use as a carry-on was more suited for her laptop, but Julien had made her leave that back in Tunis when she'd been ordered to bedrest. "No more work for you, young lady." His charming smile hadn't set her at ease when he'd taken the laptop and her smart phone and handed them to one of his servants, who'd bowed quickly and disappeared. Julien had given her a cheap flip phone for emergencies. "Our child needs all your attention."

That's when she'd started to worry. Did he know she'd discovered his secrets?

The messenger bag was already packed with the baby gear

she'd need on the long trip. She lifted the interior flap and pulled out a manila envelope. She felt the flash drive she'd slid into it, along with a handful of photocopies. Maybe they'd save her. Maybe not.

She unlocked the ornately carved box on the top of her bureau, removed the jewelry from their protective boxes, and dropped them in a paper bag. Who would store thousands of dollars' worth of gemstones in a sack from the market? It looked like a pile of trinkets one might buy at a kiosk at the mall.

Finally, Rae dug a box from deep in the closet. She'd owned these items for years, worn them in Africa to fit in where western women often wouldn't. She hated them. She'd seen what the clothes meant for women all over the world. They would be the perfect disguise. Julien's guards would never suspect it was she who hid beneath.

She pulled the loose-fitting black abaya over her jeans and T-shirt, then fastened on her baby carrier. She added the wide black scarf around her shoulders and positioned it over the baby's sling. Yes, that should work as long as Jean-Louis kept quiet.

She pulled the note she'd written from her bedside drawer and reread it, just to be sure. *The hospital called. Gram's taken a turn for the worse, and she's not expected to pull through. Forgive me, but I have to see her. I'll call when we change planes this afternoon. Love, Rae.*

Love, Rae. Those last two words had been the hardest to write, not because they weren't true, but because, on some level, they still were.

She left the note on Julien's bedside table. No going back now.

She grabbed the second note and walked to his office. He kept the door locked, but the old-fashioned locks were easy enough to pick. She'd done it enough, it took less than a minute to get the door open. She opened the file cabinet and slipped the note into a file containing information on his *other* business, the one he'd kept from her. When Julien realized Rae wasn't where she said she'd be, he'd check his files. Then he would know. Either he would leave her alone because she could expose him, or he would hunt her down. She hoped he would choose the first. She glanced at the photograph of Julien and Jean-Louis on the desk, the one she'd snapped a week earlier. The love that shone in her husband's gaze was unmistakable. Tears stung her eyes. At least she knew that wasn't a lie. Maybe Julien loved his son enough to let him go.

She wouldn't count on it.

In the bedroom, she fastened the niqab around her head so only her eyes showed. After she dragged her suitcase to the front door, she returned to the baby's room, where she changed his clothes. His eyes blinked open, and she kissed his cheek. "Shh, baby. Go back to sleep."

He scrunched up his face as if he were about to cry. At least his cry wasn't that loud yet. At two weeks old, his little lungs could only make so much noise. She lifted him and rocked him until he relaxed against her shoulder.

As she eased him into the sling, he barely stirred. She draped the scarf over him, placed the messenger bag on top of the suitcase, and slipped out.

She lugged her suitcase down the stairs, through the center courtyard, and out a side door, where the tiny cab she'd ordered the night before waited for her in the alley. The taxi driver hefted her suitcase into the trunk while she glanced left and right, straining to see in the dim light of dawn. Julien's guards were nowhere in sight. The morning was quiet. Free of weapons and violence.

"Charles de Gaul, *s'il vous plaît*."

The drive to the airport seemed to take forever. Rae didn't relax until her flight's wheels lifted off the runway.

She kissed Jean-Louis's tender head, wiped the tears that had dropped onto his thin spray of hair, and whispered, "We're safe, for now."

Nearly nine hours later, Rachel pulled her suitcase to the curb at Logan International Airport. She dropped the abaya, scarf, and niqab, along with the remaining airline ticket, into the trash can, and climbed into a beat-up yellow cab. The taxi slid onto the highway and was quickly engulfed in the chaos of the traffic headed to downtown Boston.

Rachel Adams had disappeared.

TWO

Reagan McAdams had been gone more than a decade when Rachel resurrected her.

Although how her alias could resurrect her true identity, she wasn't sure. She did know that the woman she'd become in college, Rachel Adams, had to disappear, and fast. So Rachel would be Reagan McAdams again, the name she'd been given at birth. She'd return to her hometown until she collected Gram and got what she needed. And then she'd disappear again.

At least she'd stuck with the nickname Rae through it all, or else she'd be completely confused. Right now, too many choices at the coffee shop were enough to confuse her.

They'd been traveling for two days by the time Reagan and the baby crossed into Nutfield, New Hampshire. She'd had her fill of planes, trains, and automobiles, of spaces so small she could barely get comfortable. And then there was the taxi that stank of body odor and that cheap hotel, the only one that would agree to her cash-up-front, no-ID requirement. She certainly couldn't use her current ID. She wasn't willing to leave any crumbs for Julien to follow. So she'd settled for the horrible hotel, where it was just the baby, Reagan, and the varmints that called it home. All she could think about now was her comfortable bed and her beautiful grandmother.

She couldn't imagine why Gram hadn't answered the phone. Rae had tried to reach her the day after Jean-Louis —Johnny—had arrived, healthy and beautiful, weighing in at seven pounds, eleven ounces. She'd had to cajole the nurse into giving her his weight in pounds and ounces instead of grams. It hadn't mattered, because Gram hadn't picked up. Not that day, not any day since. Rae could understand if she'd forgotten to charge her cell, but the house phone? What could account for her not answering that? Perhaps the hearing loss was worse than Rae had understood. Not a shock at her age, and she'd never wanted to try hearing aids. Whatever the reason, Gram was Rae's rock. Her comfort. As soon as they stepped into her house, Gram would wrap them in her wrinkled arms and make everything all right.

But when she turned the clunker she'd bought in Manchester down the driveway to her childhood home, the place looked deserted.

In Gram's defense, it was nearly midnight, and she wasn't expecting them. She'd always kept the porch light on, but maybe she'd gotten out of the habit. Or maybe the light bulb had burned out. Or maybe Gram was sick.

No, Reagan wouldn't consider that. She couldn't wait to introduce Gram to little Johnny. She'd adore him and tell Rae how to be a mommy. And oh, how she needed those lessons.

Reagan stepped out of the car and breathed in the chilly fall air. It smelled so clean here, so fresh. She'd loved Tunis, and if things had been different, she knew she'd have fallen in love with Paris too. But here in the woods in New Hampshire, surrounded by the tallest trees, the prettiest leaves, the greenest grass, she felt embraced by comfort.

Not that she could see much of that in the moonlight, but her memory filled in the blanks.

Reagan freed her sleeping son from his car seat and kissed his head. "We're here." Joy bubbled up with her words and, despite her fatigue, or maybe because of it, she giggled. She grabbed the diaper bag from the backseat and headed for the house. Home. For all its dark memories, for all the secrets this place hid, it would always be home.

She knocked. Rang the doorbell. Waited. Knocked again.

When no lights came on, she dug her keys out of her purse. She'd been carrying this key on her key ring since childhood, and though she hardly got to use it, having it with her had always felt right. She slid it into the lock and turned the knob.

The door creaked as it always had. No other sounds greeted her, certainly not Gram's joyful gasp. Rae carried Johnny inside. Gram would be sleeping, of course. Still, why was it so quiet? And cold. The house felt hardly warmer than the air outside. She flipped the light switch. Nothing.

"Gram?" Her voice echoed off the walls. The only answer came from Johnny, who started at her shout and whimpered. Rae kissed the top of his head and patted his back. "It's all right, baby. We'll figure it out." She inched her way into the kitchen and hit the switch. Still dark. There'd always been a flashlight in the junk drawer. She made her way to it and pulled it open, thankful for the moonlight that streamed in through the kitchen window. She felt inside until her fingers touched the thick metal shaft. Thank goodness. She shined the light around the kitchen. Everything seemed to be in place. She headed for the stairs. Perhaps a storm had knocked the lights out. She wouldn't think about that full moon outside, the cloudless skies, and the dry ground, because only a storm explained this.

Johnny fussed, his whimpers loud in the too-quiet house. She'd feed him as soon as she woke Gram. She ignored her pounding heart and called out again, "Gram? It's Reagan." She listened for sounds of stirring. Nothing but the hollow thump of her footsteps on the hardwood. The third stair from the bottom creaked. In all those years, as much as that noise had driven her nuts, Gram still hadn't had it fixed. Why, at the loud creak, hadn't Gram woken up? The woman had never slept through that noise when Rae was a teenager coming home after a date.

She called out again. "I'm coming upstairs. It's just me."

She flipped on the switch in the upper hallway. Nothing. She turned right into the master bedroom and swept the beam of light over the bed. It was empty, the blankets tucked carefully, the pillows arranged. She shouted louder, her heart pounding now. "Gram? Where are you?"

Johnny wailed, and Gram said nothing.

Maybe she was in the hospital. Rae was about to grab the house phone and call when she stopped. The goal had been to come to town, get what she needed, and leave again without anybody knowing she'd been there. How could she do that if she called the hospital? Could she find out anything without being discovered? Would it be dangerous if people discovered she was there? Julien didn't know her real name, didn't know where she was from. He'd look in California until he realized she'd kept as many secrets as he had. She should be safe here for now. Still, alerting the town to her homecoming hadn't been part of the plan.

Johnny cried louder.

"It's okay, sweetie." She bounced him, and he quieted a bit as she carried him downstairs. Too many things to worry about. Right now, she had to take care of her baby.

The circuit breaker panel was in the basement. Rae flipped the basement light switch, but of course the bulbs didn't light. She found the electrical panel. All the breakers were turned off.

She flipped each on, and when the basement lit up, she relaxed. The feeling didn't last long.

Why would Gram shut off the power? If she'd moved, she certainly would have told Rae. Or maybe not. Maybe, knowing Rae was pregnant and confined to bedrest, Gram wouldn't have said a word.

Johnny fussed, red-faced, and wound up for another wail.

She kissed his cheek. "I know, you're hungry. Let's feed you."

She carried him upstairs, grabbed her bag off the porch, and fixed the baby's bottle before collapsing on the sofa to feed him.

Halfway through the bottle, he nodded off. What to do? Gram was supposed to take over now. Tell her where the old cradle was, hold the baby while she fetched it. But Gram wasn't there.

She changed Johnny's diaper and slipped him into fuzzy pajamas. He didn't stir. She carried him upstairs and laid him in the center of Gram's king-sized bed.

He'd be fine until she located his cradle.

She glanced in her parents' old bedroom. It looked just like it had when they'd been alive.

Rae checked her old room. Her double bed was made as if Gram had expected her. Rae pulled back the quilt to find sheets beneath it. She sniffed. Not freshly-laundered, but not stale, either. Gram must have washed them regularly, just in case. The thought made Rae smile.

She grabbed her suitcases and two shopping bags out of the car and carried them upstairs to her room. From one crumpled sack she pulled the used baby monitor she'd purchased at the pawn shop in Boston. She'd walked in with thousands of dollars' worth of jewels and walked out with a used baby monitor and a wad of cash that should last until she found what she'd come for.

She went to Gram's room and plugged the monitor in, then grabbed the receiver and headed downstairs.

That old cradle had been in the barn since Rae was a child. She wasn't sure exactly where in the barn, and the ancient building had always been piled high with stuff accumulated over generations. But it was out there. Rae remembered when her mother had brought the cradle into the house eighteen years earlier. For years, the cradle had been the symbol of her mom's shattered life—and her own. Today, she would change that. Johnny would redeem the cradle.

The property had been in her father's family for generations. Gram had told her stories about secret passageways and hidden treasure. But in all her searching, Rae'd never found any passages or treasures. Gram had only tsk-tsked when Rae called her on it.

"Just because you don't see them doesn't mean they're not there."

Gram'd always had an active imagination.

There was treasure now, though not buried years before by an ancestor. Rae hoped it wasn't buried at all. She needed to find the inheritance her father had left her, and she needed to do it fast.

She turned up the thermostat to sixty-eight, as warm as Gram ever let it get in the cold months. She could hear the old woman's voice now. "If you're cold, wear more clothes. We aren't Rockefellers, you know." Rae smiled at the memory. Then her stomach dropped. Where was Gram?

When she heard the furnace kick on, she grabbed the flashlight and headed to the barn for the cradle.

THREE

Terrorists could be so unpredictable.

Julien Moreau hadn't planned to be gone overnight, but his business associates, as he preferred to think of them, had needed some convincing.

He'd told Rae it was possible he'd have to stay, but only as a precaution. He hated leaving her, and especially now, with the new baby. The huge deal he'd just closed was worth the small sacrifice.

He double-parked outside his building and stepped out of his SUV.

Hector came around from the opposite side to drive the car the few blocks to the parking garage. His suit jacket didn't mask his giant muscles, cultivated by pumping iron and swinging fists.

Julien said, "I'm going to spend the rest of the day with my family. Set up delivery and call me with the details."

"Of course." Hector nodded his shaved head and slipped into the driver's seat.

Julien turned for his apartment. He unlocked the outer door, reveling in the beauty of the building. In another life, he'd have time to research the architecture, to understand the property and the neighborhood. But he hadn't been given a choice of occupations. Being a Moreau came with expectations. Studying architecture had never been an option.

Julien jogged up the stairs to his apartment, slipped the key in the lock, and stepped inside.

Something was wrong.

The space was silent. Even the air felt stale.

He walked across the foyer and into the living room, where Rae often sat and watched the news, their child nestled in her arms. He didn't want Jean-Louis exposed to the evils on BBC, but Rae laughed when he suggested it wasn't good for the boy.

"I don't think he's worrying about the tension in the Middle East quite yet."

He'd let it go. If she'd just let the nanny take their son, it wouldn't be an issue. But Rae insisted on keeping the child with her, sending the nanny away most days. So American. He'd enjoyed watching her interact with their child. She wasn't one of those women who had children, then passed them off. She took motherhood seriously. Like his own mother had.

There was only so much a mother could do, though. He'd learned that lesson the hard way.

The living room was empty and still. He checked the kitchen. Also empty. He kept the office door locked, so there was no reason to check that room.

"Rachel?"

His voice echoed in the hallway as his footsteps clipped along the floor.

Jean-Louis's pajamas were lying on the changing table in the nursery. Julien lifted the garment, fingered the soft fabric, and looked around the room. Everything seemed in order.

He moved on to the master bedroom. From her bureau, he lifted one of her perfume bottles to his nose. It reminded him of her, but the chemicals lacked her unique scent. Where was his wife?

Her silky robe lay across the chest at the end of the bed. The housekeeper should have picked that up. So had the housekeeper not been here, or had Rae worn her robe this afternoon? Perhaps she was ill.

He lifted the robe, held the cool fabric to his cheek, and inhaled. He imagined she was in his arms, pressing into him as she so often did.

When Rachel looked at him, he felt like the man he pretended to be.

He dropped the robe and turned toward the door, but a folded piece of paper on his nightstand caught his eye.

He read the note, then read it again.

Her grandmother was sick. Rae had left. Not just the apartment, not just the city. She'd left the country, the continent. Without his permission.

He pulled out his phone and scrolled through the texts and missed calls. None from her. No voice mails, either. But he'd made it clear she shouldn't call him when he was working. Emergencies only. He crumpled the paper in his fist. Packing up their son and leaving the country would qualify.

He shoved the paper in his pocket and dialed her guards.

Lionel answered on the first ring. "Oui, monsieur?"

"Where are you?"

"Outside, of course," he said. "We are in the van."

"Do you know where my wife is?"

A pause. "We haven't seen her leave."

"When did you see her last?"

"She hasn't come out since you left yesterday morning."

"Has the housekeeper come? The nanny?"

"No, monsieur. But that isn't unusual. When you're not here—"

"Yes, yes. Has anyone else come?" Julien stalked back to the living room.

"People have come and gone from the building, but there are many apartments. We've seen nothing out of the ordinary."

"You missed something, because she's gone."

"That can't—"

Julien ended the call and dialed his wife.

It went straight to voice mail.

"It's me." He forced his voice to sound calm. "I'm sorry to hear about your grandmother. Call me as soon as you get this. I miss you."

He pressed end, pulled his computer from the case by the door, and headed for his office. He'd track her phone...

No, he wouldn't, because he'd taken her smartphone. He'd wanted her to rest, and she never rested when she had constant access to news and email. Always working on some story or looking for a new one. He couldn't track the cheap phone he'd given her, but he hadn't worried about that. He hadn't needed to insist she stay close to home since they'd come to Paris. She'd been confined to bed rest. And then she'd had a newborn. Where would she go?

California, apparently.

Without telling him. Maybe her phone wouldn't work in America. It hardly worked here. That might explain why she hadn't answered.

But why hadn't she called? There were phones in America. He knew her grandmother had one—Rae spoke to her often.

He was not accustomed to people defying him. Most knew better. Those who didn't paid the price. Nobody got away with going against his wishes. Certainly not a woman. Not even his wife.

FOUR

Brady Thomas had put up with his share of ribbing over the years, so the barbs the two officers threw at him now were nothing. He led the way as they entered the police station, then shifted around the counter toward the back, ignoring them.

"So she just outran you?" Donny said, his grin wide.

Eric sized Brady up and down, then scrunched up his baby face. "She was, what?" He held his hand at shoulder height. "About five feet tall?"

The girl had been closer to five five, but Brady wasn't about to point that out. He absolutely wouldn't defend himself, not to these two.

"Tell us about the skateboard again," Donny said, glancing at Eric. "That was the best part."

Brady crossed his arms and nodded toward the two drug dealers they'd arrested an hour earlier. "You guys better focus on your jobs. They get off on a technicality because you were goofing off, I'll have your badges."

Their smiles vanished. "Gotcha," Eric said.

Satisfied that they were on task, Brady pushed through the

door to the squad room. He hadn't taken two steps toward his desk when the chief's door swung open.

"Detective," the chief shouted. "In here."

Brady veered toward the chief's office and entered.

"Close the door."

Brady did, then stood straight and still while Chief Will Jamison returned to the leather chair behind his cluttered desk, sat back, and glared. He had the blackest eyes Brady'd ever seen. Back in the day, his hair'd been black too. Now what little fuzz was left had turned gray. His pale skin showed through, a little red now. Did everybody's scalp turn red when they got angry, or was it just the chief's?

"What happened?"

Brady detailed the bust, which had gone according to plan and resulted in two arrests and a great lead for another. "If we'd had more manpower, we could have followed—"

"I saw your request." The chief stood and hitched his pants up over his ever-growing belly. "You shouldn't be wasting time worrying about what the state police will do, not when you let one get away. You wanna tell me about that?"

Brady resisted the urge to roll his eyes. "She was in the kitchen. When we busted in, we told her to get on the floor, and she did. Donny stayed with her. But then Chubby freaked out and started resisting, and Donny stepped in to help. The girl bolted out the front. I left the guys with Marker and Chubby and followed on foot. I was closing in, but she managed to get to a longboard and take off. I didn't want to leave my officers with two dangerous criminals, so I returned to the house."

The chief's mouth moved like he was chewing on his words. After a minute, he said, "I know you're still adjusting to life after, you know..."

Brady clenched his hands tighter. "This has nothing to do with that."

"You ever have to arrest a woman in Afghanistan?" the chief asked.

"Yes."

"How about in Boston?"

Brady forced his voice to remain even. "I've arrested women here too."

"Not many."

"Most of our criminals are men."

"Some bad guys are girls, you know."

Brady tried to picture that.

Chief Jamison leaned forward. "Why didn't you tackle her?"

Brady looked at the floor. He should have. He'd told himself to, but when it came down to it, he could question women, lecture them, take them into custody, even arrest them. But he'd never been able to risk hurting one. And the chief knew that.

"I would have if I'd thought it was necessary." Brady stood taller and crossed his arms. "We ran surveillance on that house for weeks, and that girl had never been there before. You know how Marker is. He doesn't have flavors of the week, he has flavors of the hour. That girl was tonight's flavor."

"For all you know, she was the supplier." A vein was pulsing in the chief's forehead. "But we'll never know, because you didn't stop her."

"She wasn't a woman, she was a girl."

"You checked her ID?"

"She looked like a teenager."

"Eighteen is an adult." The chief sighed. "Look, I don't want to be stuck in this office forever, Detective." He ran his fingers over his buzz cut. "There's a whole load of fish in the lake just waiting for me and my new boat. I'm going to have to find someone to take over for me pretty soon. If you're not the guy, I'll need to look elsewhere."

The thought that he might lose the chief's job over this rankled. "Look, the girl looked familiar, and I can track her down. I'll have a talk with her, see if she knows anything we can use. Maybe keep her from getting into trouble again."

"Do that. Now that Marker and Chubby are behind bars, I want you to focus on the break-ins. I'll get Detective Green to finish up with those two yahoos."

Brady opened his mouth, then forced it closed. From drug dealers to petty thieves, all because he hadn't tackled a teenage girl.

"Next time you have the chance to stop a female suspect," the chief said, "stop her. Got it?"

Brady swallowed his retort. "Yes, sir."

Brady left the chief's office. He wrote up what he had to and decided to put the rest of the reports off 'til Monday before heading for the door.

"Is Gronk back tomorrow?" Donny asked from behind the counter.

"I haven't heard," Brady said through gritted teeth. When the Patriots had first drafted Tom Brady, the fact that Brady's name was so similar to the new backup QB's was sort of funny. A lark. All these years later, and Brady wished he could change his name.

"Either way, have a good game, Tommy."

"That joke never gets old."

FINALLY, Brady was headed home after his longest day in months. The clock on his dash told him it was almost one in the morning. His sandpaper eyes told him he needed a good night's sleep. Maybe he wouldn't toss and turn over all the *what-ifs* of his life tonight.

When his phone rang, he resisted the urge to throw it out

the window. Instead, he connected the bluetooth. "Thomas here."

"You home yet?" the chief asked.

"Not quite. What's up?"

"Just got a call. A neighbor reported a light on at Dorothy's place."

"In the house?"

"That's what she said. Thought maybe that prowler was back."

"Can't you send—?"

"You're driving right by."

True. And this was the third time in two weeks they'd gotten a call about a prowler over there. But what kind of prowler turned on the lights?

Brady owed it to Dorothy to check it out. Maybe if he came in low and quiet, he could catch the guy this time. "I'm on it."

Brady parked on the street beneath the trees and out of sight of Dorothy's house. He grabbed his flashlight but didn't turn it on, unholstered his Glock, and picked his way through the woods. A black Honda was parked in the driveway. He noted its temporary plate.

Burglars who parked in the driveway?

Lights lit all the windows on the front of the house, two upstairs, and a few on the side. Brady headed toward the kitchen window to peek inside. Nearly there, he heard a crash coming from the barn, followed by the faint sound of a voice. Sure enough, through the dark window on the front of the old building, he saw a flashlight beam bouncing around. Just in case, he looked in the kitchen window, then the dining room. Not a soul.

He crept to the partially open barn door and stepped inside. He'd been in here enough to know only a fool would rush through this place in the dark. The barn was so stuffed with crap, the people at that show about hoarders might want to bring out a camera crew.

Something banged, and he heard the voice again. Sounded female. Just what he needed. He'd tackle whoever it was this time. Nobody who had the nerve to break into this place would get away with it on his watch.

He heard shuffling, muttering, and a loud, "Ouch." He felt his way around an old wardrobe, past what he thought was a chest of drawers, then a couple of ladder-back chairs.

Dorothy had always referred to this as *the barn*, but it hadn't stored animals or feed in a couple generations. When Brady was a kid, this space had served as an office and, in another section, a craft room. It had also served as the scene of a thousand games of hide-and-seek. But there was nothing playful about sneaking through the space in search of a criminal.

In front of him stood the faint outline of a small form. He lifted his gun and aimed. "Police. Put your hands where I can see them."

The person startled, and the lights flickered on. He squinted and shouted. "Stop. Hands in the air."

The hands lifted away from the barn's fuse box. The woman turned, her eyes blinking in the glare. With her hands raised, she tilted her head to the side. "Brady?"

He blinked twice. The voice came straight out of the past, the face one he'd only seen in his imagination for years. It couldn't be. He studied her another moment and was about to speak when she beat him to it.

"Are you going to shoot me, or can I put my hands down?"

He lowered his gun without taking his eyes off of her. Reagan McAdams looked even better than she had in high school. Her eyes were hazel in this light, but he remembered how they seemed green sometimes, almost gold others. Those long eyelashes flicked over bloodshot eyes. She lifted a hand to push her too-dark, long hair out of her face, and a giant diamond glittered on the ring finger of her left hand. One big diamond. Lots of little diamonds on the wedding band. He forced his gaze back to her face. Pale and freckled. Her eyes were bright and studying him just like he'd been studying her. Reagan. Not a word from her for twelve years, and here she was, in the flesh.

Two weeks too late.

She eyed the gun and half-smiled. "What's new?"

He holstered his gun slowly, forcing his voice to remain neutral despite the rush of rage. "We got a call about some lights on. I was looking for a prowler. Looks like I found one. What are you doing here, Reagan? Looking for valuables?"

Her smile faded. "I was just turning on the lights, and—"

"You had to have the lights on in the barn? In the middle of the night? Couldn't wait a couple of hours 'til morning? Or did you figure you'd take what you wanted and leave before anyone discovered you?"

He knew Rae well enough to know he'd hit a nerve. If he weren't so angry, he'd back off.

She stuck her hands on her hips, and he had a flashback to high school. To Rae in her cheerleader outfit on the sidelines. The girls had always stood just like that, hands on their hips, big smiles on their faces. Nothing like the scowl he saw now.

"What are you talking about? Why would I have to steal from my own grandmother?"

"What do you need so badly that it can't wait 'til morning?"

Her gaze slid downward and landed on something out of his line of vision. Then she looked up and glared at him. "I don't know what you're so mad about, Brady, but—"

"You don't know? You take off and don't come back for twelve years."

"I've been—"

"You aren't here for birthdays or holidays. You couldn't

bother to show up when your grandmother had surgery last year—"

"I was—"

"You can't even manage to get here to bury her, but ten days later…"

Brady's words trailed off as her eyes widened and her jaw dropped. She placed her palms on the desk in front of her, then collapsed into the chair behind it.

Brady rushed across the room, skirted the desk, and knelt in front of her.

She covered her face with her hands. Her sobs filled the silent barn, and she spoke into her palms. "It can't be."

"I'm sorry, Rae. I thought you knew."

"How would I have…? What happened? How could I not…?"

He leaned forward and wrapped his arms around her. She leaned into his chest.

He stroked her hair. "I'm so sorry."

After a few minutes of sobbing, she managed a barely audible, "When?"

"Monday it'll be two weeks."

For some reason, that information made her cry harder. Deep, gut-wrenching sounds that seemed to come straight from her soul. Minutes passed before she settled into quiet weeping. He rubbed her back and waited another minute more before speaking. "I'm sorry, Rae. Dorothy told me you kept up with the local news. She said you read the paper online, so I made sure they ran a pretty big obituary. I know how you are about newspapers. I figured you saw it."

She shook her head. After a few sniffles, she said, "I've been away from my computer for a while, and…" She stopped mid-sentence and sobbed again. "I was so close. So close." Rae wiped her eyes on the sleeve of her sweatshirt and pulled away from him. She stood, so he did too.

"I'm sorry, Rae. I never would've told you like that if I'd known—"

"Doesn't matter. What happened? How did she...?"

She stopped, apparently unable to say the word, as fresh tears dripped down her cheeks.

"It was her heart." He held out his arm. "Here, let me walk you inside."

"I know the way."

Typical, stubborn Rae. Couldn't do anything for her. "We've had some prowlers around here the last two weeks, so I'd feel better if I knew you were safe."

She scanned the barn, seemed to settle on something on the far side. Who could tell what in that mess?

She took a deep breath, stifled a sob, and hooked her hand around his arm. "Okay." She walked to the barn door, and after he stepped out, she turned out the lights and locked it behind them. How was it that just a half hour earlier all he'd wanted was his own bed? Funny how priorities change.

At the front door, she paused. "Would you do me a favor?"

"Maybe."

"Don't tell anybody you saw me. I'm not ready for visitors."

"On one condition." He waited for her nod, then smiled. "I bet you don't have anything to eat in there."

"No idea. I just assumed..."

When she didn't finish the sentence, he cleared his throat. "Well, I know you don't, because I cleaned out the fridge and cabinets myself. Figured it'd be easier to do before everything spoiled. I donated what wasn't opened to the food pantry."

She swallowed hard. "Gram would have liked that."

"Yeah. I know."

She tilted her head again, studied him. "Why you?"

"We got sort of close these last few years."

"She didn't tell me. I knew you were back, knew you were a detective here, but I got that stuff from the newspaper. She never said anything about you two being friends."

"Maybe she didn't think you'd care."

A look crossed her features, and she nearly smiled. "What was your condition?"

"I'll bring over breakfast tomorrow. I'll tell you what I know about Dorothy, and you can fill me in on..." His eyes flicked to her wedding ring before he forced them back to her face. "On what you've been up to."

For a moment, he worried she might refuse. But then she nodded. "Yeah. Okay."

"See you in the morning."

FIVE

JULIEN SPUN the mobile hanging above his son's bed and watched until the jungle animals stilled. He pulled the phone from his pocket, stared at the screen, and willed it to ring.

Aside from the noises on the street below, his apartment remained silent.

If only he hadn't gone to that meeting.

Meeting. That's what he called it. In truth, he'd flown his private jet to a remote landing strip in the middle of the African desert to work out one of the largest deals of his life. His people would procure the weapons and complete the deal in the next few weeks. It would take him that long to get the volume of munitions his clients desired.

When he completed the sale, he'd be richer than he'd ever been. His father would be pleased.

Julien should be pleased as well. But with Rachel and Jean-Louis gone, no amount of money could please him.

And if his father found out Rae was missing? Or God forbid, his brother? No, he had to keep that circle small.

Why hadn't Rae called? He understood why she'd gone to

be with her grandmother, but why the note? Why not at least a text message?

And it didn't make sense that she'd slipped past her guards. Usually, she waved to them whenever she went anywhere. This time, they hadn't seen her leave.

So had they been complacent? Or had she eluded them on purpose?

Had she left today, or the day before?

Was she traveling right now, or was she already sitting at the old lady's bedside?

He imagined his wife and their tiny son in a germ-infested hospital. If anything happened to either one of them...

But Rae could handle herself, and in California, she should be safe from Julien's enemies.

And his family.

He smacked the mobile again, and it dislodged from the crib and toppled to the hardwood floor.

He had to find Rae and bring her home, sick grandmother or not. He returned to his office and dialed Farah. She answered in heavily-accented French. "Bonjour, Julien."

He forced his voice to sound casual. "I need you to do me a favor."

"Oui. Of course."

"Rae's gone to the States to see her grandmother."

"Is she ill?"

"Apparently, quite so. I'm having trouble getting in touch with her. I assume that phone I gave her doesn't work in the States. Could you find out what flights she took? I want to make sure she made it safely."

"But of course. Her family is in California, no?"

"San Diego area. I forget the name of the town, though. Maybe if we look on her smartphone? Do you have it?"

A pause, then, "I believe it's with the things I brought from Tunis. I will check."

"Good. Maybe you could get her grandmother's phone number off her smartphone. And those flights."

"I'll get right back to you."

"Merci. And Farah? This stays between us."

"*Mais oui.*"

Of course. He could always count on Farah. He ended the call and sat back in his leather chair. It would be all right. Rae wouldn't leave him. She loved him, and he her. And their child.

He lifted the photograph from the corner of his desk, traced his son's image with his finger. He'd once believed it was Rae who'd taught him to love, and indeed, he'd never truly known love until he met her. When Jean-Louis was born, it was as though Julien had grown a new heart, just for the boy. He loved them, loved them enough that he would never let them go.

The phone rang, and he snatched it, but it wasn't Farah.

"Bonjour, Papa," Julien said.

"How did it go?"

"Successfully, of course. We made the deal for more than we'd hoped."

"*Tres bien.* When do they take delivery?"

"Soon. Hector is managing the details. We should know more in the next day or so."

Julien tapped his fingers on the desk while his father went on about his own latest deal and the family business. Papa was heading to Washington, D.C., to visit with some of his contacts there.

"I expect you here for your mother's birthday," his father said.

Julien navigated to the calendar on his laptop. Maman's birthday was three weeks away. Rae would be home by then. He would make sure of it. "The baby is still too young to travel."

"Your mother is counting the days until she can meet her grandson. Surely you won't put us off again."

The warning behind his father's words was unmistakable. "Of course not. Rae and I are looking forward to it." Julien's call waiting beeped. "I have to go, Papa."

After saying *au revoir*, Julien switched to the other call. Farah.

"What did you learn?"

"Rachel has hundreds of contacts in her cell phone, none called *grandmother*."

"She called her Gram."

"Nobody with that name, either. Why don't I start with the California phone numbers?"

"Okay. What else?"

"She flew out yesterday morning. She changed planes in Boston on her way to San Diego. The flight landed last night."

"Will her phone work internationally?"

"I do not think so."

"Her last phone worked everywhere."

"Oui. But the one you made her—"

"Yes, yes, I know. I'm a terrible man because I wanted her to rest."

Farah paused. "No, monsieur." Her voice sounded timid. "You only want what is best. I just meant perhaps she isn't getting your calls."

"Perhaps."

He hung up the phone knowing Farah's explanation would make perfect sense—if Rae had called him before she'd left. Or since. But she hadn't. So something was wrong. And he had to find out what it was and get her back before his father found out she was gone.

SIX

Sunlight penetrated Rae's eyelids, and she blinked them open. Her first thought was that she was home. Her second thought, *Gram's gone*.

Tears stung, but her third thought had her gasping. Johnny hadn't eaten in hours. She glanced at the clock. Quarter 'til nine. She jerked upright and leaned over the baby, who was lying beside her on Gram's bed. She touched his chest to make sure he was breathing. His eyes popped open, and he scrunched up his tiny face and wailed.

She scooped him up and rested him against her chest, calming them both. He'd never slept so many hours straight. Poor baby. He'd been exhausted. She knew how he felt. The last two days had beaten them both.

"It's okay, baby." She patted his back. "Let's get your breakfast."

She fixed his bottle, then settled on the sofa to feed him, tears filling her eyes yet again. All those years she'd rarely seen her grandmother. What kind of person neglected the only person in the world who truly loved her? And when Rae had finally been able to come home, to talk Gram into going with her, it was too late.

Johnny finished his bottle and looked at her with a curious expression.

"We're okay, baby. We'll figure it out. We have each other. That's all we need."

She changed his diaper and clothes and tried to decide what to do next. She'd planned to stay no longer than a week, and only because she'd figured it would take her that long to convince Gram to join her. But now she had little reason to stay at all. After Brady had left the night before, Rae'd returned to the barn for the baby monitor she'd left there. She'd stood in the barn a long time, staring at the cradle before deciding she didn't have the energy to move it. Then she'd walked to the foot of the steps that led to the loft and remembered the conversation she'd had with her father, all those years ago.

"This is the best hiding space." He'd held the brown metal box in his hands and looked at her with a twinkle in his eyes. "By the time you go off to college, this will be enough to pay your way."

She couldn't remember exactly where they'd been when he'd hidden the box, but she remembered stairs, and she thought she'd been in the barn. The memory was so fuzzy, crowded out by the events of the next few days. The accident and the funeral and the insane things that followed.

The night before, she'd stood in the barn and thought, if she could just find that box, she and Johnny could be gone before Brady ever returned.

But then she'd yawned, and tears had filled her eyes, fatigue and grief blinding her. She hadn't been able to think straight last night. And it wouldn't hurt to visit with Brady one last time before she left for good.

In the harsh light of day, Rae could admit that even if she'd been well-rested, even if she'd found the box, she'd still be here. Seeing Brady again, being in his arms again, had dredged up memories she'd thought long buried.

Rae carried Johnny upstairs and laid him on the single bed in her bedroom, so she could change her clothes. Johnny was discovering his voice, and his little baby squeals made her smile, though the tears still fell. Ready to face Brady, she held the baby until he fell back to sleep, then laid him in the center of Gram's bed and surrounded him with pillows, just in case.

Back in the kitchen, she searched for any scrap of food, but Brady'd been thorough. Just when she didn't think she could wait another minute, a car pulled down the long driveway.

She swung the door open to find Brady with a cup of coffee in each hand and a plastic bag dangling from his arm. He looked even better in the light of day. Dark hair, shorter than it had been in high school. A little gray showed on the temples, which somehow made him look sexier than before. His eyes seemed darker, his face more chiseled than she remembered. In high school, he'd had boyish good looks. Now, he was all man.

She forced her gaze to the items he carried. "Thank God." She swung the door wider, and he stepped inside.

"I'd like to think that greeting was about me, but I have a feeling it was this you wanted." He held out a cup, and she snatched it.

The warm, bitter liquid slid down her throat. Needed some cream, but she couldn't wait. "Like a little sip of heaven."

She stepped into the kitchen. He followed and set the bag on the counter. "I wasn't sure what you'd like, so I bought a blueberry scone, a lemon scone, a bagel, and two egg sandwiches." He laid the items on the counter as he mentioned them.

She pulled two plates from the cabinet, set one in front of Brady, and reached for an egg sandwich. "I'll start with this and go from there."

"Hungry?"

"Very." Rae noticed the name on the bag. "McNeal's?" Place had been little more than a dive bar when she'd lived there. "Since when do they serve breakfast?"

Brady took the second egg sandwich. "You've been gone a long time, Rae."

The thought brought fresh tears to her eyes. She sat at the round kitchen table and indicated a chair for Brady. The chair he'd always sat in when they were kids.

Brady sat and his expression changed. "Hey. You okay?"

Rae nodded and wiped her eyes with her fingertips.

Brady looked around, then jumped up and grabbed a handful of napkins out of the McNeal's bag. He handed one to her. "I know it's a shock."

"It just...I can't believe she's gone." She wiped her eyes and sniffed. "What happened?"

"She died in her sleep. Doctor thought it looked like a heart attack."

"Did they do an autopsy?"

He shook his head. "She was elderly."

Steam rose from their coffees. Grief or not, Rae's stomach growled. She unwrapped her egg sandwich and took a bite. It tasted fantastic, and not just because she was so hungry. "This is delicious."

"They hired a chef a few years back. Came from Worcester or Watertown or...Weymouth or something."

Rae smiled. "Something with a W, I guess."

"Yeah."

Rae took another bite, then a sip of her coffee, before speaking again. "So where is Gram now?"

He took a long breath. "We waited for you to contact us, but when you didn't—"

"Did you try to find me?"

He leveled his gaze at her, the frown familiar. "I gave up trying to find you about eleven years ago."

She returned his glare, then looked away. Her reasons for cutting Brady out of her life all seemed so silly now. "So, Gram?"

"When you didn't show up..." He shrugged. "She'd already planned and paid for her funeral. She's in the cemetery."

"Next to Gramps and my parents?"

"Uh-huh. It was a nice service. The whole town came out."

Gram would have liked that, lying at rest beside her husband and son. And her daughter-in-law too. As much trouble as Mom had always caused, Gram had loved her. Rae felt the burn of tears again and wiped her eyes.

They both ate for a few minutes. There'd been a time when she and Brady would fill almost every moment with conversation, and the rare moments of quiet they'd shared were comfortable. Easy. Now, the silence hung like smoke.

"So." Brady finished his sandwich and wiped his fingers on a napkin. "Are you going to tell me about him?"

Rae pictured Johnny sleeping soundly upstairs. "Him?"

"The man who put that ring on your finger."

Right. Him. "What do you want to know?"

"Where is he?"

"Paris."

"Why isn't he with you?"

"Work."

Brady closed his lips in a tight line, and she recognized the look of frustration. "What?"

He blew out a breath. "You don't offer much, huh?"

She shrugged, and he continued. "So Paris. Is that where you've been living? Dorothy told me you were in Africa somewhere."

"He has an apartment in Paris, and he's there now."

Brady's eyebrows lifted, then fell. A moment passed before he said, "When are you going back?"

"Soon as I can." She grabbed the other breakfast items off the counter and set them on the table. No reason to panic. All she had to do was convince Brady that all was well with her and Julien. Rae'd perfected the art of lying when she started college. The stories that had rolled off her tongue back then had surprised even her. But lying to Brady? That was a whole different ballgame. She pasted on a smile. "You want something else?"

"You pick first."

She unwrapped the scones and took the blueberry one. "That okay?"

"I knew you'd pick that one." A tiny smile. "You always were a sucker for blueberries."

Once, she and Brady had picked enough blueberries from the bushes out back for a couple of pies, then eaten so many Gram had scolded them. They'd been nine or ten at the time, old enough to know better. They'd both paid for it with stomachaches that night.

By the look on Brady's face, he remembered too.

"Not a lot of blueberries in Tunis."

"Tunis," he repeated. "Never been there."

She smiled. "It's not a hot spot for American tourists, but it's been home for years."

He nodded and bit into the lemon scone. She had a bite of hers, and it melted in her mouth. She swallowed a sip of her coffee and enjoyed the combination of flavors. "Delicious."

"Why Africa?"

She took another bite and swallowed. "I moved to Belgium when I graduated, but it was hard to make a living there. I followed a story to Tunisia and fell in love with the place. It's in the middle of Northern Africa, so from there I could investigate stories from Cairo to Morocco. And I could afford to live there, which hadn't been so easy in Brussels."

"What's so special about it that you fell in love with it?"

"It's beautiful. The people are big-hearted. It's fairly safe, at least it was when I first moved there. It's getting more dangerous, but..." She shrugged. "It was a good place to live."

"Was?"

Oops. "We're considering staying in Paris for a while," she lied. "Julien wants to be nearer to his family." Another lie. She'd been married to the man for a year and had yet to meet any member of his family.

He set his scone on his plate. "What's his name?"

"My husband?"

One of his eyebrows lifted, and she sighed. "Julien." She said it the way her husband had taught her, with the French accent, so the J was breathy, and the N sort of fell off the back.

Now both of Brady's eyebrows lifted. "You speak French?"

She nodded. "Helps in Tunisia."

"Don't they speak Arabic there?"

She nodded slowly. "A form of Arabic. They call it *Darija*. And I've learned some of that. But almost everybody speaks French."

"I see. So he's French, this Julien," he said with no effort at the French pronunciation.

Her heartbeat quickened, but she was safe. Julien didn't know where she was. Thank God she'd kept to her cover story about her past when she'd met him. All those times she'd almost told him the truth... She'd felt guilty about her lies, which had proved so inconsequential compared to his. She sipped her coffee, calmed herself, and answered. "He was raised in the south of France. His mother was French."

"His father?"

"Other things." She bit her scone.

"Julien what?"

She set the scone down and swallowed. Then wiped her mouth. "Julien Moreau."

"Moreau. Okay. So why isn't he here?"

"Do you do a lot of interrogations for your job?"

He chuckled, and tiny lines appeared at the corners of his eyes. "I'm sorry. It's just weird you showing up like this."

"Not really," she said. "Gram quit answering her phones, and I got nervous."

He flattened those lips again. "Phones? She just had the one."

"I bought her a cell years ago. It had a good international plan, cheaper than her house phone. I tried to get her to carry it for emergencies, but I don't think she ever did."

"Oh. If I'd known..."

"It's okay."

"And then you just show up. All these years, nothing brings you home, and suddenly—"

"Just because you haven't seen me doesn't mean I haven't been home."

He nodded slowly. "Yeah, Dorothy told me about a few of your visits, but nobody else ever saw you."

"So you figured she was lying?"

Brady had the decency to look embarrassed. "Not lying. Just...covering for you."

"Because I'm a terrible granddaughter who abandoned Gram to pursue my own interests."

He shrugged.

"Gram told me to leave. It was her idea."

"And staying away for twelve years—was that her idea too?"

Rae swallowed and stared at what was left of her scone. "I've been back. Just not in a while. Tickets from Africa are expensive."

"Right."

She sighed. What was the use? She pushed back from the table and stood. "Thanks for breakfast."

He stood too. "I shouldn't have... Your life isn't my business. Just... Your grandmother missed you. I missed you."

The awkward silence was interrupted by a scratchy, metallic sound coming through the old baby monitor.

SEVEN

BRADY WHIPPED AROUND. What was that garbled noise? There, on the kitchen counter, sat the old walkie-talkie-thing he'd seen in the barn the night before. He should have realized what it was.

He turned back to Rae in time to see color rise in her face.

"What...?" He listened more closely. He recognized that sound. "Better yet, who is that?"

Rae sighed and walked out of the kitchen. He heard her footfalls on the stairs, a loud creak, and then a moment later, the soft sound of her voice through the device on the counter. Not a walkie-talkie, but a baby monitor.

"Hey, sweetie," Rae said. "How was your nap?"

The crying stopped, replaced by a scratchy cooing sound. He walked to the stairs and watched as Rae carried a tiny bundle down. She passed him with barely a glance and disappeared into the living room.

Brady followed and watched her set the bundle on the couch in the wedge between two cushions. Not that the kid was big enough to roll over, but he liked that Rae was cautious. She disappeared into the kitchen.

Soft noises drew him to the sofa. There, wiggling happily, lay a tiny, surprisingly dark-skinned baby. Brady remembered Rae's evasive answer just a few moments before. Her husband's mother was French, but his father was... How had she put it? *Other things.* Had she evaded the question because she'd thought Brady might judge? Surely she knew him better than that. Or maybe, after all these years, they didn't know each other at all.

Rae brushed by him, scooped up the baby, and sat on the sofa to feed him.

He leaned against the door jamb and crossed his arms. "So you have a baby."

"This is...Johnny."

He lifted his eyebrows, and she looked back at the child. Something was wrong. The way she'd said the baby's name, hesitant, like she hadn't been sure, the way she'd avoided telling Brady about him, the way she avoided his gaze now. And that remark from earlier about her husband—*He has an apartment in Paris.* Not *we* have, but *he* has. Something was definitely wrong. Brady could question her, wear her down, get the answers he craved. But Reagan was not his suspect. "How old is he?"

"Two weeks tomorrow."

So Johnny had been born the same day Rae's grandmother had died. The timeline suddenly made sense. Rae called to tell Gram the good news, and Gram never answered. Dorothy must've known the baby was on the way, so the fact that she'd never returned Rae's call had to have worried Rae. Still, to pack up and cross the ocean with an infant? Must've been hard.

"Dorothy would've doted on him."

Tears filled Rae's eyes, and she wiped them on the baby's shirt sleeve.

"I can't believe she didn't tell me you were expecting."

Rae never took her gaze from the baby's face. "Did she tell you I was married?"

"As a matter of fact, she didn't."

"I asked her not to share my news with the town. I've had enough of everyone knowing my business."

He could understand that, but the crazy events from Rae's childhood hadn't been Brady's fault, or Dorothy's. It hadn't been the town's fault, either, and most of the townspeople had tried their hardest to protect Rae. After what her mother had done? Well, the people who loved Rae had only been able to do so much.

And besides that, almost two decades had passed since her father's death and her mother's... "Seems you'd be over that by now."

She glanced at him before returning her gaze to the child's face. "Guess not."

"You could have called me, you know. You admitted last night you knew I was in town. You knew I was a cop. You had to know I'd help you locate Dorothy."

"Sure." Sarcasm dripped off the word like ice cream on a July day. "You were at the top of my list."

"You can trust me, you know."

She didn't say anything.

He sighed. "Are you ever going to forgive me?"

"I forgave you a long time ago. I just never understood."

"If you hadn't taken off—"

"I should have stayed so you could justify what you did? Listened to how much you loved me, how you hadn't wanted to hurt me."

"I did love you. And I didn't want to hurt you."

"You did, though."

"Seems after all we'd been through—"

"All we'd been through," she said through gritted teeth, "didn't matter an iota to you."

"So you haven't forgiven me."

They stared at each other across Dorothy's living room. Rae's living room now, not that she'd stay to take care of it. She'd probably sell it to one more rich Boston family looking to escape the big city life. Just what their town needed.

This living room, this whole house, reminded him of Dorothy. For years he'd come here and thought how empty it felt without Rae. How strange to be here with Rae and miss her grandmother.

Rae was sitting on the sofa upholstered in that soft, fuzzy brown fabric. Dorothy'd called it something once—chamois or chardonnay? No, that was wine. Whatever, it was soft. The club chairs with that yellow flowery fabric. He'd spent hours in this room, sipping a soda and eating chips. No tea and crumpets for Dorothy, no matter her age. She liked Ruffles or the Lay's Classic.

But now, Dorothy was gone, and Reagan was back. And she didn't trust him.

It didn't matter. Pretty soon she'd be gone, and he'd never see her again. Fine with him. If the previous few years had taught him anything, it was that getting too close gained him nothing and cost him everything.

Rae lifted the baby to her shoulder and softly patted his back. A moment later, the baby burped, and she shifted him to feed him the rest of his bottle. The way she looked at him, so tenderly... He'd always known she'd be a great mother. Hadn't he imagined this a million times? Only in Brady's imagination, the baby had looked like him.

He shook off the thought. Been there, done that, had the scars to prove it. "Did you get everything you needed out of the barn last night?"

She looked up. "I was going to grab the cradle, but then I found out about Gram..."

"Right." And she hadn't wanted him to know about Johnny. "It's locked?"

"The key's on the counter next to the stove."

He grabbed the key and called, "Right back," over his shoulder.

The sun had burned off the little fog he'd driven through that morning, and now it shone bright. It was probably mid-seventies, and it would warm into the eighties today. The last gasp of summer before autumn set in. With the birds chirping in the trees surrounding the house, all should be right with the world.

He crossed to the barn, unlocked the door, and entered. The room was light now that the sun was out, thanks to the many windows. But the light only managed to illuminate the piles of junk on that old wooden floor. He stopped inside the door and let his gaze roam. Too many pieces of furniture to count, cardboard boxes that looked about to disintegrate from age, plastic storage containers stacked to the ceiling, random papers and files strewn across the cavernous space. A mannequin a seamstress might use. A Persian rug, discolored from dust and age, spread out like an accent piece. Old lamps, shelves, books... He couldn't take it all in.

On the far side rested a dark brown cradle. He picked his way toward it, banged his shin against an upended nightstand. "Ouch!" He paused, took a deep breath to keep from kicking the stupid furniture and injuring himself further. Finally he reached the cradle.

It seemed sturdy. The curved spindles were close enough together that no baby's head would fit in there. He never would have thought of that before, but now he had just enough experience with babies to know how fragile they were.

He pushed that thought back down to where it belonged and tested the cradle's sturdiness. While he wiped his dusty hands on his jeans, he walked around it one last time, swiping at a spiderweb stretched along one side. Yes, that should do.

He stopped beside a trash bag leaning against the cradle. Judging from the thick layer of dust, it had been there a while. It weighed almost nothing. Holes covered it like polka dots, and through them, he saw fabric. He removed the twist-tie and peered inside.

Blue bumper pads decorated with pictures of footballs. For a baby boy. The baby boy whose presence had signaled the end of Rae's rocky childhood. And the development of the cynical, angry woman sitting in the house.

He spun the holey sack, replaced the twist tie, and carried it outside. He spied the trash cans but got a better idea. He threw the dusty sack into the bed of his blue Dodge Ram. He'd throw it out at his house, so Rae'd never have to see it. He turned back toward the barn, then froze.

The plates on Reagan's car. Temporary. As if the car had just been purchased. He'd noticed last night, but he'd forgotten.

If she'd rented it, there'd be permanent license plates. One more piece of the puzzle. Sure would help if he had a picture on a box to help him put these pieces together. Not that the puzzle or the big picture was any of his business. And he didn't want them to be, either. Rae'd already burned him once. Since then, the lesson she'd taught him had been cemented by every woman he'd ever cared for.

He returned to the barn for the cradle.

EIGHT

Rae finished feeding Johnny, then fished a notebook and pen from her messenger bag to make a list for the store. She sat beside Johnny, who was cooing and staring at the ceiling. "You need some toys, don't you?"

He met her eyes before returning his gaze to the ceiling.

She noted the food she needed on her list, then added *bouncer* and *baby gym*. She couldn't go crazy, but those things wouldn't take up too much space. She'd imagined taking Gram with her to the store and picking out all these things together. Instead, she'd be shopping alone. At least she had lots of practice being on her own.

She pushed a lock of hair out of her face, noted the dark color, and wrote *hair dye*. That job couldn't wait long.

The front door opened, and Brady carried the cradle into the kitchen. "It's pretty dusty," he called, "so I figured we should clean it up in here before we take it upstairs."

She dropped the notepad on the coffee table and joined Brady. The cradle was filthy. She grabbed a dishtowel from the drawer by the sink, wet it down, and got to work.

"I'll get the base," Brady said. She heard the door close. A moment later, he returned and set the base beside her on the floor.

"Thanks."

"No problem." He grabbed a towel and cleaned. "Lots of stuff out there."

"Yup."

"What do you plan to do with it?"

She froze mid-wipe. "What do *I* plan...?"

He sat back on his heels and tilted his head. "I just assumed Dorothy left this place to you. Gordon Boyle's been asking me if I'd heard from you."

"Mr. Boyle?"

"Your grandmother's lawyer."

Rae rubbed one of the spindles with the rag. It hadn't occurred to her, but of course Gram would leave the house to her. She had been Gram's only living relative. Which meant Rae owned a house. What in the world was she going to do with it?

The answer came before she finished the spindle. Sell it. The money would go a long way in helping to finance her new life. And her disappearance.

But could she?

Not only had she grown up here, her father had too. And Gramps. Gram had moved in when she and Gramps married, right after her twentieth birthday. Rae's great-great-grandfather had built this house somewhere around the turn of the last century. Rae figured it didn't look much like it had back then. The kitchen had been fully updated, and the living room was an addition. At some point, someone had added the pantry, which stuck out awkwardly on the side of the house. But the original home remained. The barn, the land, and the old rock wall that edged the border of the property had all been in her family for more than a hundred years. And now, because of her stupid choices, they'd all be lost.

"Hey." The concern in Brady's voice did nothing to stem the tears. He moved to sit beside her and rubbed her back gently. "You all right?"

Rae shouldn't have burrowed into his shoulder, but it felt so nice to have a moment of comfort.

"I'm sorry," he said. "I don't know what to say."

There was nothing to say. Nothing would bring Gram back. Nothing would make Julien the man she'd thought he was. Nothing could undo the damage she'd done to her own life.

When she'd cried herself out, she pulled away and dabbed at her eyes with her fingertips.

Brady grabbed the napkins off the kitchen table and handed her one. "You might have to keep tissues in your pocket."

She chuckled and wiped her eyes. "You may be right."

He watched her, the amusement gone. She turned back to the cradle and continued the task.

After a second and third wipe-down, the cradle looked clean and shiny, the dark wood gleaming in the overhead lights. Brady stood and grabbed it as if it were no heavier than a pillow. "Where do you want it?"

"My room, please."

His eyebrows rose. "You might be more comfortable in—"

"My room's the most comfortable place in the world."

He nodded and carried the furniture up the stairs.

Rae returned to the couch to check on Johnny. He was staring and cooing as if the plain white ceiling were the most fascinating thing in the world. She picked him up, and he nestled his head to her neck. She'd never known true comfort until she'd felt his cuddle. Though, a moment ago, Brady's arms had been close.

Brady returned and stood at the entry.

"Was there a mattress for it?" she asked.

"Nope. Guess you'll need to grab one."

She looked at her list. "I need to write that down."

Brady took two long steps across the room and held out his arms. "Here, let me."

She looked from the top of Johnny's head to Brady's outstretched arms. "You sure?"

"I offered, didn't I?"

"You know how to hold a baby?"

The corner of his mouth lifted in a smirk.

"Right. Your sisters have probably had babies over the years. How are they?"

Brady swallowed and smiled, but it seemed forced. "Married with kids. They both live in Manchester. Seven nieces and nephews, at last count."

She laid Johnny in his arms and braced herself for the scream that was bound to come. The baby almost always cried when Julien held him. But Johnny nestled into his neck, just like he had hers, and cooed.

"Huh."

Brady patted the baby's back. "What?"

She smiled. "Nothing." She sat and added *cradle mattress* and *bedding* to her list.

"You like that Civic?" he asked.

She shrugged. "It's fine. Gets good gas mileage."

A moment passed, but she kept her eyes trained on the list.

"So where are you going?"

She added *milk* to the list to give her fingers something to do. Then *ibuprofen*, hoping to stave off her growing headache. How could Brady know about her plans to disappear? Had she let something slip? Or maybe... "What do you mean?"

"Which store?"

Oh. She relaxed and looked up. The picture of Brady gently

rocking Johnny reminded her of all she'd once hoped for, and all she'd lost. She found she couldn't look away.

He must've seen something in her expression, because his hardened.

"Where did you disappear to all those years ago, Rae? I looked for you at Cornell, but you never enrolled."

"Went to Columbia instead."

He lifted his eyebrows. "I looked for you there too."

She tapped the pen against the pad. "I changed my name."

His forehead wrinkled. "To what?"

"Doesn't matter."

He took a deep breath and angled his gaze upward. Everybody was fascinated with the ceiling today. She stood and took Johnny back. "Thanks for coming over. I appreciate your help, and breakfast."

He nodded to the notepad she'd left on the arm of the sofa. "There's a Walmart. It'll have everything you need. It's right off the highway."

"Right." That was new since she'd left. "That'll work."

"You need some help?"

She shook her head. "I can manage."

"Might be easier with another set of hands."

It probably would, but as nice as the picture of Brady and Johnny had been, she couldn't be seen in public with him. With anybody, if she wanted to protect the people of Nutfield. "Thanks, anyway."

"I meant what I said earlier, Rae. I know you don't believe it, but you can trust me."

"I tried that once, remember? It didn't work out so well."

"One stupid kiss—"

"It's fine. It's in the past."

He walked down the hall, muttering under his breath. He pulled the door open before turning back to her. "You'll need

Gordon's number. I have it at home. If you give me your cell number, I'll text you when I get home."

"No cell phone."

The suspicion on his face faded, but not quickly enough. "No cell?"

She thought fast. "My phone doesn't work in the States."

"Right. You should add that to your list. People will need to get in touch with you."

"I'll think about it."

"Meanwhile, the house phone still works. You need to call Gordon tomorrow. Call me if you can't find his number. I should be at the station."

"Okay."

"And Samantha will want to see you."

Samantha. Her one-time best friend was still in town. Of course. "I don't have time for reunions."

"She's the town clerk. You can reach her at work. You need the number?"

"If I decide to call her, I'm sure I can find it."

"Rae—"

"Thank you for breakfast, and for the help. I appreciate it."

"Rae, I know it's hard, but you need to call Gordon and Sam."

Trouble was, the last thing anybody in this town needed was to be associated with her. When Julien came here—and she knew someday he would—the people of Nutfield would be safer if they'd never laid eyes on her.

NINE

THE TRIP to the store had been a nightmare. Rae'd managed to get Johnny in the house, then set his car seat on the kitchen table while she unloaded the groceries to the sound of his screams. She set up the new bouncer, but he wanted none of it.

This was why it took two people to make a baby. It took two to raise one. She'd sent Brady away, but she could sure use his help now. She lifted Johnny and rocked him. "How about we go outside?"

He made no argument, so she headed for the back patio. The air was in the mid-eighties, and a soft breeze rustled the leaves. The backyard was just like she remembered it, though the trees were more mature, the forest denser than it had been. The grass was spotty thanks to the sandy soil, but the hydrangea bushes against the house were lush and beautiful. The roses still held a few blooms. And across the yard, the apple trees were heavy with fruit.

Why hadn't she thought of that when her stomach had rumbled that morning?

Johnny quieted—thank God—as Rae pulled in the crisp scent of home. The cleared area of Gram's property stretched thirty or forty yards before the forest took over. Toward the right, Rae spotted something out of the corner of her eye. A figure was moving in the shadows just beyond the tree line. Rae's heart beat faster, and she turned the baby around and held him to her shoulder. The bright sunlight made it hard to see into the darkness beneath the trees, but she was sure the person was moving toward the center of the back of the property on this side of the rock wall. Whoever it was remained mostly hidden in the trees.

Rae was reaching behind her for the door handle when the figure stepped onto the yard. Relieved, Rae called out. "Hey, Caro!"

The girl had unnaturally red hair and wore a long-sleeved, oversized black T-shirt, and dark blue skinny jeans. On her feet, she wore sneakers, maybe Converse. She waved and smiled. "You're home."

"Grab me an apple while you're out there."

Caro snatched a couple of apples then headed for the back porch. "I've been coming by every few days to see if you made it back yet."

Gram had befriended the girl a few years before. Rae'd only met her once, but she'd liked her immediately.

She patted the baby's back. "This little guy kept me from getting back sooner."

Caro smiled. "Gram didn't tell me you were expecting. What's his name?"

"Johnny."

Rae sat, and Caro walked around behind her to get a better look at Johnny's face.

"Omigosh, he's so adorable. Is he adopted?"

She'd have to get used to that question. "He's mine, but he gets his coloring from his father."

Caro spoke from over her shoulder. "Like Middle Eastern or something?"

"Johnny's grandfather came from Libya, and the people there are mostly of Arab-Berber descent."

"Arab Berbers. Are they like Middle Eastern carpet makers?"

Rae chuckled. "Not exactly. Just North Africans."

Caro joined her at the table. "He's adorable. And he has that straight hair, like yours."

"Even the hair is his dad's. I'm a natural redhead."

Caro fluffed her obviously dyed hair and said, "Me, too." Then she laughed and took a huge bite of her apple. Rae had a bite of hers—utterly delicious—and studied the girl. Caro had changed since Rae'd seen her last a few years before. Black makeup lined her hazel eyes and contrasted dramatically against her fair skin. "So, how old are you now?"

"Fifteen."

"What grade?"

"Sophomore. I hate it."

"How come?"

The girl shrugged. "Boring, I guess." Caro took another bite of her apple. They ate in silence while Johnny rested on Rae's shoulder. He'd fallen asleep, but after the day they'd had, she wasn't ready to lay him down and risk him waking up to scream some more.

Caro finished her apple and looked around the deck.

Rae followed her gaze. No trash can. "You can take it inside and toss it out. You know where the trash is?"

"Yeah. You sure?"

Rae held out her apple core. "Take mine too?"

Caro returned a moment later. "Cute little bouncy seat. You want me to bring it out here for him?"

Rae patted Johnny's back. "He's fine. Thanks, though." She'd thought Caro might leave then, but the girl sat back down.

"So how come you guys lived with your grandmother when you were a kid? She never would tell me."

No, Gram wouldn't have shared their family's secrets. There was nobody left to protect now, though. "My mother was mentally ill. It started with postpartum depression—I guess I drove her over the edge." She smiled, but Caro didn't.

"Whatever happened, it wasn't your fault." Caro pointed at the baby. "Would you ever blame him for anything?"

She smiled at the astute girl. "Good point. Anyway, Mom's behavior became more erratic, and she was eventually diagnosed with bipolar disorder. Dad had to work, of course, and traveled a lot, so he moved us in here so Gram could help out."

"And then he died."

"Right. In a car accident when I was eleven. And my mom didn't handle it well."

Caro looked toward the yard and nodded slowly. "It sucks having a parent in prison. Sucks not living with your parents."

The girl was right, though Rae'd have preferred if her mother was still in prison.

"But at least I get to see him sometimes," Caro said. "And I get to see my mom sometimes, when she can get her act together for a little while. But she can't seem to stay sober for very long, so I'll probably never live with her. I can't imagine not having any of them."

Rae's eyes filled with tears.

"I'm sorry," Caro said. "I'm so stupid. Don't listen to me."

"You're not stupid. You're right. I wish they were still here—all of them. Even after my mother no longer knew who I was, when she was in prison, at least I could look at her. I could hear her voice and talk to her."

"And now even your Gram's gone."

"Are you trying to cheer me up?"

The girl cracked a smile, and Rae did too. Yes, her life was hard, but this girl didn't know the half of it.

"So, can I hold him?"

Johnny breathed evenly in her ears, resting for the first time all day. "He's been so fussy today." Rae considered the consequences of spending time with Caro and decided there wouldn't be any. Nobody would see the girl coming and going from the backyard. "Can you come back tomorrow?"

The girl brightened. "I'd love to."

"Okay, then. And do me a favor? Don't tell anybody you saw me?" She scrambled for an excuse and finally settled on one. "I have so many old friends in this town"—the lie slipped easily from her lips—"and I know they'll all descend with casseroles and kind words if they hear I'm home. I just need a little time alone first."

"I'm a great secret-keeper. Nobody will hear it from me."

Caro left, and Rae watched as the girl with the red hair disappeared in the trees. Not that Rae would be here very long, but it was good to know she had a friend.

TEN

At just after seven California time on Sunday evening, Julien, Hector, and Farah stepped out of the San Diego airport and slid into the backseat of a waiting limousine.

Hector sat in the far seat, facing them. He checked his phone for messages.

Farah yawned beside him. Julien was too wired to feel the hours. In Paris it was three in the morning, but he'd grown so accustomed to traveling, he hardly noticed the jet lag.

"You're sure you have the right address?"

Farah wiped at tired eyes. "I'm as sure as I can be. She has a common name, and there are millions of people in southern California. There were hundreds of women named Rachel Adams, but this is the only one I can find who shares our Rachel's birthday."

Our Rachel. It was good that Farah had grown fond of his wife. An awkward situation, but he'd been bound to fall in love eventually. He was pleased to see how well Farah handled it. The woman was a professional, and she'd gone beyond the call with Rachel, befriending her, making her feel welcome at his home in Tunis, then checking on her often when her pregnancy confined her to bed in Paris.

He smiled at his assistant. "You've done well, as always. I thank you."

"You're welcome," she said in practiced English.

He realized he'd spoken in English too. Didn't take long to slip back into old habits. He pulled in a deep breath of American air, then blew it out slowly. Savoring the freedom. From his father, from the business. Not that he had ever truly been free.

His cell rang. He looked at the screen, took a deep breath, and answered. "Bonjour, Papa."

"I understand you've lost your wife."

If he ever saw that inept guard again, he'd kill him. "I haven't lost her. She's visiting her grandmother. The woman has taken ill."

"So you're in the States?"

"We're on our way to her house right now."

"You have business to take care of here."

Business had to take priority. Of course if Maman were ill, Papa would drop everything to be with her. Perhaps if Julien had introduced Rachel to Papa and Maman, they would feel more affection for her. As it was, Papa was suspicious of this new woman Julien had brought into their lives and then kept from them.

He hadn't been eager to introduce Rae to his family. He would have to eventually, but there'd been no rush. He'd enjoyed having her and Johnny all to himself. Perhaps he'd isolated her too much. Perhaps that's what this was about.

He'd find out when he located her. And he'd make sure she never did anything like this again.

"Thanks to the deal I made last week," Julien said, "I'll make more money this month than I made last year. I think I can afford to take a few days off."

"If you'd be willing to expand—"

"And cut into Geoffrey's pie. No, thank you."

"Your brother is bringing a lot of income to the family."

A lot of income because the man had no morals. "He's a thug, Papa. I will not stoop as low as he. No money is worth that."

There was a long silence on the other side of the line. Julien's blood pressure ticked up with each passing second. Finally, Papa said, "That thug, as you call him, is building an empire."

"On the backs of—"

"You might be the elder son, Julien, but he has proved himself. And he has heirs to leave the business to someday."

"I have an heir."

"So you say."

Julien let the words sink in. He looked at Hector, who was studying him across the car. Farah's eyes were focused on the limo floor.

Julien looked out the window at the arid landscape, the lush foliage, the gleaming homes. Two bicyclists rode along the street toward him, the evening breeze flapping their clothes behind them.

Julien turned away. "We've nearly arrived. I will call you later."

"See that you do."

Julien waited until his father had disconnected before he slipped his phone back into his pocket.

It would work out. His father would see Julien was right about Geoffrey. He'd fall in love with Jean-Louis. Julien had been shortsighted in not introducing his parents to Rae earlier. She'd wanted to meet them, and his parents understood the situation. How did one share his line of work with an outsider? He needed to marry her first, be sure of her allegiance, before he confided in her. His father had agreed it would be better to wait until the baby was born to share the more...delicate aspects of his business. But that didn't mean they couldn't have met.

And now, she was gone, and his father was all too willing to write Rachel and Jean-Louis off in favor of Geoffrey and his little thug sons.

If only Martine hadn't been barren.

Hector cleared his throat, and Julien looked up. "What is it?"

"I'm having trouble nailing Aziz's people down."

Julien leaned forward. "What do you mean?"

"We have arranged for receipt of the goods, but Aziz is hesitating about setting a delivery date. They've put it on hold."

Julien muttered a curse. He needed this deal to go through. His hold on power was tenuous at best, but if he lost this, he might lose his father's respect along with it. "Fix this, Hector."

"I'm sure it's logistics, nothing more."

"I hope you're right."

He looked out the window again as the limousine turned down a neighborhood street. The homes were enormous, many Spanish and Mediterranean styles. In a strange way, it reminded him of Tunis. All the bright colors. So unlike Paris, where the buildings and streets were covered in a soft gray patina.

Nothing dulled this. If not for the limo's tinted windows, he'd need his sunglasses.

They pulled into the driveway of a brick single-family home. From the outside, he guessed it to be at least three hundred square meters. The Americans would call it three thousand square feet.

The driver opened the door. Julien said, "Wait here," and stepped out.

He took a path lined in dark green bushes. The air smelled

of flowers and sunshine. Had Rachel grown up in this house? She'd never told him much about her childhood. He hadn't gotten the impression her parents were wealthy, but this neighborhood reflected incomes beyond the average American standard of living. He tried to imagine Rae riding this street on her bicycle, running around on that lawn. The image wouldn't come.

Would she answer the door? If she did, would the smile that had captured him from the start greet him, or would she be more shocked than happy?

Would she try to run?

He'd been too gentle with his wife. Perhaps he'd become accustomed to Martine and her acquiescent personality. Of course she had known what he did for a living, what he was capable of. Julien had never let Rae see that side of him. As soon as he got her home, that would change.

The front door stood at least three meters high and looked aged, as though it had been taken from some ancient mission. He rang the bell. A moment later, a middle-aged woman with short, curly brown hair opened the door. She wore a blue blazer over matching slacks and silver sandals. She tilted her head when she saw him, then smiled. "May I help you?"

"Are you Mrs. Adams?"

She nodded. "I am."

"I am Julien Moreau."

Her expression didn't change. Not a good sign.

"I'm looking for Rachel."

Her smile faded, along with the pink in her cheeks.

Julien waited for her to say something, but she seemed speechless.

"I am her husband. Is she not here?"

"Here?" The woman looked behind her as if seeking help.

Then turned back to him. "She hasn't been here in..." She blinked twice, shook her head slightly. "Rachel passed away."

Passed away? "No, no. I must have the wrong house." But Farah had said this was it, and Farah was rarely mistaken. "The woman I'm looking for is thirty years old. A reporter. Attended Columbia University."

"Look, if this is some kind of a joke..." The woman grabbed the door and swung it toward him.

Julien stopped the door with his hand. "Perhaps there's been a mistake. Could you look at this photograph?"

"I don't need to look. My daughter died years ago."

The woman could be lying, but she seemed sincere. The reaction, the paling skin. He had the wrong house. "Forgive me for intruding."

He'd taken two steps toward the limo when the woman added, "But she went to Columbia."

He froze. Turned. "Columbia?"

"Got accepted. Enrolled. But then she disappeared."

"But you said she died."

"A year later. In LA."

He didn't understand. It had to be a different Rachel. But what were the chances, two women from La Jolla with the same name and birthday, both going to Columbia?

He pulled out his cell phone and scrolled through the photographs. He found one of Rachel and Jean-Louis, turned the phone to the woman. "This is my Rachel."

The woman stepped back. "Come inside." She left the door open and walked into the house.

He followed, admired the grand entrance and curving staircase. Tried to picture Rae as a little girl, playing in these rooms.

Based on the woman's reaction to the picture, Rae had never been here.

She stopped in the hallway and pointed to a portrait of a

teenager with dark brown hair and brown eyes. She had the round face of a girl who liked American cheeseburgers.

"That's Rachel's senior picture. By the time she went to college, she'd lost all the extra weight. I was so proud of her, until I realized she'd lost it because she'd started using drugs."

"I'm sorry."

"Not the same girl."

Indeed, there was no resemblance.

Seemed his wife had spun a web of lies to rival Julien's. Fortunately, he was good at ferreting out the truth.

ELEVEN

Brady slammed his laptop closed, stood, and stretched. He'd spent the morning working on the burglaries with zero luck. Now he needed to focus on what was going on with Rae. Not that it was any of his business, but something didn't feel right. If she was in danger, he needed to know so he could keep her and his town safe.

Brady shoved his hand in his pocket, felt the handful of change, and headed for the vending machine. What he needed was a jolt of caffeine.

Saturday night, the late bust, and then the shocking reunion with Rae had kept his eyes from closing until almost dawn. And Sunday night... Yeah, that was Rae's fault too. He'd spent most of his should-be-sleeping time replaying the better moments of their past, when they were children and such good friends. When they were teenagers and so much more. When Brady had finally drifted into sleep Sunday night, he'd dreamed of her.

He had to stop.

He bought his soda and poured a quarter of the sweet fizz down his throat. Better. Nothing like sugar and caffeine to reset the brain functions.

He should just accept Rae's story and let it go. A wise person would. He'd never been accused of great wisdom.

He returned to his desk, grabbed his phone, and dialed a number written on his blotter.

"Law offices."

"Hey, Ellen. Is Gordon in?"

"Sure. I'll buzz you through."

A moment later, Gordon picked up the phone. "Tell me you found Reagan."

"She came home this weekend. I take it she hasn't called you yet."

"Not a word."

"If you don't hear from her soon, call or stop by Dorothy's house."

"Surely she'll call me. She has to know we have business to discuss."

Brady ran his palm over his scalp. "But this is Reagan McAdams we're talking about. Anything's possible."

The older man's laugh rumbled through the phone. "She's a lot like Dorothy, isn't she? I'd forgotten that."

Gordon might be right. Of course it had been so long since he'd spent any time with Rae, who knew what she was like?

Brady hung up the phone and stared at his laptop. It was time to figure out what was up with her car. Rae had told him she'd come home to see about her grandmother, and that was probably true. She'd also given him the impression she wouldn't be staying long. But Rae had said she was going back to her husband, and if that were the case, then why the car with temporary plates?

One quick check of those plates revealed what Brady had already suspected. She'd bought the car. A call to the dealership in Manchester told him she'd paid cash.

"Hardly bickered at all about the price," the salesman said.

"I told her seven thousand, she offered me sixty-five hundred and started counting out Ben Franklins."

Being a cop had its privileges. "Anything else you can tell me? Anything unusual about the sale?"

"Yeah, I'd say. After she bought the car, she asked me if she could have a ride to the store 'cause she didn't have a car seat and couldn't hold the baby and drive at the same time. It was a slow day, so I drove her, and another salesman followed me. Weird, right?"

"Did you happen to see how she arrived at your dealership?"

"Taxi. With luggage to boot. She had the kid in one of those backpack kind of things, only on the front. You see someone get out of a taxi, you think cha-ching, I'm gonna make a sale. That'll be my easiest sale all month."

"Do you remember anything else about her?"

"She looked wicked tired, like she hadn't slept in days. But with a baby, maybe she didn't, you know?"

He did know. Too well.

Brady laid the phone in the cradle and rubbed his temples. His hunch had been right, but what did it mean? The sooner Brady could shut up that niggling voice in his head that told him Rae needed his help, the sooner he could return to his normal life.

Such as it was.

With a new search window open, he typed *Julien Moreau*. He spent an hour looking for information on Rae's elusive husband. A photograph, a marriage certificate, something. As unusual as the name seemed to Brady, it was fairly common in Europe, so it wasn't that the search didn't turn up anything, it was that it turned up too much. An artist studying at the Sorbonne, a chef at some restaurant in Nice. Every man named Moreau he found had to be wrong. Brady clicked on one he hadn't checked out yet. Julien Garcia Moreau, born in 1975 in Toulouse, France. He checked the map and found the city in the southern-central part of the country. She'd said he was from southern France, hadn't she? A few more clicks and Brady discovered this Julien Moreau was a businessman working in... And there it was. Tunisia. This had to be the guy.

Brady clicked on the guy's business profile. Seemed his corporation had a hand in a lot of different kinds of business, most of which were operating somewhere in Northern Africa. Brady clicked on the corporation's website, translated it into English, and read. *Bringing manufacturing and commerce opportunities to the people of Africa.*

Julien Moreau was just the type of guy Reagan would fall for. He clicked on the photograph and studied it. Moreau had a thin face, a straight, narrow nose, and dark wide-set eyes. His jet black hair was straight and cut short. He had the swarthy skin of a Middle-Eastern man, and that skin matched little Johnny's coloring. Brady supposed some women might find this Moreau guy attractive. Handsome, successful... So what was going on in their marriage?

"Brady?"

He looked up to see Samantha Messenger approach his desk with a yellow sticky note in one hand. "Sorry. I saw your note when I got in this morning, but it's been crazy today."

"No problem. You have a minute now?"

She nodded and tossed the note in the trash can.

"Have a seat."

She sat in the wooden chair beside his desk, a flicker of worry in her eyes. "Not often I get pulled into the police station. What's going on?"

"What are you talking about?" Brady grinned for the first time all day. "You're here all the time."

"Well, sure." She flicked her hand toward the door that

separated the small police station from the clerk's office. "But I'm not usually summoned. Is something wrong?"

His grin faded, and he leaned forward. "When's the last time you heard from Rae?"

She blinked twice and sat straighter. "After graduation, same as you. Did she call?"

He took a deep breath. "She's back."

Samantha's jaw dropped. "Back? Wow. I thought when she didn't turn up for the funeral—"

"She hadn't heard. I dropped that bomb on her."

Samantha tilted her head. "So if she didn't know, then why'd she come home?"

He explained Rae's reasoning.

"She could have just called someone."

"But would she? She also swears she's been home before, and Dorothy said the same thing. But she avoided everyone from town like the Ebola virus."

Samantha sat back and smiled. "She called you this time, though. See, I told you she wouldn't stay mad forever."

He shook his head slowly. "That's not exactly how it happened." He explained his late-night run-in with Rae. "I don't know what she would have done if I hadn't shown up."

"So how does she look?"

Brady pictured her for about the millionth time since Saturday night. "Good, I guess. She has... Actually..." Brady really wanted to get Samantha's impression of Rae, and he didn't want to color it with his own. Sam had developed some keen instincts, and he'd learned to trust her judgment.

"She has a—?" she prompted.

"Never mind." Brady straightened the pens and pencils on his desk. "I told her to call you."

"Of course. Do you think she will?"

He relaxed a little and shrugged.

"She still mad?"

"She said she forgave us."

Tears filled Samantha's eyes, and she looked at her hands in her lap. "I never wanted to hurt her. Neither of us did."

"It's not your fault she disappeared for twelve years."

"It was my fault, though."

"I was there too. You didn't force me." He pulled open the drawer second from the bottom and grabbed a snack-sized Snicker's bar. "Here."

She took it, unwrapped it, and popped it in her mouth. "That solves everything."

He took one himself and shrugged. "Can't hurt."

She sat back and looked down at her hands again. "So if she has forgiven us, why hasn't she ever come back? Or at least called?"

He shrugged. "Maybe she didn't care enough." Twelve years had passed, and Rae had never contacted either of them. Best friends since diapers, and then just like that, she was gone. "You'll feel better after you talk to her."

"Do you?"

He refused to feel anything, and he certainly wasn't stupid enough to get tangled up with Rae again. "So..." He grabbed a pencil and doodled on his blotter, going for casual with the only picture he knew how to make, a side-view of Snoopy he'd learned to draw in second grade. "You know Rae. She could be gone tomorrow."

"And that would be tragic."

He kept doodling. He'd learned to ignore bait like a grand-daddy trout in Clearwater Lake.

She cleared her throat. "You have a phone number for her?"

He looked up and shook his head. "She says her cell doesn't work here. You could try the house phone, or just go over there."

"I'll do it today."

TWELVE

Rae sat back on her heels and wiped her forehead with the back of her hand. Might be September, but with all the searching she'd done in the last two hours in this stifling barn, it was no wonder she was dripping in sweat. The birds' music outside and the gentle sway of the breeze blowing through the windows and door were like a soothing soundtrack to her work. And then she'd heard something that didn't belong. She stilled and listened.

Tires on the asphalt, a gentle squeak of brakes.

After a glance at Johnny snoozing soundly in his bouncy seat, Rae skulked to the door and looked. She ignored the jolt of fear. It couldn't be Julien. He couldn't have found her already.

A white Isuzu Trooper was parked in the drive. Samantha Messenger stepped out and walked toward the house. She hadn't changed much since Rae'd last seen her, twelve years earlier, except where Samantha's dark hair had been short in high school, now it was long enough to pull into a ponytail, which hung halfway down her back. Samantha'd filled out more in the years, and Rae found herself still jealous of the shorter woman's curvy figure. Sam approached the house, and Rae lost sight of her when she walked up the steps. Rae heard the faint sound of knocking. Then nothing. Then footsteps on the wooden front porch. Rae stifled the desire to sneak a peek. Maybe Sam was looking through the windows.

Rae was tempted to step out of the barn. What would it hurt to have a conversation? But then she thought of Julien. She had to maintain her distance. The last thing she wanted was to drag Sam or anyone else down with her.

Samantha returned to her SUV, stopped near its hood, and looked toward the barn. Rae stepped into the shadows and watched as Samantha stared, then slid in the car. But she didn't pull away. Rae couldn't figure out what she was doing until, a moment later, Sam stepped out and carried an envelope to the front porch. Rae heard the storm door close before Samantha returned to the truck and drove away.

When she was sure Sam was gone, Rae walked to the front door and grabbed the envelope stuck between the storm door and the jamb.

DEAR REAGAN,

I don't blame you for not wanting to talk to me. I'd probably avoid me, too, under the circumstances. But I would love to see you. Please call me. I miss you.

Samantha

BENEATH HER NAME, Samantha had jotted her cell phone number and drawn a half a heart and three tiny letters. *BFF.*

Best friends forever. After what Samantha and Brady had done, Rae had once wondered if she could ever think of Sam as a friend again. Yes, Rae'd forgiven them. And while she still felt a twinge of anger when she thought of it, their kiss was so far in the past, and so much had happened since then, that the way Rae had reacted now seemed over the top. She'd love to see Sam, but to rekindle the friendship could only bring her friend harm.

Back in the barn, Rae shook off the sadness and crossed to the old metal desk, looking down at the rug beneath her feet. It reminded her of something she'd see in the medina in Tunis. She and Julien used to love to wander the old city and visit the stalls. He'd taken her to meet a rug maker once. Amazing the details that went into real Oriental rugs. She swept her foot across the one at her feet, kicking up a little cloud of dust. This one probably wasn't authentic, but still, why would anybody unroll a nice piece like this in a dusty old barn? The thing was ruined now, the once bright reds and blues faded.

She searched the desk and was just about to push the final drawer closed when she noticed something at the bottom. She reached past all the empty folders and grabbed a little red envelope. She unwound the thin string holding it closed, lifted the flap, and tipped it over. A key slid into her hand. Printed on the envelope were the words, *Nutfield Bank and Trust*. She could picture the building on the corner of Crystal and Baldwin.

Maybe she'd find what she was looking for there.

Rae glanced at her watch. Four-thirty. Bank was probably closed for the day. She'd go tomorrow. If she found Dad's box, her plan would be back on track.

Johnny whimpered. A good excuse to quit for the day.

She stood and smiled at the baby. "You hungry?"

He worked to stick his fist in his mouth, settled for two fingers, and sucked.

"I'll take that as a yes." She wiped her hands on her jeans and lifted the bouncy seat with Johnny still inside. He'd grown attached to the thing. In the house, she set the baby on the counter and washed her hands before fixing him a bottle.

He'd finished about half when she heard a tap on the back door. Her heart beat faster, but Julien wouldn't knock. Cradling the baby in her arms, she stood and looked past the curtain to see Caro on the other side. Rae opened the door. "I'm glad you came back."

"Wow, your hair looks good."

Rae ran her hand over her light red hair. "Figured it was time to go back to my roots, so to speak."

"Why'd you dye it in the first place?"

"I started dying it when I lived in Tunis, so I'd fit in better. Not a lot of redheads there."

"But standing out is good, right?" She ran a hand through her own unique hair.

"Sometimes. But Tunis isn't America, so standing out can be dangerous."

"Oh. Well, I love it." Caro held out her hands to show two shiny apples. "You want one?"

"Definitely. Right after I finish feeding Johnny." She led the way into the kitchen, and they sat at the kitchen table. Caro set one of the apples down and took a bite of the other.

"Good day at school?"

"Except for geometry."

"I never liked math." Rae lifted Johnny to burp him. "Do you have a boyfriend?"

Caro's pale skin turned a little pink. "Kinda. Yeah. We started seeing each other this summer."

"Is it serious?"

The girl shrugged. When Caro didn't say anything, Rae changed the subject. "So you said you don't like school. Are you in any clubs?"

"Not clubs, but I do love drama."

Rae should've guessed. "Have you been in any plays?"

"Nope. They're having auditions for *Once Upon a Mattress*, but I can't do it."

"Why not?"

Caro bit her lip. "My grandparents won't let me walk in the dark, and Nana doesn't like to drive at night. And Papa doesn't like to leave the house at all."

"Couldn't you get a ride with someone else?"

"Nobody lives in my neighborhood. I asked my sister, but she can't be bothered." She pasted on a smile. "It doesn't matter. I get to practice acting in class, and that's fun."

Rae studied the girl's forced expression. Even without a mom and dad at home, Rae'd never missed out on anything. Gram had seen to that. She had the fleeting thought that she could offer to drive the girl. But Rae wouldn't be there long enough for that.

Johnny burped.

"Good baby." Rae rubbed his back and cradled him closer. His skin was so soft against her neck. "Are you a good actor?"

Caro's fake smile morphed into a real one. "Actually, Mrs. Mathison says I'm a natural."

Rae carried Johnny into the living room, where she changed his diaper on the sofa. When she finished, she saw Caro's hopeful expression. "You want to hold him?"

"Could I?"

"Sure. Would you mind washing your hands?"

Caro did, then sat on the couch, and Rae gently laid the baby in her arms. She waited, wondered if he'd scream, but Johnny simply studied the girl's joyful face.

"He likes you."

She grabbed his tiny hand. "I like him too."

"Can I get you something to drink?"

Caro brightened. "Sure, if you don't mind."

Rae filled two glasses with iced tea and returned to the

living room. She'd started to sit when another knock came, this one from the front door. Her heartbeat raced once again, and once again she reminded herself.

Julien wouldn't knock.

THIRTEEN

BRADY KNOCKED AGAIN, louder this time. "Rae, I'm not leaving. You might as well open the door."

He saw a shadow shift in the window beside the door. She was right there. He pounded on the wood. "Open up. Police."

Seemed unlikely, but he could swear he heard her sigh through the thick door before it swung open. "Really?"

Whoa, she'd colored her hair. It wasn't exactly the right color, but it was close enough to stop his breath. That was the girl he'd fallen in love with.

And that was a thought he needed to banish, immediately.

He offered what he hoped was a conciliatory smile. "Hi there."

She stepped back, and he couldn't miss the sigh this time. "Come on in."

He stepped inside, heard little Johnny cooing, and followed the sound to the living room. He stopped in the entry and regarded the red-headed girl sitting on the sofa.

"Detective Thomas," the girl said. She was holding Johnny and looking at him with a nervous smile. "What happened yesterday? In Miami, no less? How could you lose to the Dolphins?"

He scowled at her while Rae laughed. "Still?" she asked. "It's been how many years?"

Brady took in Rae's rare smile. "Too many."

"You have to admit," the girl said, "it's pretty funny." She tilted her head to the side. "You look a lot like him too. Especially with that five o'clock shadow. It could be worse. You could be named after a terrible quarterback. And who doesn't love the Patriots?"

"Fans of every other NFL team in America."

The girl shrugged. "Who cares about them?"

"It's Carolyn, right?"

Her smile faded. "I prefer Caro."

Caro. Carolyn Nolan. Fifteen. She'd been caught shoplifting a bottle of nail polish from the drug store a few months before. He'd thought she was the girl from Saturday night's bust. The face was right, and the eye color. But she looked too young. And there was something else. "Didn't you used to be blond? How long has your hair been that color?"

The girl ran her fingers through her dark red, shoulder-length hair and pulled a bit in front of her face. "A month or so. Why?"

He studied her. Might've thought she was lying, but he could see the blond roots.

Rae cleared her throat. "Did you want something?"

He kept his eyes trained on the girl. "Do you have a sister?"

Caro's eyes narrowed. He was sure she'd have crossed her arms if she hadn't been holding the baby. "Why?"

"You live near here, don't you?" He'd driven her home from the store that day and talked to her grandparents. Their last name was Allen. Didn't seem the nurturing types. "I'll just call your grandparents and ask them."

She blew out a long-suffering breath. "Yes, I have a sister."

"How old?"

She glared at him. "Nineteen."

"Name?"

"Laurie."

"Where does she work?"

"She just started at that new copy shop near the highway."

"Is she—?"

"Um, Brady?" Rae stepped between them. "What are you doing?"

He looked at Rae and relaxed. "I'm sorry." He sidestepped Rae and looked back at Caro. "I saw a girl who looked like you the other night, but her hair color was different. And she seemed older. I'm just trying to put the pieces together."

"Did she do something wrong?" Caro asked.

Rae looked from Caro to him, and he shook his head. He was sure the girl at that drug bust had just been really unlucky, and he didn't want to make a scene. "Of course not."

Caro shrugged. "Whatever."

"Are you done?" Rae asked.

He turned to her. "Yes. Sorry. I didn't... It just surprised me to see Caro here." He took in Rae's appearance. She was wearing a T-shirt with what looked like dirt across the shoulder over a pair of dusty blue jeans. Her newly-restored strawberry-blond hair was a mess. He reached for it and pulled out a paper clip.

She pulled away and glared at him. "What are you...?"

The paper clip he held out silenced her. "Did you want this in there?"

She patted the top of her head. "I have no idea where that came from."

"Been going through stuff?"

She grabbed the paper clip, tossed it on the coffee table, and dusted off her T-shirt. "What do you want?"

He eyed the two glasses on the coffee table. "Sure," he said, "I'd love a drink."

He caught her scowl as he settled in the club chair in front of the fireplace.

"I don't remember inviting you to sit," Rae said.

"Your grandmother would be appalled." He turned to Caro. "Did you know Mrs. McAdams?"

The girl looked from him to Rae and back. "Uh huh."

"She was so polite, wasn't she? Always had a smile and a snack for guests."

"Fine." Rae disappeared into the kitchen. She slammed a cabinet door, then returned a moment later with a full glass. She handed it to him—should he check for arsenic? He decided to live dangerously and took a sip.

"Sweet. You make this yourself?"

"It's from a can." She sat on the chair opposite him. "What do you want, Brady?"

He set the tea on the table. "Did you call Gordon?"

She shifted in her seat. "I was busy."

"I told him you're here. He might've tried to call you on the house phone."

"It rang a few times, but I didn't pick it up."

"Right," he continued. "And then there was Samantha."

"Look, I'm only going to be home a few days, and there's no reason for me to see her. Or you, really. I just need to take care of stuff around here and go."

"You're in such a hurry you couldn't even answer the door when she came by." At Rae's lifted eyebrows, he nodded. "Yeah, she told me."

"You two are pretty close, huh?"

"We're friends, Rae. Have been since forever, as you might recall."

She glared. "I recall you were more than friends."

He glared right back.

Rae crossed her arms and looked at Caro. "Would you like me to take Johnny so you don't have to witness this?"

Caro held the baby a little tighter. "Are you kidding? This is the most fun I've had all day."

Reagan looked at the girl a moment longer before shifting her gaze back to him. "I don't have time to visit with her or you."

He tried to keep the hurt from his eyes but figured he'd failed when he saw Caro's pitying expression. When had he gotten so pathetic that a teenager living with her crotchety grandparents felt sorry for him?

Rae took a sip of her tea. "I just need to take care of stuff and get out of... Get home."

"If you're in such a hurry to get home, then why didn't you call Gordon today?"

She opened her mouth, then snapped it shut.

Something was very wrong. He needed to speak with Rae, and not with this girl as a witness.

Brady turned to Caro. "You're a sophomore this year?"

She nodded.

"You like it?"

"She likes drama," Rae offered. "In fact, she wants to audition for a play, but she doesn't have a ride home from rehearsals. You know anybody who could help her?"

"You'll be around for a while."

She set her glass on the table. "Not that long."

He could tell Rae was hiding something by the look in her eyes, the way her gaze flicked to the ceiling. And the used car in the driveway.

He turned back to Caro. "When are auditions?"

"Tomorrow after school."

"What time will they be done?"

"Probably about seven."

He turned back to Rae. "Why don't you plan to pick her up after the auditions?" He turned to Caro. "If you get a part, I'll arrange for rides after that."

"You'd do that?" Caro's gaze shifted from him to Rae and back. Her eyes were bright and hopeful, and his heart melted just a little.

He turned to Rae. "And you'll still be here for a couple weeks, so you can help for a little while. It'll take at least until then to manage the estate."

"I don't know." A little sheen of sweat broke out on her forehead. She wasn't just hiding something.

She was scared.

She looked at Caro, then at him, and nodded. "Sure."

He stood and approached Caro and the baby. "Can I hold him?"

The girl relinquished the baby.

"Thanks. Would you mind if I spoke with Rae alone for a couple of minutes? Maybe you could just wait outside or—"

"I gotta go, anyway." The girl peered beyond him at Rae. "Thanks for the tea. And for the ride. I can't wait to tell Finn I can audition."

Rae smiled, but the corners of her mouth were tight. "Great. See you tomorrow."

As soon as the door closed, Rae glared at him. "What is wrong with you?"

He sat and breathed in the baby's scent, enjoying the feel of that fine hair against his cheek. "Offering to help her seemed like the right thing to do. Caro seemed happy, and—"

"That's not what I meant. Just...you barge in here, interrogate her like that."

He settled the baby on his shoulder and patted the tiny back.

She put her hands on her hips. "Well?"

"Are you still mad at Samantha and me? I thought you forgave us."

Her jaw dropped, but he continued before she could speak. "It's been twelve years, Rae. And from where I sit, you've got everything you ever wanted. You moved overseas, a dream of yours. You're married, you have an adorable baby. According to Dorothy, you're enjoying a very successful career. Samantha and I are both still alone, but it seems you've found your happily-ever-after."

"You don't know anything about me."

"I know you ignored Sam when she came over today."

Rae grabbed Caro's half-glass of iced tea and stomped into the kitchen. He waited until she returned, waited while she stood over him, glaring. Finally, she sat in the chair across from him. "What do you want from me?"

He leaned forward to better see those hazel eyes. They always seemed nearly gold when she was angry, and sure enough, right now Yukon Cornelius would fall in love. "I want you to forgive me."

"I told you, I already did. I just don't see any reason to rehash the past. I'm not going to be here very long, and I don't have any time to reminisce with you two."

"She just wants to talk to you. Is that too much to ask?"

Rae blinked and turned away.

"What aren't you telling me?"

She turned back to him. "There's all sorts of stuff I'm not telling you, Brady. My life is none of your business."

He absorbed that blow, tucked it away. "There was a time you trusted me."

"I said I forgave you. That'll have to be enough."

"Maybe if you'd given me the opportunity to explain." The baby squeaked at Brady's raised voice, so he lowered it. "You just took off without a word."

"What did you expect?"

He watched her a long moment, saw the defiance in her gaze and just beyond it, the pain. He softened his voice. "After all we'd been through, I expected you to talk to me. I deserved that."

FOURTEEN

Julien took a slow sip of his American beer and set the mug on the table, refusing to look at the door.

In the busy hotel lounge, Julien had chosen a seat where he could keep an eye on the lobby. He glanced at the bar's patrons, suited men and women, leather shoes, laptop cases propped against chairs. Because one can never stop working.

He'd landed at LaGuardia a few hours before. Both Farah and Hector understood the importance of secrecy, so neither of them would have told his father they hadn't located Rachel yet. What had prompted Papa's insistence on this stateside meeting?

Julien resisted the urge to tap his feet. Farah and Hector were at Columbia right now, trying to track down an address for Rae. If Farah's charms didn't work, Hector's brawn would. They'd have her address by dinner.

From the corner of his eye, Julien saw his father enter the hotel. He wasn't a tall man, and flanked by his two most loyal guards, he looked even shorter. He wore a gray suit and blue tie over a crisp white shirt, which set off his complexion. Like Julien, he could pass for nearly any dark-complexioned nationality, thanks to his Spanish, African, and French heritage. He walked with authority, and people seemed to step out of his way without even realizing they were doing so.

His guards wore designer suits too. Unlike Hector, these men were lean. One would never guess their strength. And their weapons were well-hidden beneath their jackets. They looked like three high-powered businessmen.

Julien knew the truth.

When Papa saw him, he said something to one of the guards, then left them in the lobby. He entered the lounge and slid into the seat across from Julien.

"What are you drinking?" Papa asked.

"Sam Adams Octoberfest." It was one of his favorites, and Julien didn't mind a bit that drinking beer would irritate his father. "Would you like one?"

Papa made no effort to hide his disgust. "I don't know how you can stomach it."

"I developed a taste at Princeton."

"You're no longer a college boy."

"When in Rome." He set the bottle down and signaled for the waitress. After his father gave his order in perfect English—Scotch, neat, of course—Julien said, "What are you doing here, Papa?"

"I'd hoped to meet your wife." He looked around. "She is here, no?"

"She's at her grandmother's bedside."

"In California?"

His father could not possibly have found out about what happened in California. But Julien needed an excuse for being in Manhattan. "In her haste to get here, Rae neglected to tell me her parents had moved her grandmother to New York to be closer to her sister. I'd be with my wife right now, if not for your summons."

His black eyes focused on Julien's, a hint of challenge in them. "Is that so?"

Julien tapped his fingers on the table. "What's going on?"

"Your deal fell through."

His fingers stilled. Hector had been trying to nail Aziz down on delivery and payment, but the man had been elusive. Now Julien knew why. "What happened? And how did you find out?"

"Geoffrey had a conversation with your contact. Seems Aziz was eager to make a trade, but you refused."

"It was unnecessary, and it adds more manpower and risk."

"This has nothing to do with risk."

Julien remained still, though not without effort. "Everybody has to have a line."

"Your brother has drawn his line in a place that makes me more money."

"My brother cares only about money. And power. That is not how you raised us, Papa. I take risks, but I don't take unnecessary risks just to earn your approval."

Papa leaned forward. "Maybe you should try a little harder to earn my approval."

Julien settled back against the chair. He would not grovel. "All my life, you have groomed me to take over your business."

"The job is still yours, my son. If you're willing to do it. But you need to embrace it for what it is. You need to..." His voice trailed off when the waitress delivered the drink. Papa waited until she walked away. He leaned closer to Julien and lowered his voice. "You need to adjust your *line* for the changing times." He lifted his drink to his lips, sipped slowly.

At his father's deadly calm, Julien's veins gushed with adrenaline, but Julien wouldn't back down. He'd faced men with weapons and armies and vast power, and Julien had always held his ground. Papa was a man, just like any other. Or so Julien had been telling himself as long as he could remember.

"We are equalizers, my son. We make it possible for the least among us to make their feelings heard. We keep tyrants in line."

"We have plenty of tyrants as customers."

"It's not our job to decide who—"

"Yes, yes." Julien waved off his father's mantra. "So you've always said. But how does the opium fit in?"

Papa sipped his drink, set it down. "I've never understood your opposition to that aspect of the business."

Julien looked at the customers in the bar, ordering their second and third and fourth drinks for the evening. He glanced at his own. But it was different. It was.

"I went to college with a man who sold cocaine," Julien said. "The men who bought it told themselves it was different. They weren't going to end up like those people in crack houses. A friend tried it. He told me cocaine made him his best self, amplified his skills and gave him energy to get more done. I think he'd done it four or five times. And then, one night, he had a heart attack and died. He was twenty-one."

"How people choose to use it—"

"It gets people addicted. The people who deal it are dangerous. I have worked hard to develop my business, and I want to focus my energy on what I know, deal with people I have relationships with. Dealing drugs is an ugly game, and I don't want a part of it."

"What you do kills."

"Maybe I save lives," Julien said. "Like you always said, we give the weak and defenseless a voice. We can be equalizers."

"The people who sell the opium, it's all they have. It's their livelihood."

"It's a crude and vulgar way to pay the bills."

Papa's eyes narrowed, and again Julien felt a surge of adrenaline. He hadn't given in to the flight response since he was a child. He'd been tempted when he'd been caught playing with his father's pistol at nine years old. He'd wanted to run. Fear had held him in place. He'd turned to his father and pointed the gun at the ground.

To teach him how dangerous the weapon was, Papa made him fire it.

At the family dog.

But Julien hadn't run. Not even as he'd watched his beloved German shepherd bleed to death. Not as he imagined what would have happened if he'd turned the gun on his father instead.

That night, Papa had buried the dog himself. As they stood beside the grave, his father, sweating and dirty, laid his hand on Julien's shoulder. "It's a terrible business, killing. It's not something to take lightly. When you wield a weapon, you must be prepared for the consequences. Better to learn it through the loss of a dog than a friend, no?"

It was a lesson Julien had never forgotten.

"So you're ashamed of me?" His father's words pulled him back to the moment.

"I'm proud to be your son." The words were true, most of the time. When he watched Papa kiss Maman's hand, he was proud to be his son. When he felt the respect of business associates who learned Julien was Alejandro's son, he puffed up with pride.

"Just not Geoffrey's brother," his father said.

"I would die for my brother. I would die for you, for the family. You know my commitment." Julien sipped his beer. "But I do not want to expand into the opium trade."

"Your brother is making a lot of money."

"My brother is as crude and vulgar as the drugs he deals."

Julien hadn't meant to say that. His father's stony face didn't dissuade him from continuing. "How do you justify the girls?"

Papa lifted his drink. "People are entitled to their entertainment."

Entertainment. Julien swallowed his retort. Another loathsome business fueled by perverts and addicts. He wanted no relationships with such lowly people, but now wasn't the time to argue the point. He laid his hands on the table, marveling that they were steady. He'd trained his body well. "And you approve of Geoffrey betraying me?"

"I approve of the money."

"You know he can't run your business. He doesn't have the sense you have. He doesn't have the self-control."

"He is loathsome and vulgar," Papa said, "according to you."

"Not him. The people he works with—"

"I've always felt you were a better choice to run the business, and now that you have an heir, and more, I assume, on the way, I can continue grooming you for the position. Geoffrey will need to be led. And you will need to find a way to compete with him. It's time to adjust that moral line."

"It's not about morals. It's about—"

"Dealing with people who are beneath you. But you must learn."

Julien nodded slowly. "And what if I decide I'm not willing to live with those terms?"

His father's gaze never wavered as he leaned forward. "You either choose to take over running the business, or you work for Geoffrey. But as you know, one doesn't leave the Moreau family."

Julien knew too well the truth of that. His cousin had turned against the family when Julien was a schoolboy. He'd escaped, gone to Interpol, agreed to testify in return for a new identity.

He'd never testified. His body had never been found.

What did the man expect, turning his back on his family? Trying to escape those unbreakable ties.

Rae. What was her endgame? Was this just a foolish whim to visit her grandmother, or did she know more than he realized?

Julien thought about all the files he had back Paris. In Tunis. Surely she hadn't...

He pushed back from the table. "I need to be with my wife."

"We'll see your family at your mother's birthday celebration?"

Julien stood, pulled a few bills from his wallet, and tossed them on the table. "We'll be there."

FIFTEEN

Rae turned over in bed and peeked at the clock. Nearly midnight. Johnny would wake in a couple of hours to eat. She needed to get some sleep, not rehash her conversation with Brady for the thousandth time.

He'd asked her about her husband, their home, their lives. She hated lying to him, and she really hadn't liked the fact that he'd known she was lying. He'd finally quit the interrogation, handed her the baby, and headed for the door. "Please call Samantha tomorrow. You need to talk to her."

"The only reason I'm talking to you is that you're too stubborn to go away."

He stopped, hand on the door knob, and turned to her. His eyebrows lifted so high they disappeared beneath his hair. "Are you seriously saying *I'm* stubborn? Honey, you wrote the book."

The temptation to visit with her old friend was nearly overwhelming. But what if Julien discovered their friendship? What if Julien discovered Brady had been over?

Yet, how would he?

Rae couldn't think straight.

Brady took a deep breath. "Sam will stop by tomorrow. For the sake of your friendship, talk to her."

"You can't make me."

He chuckled, but the sound died. "Sam's been punishing herself for what we did for too long. She needs to be set free of it."

Rae tried to come up with a quick-witted answer for that, but nothing came to mind as she imagined her old friend, tortured because of the way Rae had treated her. For years, she'd told herself that Sam and Brady had deserved it after betraying her the way they had. But now... Rae understood the need for freedom.

His lips had twitched, and he'd pulled out his badge and flipped it open. "I might need to take you in for questioning."

"You wouldn't dare."

He chuckled. "Don't tempt me." His grin faded. He slipped his badge into his pocket. His gaze was so tender, so reminiscent of the way he'd gazed at her when they were young and in love. That thought had her backing away.

As if he could read her mind, he took a step back. "Please talk to Sam. Maybe you don't trust me right now, but think back to when you did, to when you and I told each other everything. Try to remember what that felt like for just a minute." His hand covered his heart as if touching memories. Or maybe he was protecting it from her. "Do you remember?"

Every minute of it. She nodded, unable to speak.

"For the sake of the boy I used to be, the girl you used to be, and the friend Sam used to be, please, just talk to her."

Rae wished he'd put his detective mask back on. This vulnerable man had too much of a pull on her heart.

So of course she'd have to see Sam. Anything to make that tortured picture of Brady go away.

THE NIGHT of tossing and turning had her pouring a second cup of coffee the next morning. She'd planned to get to the bank, but Brady had called and told her Samantha would be over before lunch. Rae agreed to be there.

The sunny weather had disappeared behind a thick layer of clouds and drizzle, and though she wanted to continue her search of the barn, it was too cold. At least Julien couldn't possibly find her this fast. She still felt safe here.

Though something told her Dad had hidden his box in the barn, it wouldn't hurt to look in the house too. After breakfast, she carried the baby upstairs and laid him in the middle of what used to be her parents' bed.

She pulled open the closet door and stared at the mess within. It was packed. She quickly flipped through the musty clothes hanging from the bar. Mom's things, mostly. Some of Dad's nicer suits and ties. Rae bent and looked at the floor. There had to be fifty pairs of shoes. And every purse, pocketbook, and wallet her mother had ever owned lay in a heap on the right. On the left, boxes had been stacked halfway up the space, bumping into the clothes hanging above. Rae opened each box and looked inside. Cheap costume jewelry, old perfume bottles, belts, and purses.

She stood and peered at the shelf above the clothes rod. More shoes were piled beside a chest. Rae stood on her tiptoes and tried to work the chest off the shelf. It wouldn't budge.

Maybe that's where the treasure was hidden.

Unfortunately, she'd have to get help with that.

Rae sighed and moved on to the long bureau that had been her mother's. She opened the top drawer on the left side and found Mom's panties and bras just as her mother had left them. She ran her hand along the bottom of the drawer but found nothing unusual.

Rae glanced at Johnny, who was sucking his fingers and staring at the wall. "You like this room?"

He turned to her voice. Was that a smile? She approached and tickled his belly. "You having a good time, sweet thing?"

He bounced again, and his lips twitched. And there it was again, that almost smile, gone before she'd been sure. She picked him up and snuggled him close, amazed at the way his little head fit perfectly in the crook of her neck. She patted his tiny back and rocked him gently. All the stupid decisions she'd made, and somehow she'd still ended up with this precious, priceless life. She'd fallen in love before, had friends she'd cared very deeply about, but the feelings she had for Johnny were unexplainable. Why hadn't he been given to a better person, one who was worthy of him? She couldn't answer that, but she knew she'd never done anything to deserve this perfect child.

She could feel his soft breaths against her neck, his very life measured in tiny puffs through her hair. So small and vulnerable. She would do anything to protect her child. Anything.

She held him in front of her and looked into his dark, serious eyes. "We're not alone, my sweet child. We have each other, and that's all we need. I'm going to take care of you."

He wiggled in her arms, and she smiled and set him down, then wiped the tears from her cheeks. "Back to work for me."

She turned to the bureau, took a deep breath, and opened the second drawer, then the third, feeling around for anything hard and finding nothing but socks, pantyhose, and a girdle. The next drawer held scarves. Rae pulled them out one by one, flooded with memories. Rae still missed her mom. After she'd been sent to prison, Rae had visited her a few times, but her mother barely recognized her.

And then she'd died. Rae had become an orphan at sixteen.

She was moving on to the next drawer when she heard the

crunch of tires on the asphalt. She looked out the window. Samantha.

She turned to Johnny. "I'd be really grateful if you'd do something to make her get out of here fast. Scream or have a blowout or something."

He stared at the ceiling.

She scooped him up. "Yeah, I didn't think so." They were halfway down the stairs when she heard the knock at the door.

Rae took a deep breath, blew it out, and pulled the door open.

Samantha stood on the other side, her round face a mixture of joy and dread. She smiled, blinked twice, and said, "Thanks for opening the door this time."

The sight of her best friend, up close, stole her breath. How she'd longed for Samantha in the years since she'd seen her.

Rae stood back, and Samantha walked in and smiled at the baby. "Brady didn't tell me about this guy. How old is he?"

"A little over two weeks."

"Oh, he's precious. What's his name?"

Rae swallowed a lump of emotion. "Johnny."

Sam leaned in for a closer look, then stepped back and looked at Rae's left hand. "Quite a ring you have there. Your husband must be some guy."

Oh yeah. Julien was something.

"Let's go in the kitchen." Rae nodded in that direction, and Samantha passed, her heels clicking on the hardwood. Even with the extra couple of inches on the shoes, Sam was still shorter than Rae. Her dark brown hair was loose and curly and swung across her back as she walked. She stopped in the middle of the kitchen and looked around. "I haven't been here in so long. It's hardly changed."

The room, with its yellow walls and pine cabinets, was bright and cheery even with the drizzle outside. A shelter in the storm, just like Gram had always been. "You want some coffee? I made a fresh pot a little while ago."

"Sure."

Rae put Johnny in his bouncy seat on the kitchen table and pulled out a coffee mug. She poured the coffee and set it on the counter with a clean spoon, smiling at the picture of Sam leaning over Johnny and murmuring baby talk. This is what her life should have been.

And where had that thought come from? Hadn't she always wanted to escape this town? She shook off the questions. "Sugar? Cream?"

Samantha didn't even look up from the baby. "Do you have low-fat milk?"

Rae turned to the fridge with a comfortable smile. All these years, and Samantha was still worried about her weight. "No milk. I have some baby formula."

Samantha giggled. "Black is fine."

Rae poured herself a fresh cup and approached the table. "Shall we sit?"

Samantha sat in the chair that faced the window, the same chair she'd always chosen. If Brady were here, he'd sit in the chair against the wall, and Rae would sit between them. And when Gram had joined them, she'd sit on the opposite side. How many times had the four of them shared a plate of cookies or sipped hot chocolate right here?

"Brady said you wanted to see me."

"I'm so glad you agreed." Her gaze drifted to the baby, then to her coffee, before meeting Rae's. "I..." She blinked twice.

Were those tears? "You don't have to say anything, Sam. I don't really know what happened between you and Brady, but I know you didn't mean to hurt me."

"I tried to find you. When I couldn't, I begged Gram to tell me where you were, or at least to tell you I needed to talk to you."

"She told me."

Samantha swallowed and nodded and wiped her eyes. "I have to explain."

Rae didn't need a blow-by-blow. "Let's not rehash it. It's not important now."

Samantha sipped her coffee. Her hands trembled, and the liquid inside her cup shimmered.

Rae could hear Brady's words from the night before as if he were standing right behind her. *Samantha and I are both still alone, but it seems you've found your happily-ever after.* So many years later, she would have expected both Samantha and Brady to be married, if not to each other than to somebody. But there was no ring on either of their fingers.

"It was my fault," Sam said. "Brady's mother had said all that stuff—"

"I remember."

"You have to admit, you were acting a little crazy."

"There was a reporter in her house. After all I'd done to avoid being in the news, and Brady's mom invited that lady from the *Boston Globe* to his graduation party."

"Mrs. Thomas didn't know who she was. When Brady explained, she realized what she'd done."

"It wasn't Mrs. Thomas's fault you and Brady fooled around."

"He was ashamed of himself."

"Well, at least he felt something after cheating on me."

"No, before that," Sam said. "He should have defended you to his mom. He didn't know why you were acting like that, and he thought maybe..." She trailed off.

"Maybe I was crazy, just like my mother."

"But then he saw that woman, and he realized why you'd run out of there so fast, why you'd been so upset."

Samantha stared at her hands, unfolded them and folded them again. "We'd both had too much to drink, and he was feeling bad about you. And he thought you'd never forgive him, and I..." She looked up. "I knew you were going to leave us and never come back. You hated Nutfield and the memories here. I knew eventually it would just be Brady and me. I was already angry with you for it, even though you hadn't left yet. And I already missed you."

Rae stood and checked on the baby, who seemed about to fall asleep. Mostly, she needed a distraction for this memory. "So it was all my fault?"

"It wasn't your fault," Sam said. "I take full responsibility. I'd always had a crush on him."

"I thought you loved me too. You were my best friend. I thought I could trust you."

"You could, and you still can. It was ten minutes, Rae. We kissed, we...fooled around, and then we both felt so bad, that was the end of it."

That moment had been the end of a lot of things for Rae.

"Brady never stopped loving you," Sam said. "I didn't, either. And I've never stopped missing you. I know we hurt you, but we're both sorry."

"And like I said, I already forgave you."

"And yet, you never came home."

Rae thought of all the pain, all the choices she'd made because of what her two best friends had done. She'd altered the course of her life because of it. She'd changed colleges so they wouldn't be able to find her. She'd cut off all ties to her hometown because of that night. And for years, she'd blamed Brady and Samantha. Now she knew she'd overreacted. Now she knew she'd never have friends like them again. Yes, they'd betrayed her, but she'd betrayed them too.

She'd lost everything. And as much as she wished she could go back and undo it all, she couldn't. She had to focus on finding her dad's treasure and getting out of town. And she had to keep Brady and Sam far, far away.

Rae reached across the table and took Sam's hand. "I do forgive you, and I'm glad we're able to put it behind us."

Her friend smiled and settled in.

Rae released her hand. "Unfortunately, I've got a lot of stuff I need to do before I go home to my husband. So...thanks for stopping by."

Sam's smile faded. "Oh. Right. Well, maybe we can get together while you're here, for lunch or something."

"I don't think so."

Sam nodded slowly. "Okay, then. I guess I'll just..." She pushed away from the table, and Rae walked her to the door, careful to hide her regret behind a polite smile.

SIXTEEN

Brady walked the short block from the police station to McNeal's in the drizzle. Aside from the occasional car splashing down Maple Street, the town was silent. He'd been gone from Nutfield too long. Join the service and see the world? He'd seen enough for a lifetime. Now he was content to stay at home. Downtown Nutfield had looked very much like this as long as he could remember. Quaint and inviting, but today it seemed like an impressionist painting, all muted and blurry.

He paused in front of McNeal's. The clinking of dishes and muffled voices seeped through the closed door, and the yellow light from the diner painted the sidewalk in a warm, welcoming glow. Brady pushed the door open and stepped inside.

Sam had chosen a booth by the window. He walked across the room, nodding to familiar faces, grimacing at the remarks about the Patriots, as if not quite sharing a name with the quarterback made him somehow responsible, and slid into the booth. His smile faded at the look on her face.

"I guess it didn't go well."

"It went fine. She forgives us."

Sam didn't look like somebody who'd just had a *fine* conversation. "So what's wrong?"

The waitress kept her from answering. "Hey, Detective. What can I get you?"

He glanced at Sam's half-finished coffee. "How about more coffee for Sam and a Coke for me?" He looked at his friend. "You ready to order?"

"Soup of the day, please."

"You're going to waste away." Brady turned to Bonnie. "I'll take the club sandwich."

After she left, Brady turned back to Sam. "What did you think?"

She shrugged. "Rae seemed really guarded. Didn't tell me anything about her husband or her home." She took a sip of her coffee and set it back down. "She didn't tell me anything important."

"Did you get any impressions you wanted to share?"

Samantha shrugged. "She seemed ready for me to leave the minute I got there."

He'd gotten the same impression.

"Johnny doesn't look much like her, does he?" Her voice was soft, tentative.

"He must take after his father."

"Right. What do you know about her husband?"

He pulled out his notepad and flipped to the right page. "His name is Julien Garcia Moreau. He was born in Toulouse in seventy-five. His mother is French, his father... Well, according to the one photo I saw of him, he has the same coloring as Johnny. Moreau owns a pretty big corporation."

"How long have they been married?"

Brady set the notebook down. "I don't know. Rae said they'd been living in Tunis."

She cocked her head in question.

"It's the capital city of Tunisia, a small country on the northern coast of Africa. It's kind of tucked in between Libya and Algeria."

"Sounds lovely."

"I bet it is. It's on the Mediterranean, and according to Rae, it was one of the better places for westerners to live in Africa. For a predominantly Muslim country, they have pretty liberal policies, new women's rights laws, stuff like that. But from what I've read, it's not nearly as safe now as it was a few years ago."

She nearly smiled. "Since when do you know so much about Tunisia?"

"I just want to make sure she's all right."

"Um-hmm."

He was spared the need to further explain when Bonnie set Samantha's bowl down, then his plate. "Anything else I can get you?"

After their "no, thanks," Bonnie left.

Sam stirred her soup. She took a small sip, then peeked up at him. "You find her marriage license?"

He swallowed the first bite of his sandwich. "I haven't had enough time to dig into it."

"Okay." She held his gaze, probing. "Why exactly are you bothering to dig into it?"

"She didn't seem a little off to you? Scared?"

Sam nodded. "Yeah, I know what you mean. I can look into the license, if you want me to."

As court clerk, sometimes Samantha did research for the police. She was very good at it.

"You sure you don't mind?"

"Not one bit." She smiled. "You're telling me you don't have any feelings for her?"

He busied himself smoothing his napkin before he

answered. "I'm not getting involved with anybody, ever again. Besides, she's married."

Samantha blinked and studied her lap. "Right. Sorry."

Brady leaned forward. "Samantha?" He waited until she looked up. "It wasn't your fault she took off."

"It sort of was, though."

"It wasn't your fault. You were trying to do the right thing, to come clean before she heard it elsewhere." He tamped down long-held frustration with a sip of his drink. It didn't help. "She should have come to me, asked me what happened. What does that say about her feelings for me that she could walk away without a backward glance?"

"Still—"

"It's done. You and I are good, and she's forgiven us. Don't beat yourself up about it again. Okay?"

Samantha nodded and sipped her soup.

They finished their meals while Brady turned over everything he knew about Rae and again came to no conclusions. He'd thought maybe Sam could get more information out of her, but that hadn't worked out. And that troubled feeling he'd had about Rae since he'd seen her Saturday night wouldn't go away. Maybe, if not for that used car in her driveway, he could be convinced all was well in her world. But something wasn't right. And he was determined to find out what it was.

SEVENTEEN

Rae parked her car in front of a hair salon. At one point, this building had housed a cobbler, but she wasn't surprised to see that business gone. Who had shoes repaired anymore? Everything was disposable in America. She'd been gone long enough to be surprised and horrified by that. In Tunis, people cherished their possessions. They had so few, and there weren't Walmarts on every corner.

She lifted Johnny from his car seat and slid him into the sling fastened across her chest. Once she'd snapped him in, she draped his blanket over him to protect him from the drizzle.

She reached back in the car for her bag, then checked to make sure the manila envelope was in there. She'd be relieved to have the evidence against Julien in a safe place, and the safe deposit box seemed the best option. If Julien somehow found her, maybe she could leverage this to protect Johnny.

The thought of Julien in her hometown had her checking over her shoulder. It was only a matter of time before he followed her trail here. All she could hope was that she'd be gone by the time he did, and he wouldn't decide to find out if she'd confided in anyone.

The sidewalks were empty, but that was no surprise with the rainy weather. She peered at the buildings across the street as she walked. One used to be a dress shop. Now it sold souvenirs. With Nutfield's beautiful lake, its proximity to the ocean, and its abundance of antique shops, the town was getting its share of tourists. Gram hadn't been too keen on the outsiders, but according to the *Nutfield Gazette*, most local business owners tried to attract them.

No tourists wandered the streets today, but when the leaves exploded in fall colors in another few weeks, there'd be people everywhere. If only she could stay to witness her favorite time of the year. At least she'd miss the leaf-peeper traffic.

Across the street McNeal's was filled with diners. Rae stopped beneath an awning to stare. Yellow light spilled onto the sidewalk from the huge windows in front. She imagined the clanking of dishes and the clatter of voices. People laughing and calling to one another, friends sharing some inside joke she'd never been a part of. She hugged herself against the chill and had nearly turned away when she caught sight of the couple seated at the window.

Brady and Samantha. Bosom buddies, like they had been for years.

A car approached, splashing through a sizable puddle on the street and spraying her jeans. When the car passed, Rae looked again at the window and met Brady's eyes. Crap. If she wanted to keep Brady safe, she needed to avoid being seen with him in public.

She rushed down the sidewalk. The bank was two doors down, right past the old shoe store. Maybe she should duck in there—

"Rae, wait!"

She walked faster, knowing it was futile. Maybe Brady would trip or slip in a puddle.

Better wet than seen with her.

His hand closed on her arm, and he fell in step beside her.

"I'd like to think you didn't hear me."

She kept walking. "I'm in a hurry."

"You know, Samantha and I are just friends. I mean, I know you saw us together, so—"

"I'm not jealous, Brady."

She stopped in front of the bank's glass door. Across the street, Samantha stepped out of the diner, lifted a hand in a wave, and turned in the opposite direction.

Rae watched her for a moment before turning back to him. "I'm sorry. I have to go."

Brady's lips turned down. "She told me you two talked, but then you dismissed her."

"I was busy."

Brady looked away, and she couldn't help taking the opportunity to look around, see who was watching them. Probably every eye in downtown. This was not good.

Brady met her eyes again. "I was never attracted to her, you know. And after that night, she didn't find me very attractive, either."

A car drove past, the sound of splashing water drowning out the dripping of the rain on the sidewalk. She watched the taillights. Someone who recognized her? Someone who could tell Julien she'd been there?

She turned back to Brady. "There's no reason for me to get to know Sam again. I won't be here long enough to make it matter, and now that Gram's gone, I don't see myself coming back."

She lifted the blanket and peeked at Johnny to give her something else to look at. Sound asleep. The drizzle and cold didn't seem to bother him one bit, all cuddled up against her chest. She hadn't felt that kind of comfort since...since Brady.

"You're not planning on ever coming back?"

She looked up to see an expression cross his features. He looked...heartbroken.

"I don't see the point."

He swallowed. "As long as you're here, I can help you get things settled. I know you've been going through stuff, and I know you have a lot you need to do. I'd like to help."

She needed him to leave her alone. She needed to know she wasn't putting him in danger. She glared at him, desperate for him to believe she was angry. "I don't need your help."

"You might need a friend."

A friend. Yes, she could definitely use a friend. But the risk was too great.

She shook her head and backed away. "I have to go."

"What's going on, Rae?"

She shivered in the cold and held her child closer. "I just..." What could she say? She looked around again. The street was deserted, and they were far enough away from McNeal's not to be seen by anybody inside. Still, she had to get away from him before people started talking.

He looked around, too, as if trying to figure out what had captured her gaze. Then he looked back at her. "You can trust me, Rae. I'm not perfect, but I'm still the same guy you shared your secrets with."

She met his eyes. "What am I supposed to trust you with?"

"How about the truth?"

EIGHTEEN

Brady hoped like crazy she'd confide in him. Based on her shaking head, she had no intention of telling him anything.

She looked at the sidewalk. "There's nothing you need to know."

He tamped down his initial reaction. "Let's go somewhere and talk."

Her eyes widened. "I have stuff to do."

"I'll wait, and then we can go get a cup of coffee or something."

"No." She took a step back, and the fear was written clearly across her face now. "It's not a good idea."

"You need a friend."

"I have plenty of friends."

Really? Back in Tunis, where she claimed they no longer lived? In Paris, where her husband had an apartment she didn't consider hers? No, he didn't believe Rae had anyone to confide in. But she'd never admit it. "Fine. I need a friend. But right now, I have to go to the bank."

"I'll wait. I'm not leaving until we talk."

She looked up the street again, then down. What was she

looking for? Or maybe the better question was *who* was she looking for? Whoever it was, she was terrified.

She met his gaze. "Okay, I'll be done soon. Meet me at Dunkin' Donuts in a few minutes."

"I'll wait."

"No! I mean, just... Please, meet me there, okay?"

He nodded, and she fled into the bank lobby.

Very weird.

Brady jogged back to the police station and slipped into his truck. A few minutes later, he eased into the parking lot of Dunkin' Donuts and waited.

She pulled up in about ten minutes, and he stepped out of his truck, approached her car, and knocked on her window. She rolled it down.

"Can I help you with Johnny?"

She was staring through the glass at the restaurant. He followed her gaze. A pretty big lunchtime crowd, but then it was a cold, gray day. A perfect day for coffee. He turned back to her and lifted his eyebrows. "Want to go through the drive-through?"

She relaxed and nodded, and he climbed in the passenger seat of the tiny car. After he pushed the seat back as far as it would go, he turned to her.

"Did you get what you needed at the bank?"

"I found an old safe deposit box key in Dad's stuff. I thought I'd see if there was anything interesting in the box."

"And?"

She glanced in the rearview mirror, then back at him. "Just some paperwork. I'll go through it later. Looks like Dad owned some stocks. Not sure if it's worth anything."

"Seemed your grandmother was on top of things."

In the drive-through, Rae ordered a sandwich and two coffees. With the coffee safe in the drink holder and the food on the console between them, she drove to a nearly empty parking lot outside a bait-and-tackle shop on the outskirts of town. She pushed her seat all the way back, pulled her knee up, and faced him.

"Cozy," he said. And with the rain outside and the steam from the coffees, it was.

She sipped her drink. "Mmmm."

With her mouth, she smiled. But her eyes hinted a different emotion altogether. Fear, he thought. "So, have you decided yet?"

She took the paper off her sandwich. Her fingers were trembling. "Decided what?"

"Whether or not to tell me what's going on."

She sighed deeply and set the sandwich back down. "Why are you so certain that I'm not telling you the truth?"

"The car."

She looked around its interior. "What about it? I know it's not the nicest rental—"

"It's not a rental." She opened her mouth to argue, but he cut her off. "You bought it on Saturday, paid cash."

"How did you—?"

"I'm a detective, Rae. I detected." He let that hang in the air, hoping she'd explain. When she said nothing, he continued. "So, why would you buy a car if you were planning to go back?"

"I...I just..." A moment passed. "I thought... I just thought maybe Gram—"

"Your grandmother hasn't driven in years. If you've been home like you say you have, then you know that."

"I needed a car while I was here."

"Ever heard of Enterprise?"

She stared out the window.

He wanted to reach out to her, to calm whatever fears were keeping her quiet. He wanted to make everything better, but how could he if she wouldn't confide in him? He was impotent, unable to fix anything. Seemed the story of his life. And it wasn't going to change, because she was about to lie to him. Again. "Why don't I drink my coffee while you come up with a plausible story?" He sipped, never taking his eyes off her.

"It's hard to explain."

He looked at his watch and relaxed against the seat back. "I have time."

She nibbled a tiny bite of her sandwich and set it back on her lap. She swallowed some coffee and looked down at the plastic lid.

"Rae?"

When she turned to him, he said, "Julien Garcia Moreau."

She narrowed her eyes.

"Is that him? From Toulouse? He's the CEO of—"

"Are you investigating me for something?"

"I'm worried about you."

"What did you do?"

"Just some surfing the web. I didn't learn much."

Johnny shifted and squeaked.

She looked behind her toward the baby. With the backward-facing seat, she couldn't see him from where she sat, but Brady could. The child was sound asleep. Brady looked back at Rae.

"I'm fine." As if to prove her point, she took another bite of her sandwich. After she swallowed, she sipped her coffee, then wiped her mouth. She stared at the dashboard. He could see her wheels spinning a story. And he didn't want to hear it.

"So this Julien," he said. "Did he hurt you?"

She whipped her head toward him. "What? Never. Why would you even—?"

"Because you look scared." He took in their surroundings, the deserted parking lot far from town. "You're afraid to be seen."

"Not really. Just—"

"Or maybe you're afraid to be seen with me. Is he the jealous type?"

When she didn't say anything, he continued. "You've been lying to me since you got here."

"Just because I haven't told you my secrets doesn't make me a liar." She wrapped the sandwich in the paper and set it in the center console. "Johnny's going to need to eat soon." She moved her seat forward, shifted into drive, and pulled out of the parking lot.

They drove in silence. He tried to think of something to say, anything that would convince her to confide in him. But he came up short.

When she stopped beside his truck, Brady turned to her. "So you still don't trust me."

"This isn't about trust."

"Did you leave your husband?"

She pulled in a deep breath, blew it out slowly, and nodded.

"Does he know where you are?"

She shook her head.

"Are you going to tell me why?"

She seemed to wrestle with her answer. After a moment, she said, "No."

He processed that. At least he'd made a little progress. He stepped out of the car, then leaned back in. "I'm not going away, Rae. We'll talk more later."

NINETEEN

Why, why, why had she told Brady she'd left Julien?

Rae sat in the passenger seat of her Honda and rocked Johnny, hoping the motion would calm her down. She'd left Brady at Dunkin' Donuts, driven back to downtown Nutfield, and parked in front of a red brick building. A gold placard on the door read, *Gordon Boyle, Attorney-at-Law*.

Twelve years had passed, and Brady could still read her like a well-worn novel. But what Brady knew or guessed was irrelevant. Even if he knew she was leaving Julien, it didn't matter. She couldn't let it matter, because as soon as Rae found what she was looking for, she'd never see him again.

The thought made her want to cry.

She'd loved him once. Maybe, deep down, she'd never stopped loving him. What she'd had with Julien had been nothing compared with the intimacy she and Brady had shared. Maybe he was right, and she should have let him explain himself twelve years ago. She still would have left town for college, but they could have salvaged their friendship. Then she wouldn't have cut off everybody from Nutfield, and perhaps she wouldn't have been so quick to move to Europe, to get away from everyone she'd ever loved.

She kissed Johnny's head. Whatever she'd been through, it had all been worth it. "Because now I have you."

The baby cooed, and Rae hugged him to her chest.

The more time she spent with Brady, the less she wanted to leave town. Unfortunately, Brady and Nutfield were a package deal, and though she might still care for Brady, she couldn't tolerate the people of this town. Aside from Brady and Sam, maybe Gordon and Ellen Boyle, she wasn't welcome here. Even if Julien weren't chasing her, she'd leave. The people here knew her past. She'd never forget the stares she always felt growing up, the whispers behind her back. *There she is, the girl with the crazy mother.* The last thing she needed was to relive it every day of her life.

She looked through the drizzle at the attorney's office. She wanted to go inside, to visit with Gordon Boyle, her grandmother's attorney and her father's best friend. His wife probably still worked there. Rae had never known Ellen well, but Nate had spoken highly of his stepmother. Rae had known the Boyles as long as she could remember, and even though she and Nate hadn't become good friends until she'd gone to Columbia, they had shared a common bond.

Most high schoolers didn't know what it felt like to lose a mother. She and Nate knew, though. They knew.

Gordon and Ellen would embrace her, and the three of them would share stories about Gram. She'd find acceptance and comfort inside that building.

But it would be the first place Julien would go. If Gordon and Ellen could say she'd never come by, never seen the will, never taken possession of her inheritance, then Julien would leave them alone.

Maybe. Probably.

So she'd never receive her inheritance. Never own the home that had been hers all her life. She'd take what she could sell and leave it forever. What would happen to it, when she never returned? Would it eventually crumble to the ground from lack of love, lack of the family that had cared for it for generations?

Tears filled her eyes one more time that day as she settled Johnny back into his car seat. She climbed behind the wheel and drove away from one more crushing loss.

TWENTY

The afternoon rain pattered against the police station roof and seeped into Brady's mood. At least he'd gotten her to admit she'd left her husband. That was something. He'd need to gain her trust if he was going to help her.

He'd worked on the burglary cases all afternoon, but that wasn't why he was exhausted. Tonight, he needed to relax. Go home, make dinner, catch up on some TV, and get into bed early. That was the plan. And he wasn't going to get depressed about doing all of that by himself. He was learning to live alone again, and he'd eventually learn to like it.

Having Rae in town didn't make it easier.

The door to the town offices opened. "You busy?"

Brady looked up from his paperwork to see Samantha crossing the room, a notepad dangling from her right hand. Her frown wasn't encouraging.

"Just finishing up. Have a seat."

"Can I sit there?" She nodded to his chair. "I have a couple things to show you."

He stood and stepped out of her way. "Have at it."

Samantha settled in front of his laptop, set the notebook on his desk, and typed. A web page popped up. "This is an article about Julien Moreau. It was written about eighteen months ago. Do you know when Rae and Julien married?"

"She didn't tell me much."

Samantha scrolled down. "It's a pretty comprehensive article about his business and his life, but there's no mention of a wife or family."

Brady leaned closer, trying to catch a few of the words on the page as she whizzed past.

"I just wanted to show you that so you understand that this Julien Moreau is a pretty public guy. I've read a lot of articles about him. It doesn't surprise me Rae married him. He's wealthy and powerful, but he seems to have a heart for people."

When Samantha turned to him, he nodded. Great, she'd married a Boy Scout. So why was she running away?

Samantha continued. "I've made some calls and searched a lot of records today, and I can't find any record of him marrying anyone in Africa in the last decade."

"Okay. But maybe—"

"And so I checked in France, and I found this."

Brady peered at the page. It was a marriage license between Julien Garcia Moreau and a woman named Martine Desjardins."

"So is that her alias?"

"No. Moreau and that woman have been married for eight years."

Eight years. That was a long time, but it could still be possible. Maybe they'd met when she was in college. But wait, hadn't she told him she'd lived in Belgium before?

Samantha turned back to the computer. "I've perused a dozen articles about him, and he never mentions that he's married, much less the woman's name. So I dug a little deeper, and then I called just to be sure. There's no record that they divorced or that their marriage was annulled."

"Wait, who did you call?"

She sighed. "It was a pain in the neck. I started with a number I found for the city clerk or whatever they call it in Toulouse, but they gave me a different number, so—"

"Forget it." He shook his head. "Your resourcefulness knows no bounds."

Samantha nearly smiled, but there was no joy in it. "So Martine has an online presence. Like her husband, she's deeply involved in philanthropic activities, but she lives on a vineyard in France." Samantha clicked on a link, and a picture filled the screen. "That's her."

Brady peered at the photograph of an elegant woman who had to be in her mid-forties. Lines fanned out from her nearly black eyes. Her face was thin and angular. She looked nothing like Reagan.

They had the right guy—Rae had confirmed the name in the car. But the guy was married to another woman.

TWENTY-ONE

Rae buckled Johnny into his car seat that evening and headed to the high school to pick up Caro. The drizzle was coming down just hard enough that she needed her windshield wipers, but not enough to keep them from squeaking.

Rae had barely been home long enough to feed and bathe the baby. This wouldn't take long, though, and it felt good to be needed.

Out the driveway, across the short bridge, and down the windy road, and there it was, that low brick school that had glared at her every time she'd come home for a visit. Any chance she'd had of feeling at home in Nutfield had disappeared when her mother'd lost her mind. After that, no matter how many years passed, Rae had been the girl who'd called the police. The girl who'd brought their little one-stoplight town national attention. The girl who'd sent her own mother to prison.

If she had to do it again, what would she do?

Rae'd been asking herself that question for almost two decades. The answer was always obvious. Unfortunately, it wasn't always the same.

She parked, stepped out of the car, bundled Johnny close to

shelter him from the drizzle, and stepped inside the cafeteria doors.

The room seemed smaller than it had when she'd been in school. It smelled the same, though. Some combination of cleaning solution and sour milk. Most of the lights were off, and on the stage, the lights seemed over-bright, making the rest of the room even darker. All but one of the tables had been folded and pushed against the far wall near the opening that led to the kitchen. Three people sat at the table. Two were watching the stage. One turned to glare at Rae. She guided the door to a soft close behind her.

A tall boy was rattling off a monologue that sounded vaguely familiar. But his delivery was dry as Tunisian sand. She hoped he wasn't indicative of the talent at Nutfield High.

Rae slipped past the stage and through the door leading to the rest of the school. The hallway was bright and lined with signs and posters. When she'd been here, most of the signs on the walls had been handmade. She could picture the cheerleaders sitting on the floor of the gym, coloring the banner the football players, with Brady in the lead, would run through on their way to the first playoff game the school had ever been in. An explosion of orange and black and white, little brown nuts drawn all over it. And somebody's hideous rendition of a squirrel.

Johnny cooed, and she turned him to see the perfect, machine-made posters that had replaced the homemade ones from her youth. "See the squirrel?" She pointed, then looked at Johnny, who was staring at her with something like awe. She squeezed him tighter and kissed his head.

She continued down the hallway and, following a din of voices, found a crowd of students outside the stage doors. Rae searched for Caro's bright red hair. No luck. She should've gotten the girl's cell phone number. She'd activated one of the disposables she'd purchased at Walmart on Sunday, and she may as well use it. She'd toss it when she left town, anyway.

She turned and wandered down the hallway. Caro would come out soon enough.

Down a short ramp, Rae entered what used to be the science wing. Based on that nauseating smell, it still was. Science and math—two subjects she'd struggled with. Thank heavens for history and English.

The lights were off here, and she probably shouldn't be snooping. Rae'd never been great at *not* snooping, and the memories were too compelling to pass up. She stopped in front of a familiar door. Chemistry with Mrs. Manning. Brady, Samantha, and she had been lab partners. Samantha had been great at following directions, and Brady had always understood...well, everything. Rae had written the lab report, carefully copying exactly what they said. At least she hadn't been useless. The reports always had perfect grammar.

Angry voices coming from the English hallway caught her attention. Her nosiness was a bad habit that would eventually get her in trouble.

Eventually? She was running for her life.

Compared to that, how bad could this be? She peered down the corridor.

Two boys were staring each other down, one tall with curly light brown hair, the other slightly shorter with black hair. Both wore muddy practice football uniforms. Odd, since the gym was on the far side of the school. They must've been looking for privacy.

"If it happens again," the curly-haired one said, "I'll call the cops."

"You wouldn't dare." The darker one backed up a step, and Rae saw who stood beyond the two boys.

Caro. The girl stepped forward. "What are you two—?"

"Go back to the caf, Caro." Curly barely glanced at her. "This doesn't concern you."

"But what—?"

The dark-haired boy turned and caught Rae watching.

She pasted on a smile. "Hey, Caro. I was just looking for you."

"Oh. Hi. Uh...Finn?" Caro turned to the curly-haired boy. "This is Reagan."

The boy turned to her with a short nod. "Hey."

The other boy took off in the opposite direction.

Rae stepped forward and held out her free hand. "Nice to meet you."

His hand was warm and sweaty. "Are you the lady who's helping Caro with the auditions?" When she nodded, he said, "Thanks for doing that. It means a lot." He turned and kissed Caro on the cheek. "I gotta go." He brushed past Rae with barely a glance.

Caro stood beside her and stared at the spot where her boyfriend had disappeared.

"What was that about?" Rae asked.

"I have no idea. Trent is his best friend."

"Didn't look like friends to me."

"Something's going on, but Finn won't tell me what."

Rae shrugged. "People fight. Maybe he'll tell you later. How'd your audition go?"

She turned to Rae with a bright smile. "Omigosh, so good. I'm sure I'm going to get a part."

Caro prattled about her audition until they reached the car. Rae strapped Johnny in, then climbed in beside the girl. "Before I forget, why don't you give me your cell phone number?"

"Sure."

They exchanged numbers, then Rae said, "You hungry?"

"Starved. I'm sure Nana has something I can heat up."

"I thought we'd grab dinner somewhere."

Caro brightened even more and pulled out her phone. While she called her grandmother, Rae pulled out of the school parking lot. She turned to Caro and lifted her eyebrows in question. The girl gave her a thumbs-up, then told her grandmother how the audition went.

Rae turned toward town. She didn't want to run into anybody she knew, and the Kentucky Fried Chicken lot was empty except for a few cars in the back. Seemed safe enough, and chicken sounded good.

They grabbed their meals and chose a booth near the window. Rae lifted Johnny's carseat and set it on the table. Caro was practically giddy with delight.

"Nana and Papa never want to go out to eat." She grabbed a piece of golden goodness from the box. "This is a treat."

Rae bit a piece. "For me too. I forgot how much I liked fried chicken."

"They don't have fried chicken in Africa?"

Rae savored the yummy, salty flavor. "Nothing like this. This is very American."

Caro looked down at her chicken, then up at Rae. Then back down again.

"What?"

The girl shrugged. "I just wanted to know..." She seemed to force her gaze up. "I'm sorry. I know you asked me not to tell anybody you were home, but I sort of told Finn, just because he wanted to know about the auditions and stuff, but he won't tell anybody."

"It's fine," Rae said.

"So he told me a story about your family."

"Oh." Rae swallowed a sip of her soda. "What did he tell you?"

She turned a little pink. "It's not my business."

The whole town knew her business. What was one more?

"About my mom?"

She nodded but didn't make eye contact.

"My mom was bipolar. Have you heard of that?"

Caro looked up. "Yeah. We talked about a lot of mental stuff in my health class."

"Okay. Well, she lived right on the edge. We—Dad and Gram and I—we sort of tiptoed around her, always wondering which Mom was going to wake up any given day. She had medication, and it helped a lot. But it didn't make her sane. Not really. And she hated taking it. Sometimes when Dad would go out of town or be gone for a while..." Rae thought of her father's other women. Dad had found a way to escape the madness. Rae hadn't had the option.

Caro paused, chicken halfway to her lips, and tilted her head to the side.

Rae continued. "When Dad would be gone for a while, Mom wouldn't take her meds. When he died, she went off them altogether. And her illness got really bad."

Caro grabbed a potato wedge. "My grandparents are sort of grouchy, but they're..." She seemed to grope for a word and finally finished with "solid."

"Gram was solid," Rae said. "Thank God for Gram." A rush of emotion had her pausing again.

"Anyway," Rae said, "Mom lost her mind. Gram had gone to her sister's for the weekend, because her sister'd had surgery. Gram didn't know Mom had quit taking her medicine, and for the previous few weeks, she'd been amazingly steady. While Gram was gone, Mom drove to Portsmouth. She parked near downtown, walked around the little shops." This memory used to make Rae ill, but so many things had happened since then.

"A congressman from New York and his family were vacationing in Portsmouth," Rae said. "They were in this tiny store, and their baby was in a stroller. According to the news, the parents had walked around the corner to look at something with another one of their kids. They left the baby in his stroller, and my mom just pushed the baby out of the store. I'm sure there was more to it than that." She glanced at Johnny. His eyes were open, taking in the new environment. "Who would leave their child, even to step a few feet away?"

"You must have freaked out."

"I was spending the night with a friend." Rae remembered the evening at Samantha's house. It felt like the last night of Rae's childhood. "When I came home the next day, the baby was lying in the cradle. She said the baby was God's way of replacing my father. I'd seen the news. I knew. I tried to get in touch with Gram, but they didn't answer the phone. That was before cell phones."

"So you called the police."

"There was a report on TV about it, and this special number to call. I thought… Well, I don't know what I thought. That Mom would go to a hospital and get some help. That we could trust the police."

Caro nodded. "My mother doesn't trust the police, but Nana says that's just because she uses drugs, and they're illegal."

"That must be hard."

"I think it could be worse."

"Yeah." She smiled at the girl, understanding what Caro was going through. "I really thought they'd put her in a hospital."

"They should have."

Rae shrugged.

"And then?" Caro prompted.

"The story was national news, and suddenly my face was on every screen in America, the girl who rescued the congressman's kid. And got her mother sent to prison. Reporters descended on Nutfield like mosquitoes in a swamp. They shouted questions at me everywhere I went for weeks. They dug into our family's lives. My father... He'd been involved with some women over the years. I guess it was hard being married to my mom." Rae sipped her drink. "Anyway, one of his former mistresses decided to turn our family's misfortune into her fifteen minutes of fame. She gave interviews, wrote a tell-all book with details about my mother's illness. Details she could only have gotten from my father."

Caro's eyes filled. She shook her head. "I can't... That just sucks. What a witch."

Rae managed a smile. "She was."

"That's not the word I wanted to use."

"I appreciate your restraint."

"So they made you out to be a hero for turning your mother in."

"Not all of them. Some figured I did it to be free of her insanity. Some assumed I was crazy too. It occurred to very few people that I was just an eleven-year-old girl who'd now lost both her parents. That didn't sell any newspapers."

"I can't believe you became a reporter after that."

"Ironic, I know. Considering how much I hated them."

"So your mom went to prison."

"Right. I was sixteen when she killed herself."

TWENTY-TWO

Julien sat in the office of his Paris apartment. Rae and Jean-Louis had only been gone a few days, and already the place felt cold and abandoned. Dust motes floated in the sunlight streaming in through the window. His lamp illuminated a small circle on his desk, and he stared at the note Rae had tucked into the file cabinet.

She'd copied and stolen evidence against him, evidence regarding his business, evidence that could implicate his family.

He crumpled the note and squeezed it, forcing himself to face the truth. He'd made excuses for her. He'd lied to himself about what she was doing, because he'd made the mistake of caring for her.

All the while, she had disobeyed him, spied on him, betrayed him, and left him for a fool.

Almost left him for a fool. He'd make sure she wouldn't get away with it.

Julien had flown to Paris right after his father left the hotel the night before, leaving word with Farah that he'd be back the next evening. They were to continue to search for Rae, to find her using any means necessary.

He'd arrived at his apartment by eleven. It only took fifteen minutes to find the note.

He stared back in time to the first moment he'd seen Rachel, walking into that Tunisian cafe. He'd thought she must lack sense to not be nervous, surrounded as she had been by locals, Muslims who hated the very sight of her, a woman proudly sporting her modern clothes. The hijab covered her head, but her Western ways were too evident in the khakis and T-shirt. Rae had seemed so confident. Now he knew she was a master at hiding fear. Just like he was.

How long had she known the truth? Had their marriage been a ruse to get information? He'd seen the lengths she'd go to when she was working on a story, but he couldn't imagine she'd have been willing to have his child on pretense. No, she must have learned the truth afterward. Had one of his enemies tipped her off, or had she simply decided to snoop?

Both seemed possible. She was an investigative journalist, after all. He should never have trusted her.

He flattened the note on his desk and reread it. Rachel was naive to think he would let her go. As if he could, even if he wanted to. He needed Jean-Louis, his only heir. And he needed her caught and punished. Nobody escaped the Moreau family, evidence or not.

She wouldn't dare take that paltry information to the authorities. His files didn't prove anything. They could make life complicated for him in the short term, but they wouldn't bring him down. He'd been too careful with what he kept around. Would she know that? Certainly she would. She was a master at gathering evidence.

Perhaps she'd gathered more. She must have known he'd follow her. Maybe that's what she wanted—for him to come after her. Maybe this was a game.

A very dangerous game.

He remembered the feeling of holding Rae in his arms the night they'd married. They'd docked the yacht just long enough to send the guests and most of the staff on their way. Then he'd carried her to the bedroom, made her his. Would he have married her if she'd been willing to join him in his bed before that? It wasn't as if he couldn't satisfy that particular urge with any number of women, but he'd wanted Rae. Probably more because she'd refused him.

That night, he'd studied her body while she lay beside him. She belonged to him now. The pale skin, the spray of freckles across her shoulders, the tiny mole on her hip. Even now he could imagine her sun-kissed red hair splayed across the rumpled sheets, her hazel eyes dancing in the pale light that filtered in through the porthole. He could hear her broken French. He'd laughed at her terrible attempt at his language. She'd swooned when he'd romanced her in words she didn't even understand.

She was his. She always would be, whatever her reasons for marrying him. She was his to do with as he pleased.

If Papa knew, he'd insist Julien kill her. But no. Julien would find her, and he'd take her back to Tunis, and he'd keep her there. He'd give her child after child, and she'd be safe as long as she stayed put and kept quiet. And if he felt she might whisper the truth in somebody's ear? Well, death wasn't the only way to silence a person. People could be broken.

He touched the image of his son in the photograph on his desk. He missed him. And he needed the boy to solidify his place in the family. Without his son, all would be lost. If anything happened to his child while Rae had her little escapade, she would pay dearly. She would pray for death if anything happened to his son.

He stood, shoved the note in his pocket, and opened his safe. The flash drive rested right where he'd left it. Thank God she hadn't found that. He slipped it into his pocket with the note. He might need it sooner than he'd thought.

One day, Julien would run the business. He would legitimize segments, and he would end the distasteful trades Geoffrey had begun, focus on what his grandfather had started. To be equalizers, to give the lowest among them a voice, so they could fight back against tyrants. It was the American second amendment—applied to the world. It was fair. It was just.

It was profitable.

One day, Rae would understand. She would stand beside him like Maman stood with Papa. Rae would be his partner. Or she would be his captive, perhaps his victim.

She would not be his downfall.

TWENTY-THREE

SOMETHING WAS DIFFERENT. Rae waited for the fluorescent lights in the barn to brighten the space. Rain tapped against the shingled roof in a low hum, mingling with Johnny's soft snoring, which was coming through the monitor in her left hand. She didn't love the idea of leaving him in the house, but he'd fallen asleep in his bouncer on the kitchen table, and she hadn't wanted to wake him.

The brighter the lights became, the more Rae could tell that someone had been there.

She studied the desk, the papers she'd planned to go through. Too neat. The old leather chair was pushed beneath the desk, but she'd moved it out of the way to crawl under the desk. A futile attempt to find a hidden box that didn't seem to be anywhere.

Her gaze landed on the furniture beneath the stairs. The two doors of the buffet sat ajar. Had they been like that the day before?

Rae had no idea. But something was off.

A chill ran down her spine. Surely if Julien had found her, he wouldn't waste his time in the old barn. There was nothing in here he'd want. No, if Julien had found her, Rae wouldn't be around to contemplate her barn.

Still, someone had been here. They were gone now. Nice of them to lock up when they left.

She checked the windows. All closed, all locked. How in the world...?

There was no way she was leaving Johnny alone in the house, knowing there'd been someone in the barn. She ran back, grabbed the afghan off the back of the club chair, and tucked the blanket around her baby. Then she lifted the bouncer—baby and all—and carried it to the barn with her. Sweet Johnny barely stirred.

She hated to risk waking him, but she had to find that treasure. She'd spent too much time in town as it was.

She looked at the papers she'd left on the desk. She'd dealt with enough paperwork today after looking through the stuff she'd found in the safe deposit box, hoping for some clue as to the whereabouts of the treasure. She'd made some phone calls and discovered the papers had turned out to be nothing helpful, a few stocks her father had liquidated before his death, a bank account that had been closed for years.

Might as well see if the prowlers had left anything in that buffet.

She froze halfway across the room. What if the prowlers had been looking for the treasure? How could they have found out about it? The treasure had been her and Dad's secret. In all the years since his death, Rae'd never told a soul, not even Brady. It had been hidden on the property for all that time. If someone knew about it, why had that person waited eighteen years to search for it?

Maybe the prowlers had just picked Gram's house at random, decided to go exploring. Or maybe, if they did know about the treasure but continued to break in, that meant they hadn't found it. So it must still be here.

It had to be.

She searched the buffet, then moved on to other pieces of furniture. She found nothing worthwhile. By the time she heard a car door slam, Rae was coated in a thick layer of dust and memories. She checked her watch. Four o'clock. She peeked at Johnny. He'd been asleep an hour, but he'd wake soon. It was nearly time for his dinner.

She was brushing dust off her jeans when it occurred to her that the slamming of the car door hadn't set her heart beating too fast. She'd become comfortable in this house, as if she were safe here.

She wasn't safe. As long as Julien was searching for her, she'd never be safe. She couldn't let her guard down.

She made her way to the window and looked out in time to see Brady approaching the house. She stepped out the door. "Hey."

He stopped on the porch steps and turned. "Hey." No smile. He leaned against the railing. "What are you doing out there?"

"Just going through stuff."

"You have a few minutes?"

"Just let me grab Johnny." She ducked inside, grabbing the key from her pocket on the way. She dangled the key ring from her pinkie and grabbed the baby's bouncer. She reached the heavy door, and Brady closed it behind her.

She jingled the key ring. "Would you mind?"

He locked it, and they started for the house. The rain had given way to a light drizzle.

"Want me to carry him?" Brady asked.

"He's fine. Thanks, though."

They reached the house, and he tried the front door, but it

was locked. He unlocked it and stood aside so she could step in. He closed the door behind them.

"Lock that, would you?" she said.

He locked it, then turned with one eyebrow raised.

"Be right back." Johnny was still sleeping, so she carried him upstairs and rested his bouncer in the middle of her bed.

When she came back down, Brady was still standing in the foyer.

"The other night," she said, "did you say there'd been prowlers?"

"What happened?"

She led the way into the kitchen. "I'm going to make some coffee. It's chilly in that barn. Want some?"

"Sure."

She started on the coffee. "A couple of things had been moved around in the barn. Nothing obvious, but it was different." She kept her voice level, as if the thought of strangers poking around her space didn't scare her to death.

"Anything missing?"

She turned to him and smirked. "Seriously?"

"Not that you could tell, I take it."

"For all I know, they nicked the family jewels."

He pulled a notebook and pen from his pocket. At least he was taking her seriously. He tapped the pen against the counter top. "Are there family jewels, Rae?"

His question seemed so serious, she nearly laughed. And then she thought of Dad's treasure and stopped herself. She shrugged.

"Someone is looking for something."

"Why do you think that?"

"If they were just looking to rob you, they'd have done it when the house was empty. Instead, they come in and search. I've never met a tidy thief before. But what you're describing,

Dorothy said the same thing. She knew someone had been here, but she didn't think anything had been stolen."

"How often did it happen?"

"I'd have to check the records at the station to be sure, but maybe..." He looked at the ceiling, then back at her. "Five times?"

"Five times! Why didn't she tell me?"

"Why would she worry you?"

Good point. "Any idea who it might be?"

He tapped the pen again. "Nope. It's strange, isn't it, that they're so polite? Leads me to believe they knew Dorothy. She was so kind to everyone."

"So if she was nice to these thieves, then why would they break into her barn?"

"At first we thought maybe it was someone looking for a place to sleep. Not that we have a lot of vagrants around here, but you never know. But then, she suspected they'd been in her house."

The bottom dropped out of her stomach. She looked at the monitor, saw the red lights flickering up and down with her son's steady breathing. "I should get an alarm."

"I thought you weren't staying."

"I'm not, but until we go—"

"Why can't you stay?"

Rae turned her back to him and grabbed two mugs. They fixed their coffees. She lifted her cup and sipped. It warmed her immediately. "I just assumed, when I saw you the other night... I don't know anything about your life, Brady. You never married, right?"

He turned the cup in slow circles on the counter. "We were talking about you."

"Where are you living? What's your life like?"

"I'm a detective. I live here."

"I don't mean what town. I mean where? A house, an apartment? One of those new condos by the highway?"

He sipped his coffee, set the cup down, and spun it again. "I'm not really a condo person. I was actually hoping to buy a house."

If only she could give him this one. Would he take care of it when she disappeared?

He continued. "I rent a house out on Gilcreast."

Gilcreast. Even further out of town than this place. "You live alone?"

He nodded.

"How long?"

"Since I moved back."

"You were in the service, right?"

He took a not-so-patient breath. "For four years after college. MP in the Army. And then I worked in Boston."

"And then you came home. How come?"

"We need to talk about you."

She couldn't talk about her. And if this was all the time she was going to get with Brady, she wanted to learn something about him. "I've had my fill of my problems."

"Was I right about your husband's name?"

She sipped her coffee, considered lying to him, then didn't. "Yes."

Brady tapped his fingers against mug. "Why did you leave him?"

"Why did you move back to Nutfield?"

"Look, this isn't about me—"

"Come on. It won't hurt to tell me something about your life. You're asking me to share all my secrets, but you won't tell me anything about you."

"Who said you had secrets, Rae? I'm just trying to figure out what's going on with you and your husband."

She turned toward the kitchen table but didn't move to sit down. "That's none of your business."

"You're hiding from him. You're scared."

She turned back and leaned against the counter. "I'm not scared—"

"I know you too well."

Through the monitor, the baby cooed, quieted, and cooed again.

"He's hungry," Rae said.

"I'll wait."

She looked at the monitor and willed the baby to make another noise. Silence.

"What are you looking for in the barn?"

She turned back to Brady. "I told you—"

"A normal person would start going through the stuff in the house first, then tackle the barn."

"Since when have I been normal?"

The baby cried. She set her cup on the counter. "I need your help."

He pushed himself off the counter. "That's why I'm here. I want to help."

She tried to smile and knew he wouldn't return it. "There's a box in my parents' room, and I can't lift it. Would you get it down for me?"

Through gritted teeth, he said, "Whatever."

He followed her up the stairs to her bedroom. She stepped inside. "Hey, baby."

Johnny turned toward her voice and quieted. He had to be the most beautiful child who'd ever lived. She lifted him, snuggled him close, and inhaled his baby scent. She got more than just the sweet smell of baby. She laid him on the towel she kept stretched on her bed and changed his dirty diaper, trying not to think about Brady, who was leaning against the door jamb, watching her.

When Johnny was clean, she lifted him to her shoulder and straightened. "My parents' room is—"

"I remember."

"Right." It was funny being here with him after so many years. Before her mother had lost her mind, she and Brady's mom had been best friends, so Rae and Brady had grown up together. Samantha had made their group a threesome in kindergarten, and they'd been inseparable all through school. Until that terrible night.

Rae followed Brady to her parents' room. He went inside and peered into the open closet, stopping when his gaze reached the chest on the top shelf. "That?"

"If you can. I can help, if you need me to."

He shook his head and stepped into the closet, then stepped back out. He looked down at the pile of shoes on the floor and turned to Rae with both eyebrows at attention. "Seriously?"

"Apparently Gram couldn't part with their shoes."

"Apparently." He crouched down and pulled shoes out of the closet, tossing them to the side.

Rae held her baby and watched him work. Such a funny thing, lifting and tossing random shoes. Yet she couldn't seem to turn away. Here was the man she'd been friends with since they were both Johnny's age. Though she didn't remember it, she figured they'd practiced crawling together, then walking, probably even potty trained at around the same time. She did remember the trouble they used to get into when they were together. Once, they'd managed to climb onto some boxes in Gram's closet, through the hatch in the ceiling, and into the attic. They'd closed the hatch, then snickered while their mothers called their names frantically. Dust bunnies danced in the air and boxes were piled in all the corners as a tiny bit of sunlight streamed in through the hexagonal window. She might have been afraid, if not for Brady.

When Brady's mother had threatened to call his father, Brady tried to move the wood that served as the hatch, but it was stuck. Frantic, knowing his father would punish him, he'd shoved his little fingers into the narrow groove and tried to pull up the plywood. It wouldn't budge.

Suddenly, those dust bunnies had seemed alive, and the musty smell filled her nose until she thought she might choke. They screamed and yelled and pounded until Rae's mother found them.

Had they been five at the time? Maybe six?

When Rae's mother's episodes had gotten worse, it had been Brady who'd encouraged her. When she'd struggled with math in seventh grade, Brady had tutored her. When she'd worried about her mother spending days at a time in bed, Brady had found a book on depression in the library. The book had been too advanced for her, but knowing her mother wasn't the only woman in the world with mental problems had helped.

Brady had done that.

Now, as he lifted the chest from the top shelf, his grown-up muscles so much more impressive than his little-boy ones had been, she couldn't take her eyes off of him. Brady had been her best friend and her lifeline. He'd always held her secrets. Her heart.

Yes, he'd kissed Samantha. They'd taken refuge with each other after Rae had freaked out on them that night. Ten minutes, he'd said. Ten minutes, and the next day, Samantha'd confessed. He would have, too, if she hadn't run away.

He didn't deserve the way she'd abandoned him.

He wouldn't trust her with the details of his life because she still hadn't proved she trusted him with hers. Maybe she couldn't stay, and maybe they could never be what they'd once been, but Brady could be trusted.

And she really needed a friend.

He turned, the heavy box bulging his biceps. "Where do you want it?"

"Just set it on the bed."

He did, then wiped the dust off the top of the chest with his capable hands.

Brady had stood by her through everything. She owed him so much, but right now, the truth was all she had to offer. At least she could give him that. She'd tell him everything.

TWENTY-FOUR

Brady looked up from the chest to find Rae with a funny look on her face.

"What?"

She shook her head. "Thank you. I never could've gotten that down by myself."

"Glad you can admit you need help sometimes."

He expected a smirk, so the smile surprised him. He'd blame that sudden rush of warmth on the heavy lifting.

"Let's go back downstairs." Her expression grew serious as she shifted the baby over her shoulder and walked away. He glanced at the chest. Apparently having lifted it didn't give him the right to see inside. He'd like to think she'd tell him later.

Yeah, right.

He followed her into the living room, where she laid little Johnny on the couch. "Can I hold him?"

She turned, tilted her head to the side. "If you don't mind. I need to fix his bottle."

She settled the baby in his arms, and Brady maneuvered him so that Johnny's tiny head nestled into Brady's neck. He inhaled that familiar scent, some combination of baby wipes and that yellow baby bath soap. Memories flooded his senses and prickled his eyes. He wasn't going to cry, no way. He carried Johnny to the door that led to the backyard and looked outside as the memories washed over him, bringing waves of grief and shame and guilt.

"Gram's apples are ripe," Rae said. "And they're delicious. Help yourself. Take as many as you like."

He sniffed and kissed the baby's head, staring at the trees heavy with fruit. "Yeah, okay. Maybe when it's not so wet."

The activity behind him seemed to stop. A moment later, Rae said, "You okay?"

"Sure." He glanced at Rae and smiled before turning back to the window. "I'm fine." He could hear her mixing the formula and water in the bottle behind him. He stuffed his emotions back where they belonged. He'd give anything to feed little Johnny, but with all the memories swirling, maybe not with an audience.

"Let's go in the living room."

She settled on the sofa, and he handed her Johnny, refusing to linger on that image of mother and child. He returned to the kitchen for their mugs, set hers in front of her, and sat on the chair next to her.

Johnny sucked on the bottle like he hadn't eaten in a month while Rae stared into his tiny eyes, a look of peace on her face he hadn't seen since she'd returned.

He remembered that peace. How powerful it had felt, and how tenuous it had been.

The baby had sucked down half the bottle when Rae lifted him to her shoulder to burp him. She caught Brady staring and smiled.

He smiled back. "He looks a lot like his father."

Johnny burped, and she giggled. "Gotta work on those manners."

So much for his subtle attempt to get more information. He was about to ask outright when she sighed.

"I was working on a story." She returned Johnny to her arms and offered him the rest of the bottle. Her smile faded. "I had a friend. She worked for the BBC and lived in the same complex as I did. Her name was Margot, and she was the only friend I had in Africa. She had to go to Cairo for a story. Just a follow-up on something she'd done before we met. I never knew the details. I went with her because she wanted to introduce me to a few people. She was like that, you know? I mean, we were rivals, but she was older than I was, and she had the backing of a major news outlet, while I was freelance."

Brady was almost afraid, afraid she'd change her mind about telling him.

"Margot had a meeting that day and told me she'd meet me afterward. I wanted to go with her, but she insisted that this was not somebody I needed to meet."

Rae turned her gaze down to Johnny. Her voice quieted a bit, and he leaned forward to hear her better.

"I got the feeling her contact was dangerous. I was tempted..." She looked up, nearly smiled. "You know me. I'm no respecter of secrets."

Nosiest person he'd ever met.

"But she'd been so good to me, and I didn't want to jeopardize our friendship, so I did what she asked. I waited at the hotel until after midday prayers."

She glanced at him and added, "After lunch. Muslims have these prayer times—"

"I was stationed in Afghanistan."

"Oh, right. Okay."

The bottle was empty, so Rae set it on the coffee table and lifted Johnny again, tapping his back rhythmically. "I was on my way to the restaurant where we were supposed to meet. But I got lost. I'd just spotted the place when..." She paused, and he watched some emotion play across her face. She swiped a knuckle beneath her eyes. "It exploded."

Acid filled his stomach. "The restaurant where your friend—?"

"Some little two-bit terrorist group had gotten their hands on explosives. The bomb just took out a few tables. Margot was killed."

He stood and sat beside her, wrapped his arm around her shoulders. "I'm so sorry."

She shook her head, like she was trying to shake it off. Then she leaned into him. "It was awful."

He froze, afraid the slightest movement might prompt her to retreat. He inhaled the strawberry scent of her shampoo and forced himself not to wrap her more tightly. He peered down at Johnny, who was looking at his mother with those serious baby eyes.

She straightened and wiped her tears, then stood and carried Johnny upstairs. He hoped like crazy she'd tell him the rest of the story. A moment later, she returned carrying the bouncy seat with the baby inside. She set the bouncer on the coffee table.

"Was it just random," he asked, "or was there a target?"

"They thought the target was the man Margot had been meeting with. Long story that no longer matters. Apparently the terrorists didn't appreciate him sharing information with a British journalist."

"Wow."

"Thing is, the group responsible, they were just a bunch of dumb, dangerous teenagers. They claimed responsibility. Within a couple of hours, the authorities had them in custody. But I wasn't satisfied with that. I wanted to know...What kind of a person sells bombs to teenagers? What kind of a man...?"

She paced across the room. "To me, he was the real bad guy. And I was angry. I started investigating arms dealers, and my search led me to Julien."

Brady leaned back against the sofa and forced himself not to speak.

"Julien had been doing business in Africa for more than a decade, and he knew everybody. I finally got him to agree to a meeting with me. We met at this little off-the-beaten-path cafe. I think he thought he'd scare me away. It was definitely not a place frequented by foreigners. And he wasn't keen on meeting with me at all, but I'd insisted. I was angry and careless. I walked in there like I owned the place." She blew out a breath and gave a wry laugh. "I was so stupid."

She paced another circuit, then another, before she spoke again.

"I think I fell a little bit in love with Julien before our meals were delivered. He was so charming, so kind."

Brady's spine stiffened. He forced himself to relax.

"Julien gave me a lead. An arms dealer they called the Spaniard. I never proved he'd sold the munitions that killed my friend, but I did tie him to another bombing. My story was the impetus that got him arrested and sent to prison for life."

"Wow."

Rae stopped and looked at him as though she'd forgotten he was there.

Brady clamped his mouth shut.

She paced again. "Julien and I started seeing each other. He..." She blushed and looked away. "Swept me off my feet, I guess. Six weeks later, he invited me to join him on his yacht." She stopped, stared at the cold fireplace, and fiddled with the wedding ring on her finger. She pulled it up to the knuckle, then pushed it back. Over and over. "He'd invited all his friends. They were mostly European, a few locals, but they all spoke

English. They were funny and smart and so...cosmopolitan. That's the world he lives in." She shook her head. "Lifestyles of the rich and..." Her voice tailed off. "In the few weeks we'd been dating, I'd gotten to know his friends. It felt like, for the first time since..." She looked at Brady, nearly smiled, and turned back to the fireplace. "For the first time in a long time, I had a group of friends, a place where I almost fit in. I was educated. I could keep up with their discussions. I got along with the women, joked with the men. I was one of them."

Rae paused in her circuit.

If only Brady knew what she was thinking.

"He asked me to marry him in front of everybody." Rae blushed. Beautiful, radiant.

Not his.

Brady kept his expression blank and nodded for her to continue.

"When I said yes..." She shook her head and stared at the fireplace again. "He had it all planned out. He'd bought me a gorgeous dress, and the rings. My friends whisked me downstairs to the stateroom and dressed me, did my hair and makeup." She looked at the floor. When she looked up again, her gaze had hardened. "We were married that day, on the boat. It was a surprise wedding, a surprise to the bride. I thought..."

She started pacing again. "It wasn't what I thought."

Rae crossed to the wall, then back to the fireplace, four times, then five.

"I'd made some stupid decisions back in college, decisions with"—her eyes flicked up, met his, then turned away—"with a guy."

She seemed to be waiting for a response. "I won't judge you, Rae. You and I did everything but back then."

She shrugged.

"I've been no saint," he said, "believe me." The heartache of those choices still haunted him. Maybe if he'd been a stronger man.

"Anyway, I'd decided not to be intimate with anyone..." She stopped in front of the empty fireplace and shrugged. "I'd decided not to. And then I got married."

Brady willed himself to push away the image of Rae with the man on his computer screen.

She turned to face him, tears in her eyes. "If I'd had a little notice, I'd have done my homework. I'd have known..."

He thought of the information Samantha had dug up, the photograph of the real Mrs. Julien Moreau. Brady stood, walked around the coffee table, and stopped beside her. "You might as well tell me the rest. I think I already know."

Her eyes narrowed. "What?"

"You didn't know, right? About...?" Maybe she still didn't know, though. Maybe he was about to drop another pile of bad news on her that he thought she already knew, like he'd done with the news of her grandmother's death.

"What would you have known if you'd done your homework?"

She stepped back. "What did you do?"

He raked his hands through his short hair and groaned. "We did some checking. It looks like—"

"Who is *we*?" Her voice rose, and the baby squeaked.

"Um, well, because we both love you and want to make sure you're okay..."

She took another step back. Her eyes were wide. "Who. Is. We?"

"Samantha and I... She's really good at research."

"You had Samantha investigating me?"

Crap. Why hadn't he kept his mouth shut? "I just... She's so sorry, and she loves you, and I knew you were in trouble, and Samantha'd be able—"

"What did she do?"

"She just made some calls."

Rae closed her eyes and shook her head.

"We just wanted to find out what was going on with you," he said. "Protect you from whatever it is you're running from."

She opened her eyes. They were wide and fearful now. "Who did she call?"

He thought back to their conversation. Samantha hadn't said much. "She said something about a court clerk in Toulouse. But I think there were others."

The color drained from Rae's face, and she sat heavily on the hearth. She dropped her head into her hands.

Brady crouched beside her. "I shouldn't have brought Sam into this without asking you."

"You have to go."

"You can trust me, you can." He grabbed her hands. They were freezing, and he rubbed them to warm them. "You need to trust me. I don't know what the deal is with this guy, but if you and Johnny need protection, I can help."

She yanked her hands away. "You have to go. Now."

He stood and blinked. How had they gone from there to here, so fast?

"I don't understand."

She stood and walked toward the door. "No, you don't."

He followed. "Explain it to me then."

She opened the door. "I'm sorry. I can't. Please, don't make any more calls to anybody, and don't tell anybody you've seen me. And tell Samantha the same. In fact, you both need to tell everybody...something. How you reached out to me and I turned you away. How I'm the same old Rae, closed off and distant. Everybody will believe that."

Closed off and distant? Nobody would believe that.

"You need to tell anybody who asks that you don't know anything about me."

"I don't know anything, Rae."

"He won't believe that."

"Julien?"

She didn't respond.

"Rae, tell me what's going on."

She glared at him. "Get. Out."

He seemed to have no other option. He stepped outside and turned back to argue.

"Goodbye, Brady."

She closed the door in his face. A moment later, the deadbolt clicked.

TWENTY-FIVE

Julien arrived back at his Manhattan hotel at nine o'clock that evening. Farah and Hector were waiting by his door.

"You have found her?"

Farah shook her head. "I'm sorry."

He bit back the ugly retort and went inside. He stepped into the bedroom. The bed had been turned down, and the room smelled faintly of the fresh flowers the staff had left on the bureau. The curtains were drawn, blocking the view of Central Park. From this floor, he could barely make out the noises of the city below. He returned to the living area and sat at the round table. He nodded to the other chairs. "What did you learn?"

Farah joined him at the table and pulled out a notebook. "Hector did much of the work."

Julien turned his attention to Hector, who was leaning against the wall, his meaty arms crossed, his bald head glistening in the artificial light. "I managed to find a file in the university's storage facility."

"You broke in?"

"I left no evidence."

"And?"

Hector nodded to Farah, who consulted her notes.

"The most recent address the university had was an apartment near campus. We spoke with the young men who live there now. Students. They've never heard of her." Farah brushed a few loose strands of her dark hair behind her ears. Her hands were trembling. "We spoke with the landlord, and he recognized her photograph. He assured us that she moved away years ago. He had no forwarding address."

Julien grabbed a bottle of Evian from the mini-fridge, downed a long swig, and snagged a can of macadamia nuts off the shelf.

"Surely you have more information than that. I asked you to find her family's address."

Farah swallowed. "Oui. The address the university has is the La Jolla house."

"You're looking into the wrong Rachel Adams." Did he have to do everything himself? "The girl from La Jolla didn't even graduate. Surely you can find the Rachel Adams who did."

"Monsieur, this is the information we have on the Rachel Adams who graduated twelve years ago from Columbia."

He looked from Farah to Hector, who shrugged.

"How do you explain that?" Julien asked.

Farah closed her notebook. "The real Rachel Adams died in California of a drug overdose. The mother identified the body. She was the Rachel Adams the university believed was attending. The woman claiming to be Rachel Adams changed the contact information, had everything mailed directly to her at that address here in the city."

"So what are you saying?"

"That our Rachel stole her identity."

Julien let those words sink in. Seems he wasn't the only one in their marriage with secrets. Why would she lie, if not to throw him off her track? Which meant she'd intended to betray him from the very beginning. Their entire marriage had been a lie, some kind of ruse. For what? To steal the paltry evidence she'd found against him? Or did she have some grander purpose. To bring him to justice? To sell him out to his enemies? Or perhaps just to get a juicy story.

He thought of all the times they'd made love, limbs intertwined, sharing secrets. Whispered words of affection and devotion. In his case, those words had been true. Yes, he'd lied, but his love for her had been real.

And what part did his son play in all of it? Why have the child only to snatch him away? But perhaps she'd needed access to his Paris apartment, and by the time she arrived, her pregnancy had prevented her escaping. The moment she'd gotten her chance, she had.

She'd made a fool of him.

He stared at the wall as a swell of rage gushed over him. When it passed, he schooled his voice and said, "That...complicates things."

"Indeed." Farah's gaze flicked to Hector. The man's jaw was clenched.

He turned back to Farah. "Anything else?"

She shook her head. "Forgive me."

Julien glanced back at Hector, then turned to her. "Would you excuse us?"

"*Mais oui.*"

After the door closed behind her, Julien turned to Hector. "Before you start, what did you hear from Carson?"

"I had him pass along your suggestion that Aziz put our deal back on the table, explained that Aziz has placed himself in a precarious position by pitting brothers against each other, and reminded him of your handshake. I also suggested that Aziz might not want to make an enemy of the *elder* brother if he wanted to continue to do business with the Moreau family." Hector shrugged. "And if he wanted to continue to breathe."

This debacle with Aziz suddenly seemed more than what he'd originally thought. Could Carson put the deal back together, or was this more than just a play to save money? Was Rae working with the terrorist? Had she been in communication with Geoffrey too? Was it all connected somehow, and if so, how?

All of those questions would be answered, but now, he had to deal with the crisis before him. "Go on."

"Carson is to meet with Aziz tomorrow." Hector checked his watch. "We should know something soon."

"And you're sure Carson is loyal?"

"As sure as I can be." Hector stepped to the table and laid a revolver and a box of ammunition in front of Julien.

Julien eyed it. "You know I don't like guns."

"Don't tell your clients that."

Julien turned his glare to Hector.

"Just in case," Hector said. "You may need it."

Julien lifted the gun. For an arms dealer, he didn't know much about pistols. His clients preferred more powerful munitions. Julien turned the cold, smooth weapon in his hands and saw it was loaded.

Hector leaned against the wall again.

"You have something to say?"

"I warned you about her, whatever her name is."

"Very helpful."

Hector pushed off the wall and took Farah's seat at the table. "I told you Rachel was too American. Too independent."

"You're a wealth of observations tonight."

"If you had done even a cursory check of her background—"

"I indulge your comments because of our friendship, but don't forget your place."

Hector nodded once. "It's like with Claire. You remember?"

Ah, Claire. Julien had fallen hard for her. Would have given her the moon, if only she'd asked.

"I was fifteen, Hector. Surely you can understand the whims of a foolish teenager. Not that you ever had any."

"I had whims. I satisfied them. I moved on."

"Are you even capable of love?"

"I'm capable of loyalty, unlike your wife."

Julien let the insult to his wife go because Hector had been his best friend since they were schoolmates. He'd attended the private academy on a scholarship he received from the orphanage where he'd been raised. They'd been best friends since before their voices changed. Even Farah's devotion was questionable—Julien had broken her heart. Hector was the only true friend he had. Which was why Julien let him get away with challenging him.

"Let's get past all my flaws," Julien said, "and figure out how to fix this. Looks like we'll have to involve the reporter."

"Thousands of people work at the *Times*. The reporter, he was in Africa on a story, yes?"

"That's what Rae told me."

"We know what her word is worth. Did you learn anything in Paris?"

Julien hesitated a moment before pulling the crumpled note from his pocket. He handed it to Hector.

The man's jaw clenched. That vein in his forehead throbbed. "I will take care of her for you."

"Find her. That's all I ask."

"Surely you aren't planning to let her live."

Julien snatched the note and slid it back into his pocket. "What I intend to do to my wife is none of your concern. The plan?"

A moment passed before Hector spoke again, though his

rage played across his face. "Farah and I will search the *Times* website and narrow the list, then show you photographs. It's too risky to try to plant bugs in the building. I presume this friend of hers doesn't know where she is. We'll have to get her to contact him, and to do that, we'll apply pressure."

"What kind of pressure?"

"She is an American. Sentimental. It is her weakness."

TWENTY-SIX

Rae sat up in bed. It was nearly four in the morning. She'd worried for hours after Brady left. What danger had she put him and Samantha in by seeing them? What if people found out Brady had been over so often? Would Julien ask around, try to figure out who Rae had spoken to?

Would he track Brady down? Would Sam get pulled into it?

She had to escape, and soon. The less time she spent here, the less chance Julien would hunt down her old friends. She'd give it one more day of searching, then she'd give up. If she didn't find her father's treasure by this time tomorrow, she'd leave with what she had.

At least she had Johnny.

She'd finally fallen asleep after Johnny's midnight feeding. So what had woken her now? She stretched, leaned across the bed, and looked at Johnny in his cradle. Sound asleep.

She strained to listen for anything that didn't belong, but all she heard were the sounds of the night slipping through the closed window.

She thought about the chest in her parents' room. Rae stood, slipped on her socks, and padded to their bedroom, where she flipped on the light and climbed on their bed beside the old chest. She unlatched it and opened the top.

Photo albums.

She pulled out the one on top, a picture of her parents at their wedding. Her mother was gazing up at her father with the most loving expression. He was looking back at her, eyes twinkling as if he had a secret.

Oh, he'd had plenty of secrets, some good. The treasure fit in that category. Others, not so much.

Not that she didn't understand the temptation. Her mother had been beautiful and enchanting and wondrous. Sometimes. Other times, she'd been ugly and angry and accusatory. Hurling insults and slurs like stones into a lake, and Rae still felt the ripples today. The difference was that her mother couldn't control her mental health. But her father—those women had been his choice.

Rae was turning the page when a creak startled her. She set the album on the bed beside her, then listened.

A whispered word. "Hurry."

Rae's pulse raced. Had Julien found her? Had she waited a day too long?

She slid off the bed and tiptoed down the hall and into the bedroom where her phone was charging. She closed the door behind her, then grabbed the cell and dialed 9-1-1.

"What's your emergen—"

"There someone in my house," she whispered. "At least two people." She stepped in front of the cradle, stared at the door, and recited her address.

After the operator had asked all the required questions, Rae dropped the phone on the bed. She flipped on the closet light. The baby snored gently while Rae searched her old closet for something, anything... She grabbed an award she'd won for an article in the local paper—an oversize brass pen on a stone stand. That might do some damage. She returned to her place between the door and her child, lifted the award in her right hand, and prepared to swing it.

Seconds ticked by. She heard nothing. No voices. No footsteps. No doors opening or closing. Minutes passed. Years. She pleaded with the silence. *Protect Johnny, please. Just keep him safe.*

The silence didn't answer.

A door creaked downstairs, then another, and then a slam. Footsteps pounded across the hardwood, and another slam.

Rae rushed to the window in time to see two figures running across the backyard. They both wore black clothes and black hats and disappeared into the forest. A larger man bolted across the lawn. She watched him until he, too, was lost in the shadows.

Rae stared at the space where they'd gone.

How could the baby still be sleeping? But aside from the two slammed doors, it had all been very quiet. Still was. Too quiet.

A few minutes passed before the larger man emerged from the woods and jogged to her back door.

TWENTY-SEVEN

Brady searched the downstairs. Nothing seemed out of place. The pantry door was open in the kitchen, but otherwise, everything was as it had been earlier.

He climbed the stairs and peeked in Dorothy's room. Empty. The light was on in Rae's parents' room. The chest he'd helped her with earlier lay open on the bed.

He continued down the hallway and knocked on Rae's door. "It's Brady," he whispered.

He pushed the door open and peeked inside.

It was dark, the only light coming from the full moon outside her window. Rae was standing in front of the crib, a sheer white nightgown ending above her knees. The moonlight shining behind lit her silhouette.

Oh, boy.

He blinked. Forced his gaze to her face. Her eyes were wide, her jaw set. Then he looked at the thing she held high in her right hand. Was that a giant brass pen?

"You can put that down now."

She lowered the thing in her hand, tossed it on the bed.

"You know," he whispered, "that's just an expression. The pen really isn't mightier than—"

"I didn't have a sword." Then she started to giggle.

He grabbed her hand and pulled her out of the room and down the stairs. No need to wake Johnny because of his mother's sudden fit of laughter.

She was hysterical, and not in a good way. Panic had always given her the giggles.

He got her to the sofa in the living room. "Sit."

She sat, laughed harder.

"What is so funny?"

"I like your pants."

He looked down at his clothes. Red and black plaid pajama pants and a gray Patriots T-shirt. "There was an accident on the highway, so the guys on duty tonight were busy. The chief knows I don't live far from you. I didn't take the time to change."

She nodded, still laughing.

"There were two men in your house, Reagan. It isn't funny."

A sob escaped her throat. She wiped the tears streaming down her face. Panic always made her cry too. "I don't know what's wrong with me."

She swayed, then fell sideways on the couch.

Brady sat beside her. "You all right?"

She folded into a fetal position.

He focused on her face, not allowing himself to see anything the flimsy nightgown wasn't covering. "You're safe now."

He rubbed her back until the sobs subsided. Finally, she sat up and straightened her clothes. "Sorry. I'm a mess."

He bumped her shoulder with his. "You're safe."

Another sob.

"Hey, really. They're gone."

She leaned against his shoulder. He could feel her trembling and wrapped his arms around her. The thin material of her nightgown wasn't leaving nearly enough to his imagination, and his imagination didn't need any more material to work with. He stood, grabbed an afghan from the back of the club chair, and tucked it around her. Then he sat and pulled her back into an embrace.

Perfect.

Except that he'd just chased two men from inside her home. Whoever these prowlers were, they were getting bolder.

What were they looking for?

TWENTY-EIGHT

Johnny's cry seemed louder in the mornings.

"Shh." Rae patted his back while she walked down the stairs, whispering, "We have to be quiet."

The baby babbled louder.

She rushed across the foyer and into the kitchen, glancing at Brady on her way. Lying on his side, he faced the back of the couch. The house was cold, and that thin afghan didn't seem warm enough. Maybe she'd get him another. It was too early for normal people to face the day. The sun had barely cut into the darkness.

She settled the baby in the bouncy seat and had grabbed the formula when Brady stepped in the kitchen. "Morning."

She blushed and turned away. Pajama pants, crumpled T-shirt, and bedhead. He probably had morning breath too. So why had the word *sexy* popped in her mind?

"Sorry about the hour. Coffee?"

"Sure. Right back."

She shook her head. Too early for those thoughts. Not that there was a good time. She started the coffee and fixed a bottle.

She was seated at the kitchen table feeding Johnny when he returned.

Brady pulled two mugs from the dishwasher and poured their coffees, adding cream to hers. Observant, that man. He placed a mug in front of her before he sat.

"Thanks."

"Sure."

He sipped, set the cup down.

She said, "We have to stop—"

"Just what the doctor—"

They'd both spoken at the same time. He nodded to her, so she started again. "We keep having coffee together. We're like boring characters in a chick flick."

"Gee, thanks."

She stared at her coffee mug, calling to her from just a few inches away on the kitchen table. If only she had a straw.

"Thanks for staying," she said. "Seems stupid now, but last night..."

"What are they looking for, Rae?"

"How would I know?"

"They're looking for the same thing you're looking for. Out in the barn. In your parents' closet. What is it?"

She studied her baby's face, considered lying, and kept quiet.

"At least you're not denying it." He pushed his chair back. "Mind if I make some food?"

"Not much to choose from."

He opened the fridge and pulled out the carton of eggs. "How do you like them?"

"Whatever you want is fine."

He grabbed a package of cheese. "No ham? Bacon?"

"Sorry."

He grabbed a bowl from the cabinet. "You're not the only one who's had bad things happen, you know."

She sighed. "I'm a reporter. I make my living reporting bad things."

He pulled a fork from the drawer. "You need to trust me."

"It's not about trust. You don't understand."

"How can I?" He broke the eggs in the bowl. "You won't tell me anything. I know you're still angry with me about what happened with Sam. You took off without a word after eighteen years of friendship. Forget the fact that we'd been dating for three years. Forget the fact that we'd made promises to each other...plans. We were friends, Rae. You were the best friend I ever had." He snapped his fingers. "Just like that, you were gone."

"You and Samantha. And that reporter—"

"I know, okay? I was there. And Mom didn't know who the woman was. They'd met at the supermarket. The woman played her."

"I realize that now, but—"

"And either way, *I* didn't invite her."

"You could have stood up for me."

He blew out a long breath. "I should have. You shouldn't have thrown away eighteen years of friendship because of two stupid things I did." He looked into the bowl like he'd forgotten what he was doing. Then he pointed the fork at her. "But you did, and I forgave you. I've had too much crap in my life. Holding onto that anger just made me miserable."

She shifted Johnny to her shoulder and patted his back until he burped. Then she offered him the rest of his bottle. "You're right. I'm sorry."

He started to say something, then stopped. He grabbed a pan from the cabinet and heated it on the stove. He beat the eggs as if the whole situation were their fault, then poured the mixture into the pan, where they sizzled and quieted.

She wondered about his comment. He'd had too much crap in his life. What was that about? Maybe she could just ask.

Johnny finished his bottle. She burped him and settled him in her arms. She wanted to ask Brady more about his life. She wanted to know everything. But what good would it do? Maybe it was better if she didn't know. Once she found the treasure, she'd leave Nutfield forever.

He slid half of an enormous cheese omelet in front of her and handed her a fork. She tasted it. It was shockingly good. She'd already eaten three bites by the time he sat at the table beside her.

"Wow."

"Thanks." He had a bite, a sip of coffee. "What are they looking for, Rae?"

She sighed. She wanted to trust him, but what good would come of him knowing her secrets? If Julien found out about their friendship, it could only cause him trouble. She should have insisted he leave the night before, but she'd been too afraid to be alone.

So what would it hurt to share her secrets? And to learn a few of his.

"You first."

He lifted one eyebrow.

"Tell me about the crap you referred to earlier. What happened?"

"Doesn't matter."

She should drop it, of course. So why did she lean toward him? Why did she look into those beautiful eyes? Before she could stop herself, she said, "It matters to me."

TWENTY-NINE

Brady leaned back, away from that imploring gaze. He sipped his coffee then poured himself a glass of juice without asking if Rae wanted any.

He couldn't talk to her.

Rae wanted to know his secrets. Not that they were secrets, really. Anybody in town could tell her. Chances were good she wouldn't ask anybody in town. He'd like to think that would stop her from finding out. But Rae was resourceful. It was only a matter of time before she learned about his tragedy. He should just tell her.

And why not? She'd trusted him, to a point, the night before. And he was asking her to trust him again. It's not like he had anything to be ashamed of, not as far as most people knew. His family and friends felt sorry for him. But they didn't know everything.

If anybody would understand how he felt, Rae would. She'd lived through tragedy upon tragedy in her life, and if he weren't mistaken, she was bearing up under another one right now. She'd sympathize with him like most people couldn't.

She'd get it.

So why was he chewing so slowly? He could've inhaled the whole omelet. Instead, he cut another tiny piece and popped it into his mouth, oblivious to the taste.

He worked through the story in his mind, working out how he'd tell her. Working out why he wanted to hold back. Didn't take him long to figure it out.

What an idiot.

Rae was a married woman. Well, she thought she was. Or had thought. Or... Whatever. She sure as heck hadn't been waiting for him. Nor he her. Hadn't there been a string of women to take her place over the years? No one-night-stands for him, though. Nope. One of his girlfriends had called him a serial monogamist after he'd dumped her. "From one I-love-you-forever to the next so fast you never have time to update your Facebook status."

Not entirely true. He'd never used Facebook. And besides, it wasn't like he'd been dumping one woman to start up with another. But every relationship had reached that fish-or-cut-bait point, and he'd always cut bait.

Until Ashley. He hadn't cut bait in time with her. Not that he hadn't cared for her. He'd cared for all of them. Ashley had been beautiful. Pale skin. Strawberry-blonde hair. Hazel eyes. Freckles.

He looked across the table at Rae, who met his gaze.

He cut another bite of eggs. His attraction to Ashley had nothing to do with the fact that she'd resembled Rae.

So what if he had a type he liked? That didn't mean anything.

He'd have cut bait with Ashley too.

And none of that was Rae's business. If she wanted to know his secrets that badly, she could find out on her own. He couldn't open himself up to her, not again. She'd already left him once, ripped a good part of him to shreds when she did. His heart couldn't take any more mutilation at the hands of Reagan McAdams.

She carried her plate to the sink, rinsed it, then set about emptying the dishwasher before putting her dirty plate in the rack. She grabbed the pan from the stove and scrubbed it. "Have you decided yet?"

"The prowlers are looking for something. If you want me to figure out who they are—"

"I'll figure it out." She rinsed the pan and set it on a towel to dry. "Or I won't. It's not going to matter much longer."

"Rae."

"Caro will find out today if she got a part in the play." Rae grabbed the eggs and cheese and returned them to the fridge. "If she does, I'll have her contact you about the rehearsal schedule."

Brady thought of all his good reasons to keep his story to himself. Were his secrets worth keeping if it meant she wouldn't confide in him? "Look, I'll tell you what's been going on with me, okay? But I have to get home and shower if I'm going to get to work on time. Can I tell you later?"

She leaned against the counter and shrugged. "It's none of my business."

He waited while a wave of anger coursed through him. "Five minutes ago," he said, forcing his voice to stay even, "you wanted to know all about me, and now it's none of your business?"

"It'll just make it harder."

Make what harder? She was driving him crazy. "We still have to figure out what to do about the prowlers. I'm worried about you."

"When I hear from Caro about the auditions, I'll call you at the station and let you know." She wrung out the dish towel and draped it over the spigot. "You're going to be able to work out rides for her, right?"

"I wish you'd stay."

The baby cooed in the silence.

She crossed her arms. "Thanks for being here last night."

"Are you calling the alarm company, or shall I?"

"I'm not going to be here long enough to worry about it."

"An alarm is always a good idea."

She shrugged, and he forced his voice to stay calm. "If it's the money—"

"I'll consider it."

"There are people breaking into your house. What are you going to do about that? You could stay somewhere else. You could—"

"I'm going to finish up here and hope they don't get any bolder."

"They were in your house, when you were home. I'd say that's pretty bold."

She nodded slowly. A normal person would be frightened by that. Rae had been the night before. But now, in the light of day...seemed Rae had something much bigger to fear.

THIRTY

She had to put a stop to this growing...whatever it was with Brady. Right now.

He'd finally agreed to tell her his story, and she'd turned him down. Not that she didn't want to know. She did, desperately. But the last thing she needed was one more tether holding her in Nutfield, and whatever Brady's story was, no doubt it would grab her, make her want to soothe all the hurts in his life.

It was better this way. She had to move forward with her plan and keep a good distance from Brady Thomas. If they stayed away from each other, Julien wouldn't discover their shared pasts. And she wouldn't have her heart broken. Again.

After she put Johnny down for his morning nap, she headed downstairs, cringing on the creaky step, and paused in the entryway.

She was sure Dad had said something about stairs when he'd told her about the treasure. Rae had searched all around the stairs in the barn, the furniture beneath them, the stuff near the bottom of them, and right at the top in the loft. She'd climbed into the attic of the house and searched near the hatch.

She'd found nothing but a few trinkets and a whole bunch of junk.

So now she looked at the staircase in the house. A barrister bookcase stood on the wall adjacent to the stairs. Could it be that easy?

Rae grabbed the baby monitor and rested it on a table in the living room. Then she turned the TV to a news program—she felt so out-of-touch with the goings on in the world—and returned to the bookshelf. She began at the top, pulling out each volume, one at a time. Maybe Dad had removed the pages from one of the books and hidden the treasure there.

Right. Dad had been a computer programmer, not a spy.

She'd spent too much time investigating criminals. How did normal people think?

The top shelf held a collection of encyclopedias. Their covers were worn and cracked. None of them held a secret stash.

Something on the news piqued her interest. "In Tunis late last night," said a male voice. "The bombing occurred at a small cafe far from the city center..."

Rae rushed into the living room to hear. She stared at the screen, at the sign in front of the familiar cafe, the smoke, the wreckage.

The encyclopedia slipped from her fingers and crashed on the floor.

Rae sank on the sofa.

"Four dead...seventeen injured...expecting the body count to rise."

She recognized the name of the terrorist group that had taken credit for the bombing, Ansar al-Tunis. AAT. She leaned forward, hoping for more, but the newsreader moved on to another story.

She flipped to another station. Nothing about the bombing.

It was odd the first station had covered it—a bombing in an obscure part of a city in a country most Americans wouldn't be able to place on a map?

What had made it newsworthy?

She ran upstairs, grabbed her cell, and navigated to the *New York Times* website. She found the story, which confirmed what she already knew and gave the text of the AAT's message. Typical stuff about the evil West. She'd covered AAT before. Bombings weren't their thing. They'd shot a government official they thought had become enamored with the West. They'd assassinated a foreigner who'd been too outspoken about bringing freedom to Tunisia, but that had been done with a high-powered rifle. She couldn't remember them ever using bombs. Bombs couldn't be trusted to take out your target. Bombs were messy. This group wasn't messy.

But the thing that bothered her most was the location of the bombing. It was the restaurant where she and Julien had met.

The news report said no specific target had been identified.

The whole thing made no sense.

She learned nothing else of value. She ought to let it go. She didn't live there anymore and never would again. So why did she care?

Because it was too much of a coincidence.

She dialed a number from memory.

He answered on the third ring. "Walter Boyle."

"Hi, Nate. It's me."

"Rae? Where have you been? I've been trying to reach you for—"

"It's a long story. Listen, what can you tell me about the bombing in Tunis?"

A long pause. "I don't hear from you in months. You don't return my calls. You fall off the face of the earth."

"I didn't. I just—"

"You stopped sending stories," Nate said. "You just disappeared."

"Look—"

"Where have you been?"

"I've been..." She thought of the events of the previous few weeks, months. There was no time to explain. "Tied up."

"Literally? Because anything less and you could've returned my calls."

"I don't have my phone."

"They sell phones on every street corner."

"Look, I'll tell you, but—"

"You married that guy from the market, right? Moreau?"

Rae froze. Swallowed. "How did you—?"

"The way you talked about him, when you quit calling, I did some checking. It's not like it was a state secret."

"I know. I—"

"You could've told me."

She ran her fingers through her hair and paced. "I should have. It was awkward."

"And this isn't? You disappear, then call for information as if nothing happened."

"I'm sorry." Rae collapsed on the sofa. "You're right. I'm just...I need your help."

"Don't you always?"

"That's not fair," she said, though she knew Nate was right. She had no right to expect anything from him.

"Is he...?" His voice softened, and he started again. "Is he good to you?"

His concern nearly brought tears to her eyes. "You and I have been over for a long time, Nate. You ended it."

"Because I was the only one really in it."

She thought of him then, not just as her conduit to information, but as her friend. As more than her friend. She'd blown it with Nate like she'd blown it with everybody she'd ever loved. She'd been so focused on protecting her heart over the years, she'd trampled on other people's. Especially Nate's. She'd always believed she'd be able to make it up to him someday. But now, she had to leave. There was no fixing it.

The regrets were piling up like bags of garbage on the curb. "I'm sorry. I don't know what to say."

Nate sighed. "Are you worried Moreau was at that cafe? I can check the names."

"He's in Paris. I think."

"You think?" Nate paused. Seemed to be waiting for her to say something. When she didn't, he said, "I guess it is a long story."

Rae couldn't handle more verbal volleyball. She needed information, not the third degree.

"So you're not in Tunis," he said.

"I'm home."

"Home as in…?"

"Your dad is handling Gram's estate."

"Her estate?" He blew out a long breath. "I'm so sorry, Rae. I hadn't heard."

"Thank you."

"So what's so important about this bombing?"

"Do you have any more information?"

Finally, she heard him typing.

"Here's the latest." He blew out a long breath. "One of the dead was a five-year-old."

She closed her eyes. A child. They'd killed a child.

Walter said, "What kind of people—?"

"The message the terrorists left, can you find out if there was any more to it?"

"According to this—"

"I know what the story says. Can you make some calls, find out if the reporter left anything out?"

Another short pause. "It'll take me some time. This number works for you?"

"Yes. Please don't share it."

Another pause. She heard him take a deep breath. "Who are you hiding from?"

"It's just—"

"Rachel?"

She bristled at the name. "It's Reagan again."

"Wow," he said. "Things really have changed."

She thought of Johnny, asleep upstairs. "You have no idea."

He paused, seemed to process that, and said, "Okay. I'll call you back."

THIRTY-ONE

Rae ended the call and slipped the phone in her pocket.

Her hands were shaking. It was stupid. The bombing had happened thousands of miles away on another continent, in another world.

So why had the impact hit her all the way in New Hampshire?

She walked past the bookshelf she'd been searching just a few minutes before and looked out the window beside the front door. Nobody there. She was safe here. Julien didn't know where she was.

But soon enough, he would find her.

She returned to the bookshelf. She yanked each book off and looked at it before tossing it on the floor. There was no secret hiding place. Nothing heavier than it should be. Nothing at all. She studied the shelves. Just old wood and glass doors. She slid the shelf away from the wall to look behind. Maybe there was a secret hiding place back there.

How could she have forgotten?

A small door opened to the tiny space beneath the stairs.

This house did have a secret compartment. Secret because the bookshelf had blocked the door as long as she could remember. The door was old and ugly. Barely a door, really. Just sheetrock painted the same butter yellow as the rest of the wall. It was attached with two-by-fours and rusted hinges. Gram had hated it.

There was no handle. Rae pried it open with her fingers. This had to be Dad's hiding space. He'd said something about stairs, hadn't he?

She crawled inside. Boxes everywhere. The first looked like it was filled with more books. She pushed it into the hallway, past the other books, and dumped it over, just to be sure. Hardcovers fell all over the floor. Old spy novels and mysteries, Dad's favorites.

She rushed back in. This was definitely his stuff.

She grabbed the next box, pushed it beyond her previous mess in the foyer, and dumped it.

More books. Nothing else.

That old metal box had to be here somewhere.

She did it again with the third box, then the fourth. Dumping piles of books and other mementos of her father's life all over the floor. Somewhere in the back of her mind, she registered that she was losing it. But she couldn't stop.

One box left. She was just dumping it when her phone rang.

She snatched it out of her pocket, saw the caller ID, and answered. "Did you find anything?"

Nate sighed. "I'm fine. Thanks for asking."

She stood in the foyer, surrounded by the wreckage of her panic. "Nate."

"I have a contact at the State Department. There was one thing in the message they didn't release to the media. They didn't know what it meant. He'd only tell me off-the-record, and I promised—"

"I'm not working on a story. It's just a hunch."

"Okay." Nate paused. Rae heard papers shuffling. "Want to tell me your hunch?" he asked.

"It's personal."

"Personal? A bombing in Tunis is personal?"

"It's a long—"

"Story. Right. So you've said."

She resisted the urge to scream. "So can you...?"

The doorbell rang. She stared at it. It wasn't Julien. He wouldn't ring the bell. Still...

"Rae?"

"Just a sec." She peeked out the window.

Brady.

Crap.

She pulled it open and stepped aside.

Brady entered, looked at the chaos of her entry, and gave her a *what the heck is going on* look.

"Just a sec, Brady." She picked her way over the mess of books and into the living room. "Nate, please tell me the message."

Nate said, "Brady Thomas? What's he doing there?"

"I have no idea. The message?"

A pause. "Fine," he said, irritated. Nothing she could do about that. "It wasn't a message. Just a string of numbers. Let's see." She heard paper again, then, "Here we go. Eight-one-seven-one-five."

There was a moment, as if she'd drifted out of her body. As if she were living someone else's life. Because how was she supposed to react to that message? Four people had been killed. Seventeen wounded. Some critically. A business destroyed.

And it had everything to do with her.

Should she scream or faint? Should she cry?

She should run.

Nate's voice filtered through her thoughts. "Rae. You still with me?"

She swallowed. "Yeah."

"I take it those numbers mean something to you."

She shook her head. She had to think. Now. "Nate, listen. It's—" A trap, she wanted to say. But was it? What did it mean? "It's very important that you not tell anybody we spoke. Don't tell anybody my real name or where I am. Even a cop or a federal agent."

"What have you gotten yourself into?"

"I haven't done anything illegal. But you can't trust anybody, okay? It's very important."

"Who are you hiding from?"

She sat on the sofa, leaned forward. Nausea overwhelmed her, and she breathed in slowly through her mouth, then blew it out.

"Rae?"

"He has contacts. If the FBI or somebody contacts you, just... I'm not asking you to lie, Nate. I just need a heads-up. Okay? Can you promise me? Put them off until you can warn me?"

"Is it Moreau?"

"I'll call you back in a couple of days, okay?"

"What did he do?" When she didn't answer, he said, "Rae, you're scaring me."

"You've been a good friend to me. I couldn't have asked for more. Please, just this one last thing."

"Anything."

"I have to go."

She ended the call, then shut off the phone. She fumbled with shaking fingers to get the back off. She opened the battery compartment and shook the battery to the floor.

Then she rolled over and held her stomach and wondered what in the world she was supposed to do now.

THIRTY-TWO

Julien stared at the photograph on the screen. Definitely the man Rae had introduced him to. He walked to the window and allowed himself to remember.

They'd only been together a few weeks, and Rae already seemed at home at his estate in Tunis. His wealth and social circles were foreign to her, but she adjusted quickly. He'd bought her a few clothing items, which she accepted only when he insisted. Those shabby rags she went around town in would not do if she were to fit in with his friends. And though she'd seemed comfortable in ghastly khaki cargo pants and T-shirts, when she wore the designs Farah picked out for her, she looked as if she'd worn them all her life.

They were enjoying a day together in the medina, wandering the old city through a labyrinth of vendors, their booths so colorful and bright, it was nearly an assault on his senses. Scents from the spice vendors and the souks serving mint tea and snacks only seemed to energize her. She was charmed, stopping at booth after booth to converse with the locals, purchasing items for far more than their value and laughing at him when he told her she was a terrible negotiator.

"In the States," she said, "we pay what they ask."

"This is not the States."

She only giggled and continued, like a child in a toy store.

She'd chosen to wear her horrible khakis that day, because she'd met with a source that morning. The very idea of it set his nerves on edge. Were these dangerous people? And if they were, what kind of information might they be giving her? He wasn't ready for her to know the truth about himself. He was falling for her. Already considering marrying her. Of course, if he married her, she'd have to give up investigative journalism. And he would have to somehow make it her idea. That was the downside of falling for an American with such a free spirit. But that was a problem for another day. This day was for simply enjoying her company.

She stopped at a booth so she could admire the pottery. Cheap stuff made for tourists, but she didn't seem to care. He was standing a few feet away to watch her, his new favorite sport, when a man approached her and spoke in her ear.

The fear and fury surprised Julien, and he was about to intervene when she turned and threw her arms around the stranger.

Julien froze, but Rae disengaged from the stranger and waved Julien over.

"Julien, I'd like you to meet Nate. He's an old friend."

Julien shook his hand and forced a friendly tone. "What brings you to Tunisia?"

The man was tall, slender, about Rachel's age. He wore a perfectly tailored suit and carried himself with confidence as he glanced around the market. Finally, his gaze settled on Julien. "Working on a story."

Rae stepped nearer to Julien. "Nate works for the *New York Times*. We've known each other a long time."

Julien kept his smile firmly in place when he nodded to the man. "Maybe I can help. I know a lot of locals."

Nate laughed. "I suspect you don't run in the same crowds as the people I'm talking to."

Obviously this Nate fellow had no idea who Julien was. A good thing.

Julien shook off the memory and stared out the window at Central Park. Millions of people were down there. Was Rae one of them?

"Monsieur? Is this him?"

He turned to Farah, then back to the laptop. The photograph filled the screen. The face was right, though the name below it read *Walter Boyle*. Apparently Walter was a pen name. "That's him."

She lifted the computer and stood. "I'll let Hector know we found him."

"Where is Hector?"

"He didn't say."

Julien bit back his remark. It wasn't Farah's job to watch his guard. Still.

"Do you know if he's heard back from Carson?"

"He wouldn't tell me," she said, eyes lowered, "even if he had."

"Yes, yes. Thank you, Farah."

She left the suite, and Julien picked up the phone to call Hector, but it rang before he could dial. He looked at the screen before answering. "Bonjour, Maman."

"Dieu merci! Thank God you're all right."

"Why would you think otherwise?"

"You're not in Tunis, correct? Your father told me you were in the States, but I know how you loved that cafe."

"What are you talking about?"

"Have you not heard? That cafe you like so much. There has been an explosion. It is on the news."

He flipped on the television set, found BBC, and watched in horror as bodies were carried out of his favorite cafe. He caught a glimpse of the owner's son. *"Mon dieu.* I had no idea. Have you heard what happened?"

"Terrorists, of course," his mother said. "I am just thanking God you were not there."

"I have to go."

"Be safe."

He hung up and dialed Hector. The man didn't answer, but a moment later, a knock sounded at his door.

Julien looked through the peephole, then swung the door open.

Hector passed him, stepped inside, and stared at the television.

Julien slammed the door, followed Hector into the sitting room, and pointed at the TV. "Tell me you had nothing to do with that."

"I told you, your wife is sentimental. This will smoke her out."

"Do you know how many were killed?"

Hector shrugged. "You told me to use whatever means were necessary. This was necessary."

"How does killing innocent people a half a world away draw her out?"

Hector's lips twitched in a smile. "Trust me."

THIRTY-THREE

Books were scattered all over the foyer. Brady stood in the midst of them and watched.

Rae had forgotten him.

After she ended her call, she took its battery out of the cell. Worried someone would trace it? Through that person on the phone?

Nate.

Must have been a different Nate.

Rae tipped onto her side on the sofa and held her stomach.

Brady picked his way over the books into the living room and sat down beside her.

She startled, and he laid his hand gently on her shoulder. "It's just me."

Her breath hitched.

"Rae, what happened?"

She shook her head.

He brushed her hair away from her face. "You need to tell me what's going on."

Rae sat up and wiped her eyes on her sweatshirt. "Why are you here?"

"I left my phone." He stood and looked around. There it was, on top of the entertainment center. He slid it in his pocket, then sat. Not too close. She was like a deer. Any sudden movement, and she'd spook.

Whose crosshairs was she trying to avoid?

He kept his voice low, soothing, as if he were interviewing a victim. "It's Julien, right? Did he hurt you?"

She shook her head, then nodded. "Not like that."

"Okay."

"You already know, right? That we're not married?"

He nodded. "He was already married when he married you. You didn't know?"

She sat up and moved out of his reach. "Of course not."

"Is that what this is about?"

"No. Just. No. He was a liar. He lied about everything, from the first moment I met him."

She paused, and Brady resisted the urge to press her.

She kept her gaze on the floor. "I started to suspect something was wrong last spring. I was pregnant. Our first few months of marriage were sort of a blur. We took a lot of trips together. When we were in Tunis, it was like one big party, all the time. People at our house, going in and out. Rich and famous people, you know? I was still working, but not like I had been. I think he was trying to keep me busy, so I couldn't work. And I let him."

Rae brushed the hair out of her face with both hands. They were trembling. "He always kept his office locked. There were people in Tunis who didn't like what he was trying to do. Bringing in jobs wasn't wrong. But bringing in European companies... Some people hate everything about the West. And Julien wasn't Muslim, which made him the enemy, even if he had been a local. He told me to stay out of his office, that knowing stuff about his business could put me in danger."

"But locked? All the time? That's a red flag."

"He had a lot of staff. They worked there before I moved in. Housekeepers, a cook. There were about ten people besides Julien and me who had access to the house. He kept his office locked to keep them out. That's what he said. He wasn't paranoid. Just careful."

"If he kept it locked, then how did you get in?"

"I picked it."

Before he could ask about that new skill, Rae continued. "It was June. I was seven weeks from my due date. And feeling sick. Very swollen. And irritable. And it made me mad that he kept an entire room from me. It was my house, too, right?"

"And you never could stand a secret."

"Oh, I love secrets," Rae said. No smile. "Exposing them."

The dull ache that had begun the moment he'd walked in sharpened now. They were getting close. And he wasn't going to like it. "So what'd you find out?"

She leaned back. "We'd been married almost a year, and I'd never met any of his family."

"Okay."

"In his office, I found a name. Alejandro Castellano Garcia Moreau. I'd heard rumors about him. He ran a crime family. Ran drugs and arms. His organization is responsible for smuggling hundreds of girls from Eastern Bloc countries, girls sold into the sex trade. Alejandro Moreau is..." Her voice trailed off.

"He's a criminal."

"He's my father-in-law."

The ache in his gut sharpened as the words hit home. "No."

"Technically, he's Julien's real wife's father-in-law. He's Johnny's grandfather."

"But Julien isn't involved in his father's company, right? Looks like he's a legitimate businessman."

"That's what I thought. But I had to be sure. I picked the lock on his file cabinet."

"Where'd you learn to do that?"

She nearly smiled. "I have skills."

He opened his mouth, snapped it shut, and said, "Go on."

"Julien's business is legitimate. It's also a great way to launder money for his other business."

"Which is?"

She sighed. "Remember I told you how we met? I was looking for an arms dealer, the man who sold the bomb that killed my friend in Cairo?"

He nodded.

"He did it." Tears filled her eyes. "My husband killed my friend. The people he arms... These are bad people, Brady. Terrorists. He plays himself off as this businessman, when, really, he's arming...everyone. He has no political leanings. He's in favor of whoever will pay him the most money."

"So he knew when he met you that you were looking for that arms dealer. Why do you think he—?"

"Lied to me? Married me? I have no idea. I can't begin to imagine what he was thinking. I mean, he had to know I'd hate him when I found out. And obviously I would eventually. But Julien does like a risk. I thought...it seemed like he really loved me. I felt loved. He acted like... But it was all a lie."

Brady nodded slowly as the enormity of her words sank in. She wasn't just running from her husband. She was running from a murderous criminal. "So what happened today?"

"A bomb exploded in Tunis."

"Okay."

"In the cafe where we met."

Brady remembered what she'd said, that it was a little out-of-the-way place, not a place for foreigners. "You don't think it was a coincidence?"

"I know it wasn't. That call? That was"—she hesitated slightly—"a contact. He found out the rest of the message the AAT gave when they claimed responsibility."

Brady had no idea what the AAT was but didn't interrupt to ask.

She studied her knees. "There was a string of numbers."

"What does that mean?"

"August seventeenth, two thousand fifteen." She took a long breath and met his eyes. "It's our anniversary."

THIRTY-FOUR

THEIR ANNIVERSARY. The bombing had been a message. Rae had given Julien a choice—leave us alone or she'd expose him. He was calling her bluff.

The information she'd stolen from his office showed he'd been involved with selling arms to people who'd killed not just Margot, a British citizen, but American citizens as well. And hundreds of others. But would it be enough to put him away? No. It was circumstantial. Enough to write a good story for a newspaper, but not enough to convict. Julien would get away with it. And even if he didn't, taking Julien out wouldn't kill the snake. His father would be free to continue his work. To track her down. And based on what she knew about him, Alejandro Moreau showed no mercy to his adversaries.

She had to run.

She stood and started toward the stairs.

Brady grabbed her arm. "What are you doing?"

She tried to wrench out of his grip. "We have to go."

"Let's think about this."

Panic rose, squeezed. She swallowed it, looked into Brady's

eyes. "He's going to find me. He's coming. He'll take Jean-Louis, he'll—"

"Reagan, stop." Brady grabbed her other arm. "We have to think."

Her heart hammered. She forced her voice to remain neutral. Nothing to get excited about now. He'd find her, or he wouldn't. Either way, she had to go. She quit fighting. "You don't understand."

"If he knew where you were, he wouldn't have bombed a cafe in Tunis."

True. If Julien knew, she'd already be dead. Johnny would be back with him. Still... "He's trying to find me. That bombing was a message. And I played right into his hands. I called Nate. I have to go. Right now."

The panic bubbled again. She tried to get away, but Brady didn't loosen his grip. She managed to free one hand and swung at his head, feeling more desperate, more panicked every second.

He grabbed her arm before she made contact, then wrapped both arms around her, trapping her. "Stop."

"Let me go."

"You have to think. He'll find you if you don't think it through." Brady pulled her closer. "I'll help you." His voice was low and soothing in her ear. "Please, just let me help you. We'll work out a plan."

A plan? There was no plan that would counteract Julien. Rae's will to fight drained away, leaving her limp and useless. She laid her head on Brady's chest and wept.

"Shh, it's okay." He rubbed circles on her back. "It's going to be okay."

No, it wouldn't. Nothing would be okay.

Minutes passed. The tears dried. She sniffed. She should

pull away. She had so much to do. But right now, being in Brady's arms, she felt safer than she had in months. Years.

He ran his fingers down the length of her hair, brushed it aside, and touched her neck.

A tingle slid down her spine, and she shuddered.

"Rae." His voice was lower, husky. "Look at me."

She tilted her face upward.

Their eyes met. His were warm and brown and filled with tenderness and desire. Filled with love. That's what she'd spent twelve years searching for. She'd never found it in another man.

He leaned closer. "You're not married."

Rae swallowed. She should move. She would, because this wouldn't help either of them. She'd pull away. Just one more second.

His lips met hers, and she melted into his kiss. Twelve years disappeared, and in that moment, she belonged to Brady, and he to her. Everything would be all right. Brady would protect her.

He caressed her neck with one hand, held her close with the other. She had no strength to fight. She was Brady's, had always been Brady's. Her love for him burst within her like the sun over the sea, reflecting beauty on everything it touched. She tilted her head and deepened the kiss, coaxing a groan from his throat. Compared to her feelings for Brady, what she'd felt for Julien was a flickering candle.

Julien.

She ended the kiss, tried to pull away.

"Don't," Brady said.

"Let me go."

He did.

She could hardly walk straight. The world had tilted on its axis. She staggered into the kitchen and sat at the table.

"Rae."

She couldn't look at him. "You need to go."

He stood beside her, touched her hair again.

She ducked away. "Stop."

"Why?"

"This is... I can't. I have to make a plan."

"We'll figure it out."

Johnny wailed, the sound screeching through the baby monitor. She wasn't sure she could muster the energy to stand. She pushed back in her chair, but Brady laid his hand on her shoulder.

"Let me."

She nodded, and he walked out.

She stared at the sunny yellow wall. Tried to make a mental list of all she had to do. She couldn't think. A moment later, she heard Brady's voice through the monitor. Soothing and kind, like a father would be.

Like the father Johnny would never have.

What should she do? Run now? Try to find the treasure and hope Julien didn't track her down while she searched? She needed to focus on figuring out what her next move should be. But she already knew. She lifted her fingertips, touched her lips, and blinked back fresh tears.

She heard Brady return but couldn't seem to tear her eyes away from that yellow wall.

Brady cleared his throat, and she turned to see him cradling Johnny in one arm. With his opposite hand, he patted the baby's back. "You okay?"

"It's not time for him to eat."

"He had a dirty diaper. I bet that's what woke him." He sat in the chair beside her, then shifted the baby to look at his face. Johnny's eyes were closed. "See, he's back to sleep already."

She watched them, the way Brady's large hand cradled little Johnny's rump. Brady stroked Johnny's face, brushed a teardrop from his tiny cheek.

This was what she'd been searching for. She'd gone to New York, to Europe, to Africa, married a man she barely knew, all in a quest for something she'd had all along, right here at home.

Someday, a long time from now, when she'd found a new place to live, a shack in an obscure village in some remote jungle, she'd huddle over an old stove and cook cornmeal mush and watch her son grow up. And this would be the moment she'd remember. Of everything she'd lost—her career, her family, this house, the wealth—it would be this image, Brady cradling her child, that would stay with her. Losing her life with Julien, losing all of it, was nothing. Losing this. That was everything.

THIRTY-FIVE

Brady looked at her tear-stained face, saw the terror in her eyes.

"We'll figure it out."

"You have to go. If he gets any inkling of that"—Rae waved her hand toward the other room—"of what just happened, he'll make you wish you were dead."

Brady didn't care. Hadn't he been dead for years already? Hadn't he only half lived, half loved, half existed since Rae left? By staying with her, he was putting himself in danger. That didn't matter. He put himself in danger every time he pinned on his badge. Sure, he was safer in Nutfield than he'd been in Boston, safer than in Afghanistan. But safety was an illusion. He wasn't afraid to put his life on the line. He wasn't sure if that made him brave or stupid or just incredibly stubborn, but there it was.

So it wasn't fear of dying that held him back now. It was her.

He looked into the face of Rae's child. Jean-Louis, she'd called him. A beautiful child, and Brady had fallen in love already. And when he glanced at Rae again, he admitted the truth. He hadn't fallen *in* love with her, because he'd never fallen *out of* love with her.

Rae was the only woman for him. All the women since had been poor substitutes. But could he throw away everything he'd fought for to be with her? A few days before, all he'd wanted was to stay in Nutfield forever.

And what for? To catch burglars? To put drug dealers behind bars? To fight for the chief's position? Once, that had been all he'd wanted. Yes, Nutfield was home. But why was he back? To protect his fine town? Or was that just his excuse to drop out of life? To cocoon himself. Drugs and knives and guns, no problem. But could he risk his heart again?

Rae wiped a tear from her cheek while she watched him. Did she really think he'd just walk away? Could he, when all he'd ever wanted was to be by her side?

No.

He would stay with her, die with her, if that's what it took. And based on what he'd learned, that was probably the future they had coming. So be it.

Rae reached for Johnny, but Brady held him closer.

She dropped her hand on the table. "You have to go. He'll kill you if he knows we were together."

He laid his hand over hers. "I can live with that."

She glared at him. "You're not listening to me."

"I heard every word you said."

"Brady."

"I'll come with you."

She blinked. Shook her head. "No. He'll... No. That's a bad idea."

"Because you're afraid for my life, or because you don't want me?"

She looked at their joined hands, swallowed, and pulled hers away. "I don't want you."

He chuckled and felt his first real smile in a long, long time. "I don't believe you."

THIRTY-SIX

If Julien didn't get out of this hotel soon, he'd go crazy. He couldn't stand the confined space, the high-rise. He needed fresh air and sunshine. He needed to find Rae and Jean-Louis. Now.

He needed a diversion.

He grabbed the flash drive he'd brought from Paris and slipped it into the USB port on his laptop, then perused the files. He'd been gathering evidence to use against Geoffrey if the need ever arose. Geoffrey was a thug, and not a very smart one at that. Julien didn't want to use this information, but he would if it were necessary. Proving to Papa that Geoffrey was holding out on him ought to convince Papa that Julien was the better choice to lead the company.

Thank God Rae hadn't gotten into his safe. If she'd found this, she could have taken down the whole organization. Julien had been a fool to gather this stuff against his own brother. If it fell into the hands of the authorities, it would ruin Geoffrey. It would ruin his father too. Julien wouldn't be immune to the investigation, either. No, this was for his father's eyes only.

Would Papa thank him, or destroy him?

It wasn't worth the risk. Julien selected all the files, then hovered over the delete key. He should delete it all.

Somehow, he couldn't bring himself to do it. Not yet.

A knock sounded on his door.

He closed the program, files intact, and slipped the flash drive into his pocket. He crossed the room to open the door. Hector. "Well?"

"May I come in?"

Julien stepped aside, and Hector passed him.

"I got a message from Qasim. You remember him?"

Julien closed the door and turned. "Works with Carson, yes?"

Hector stopped at the table. "Worked."

What else could possibly go wrong?

Hector ran a hand over his bald head, offering a rare glimpse of frustration. "Qasim identified Carson's body this morning. He was found last night in an alley in Marrakesh."

Julien swore in French. "That's where he met with Aziz?"

Hector nodded once, and Julien blew out a long breath. "We're sure it was them?"

"A poker chip was found in his pocket."

Aziz's calling card. Always the thousand dollar value, as if he had money to burn. The man's arrogance knew no bounds.

So Julien was in a war, but with whom? With Aziz alone, or was Geoffrey involved? Would his own brother turn against him? Had they teamed up? And if so, what did Aziz have to gain?

Money. And power.

Julien stroked the smooth edge of the flash drive in his pocket. He had ammunition of his own.

He didn't bother to ask about leads. No one would pin Carson's murder on Aziz or his men. Who would dare? Aziz's tentacles had gripped too many in power. He'd expanded beyond diamonds, joined the drug trade. That's why he'd wanted to give Julien drugs in exchange for the weapons, but Julien had refused. He didn't consider opium currency.

But Geoffrey did.

If Julien weren't careful, his would be the next body found with a bloody poker chip. He blew out a breath. "Is Geoffrey involved?"

"Qasim is learning all he can, and I've called in a few favors. We should know something soon. If you would stop being so stubborn—"

"You've made your opinion clear. What about Rae?"

"Farah has done some research and doesn't believe the reporter will be persuaded by money. She can't find any leverage to use against him."

"So what do you suggest?"

"We grab him."

It was risky, but Hector was right. Julien opened the door. "Come up with a plan, quickly. We're running out of time."

Hector walked out, and Julien snatched his phone from the desktop and paced to the window. Papa had called earlier, again. He was far too involved in this deal.

Julien thought of Carson. Dead. Julien hadn't anticipated that. If he were in Tunis, he'd visit Aziz himself. Just walk right into the man's desert compound and have a chat. Aziz wouldn't dare hurt him, not if he wanted to survive Alejandro's wrath. If it was war the man wanted, Julien would oblige, but surely they could reach an understanding without it coming to that. Assuming Geoffrey wasn't whispering in the old man's ear.

He stared down at the treetops in Central Park, but all he could see was his wife's mocking smile. Was she involved in all of this?

She would need to be taught a lesson. Rae had to fear him

enough to stay loyal to him. To stay, and to keep her mouth shut. Or she would have to die.

THIRTY-SEVEN

Johnny wouldn't eat. And he wouldn't stop crying.

Rae bounced him, jiggled him, and patted his back, but nothing helped.

Brady sat at the table. "You sure he doesn't have a fever?"

"I've taken his temperature twice. It's normal." She shifted the baby so he was facing out. He liked to be held like that. Usually. Now it just made him scream louder. "Maybe it's gas."

"You have that medicine?"

She stared at Brady. How did he know so much about babies? She would ask him, if not for the screaming child. She grabbed the diaper bag and tossed it on the table in front of him. "It's in a plastic pouch."

He found the medicine, shook it, and squeezed the right amount into the dropper. "Tip his head back."

"I can manage."

"Just do it."

She did, and Brady squeezed the medicine into the baby's mouth. Johnny scrunched up his little face, swallowed the medicine, and wailed.

"See," she said. "Better already."

Brady paced across the kitchen. "Shouldn't we take him to the doctor?"

"He just has a little cough. I think we should wait."

Brady ran his fingers through his hair.

"He's done this before." Rae thought back. Had it really just been ten days before? Paris seemed a lifetime ago. "He refused to eat, screamed all night. We rushed him to the hospital. The ER nurse laughed. 'Babies cry,' she said. And she was right. He screamed himself to sleep, and when he woke up a few hours later, he was fine."

"They're not always fine."

"What's with you?"

He sat and stared at the floor.

Finally, the baby quieted. He whimpered, still didn't sleep. But it was better.

Rae studied Brady. "I'm the new mama, I'm the one who should be freaking out."

"I know you're scared Julien's going to find you, but maybe a doctor—"

"Let's go for a walk. He'll fall asleep. If he doesn't, or if he gets fussy later, then we'll take him. Okay?"

Brady stood. "Grab a jacket and wrap him up."

"I got it." She wrapped Johnny in a thick blanket and pulled a hat over his head. While Brady held him, she ran upstairs and grabbed her coat.

She ran back downstairs, fearing Johnny would scream. Instead, the baby settled into Brady's arms. He was the picture of contentment. She looked at Brady and smirked. "How'd you do that?"

He shrugged. "He likes me."

"Apparently." She led the way to the back door. "Let's go."

Rae crossed the yard, passed the apple trees, and stepped onto the narrow trail that led the way to the stream. The scent of fallen pine needles transported her back to her childhood. She focused on the sound of her footsteps squishing along the moist path. How long had it been since she'd walked this way? A decade, at least.

A low-hanging branch hung near the path. She snatched a maple leaf just starting to turn red and felt its soft ruggedness in her fingers.

Brady followed, murmuring to the baby so quietly that she couldn't make out what he was saying.

The scent of the woods brought back a thousand childhood memories. The trail hadn't been used much, and the trees on either side were encroaching. When they were kids, they could run this trail at top speed with hardly anything in their way. Brady, Sam, and she had spent hours at a time in these woods. They knew every hiding place, every fallen log and climbing tree within a hundred yards.

A branch had fallen across the path. She maneuvered her way over it, then turned. "Watch out."

"I see it," he said, and stepped over it easily. His height didn't hurt. Those long legs. Strong arms. Her child nestled there...

Had he meant it? Would he really go with her?

It didn't matter. She wouldn't let him throw his life away. This was his home. He belonged in Nutfield, not running with her.

They reached the stream and turned right. The trail widened here a bit, and Brady stepped beside her. "You were right. He's sound asleep."

"Maybe he just wanted you." She glanced in time to see him smile.

The smile disappeared too fast. "So, Julien."

"Julien."

"Would your husband really attack all those people, kill people, just to scare you?"

"The man I knew was a lie. Whether I could've believed it yesterday, it's pretty obvious today."

"What do you think he's trying to do?"

She sighed. "I hate to admit it." She glanced at him and shrugged. "But you were right. I think he's trying to scare me, send me into a panic, maybe get me to make a mistake."

"I'm glad I was here to stop you."

The trail led to a huge boulder. "It's still here," Brady said.

"Where would it go?" She climbed up and reached for the baby.

"I can do it." Brady managed to climb onto the boulder without waking Johnny.

She sat and pulled her knees up to her chest. The stone was freezing, and the cold seeped through her jeans. She'd be numb soon enough.

"Remember when we thought this thing was so huge?" Brady settled in beside her and dangled his feet over the edge. "It was a mountain."

"We were smaller then. You were a lot smaller."

"You've grown. A little."

She glanced at him, then down at the tiny stream. "Life was easy."

"Your life was never easy, Rae. Mine was."

"What's your story, Brady? You have a child? A wife? You seem to know a lot—"

"No."

"Then how—?"

"I don't want to talk about it."

"You said you'd tell me."

"I know. I will. Just not right now."

She started to press him, but the look on his face stopped her.

He held the child a little tighter. "Why didn't you leave Julien when you first found out about his illegal activities?"

Could they talk about nothing else? "Remember I said I was feeling terrible?" He nodded. "I had preeclampsia. I ended up in the hospital that night."

"That's pretty serious, right?"

"Very."

Brady nodded. "You stayed for the baby's health."

"It could've killed both of us. I was ordered to bedrest."

A long pause while he processed that. "Must've been scary."

"Julien used the company jet and got us to Paris. Better medical care."

Brady studied the baby. "He's healthy, though? And you're okay?"

She smiled. "Johnny's perfect. And they caught it in time. No permanent damage."

He blew out a breath. A moment passed before he said, "Johnny isn't his real name."

"Jean-Louis Garcia Moreau."

The baby hadn't stirred. Brady rocked gently, back and forth. "What have you been looking for?"

There was no use trying to convince Brady she wasn't looking for anything. He'd picked up all the books earlier while she'd tried to feed Johnny.

She studied the stream below. The water tumbling over the rocks was as clear as glass. The sandy New Hampshire soil did that. Growing up, she'd thought all water was that clear, but she'd seen enough muddy water in her life to know better now. "I've never told anybody."

"You were always good at keeping your own secrets. It was other peoples' you couldn't tolerate."

She allowed a small smile. "Before my father died, he showed me something. He said it was our secret. He'd been buying one-ounce gold coins since I was born. One a month. They were in this tan metal box." She could still picture it. Nothing like the pictures of treasure in all the movies, with gold coins sparkling and spilling out of wooden treasure chests. These coins had all been in plastic sleeves, lined up like a collection of slides. "Gold was around three hundred an ounce back then. He said it was for my future, for college. He was convinced the price of gold would skyrocket."

Brady whistled. "One a month... You were eleven when he died, so..."

"Should be about a hundred and thirty ounces."

"Wow." Brady stared at the forest on the opposite side of the stream. "What's the price of gold now? About twelve hundred?"

"It fluctuates, but yeah."

"So you're thinking you've got over a hundred grand somewhere in that house."

"I hoped. But I can't find it. I remember Dad said something about stairs." She shrugged. "Maybe I made the whole thing up. I was sure it was in the barn. I guess because I think, if I remember right, we had the conversation in there. But I searched all around the loft stairs and came up with nothing. And today—"

"I saw what you did today."

"It doesn't matter now. If I don't go, Julien will find me."

"Why the sudden urgency?"

"I screwed up. I did just what he must've known I'd do. I called Nate."

Brady turned to face her. "Who is Nate?"

She swallowed. "Boyle."

His eyebrows lifted. He turned back to the stream. "All this time, he knew?"

"Most of it."

"You confided in him. After everything you and I went through."

"It wasn't like that."

Silence.

"I wouldn't have told Nate anything," she said. "We'd been friends back in high school for a little while, but only because our mothers both died the same year. You can't know how that isolates you. People don't know what to say."

"I didn't realize you two were that close."

"We weren't. When I was in college, I did this internship at a local paper. He worked there. He recognized my face, but I'd changed my name by then. I had to explain."

"Why all the secrecy? Why the changed name?"

She brushed a spot of dirt off her jeans, wishing she could brush off this conversation. This wasn't easy to talk about, even to Brady. "I was tired of being famous for rescuing the congressman's kid. Infamous. I was tired of everybody knowing who I was, of people judging me. I thought if I changed my name, since I looked older, I could just blend in."

He blew out a breath. "Did it work?"

She nodded.

"So you and Nate have been friends all these years?"

She kicked her feet and let them fall against the rock. "We were...close."

"Is he the guy you told me about earlier?"

"I don't think—"

"Scared I'll be jealous? I am."

"Brady."

He stared into the woods and said nothing.

She sighed. "Anyway, he works for the *Times* now, and he has lots of great connections. I knew he'd be able to find out what I was looking for."

"Okay."

"And he did. But now... You have to understand, I never told Julien the truth about my past. It wasn't because I was trying to lie to him. Fact is, I'd adopted this new persona. Everybody got the same story. I grew up in San Diego, I got a scholarship to Columbia, I was the second of three kids—"

"Someday you'll have to tell me how you did that. Changed your name and disappeared."

She thought about the real Rachel Adams. Where was she now? "I thought about telling him the truth all the time. I felt guilty." She laughed darkly. "Who knew my lies were nothing compared to his."

"Birds of a feather—"

"Shut up, Brady."

He did.

"Anyway, I wasn't trying to hide anything from him. I didn't know I had to. Nate was covering a story in Tunisia. Julien and I had just started dating, and we were shopping in the medina. It was just a weird coincidence that we ran into Nate that day. I introduced them. Now, it's just a matter of time..." Her voice trailed. "If I put him in danger... I'm so stupid. I need to call him. To warn him."

"You think he'll listen?"

She stared at the woods in front of her but saw only Nate's face. Her friend. In danger, because of her. "I hope so."

She pulled her phone from her pocket and dialed, ignoring Brady's watching eyes. She got Nate's voicemail.

"Nate, it's me. Listen, I should have explained more earlier. There are people looking for me, and you're the only connection between my old life and my new one. I know I told you not to tell anyone where I was, but it's more serious than that. You need to... Do you think you could get out of town for a few days?

Just make yourself scarce until..." She paused, took a deep breath. "Call me back, okay?"

She hung up and dialed information to get the phone number to the *New York Times*, then dialed and asked for him.

Voicemail again. She left a similar message, ended the call, and sighed. "What if Julien hurts him?"

"Do you think he will?"

"He'll probably just call him and ask if he knows where I am. He doesn't know Nate and I know each other from our childhood. I introduced him as an old friend, that's all. Maybe Julien won't even reach out to him."

Brady said, "Probably."

Rae feared Brady was just trying to make her feel better.

"There's nothing you can do until Nate calls you back," Brady said.

She nodded. Too true.

"What was your alias?"

"Rachel Adams."

He whistled. "Close."

"Too close."

Rae leaned over and peered at the baby. His little cheeks were flushed, his mouth working like he was dreaming of food. "I don't think he's sick."

"Too soon to tell."

"Johnny and I should leave. I'm never going to find the gold. For all I know, the prowlers offed with it months ago."

"Your grandmother never mentioned anything about gold."

"Dad only told me. At least that's what he said." She thought back, tried to remember the conversation. "Actually, he said he hadn't told Gram or Mom. Maybe he did tell someone else."

"Considering the prowlers, I think it's safe to say he did."

She needed that gold, but if Julien found her and Johnny, it would be irrelevant. She had to run. Maybe Brady would help her pack up the car. She'd have to stop somewhere and grab some food for the road, a couple cans of formula. She'd head to Canada. Throw Julien off her trail.

She glanced at Brady. She wouldn't think about how nice it would be to stay here beside him forever. Or have him come with her.

She slid down the rock and landed on the soft ground. "I have to pack."

"We're not leaving tonight."

She brushed the dust from the boulder off her jeans. "You're not leaving ever. And you don't have that kind of authority over me."

Brady slid down beside her. The baby shifted, whimpered, and drifted off again.

"Let's not argue. I'll stay again tonight."

He must've seen the shock in her face, because he smiled and said, "On the couch."

"We have to go."

Brady stepped in front of her. "One night, Rae. Let's make sure the baby isn't sick. Let's sleep on it. Maybe tomorrow, we'll come up with a plan."

"Maybe tomorrow Julien will—"

"I won't let anything happen to you." He hugged the baby closer. "Or him."

What if something happened to Brady? She'd already risked Nate's life.

But just one more night here. Her last night in her home with this man she... No, she wouldn't finish that thought. Then she'd never want to leave.

"One more night."

THIRTY-EIGHT

Brady heard the baby cry. "I'll get him," he said. When Ashley didn't answer, he tried to roll over to check on her. He couldn't move. The baby's screams grew louder, and he was wrapped in blankets. Trapped. Unable to save him.

He fought against the restraints, pushed off the blankets, and sat up in bed.

Only he wasn't in bed. He found himself on the couch in Reagan's living room. Just a dream.

Except for the crying baby.

Brady glanced at the clock. Two forty-five. He climbed the steps in his stocking feet and knocked softly on Rae's door. No answer. How could she hear his knock over Johnny's wails?

He turned the knob and pushed the door open just wide enough to reach his hand through. Didn't want to scare her, and he certainly didn't need the picture of her in that see-through thing she slept in. He waved his hand to get her attention. "Hey, can I come in?"

"Oh." Rae pulled the door open. She was wearing jeans and a sweatshirt. He shouldn't have been sorry not to see that nightie.

"What's going on?"

Rae's eyes were bloodshot and wide. "He won't stop screaming. I was just about to get you."

"How can I help?"

Rae handed him the baby, who whimpered, blinked twice, and wailed. Through the little onesie, Brady could feel his fever. "He's burning up."

"I know." She brushed past him. "Thermometer's in the kitchen."

He followed her downstairs, where she swiped the infant thermometer across Johnny's forehead. "One-oh-two point four."

"Yikes," Brady said.

"But it's his breathing that scares me. Can you hear that?"

Brady listened to the baby's breaths. When Johnny wasn't screaming, he was wheezing. "Get your shoes on."

She bolted upstairs.

Brady laid the baby on the sofa and threw on his sweatshirt. By the time Rae returned, he was holding Johnny again. "Here, you take him, and I'll go start the car."

Her eyes were wide and terrified.

"It's going to be all right," he said.

"You were right. I'm the worst mother—"

"No." He sat, pulled his shoes on. "Where are your keys?"

"Kitchen counter."

Two minutes later, they were backing out of the driveway.

"Where are we going?" Rae was sitting in the backseat, trying to soothe little Johnny. The baby had calmed enough for Brady to hear the tears in her voice.

"He's going to be okay."

He wouldn't think about the last time he'd rushed a baby to the hospital in the middle of the night. That wouldn't happen this time. Babies were resilient. Most of them, anyway.

He turned onto the highway.

"Wait, isn't Exeter closer?"

"We're going to the children's hospital in Manchester."

"I don't remember—"

"They're very good."

She didn't ask how he knew. Now was not the time to tell that story. And this situation was completely different. So why were his hands shaking?

Seemed like hours before they pulled up to the emergency room entrance. She grabbed Johnny's car seat and ran inside. By the time he parked the car, Rae'd hurried through the paperwork. He hadn't been in the waiting room five minutes when they called Rae and Johnny back. Brady stood, unsure.

She stopped just before the double doors. "Please come with us."

Thank God. He followed her in.

Half an hour later, the doctor, a blond woman who looked fresh out of med school, explained her diagnosis. "It's called RSV, Respiratory Syncytial Virus. It's fairly common."

Rae was seated in a rocking chair, soothing the whimpering baby. "Is there a cure?"

The woman smiled. "It'll run its course, like any other virus. Considering how young he is, he's doing very well. He should make a full recovery."

"So there's nothing you can do?" She looked at Brady as if he were supposed to fix it. "We can't just leave him like this. He's miserable."

"The nurse will give him something to reduce the fever. You'll stay for a couple hours, just to make sure that wheezing doesn't get worse."

Rae narrowed her eyes as if the sickness were the doctor's fault.

Brady cleared his throat. "What if it does get worse?"

"Then we'll get him a nebulizer." She turned to Rae. "That's a breathing machine that'll help open his airways."

"Does it hurt?"

The doctor shook her head. "You just hold the nebulizer over his nose and mouth, and he breathes the medicine in. He might not like it, but it won't hurt him. And we probably won't even have to do that."

Rae nodded, and more tears streamed. "This is all my fault."

"No, honey." Brady wished he could reach her, but the doctor was in the way. "Babies get sick. That's not your fault."

"Listen to your husband." The doctor winked at Rae. "Some daddies can be pretty wise."

Rae opened her mouth, closed it, and nodded. "I don't know what I'm doing."

The doctor ran her fingers over Johnny's forehead, then looked at Rae. "It comes with the territory." She patted Rae's shoulder. "You're doing a great job. He seems content, and you two obviously adore him. What else could the little guy ask for?"

Fresh tears trickled down Rae's cheeks as the doctor stepped out.

A moment later, the nurse stepped into the room with a medicine bottle in one hand, a dropper in the other. She had Johnny swallowing that medicine before he knew what was happening. "Give that a little while to go to work. He'll be all right." The nurse stepped out and closed the door.

Brady stepped beside Rae. He kissed her forehead and ran his hand down her hair. "This wasn't your fault."

"I should've waited until he was older to travel."

"You don't know where he got it. And you left Paris to protect him, not to hurt him. You have no control over the germs in the air."

"No control. My life story."

Brady pulled his chair across the linoleum floor. The scent of antiseptic and disease permeated the space and brought memories he'd prefer to forget. The room was nearly silent, just the sound of Johnny's labored breathing punctuating the seconds.

Brady could imagine how Rae was feeling. He massaged the tense muscles in the back of her neck.

Rae sighed and stopped rocking. "He's asleep."

He let his hand drop. "Sleep will help."

"I could use some."

They both could. He tugged Rae to lean on his shoulder, rested his head against the wall, and closed his eyes.

"So," Rae said, "are you going to tell me?"

He opened his eyes. "Tell you what?"

"How do you know about the children's hospital?"

"I'm a cop. We know stuff."

"You know an awful lot about babies. Their medicine, the best doctors. I have a feeling there's a story there."

He leaned his head back again. "Let it go, Rae."

"You know me better than that."

True.

He blew out a long breath. "I was married. For about a year. Before I moved back."

She pulled away and looked at him, eyebrows lifted.

"We had a baby."

He watched for her reaction. Either she didn't care, or she'd put on her reporter face. Probably the second. Their time together, and that kiss, proved she cared.

He stared at the empty bed in the middle of the room, but all he saw was his son. "Charlie was born with a weak heart. He had open-heart surgery when he was a few days old. And then he was fine. Grew stronger, seemed healthy. When he was six months old, he got sick. A virus, probably not too different from what Johnny has. But his heart couldn't handle it."

He glanced at Rae. Tears were dripping down her cheeks. Brady grabbed a tissue for her, but her hands were full, holding the baby. He dabbed her eyes, then his own.

"We rushed him to the hospital."

"Here?"

"We were living in Boston. We took him to Children's."

"Good hospital?"

"The best. They did everything they could."

She sniffed. "Brady, I'm so sorry. I had no idea."

"How could you have?"

"Did Gram know?"

He nodded. "She was a great comfort."

They sat in silence, the only sound Johnny's quiet wheezing. Poor baby. But he would get over this. He was strong. Healthy. He wasn't like Charlie.

"And your wife?" Rae asked.

"After the funeral, we went back to Boston. I came home after my first day back to work, and she was gone. Cleaned out the savings account, took nearly everything."

"I can't imagine."

"I have no idea where she is now. We only married because she was pregnant. I loved her, but not like..." He closed his mouth and let the unspoken words float away before continuing. "I wouldn't have proposed if not for the baby. She knew that. Our marriage was fine. But I think a marriage should be more than that. I wasn't surprised she divorced me. God help me, I was relieved."

She sniffed, and he wiped her tears again. He'd never known her to wear her emotions so close to the surface. On the other hand, it had been a roller-coaster day. She probably wanted off the ride.

Rae smiled and swallowed. "Thanks."

"Sure."

"When did that happen?"

"Couple years ago. After Ashley left, I couldn't stand to be in Boston anymore. I hated being so far from Charlie." She raised her eyebrows. "He's buried pretty close to Gram."

"Oh."

"I called the Chief of Police in Nutfield, asked him if they had an opening for me. They'd been searching for a good detective for a while. I quit my job and moved back."

"And you're happy?"

"I haven't been happy in a long time, Rae." He looked at her and realized, despite everything, he'd been happier in the last few days than he had in years. But the last time his happiness had depended on Rae, she'd disappeared.

They sat in silence. If Rae had more questions, she didn't ask them.

He looked at the baby, snoozing in her arms as if he hadn't a care in the world. "Seems better."

"I hope."

She shifted. Light as he was, the baby was probably starting to get heavy. Brady grabbed a pillow from the bed and propped it between her arm and the armrest.

"Thank you," she said. "That helps."

"Sure." He studied her ashen face. "It's scary when they're sick."

"Everything about parenting is terrifying. This is the scariest thing I've ever done."

"Scarier than Julien?"

"If it were just me, running for my life... Yeah, I'd be scared. But trying to protect Johnny is terrifying. Knowing if something happens to me, all he has left is his father."

"Julien. You said he wasn't violent with you."

"Never."

"He wouldn't hurt Johnny, right?"

"He wouldn't hit him. But raising him to be an international arms dealer wouldn't win him any parent-of-the-year awards."

Brady had lost one baby boy. No way he was going to lose another. "We're not going to let that happen."

THIRTY-NINE

Julien followed Farah and Hector from the hotel to the waiting Ford sedan, stolen earlier that morning. It was risky to use a stolen vehicle, but if their assumptions were correct, the owner had parked the car for the day, and it wouldn't be reported missing until long after they'd abandoned it. As Julien felt the revolver tucked into the waist of his slacks, he hoped they were right. He didn't want any more blood on his hands.

He slid into the driver's seat. The car was decent but far from the luxurious feel Julien was accustomed to. The faint scent of fast food hung in the air.

Farah sat beside him while Hector folded his too-bulky body into the backseat. Normally, Hector would drive, but Hector and Farah would need to get out of the car to grab Boyle. Julien wouldn't show his face until the reporter was under their control. The man might recognize him and run before they could get this done.

They started toward the reporter's home in Queens. It was too risky to capture him outside the New York Times Tower, but according to Farah, he lived in a single family home on a quiet street. It shouldn't be too hard to yank him into the car as long as nobody was watching.

They were inching along in traffic when Julien's phone rang. He pulled it from his shirt pocket and looked at the caller ID. Papa. Again.

"Boujour, Papa."

"Isn't that woman dead yet?"

Julien's heart nearly stopped before he realized what his father meant. "Rae's grandmother is a fighter."

"Is that so? Well then, perhaps it's time you put an end to this little family reunion and come home. You have business to attend to."

"Not as much, now that Geoffrey is undercutting me. Papa, is it a good idea for your sons to compete against one another? We are only hurting ourselves."

"Geoffrey's way makes me more money."

"When he unloads the drugs. But up front—"

"Seems you have bigger worries right now than your brother's business."

His brother's business? "Papa, it is your business, not Geoffrey's, not mine. If you want me to take over someday, you'll need to make sure he understands that."

"Take over my business? You can't even manage your own household."

The words registered slowly, seemed to latch onto his insides and twist. Julien swallowed, told himself to remain calm. "My household is fine, Papa. But your youngest son is out of control."

Julien accelerated through a light. "We have arrived at the hospital." He forced a casual tone into his lie. "Let me know what you intend to do about Geoffrey." He ended the call and tossed the phone into the center console.

Papa knew Rae was missing. There was no other explanation for his words, for all the phone calls, for that comment about Julien's household.

"Is everything all right?" Farah reached across the space and touched his hand.

He loosened his grip on the steering wheel and shifted away from her fingers. "Of course."

Julien looked in the rearview mirror at Hector. His best friend since grade school. Surely Hector hadn't betrayed him.

He shifted his gaze to Farah. She'd been in love with him for years, since long before Rachel entered the picture. Their short affair had ended amicably, or so he'd thought. Would she stoop to working for his father to get back at him? Surely she knew there'd never been a chance for the two of them.

But one of them, Hector or Farah, had betrayed him, because his father knew Rae was missing, and they were the only two he'd told.

FORTY

Rae yawned and lifted the sleeping baby from his car seat, then stood in the early morning chill to survey the area.

The little log cabin sat surrounded on three sides by pines and maples and oaks that towered above it like overprotective parents. Between the trees and beyond the cabin, Rae could see the sunrise reflecting across Clearwater Lake. It promised to be a beautiful day.

The screen door squeaked open. Brady crossed the front porch and jogged down the stairs. "I've got the heat cranking."

Rae shivered in the cold. "Samantha owns this?"

He nodded toward the south, and she followed his gaze to the row of cabins along the lake. "She owns this and the next two. She has a few more by the marina."

"And it just sits here, empty?"

He grabbed Rae's bags out of the trunk. "The rest are rented or will be occupied soon. This was the only one that's supposed to be empty all weekend."

"What if someone wants to rent it?"

He slammed the trunk closed. "She's your best friend, Rae. She doesn't mind losing a weekend's rent."

"But—"

"Let's go."

He climbed the steps and disappeared into the cabin.

She looked at her sleeping child and whispered, "We'll be safe here." For now.

Brady had called Sam before they'd left the hospital almost two hours earlier. With the baby too sick to travel, it was clear Rae was going to stay for a while. She'd planned to find a motel in Manchester, but Brady'd had a better idea.

He'd taken her to her house to pack her things and get his truck, then she'd followed him to Sam's condo, where he ran inside to get the key to this cabin.

And now here they were, just a couple miles from Rae's house, but it felt like a different world. Cabins, from luxurious to quaint, lined the lake almost all the way around, only interrupted by the marina and a few restaurants nearer town. Rae'd spent many hours on this lake.

Brady jogged to the car for another load. "Are you going to stand out here all day?"

"I'm coming."

She walked around to the side of the cabin and peered at the water reflecting the fading colors of the sunrise. It was beautiful. Mesmerizing.

Funny the assumptions Rae'd made about Brady and Samantha. She'd thought of them as provincial, especially Sam, who'd returned to Nutfield right after college. And yet Rae's provincial friend had somehow managed to purchase multiple vacation homes along the lake. She'd made a life for herself in Nutfield, a good life, while Rae was out seeing the world. And getting into trouble.

Brady took the final load inside, and the screen slammed behind him. Johnny stirred in her arms.

She climbed the three steps to the front porch, surveying the

Adirondack chairs that graced the space before stepping into the cabin.

"It should warm up pretty soon." Brady was placing the little food that had been at Rae's into the refrigerator from a box on the floor.

"Okay." Rae shook herself out of her daze. Lack of sleep was playing havoc on her ability to focus.

Brady closed the refrigerator door and stepped beside her. "Come on." He placed his hand on her back, and it was all she could do not to collapse. He urged her across the living room and through a door, where a king-sized bed waited. "Put him on one side, and then you can sleep on the other. Will that work?"

She nodded and watched as Brady lined the far side of the bed with pillows.

Rae laid the baby safely in the center. "Chances are good he won't roll off."

"Why don't you lie down too?"

"But I should..." Her voice trailed off. What should she do? She had no idea.

"Go to bed, Rae. I'm here. You're safe, the baby's sleeping, and when he wakes up, he'll need you to be rested."

She collapsed beside the baby and fell asleep instantly.

Johnny's fussing woke her.

She opened her eyes and looked around the small bedroom with the big bed. Log walls surrounded her. There was a small dresser with a mirror hanging above it. Hardwood on the floors, and a closet on the far side. She could live in a place like this.

Johnny's fuss turned to a cry. She stood, lifted the baby, and felt his fever through his pajamas. Seemed the medicine had worn off. She soothed him until he quieted, whimpering in her arms.

She stepped into the living room. Brady stood on the far side, talking on the phone.

"It's a long story." Brady paused. "Look, Chief, I'll let you in on it when the time is..." He paced and listened. Rae could just make out the man's voice through the speaker, though not the words. Brady sighed. "Right now, I need to be here. The town of Nutfield will survive without me for one day."

Rae soothed the baby and waited for Brady to hang up.

"You didn't have to do that," she said.

He turned and smiled. "You're up."

"His fever is back. You don't have to babysit me. We can manage."

"I'm not going to leave you here unprotected."

She was too groggy to argue.

He stared at her. "Johnny's sick. You can't leave now. You know that, right?"

She nodded, and tears stung her eyes. She was still so tired, she couldn't think straight.

"Sit. I'll get his medicine."

She studied the space. More log walls all around. Hardwood floors stretched across the living room and into the small kitchen, which was separated by an island covered with black granite countertops. A round table and four chairs were nestled in the alcove at the back of the cabin in front of the bay window, which looked out over the lake.

Rae turned back to the living room. She'd expected rustic couches, maybe plaid. She walked to the back of one and touched it. Butter-colored microfiber so soft and squishy, Rae wondered if it might swallow her whole. A coffee table that looked like the cross-section of a huge tree sat in front of the larger sofa. The gray stone fireplace stretched to the ceiling. Its hearth had a stack of firewood on one side, fireplace tools on the other. Above the simple wood mantle hung a giant flatscreen TV.

"It's... Wow."

"Not what you expected?"

She hadn't realized how close Brady was until she heard his voice in her ear. She turned to find him right behind her.

"When I think *cabin*, I think rustic." Rae turned back to the big room. "This is anything but."

"Sam doesn't do rustic."

"I guess not."

"Please sit."

She chose the sofa that faced the bay windows. It was as soft as she'd expected. Brady sat beside her and gave Johnny his medicine. The baby wailed.

"A bottle, I think." She started to stand.

"I'll get it." Brady was halfway to the kitchen before Rae could react. She rocked the baby and listened to the sounds of Brady preparing the formula just beyond the kitchen island. Through the bay window, trees swayed in the soft breeze, water lapped against the dock that stretched into the lake. Johnny whimpered but seemed too tired to do much more. Rae was thankful for that.

If only she could stay here forever. It wasn't home—nothing would ever feel like home as Gram's house had—but this was a close second. And she felt safe here.

But that was a lie.

It was only a matter of time before Julien found Nate, and Nate knew where she was from. Julien would come to Nutfield, and when he did, he'd find her.

Brady sat on the sofa and handed her the bottle.

"Thanks."

"Sure."

She coaxed the baby's mouth open. Finally, Johnny settled

in with his formula. "How can I look for the gold if I'm stuck here?"

"Sam and I are working on that."

"No. You two need to stay as far from me as possible. I don't want Julien coming after you."

"Nate won't tell him anything. You're safe here."

"Julien won't play nice."

Brady slid his arm around her shoulder, and she fell into him and fought a fresh round of tears. What if Brady hadn't come over yesterday when she'd talked to Nate? She'd have left, and then when Johnny had gotten sick, where would she have been? In some lousy cash-only rat-infested dump, too scared to visit a hospital. What if Johnny had stopped breathing? A sob bubbled up at the thought. What if...?

Brady tightened his hold. "Hey, it's okay."

But it wasn't. She couldn't do this alone. She needed Gram. She needed Brady. Johnny needed someone in his life besides Rae. She didn't know what she was doing. She'd disappeared once, but that had been easy. It had just been her. Circumstances had worked in her favor. Meeting Rachel Adams had felt like a gift from God. And back then, if she'd been found out, she only risked media exposure. Not death. Not the loss of her child.

Brady caressed her shoulder and whispered, "Shh."

She sniffed and wiped her eyes on the shoulder of her sweatshirt. Johnny paused his eating to look at her. "It's okay," she told him. "You're safe here."

He stared another minute, then returned to his bottle, his tiny red lips puckering with each sip.

"Tell me about Julien," Brady said. "Why do you say he won't play nice?"

Rae sat up and took a deep breath. "There was this guy who works for him, Hector del Bosque. He's dangerous."

"How so?"

She thought back to the first time she'd seen Hector. He'd been reading a newspaper at an adjacent table at the cafe the day she met Julien. She'd had no idea the man was with Julien until Julien snapped his fingers. "Hector."

The man stood beside them an instant later, as if he'd been listening to their conversation all along. And he must have been, because how else would he have heard Julien's quiet summons?

"Please have all the information you have on the Spaniard sent to Miss Adams right away," Julien said.

Hector had rattled off something in Spanish, and Julien had tsk-tsked. "English in front of the lady, please."

"Yes, sir." And then Hector had held her gaze. It had taken all her self-control not to lean away.

Hector was always there, doing Julien's bidding. When she'd told Julien he gave her the creeps, he'd laughed. "As well he should, *ma cherie*. Hector is not somebody you want to cross."

When Rae had discovered Julien's illegal business, Hector's presence in their lives made more sense. Julien was the brains. Hector was the brawn.

Brady nudged her with his elbow. "You still with me?"

She scooted away and lifted her knee to the couch so she could face him. She had to deal with this, and she'd have to figure out how to do it alone. Leaning on Brady, physically or metaphorically, wasn't going to help. "Hector is dangerous. Like I told you, Julien always had people at the house. I'd come home from working on a story and there'd be ten, fifteen people sitting around the pool or sipping wine on the back deck or eating in the dining room. Half the time, Julien wasn't even home. The housekeeper knew who was allowed in and who wasn't, and Julien liked the open door. The people were mostly European. He was buddies with some Americans from the embassy. A few locals were welcome, but even they almost all wore western clothes and spoke English."

"Okay."

"Once last winter, a man came to the house. Looked like all the other visitors. Older guy, gray hair, wearing khakis and an orange golf shirt. He had a white cardigan slung over his shoulders. The kind of guy you could picture with a martini in one hand, a putter in the other. Know what I mean?"

Brady shrugged.

"An older woman, a regular, brought him. Apparently the man wasn't welcome. Julien nodded to Hector, and then Hector..." She shuddered as the scene filled her mind's eye. There'd been ten or twelve guests on the deck. Glasses shimmering with French wine, trays of cheese and caviar and crackers and seafood. Typical Tuesday appetizers. Someone had just told a joke, and the laughter still hung in the air when Hector grabbed the man from behind. Then gasps, the crash of a wine glass on the deck, the sound of designer heels tapping on wood, then clicking across the marble floor as people scurried to get away. Shocked expressions, the debris of a party gone horribly awry. Rae'd stood frozen. She hadn't been able to tear her eyes away.

Julien had watched the scene with a terrifying insouciance.

Brady listened patiently as she shared the story.

"The guy'd brought a gun. He'd hidden it in the waistline of his pants, against the small of his back. Hector spotted it. He dragged the man down the patio steps where the guests couldn't see what was happening, and then beat him with the gun. I didn't appreciate the guy bringing a weapon into my home, but still... I wanted to call the police, but Julien wouldn't let me. When the guy was unconscious, Hector tossed him over his shoulder and carried him around the house. The guests never knew what happened. I never saw that guy again." Rae ran her fingers through her hair, shocked to find them trembling at the memory. "I can still see the look on Hector's face when he was hitting that guy. It was the first time I'd ever seen him smile."

Brady nodded once. He looked away for a moment before he looked back with narrowed eyes. "So Julien employs psychopaths."

She shrugged. "Just the one, as far as I know. He said he needed to make sure we were safe, that our home was safe. Before I knew the truth about Julien, I appreciated the guards he always had around."

"But Hector is more than just a guard."

"I'd been suspicious before, but when I found Julien's files, I saw references to problems he'd had eliminated. The problems were people's names. Most of the names, I didn't recognize, but one stood out. He'd been a business associate of Julien's, and the story was that he killed himself. But now I know that Julien..." The tears filled her eyes again. "The man I'd vowed to share my life with—he ordered people killed, and I'm pretty sure Hector did it."

"And if Julien asked him to, you think Hector is capable of hurting you?"

She uttered a dark chuckle. "Capable? The guy hates me. He'd love it."

FORTY-ONE

Walter Boyle refused to talk, and Julien wasn't surprised. Rae garnered that kind of loyalty in people. Fierce. Dependable. In Walter's case, suicidal.

Maybe in Julien's case too.

No. Julien wouldn't be brought down by a woman. Not even his wife.

Farah had located a dingy motel right off the highway. This was Julien's first visit to a by-the-hour hotel. It stank of stale cigarettes and cheap perfume. Julien didn't want to think about all that had transpired in the bed he was lounging on. Not that he'd pull back this terrible multi-colored, polyester bedspread and touch the sheets. The very thought made him shudder.

His legs were crossed at the ankles, his head was leaning against his crossed arms, propped on the lumpy pillows, as though he witnessed torture every day. He could tell by the way Hector kept glancing at him and smiling that none of Julien's horror was showing on his face.

Hector derived far too much pleasure from hurting people. Still, after all of Hector's blows, Walter Boyle insisted he had no idea where Rachel was.

Obviously, he was lying. Even Julien could tell that.

The reporter's phone had rung and beeped all day. Most of the calls came from the same person. Finally after an Internet search, Farah discovered the caller was another reporter at the *Times*. She'd texted the woman from Boyle's phone that something had come up, and he'd call later.

They read texts and listened to the phone messages, just in case they should get lucky and hear from Rachel. One text came from someone named Finn, and after a little persuading, the reporter admitted it was his little brother. They allowed Walter to answer those, general texts Julien approved before the man hit send.

No reason to alert anybody that Walter was missing.

Most of the time, Farah stayed in the car, and Julien was glad for that one small mercy. He might not love the woman, but he would never subject her to such terrible violence. She was an efficient assistant, but she was also a woman, and by the look on her face when she saw Boyle's injuries, she was squeamish. Julien knew how she felt. If he thought he could do so and still save face, he'd be in the car too.

He was surprised when Hector stood and wiped his bloody hands on his jeans.

"I have another plan. It will make him talk."

"What is it?"

Hector looked at Boyle with an ugly sneer, then back at Julien. "You don't want to know."

Julien swung his legs to the floor. "What are you going to do?"

"You won't approve, *mon amis*. But it needs to be done."

Julien looked at Rae's friend's bruised face. One eye was nearly swollen shut. His lip was thick, and blood dripped from both nostrils. When Boyle noticed Julien watching him, he returned the stare. Fearless or stupid, Julien wasn't sure.

He turned to Hector. Julien had known about Hector's evil streak since grammar school. He could still remember the older boys who'd taunted Hector, who was just seven years old, for being the scholarship kid. A school full of rich kids and the little orphan, Hector. They'd hurled insults, and Hector'd taken it silently. Waited until the boys moved on. Then tackled the ringleader from behind. He'd landed on top of him, straddled his back, and crushed the boy's face against the concrete sidewalk while other boys stood in a circle and watched. Hector had grabbed the boy by his hair, lifted his head, and smashed it down again. And again. By the time the teachers pulled him away, the bully's face was bloodied, the bully unconscious. The kid had needed plastic surgery to repair the damage.

Hector had been suspended for a week.

He'd never been bullied again.

Julien should insist that Hector tell him his plan, but he probably wouldn't approve. He turned to Walter again, studied the swollen lip and bloody eye. Julien didn't think he could watch any more, and out of the one eye the man could still open, Boyle seemed to be pleading for a reprieve.

This wasn't Julien. Kidnapping, torture, murder. This was the sort of thing his brother did. Taking out enemies was one thing, but this man wasn't an enemy, just guilty of knowing Rachel.

She was so close. He had to get to her, to get her back to Tunis. To keep her. To break her.

Julien forced his gaze back to Hector. "How long will you be gone?"

"Couple hours."

"And then?"

Hector's rare smile widened. "And then he will tell us everything."

Julien glanced at the reporter as the man dropped his head to his chest.

"Tie him to the bed so he can get some rest while you're gone."

Hector's smile vanished. "Why bother? The chair is—"

"Because I said."

Hector stared at him a moment before nodding once. "Oui."

FORTY-TWO

Brady had slept a couple of hours when he woke on the sofa that afternoon.

Rae and the baby were still resting in the other room, so it seemed a good time to call Samantha. Rae wouldn't like it, but he needed more information, and since he was without his computer, Samantha was his best bet. He filled her in on what he knew and asked her to do a little more digging about Julien Moreau's business, his father's illegal activities, and Hector del Bosque.

"Are you looking for anything specific?" Samantha asked.

"We need to figure out a way to defeat this guy. Rae thinks she has to run, but maybe we can come up with something to fight him with."

When Samantha responded, her voice was soft. "Maybe Rae should run."

He started to argue, then stopped. Samantha's honesty was refreshing, if frustrating.

Fine. If Rae had to hide from Julien, Brady would hide with her. Whatever it took to keep her and Johnny safe. "We can't run forever."

"We?"

He exhaled a long breath. "I can't lose her again."

A pause, then, "Brady?"

"Yeah."

"I know this doesn't mean much to you, but I'm praying. God can make a way for you to be together and safe."

Together and safe. Would that ever be possible?

He slid his phone into his pocket and paced. There had to be a way for Rae to defeat this guy. Running was too dangerous. Moreau would eventually catch them. Would he kill him and Rae, or would he simply kill Brady and reclaim Rae and the baby? Did Moreau marry her for love, or was there another reason, a more sinister reason?

And how could Brady protect her if he didn't understand the threat?

He'd been covering the same ground both in his mind and across the carpet for an hour when he heard the baby cry. He tiptoed into the bedroom and lifted Johnny from his nest beside Rae. As soon as Brady held him, the baby settled into a low whimper.

On his way out of the bedroom, Brady paused to look at Rae, snuggled beneath the blankets, one strand of hair falling across her cheek. He resisted the urge to brush it back. She hadn't stirred at Johnny's cry. She had to be exhausted after the events of the previous two nights. First the prowlers, then the sick baby. Not to mention the fear she'd lived with for months after discovering Moreau's secret.

Brady crept out of the room and set Johnny in his bouncy seat on the island in the kitchen. He took the baby's temperature. Slightly high, but not alarmingly so.

"Hungry, little man?"

Johnny watched him, expressionless, while Brady fixed Johnny's bottle and lifted him again. "Let's see if I can do this as well as Mommy." He carried the baby into the living room, sank on the couch, and fed him.

The memories came flooding back. He might not have loved his ex-wife the way he should have, but Charlie? Brady'd fallen head-over-heels with his son the instant he'd laid eyes on him. He'd have stayed with Ashley forever just to make a home for his child. And though Johnny looked nothing like Charlie, Brady had already fallen in love all over again.

The last time, he'd lost the baby and the girl. He couldn't imagine losing either one this time. He *wouldn't* lose them.

A couple hours later, Rae stumbled out of the bedroom, eyes wide and frantic, and burst into tears when she saw her son sleeping soundly in the bouncy seat.

"When I woke up and he wasn't there, I thought..." She turned to Brady, sitting on the sofa.

"You were so tired, Rae. I fed him and changed him."

She wiped her tears. "You took care of him?"

He nodded, studied that perplexed expression. "It wasn't so long ago I had my own son."

"I know. I just... Julien never did that. Johnny's not even yours."

He shrugged. "Julien is an idiot."

She nodded. "Obviously." She felt the baby's forehead. "He seems better."

"I took his temperature. Fever's gone right now. It'll probably come back later, but it's a good start."

She stared at Johnny, seemed to be itching to pick him up. Considering it had taken Brady an hour to get him to sleep, he didn't think that was such a great idea.

"You hungry?"

She smiled. "We don't have much."

"Hardly anything. You didn't think you'd be here this long, huh?"

She shrugged but didn't meet his eyes.

He nodded toward the sofa. "There's still a lot to talk about."

She stepped into the kitchen and grabbed a can of soda from the fridge. She settled onto the sofa on the far side of the room.

Seemed she'd reconstructed her guard during that nap.

Brady lifted a notebook and pen he'd left on the coffee table earlier, trying to make sense of the stories Rae'd told him. "Tell me about the other people Julien has working for him."

She popped the can open, sipped her drink, and set it on the coffee table. "Well, of course there are all the people at the factories and office buildings. And the people who work at the house in Tunis, and there's a housekeeper in Paris."

"I mean people who work with him on his illegal business."

"He has a couple of bodyguards, besides Hector. And the two guards he had protecting me. And his personal assistant."

"Tell me about him."

"Her. Farah Hanachi. She keeps his calendar, runs errands for him."

"Does she know about his illegal activities?"

"I don't know. She's just this sweet lady. She's older than we are—late forties, early fifties. She's a widow and went to work for Julien's company—well, I guess it was his father's company back then. Even then it was a front for illegal activities. Anyway, Farah was in her twenties when her husband died, and she had to get a job."

"You seem to know a lot about her."

Rae gave him a sad smile. "We were friends. When Julien and I started seeing each other, I had a lot of contact with her. And we hit it off. So when she wasn't working for him, she was hanging out with me. I told you about the parties Julien always had? Farah was there often, and the two of us would talk." She shrugged as though it didn't matter, but he knew her better than that. "She helped Julien pick out my wedding gown and ring."

"So you don't think she could be involved?"

"I don't know. At first, I thought not. But how could she have worked so closely with him and not known?" She sighed. "I'm not certain of anything."

He tapped his pen against his leg. "Doesn't help us much."

"But Farah's my friend. I can't imagine that she'd be working against me."

"She was his assistant first, though. And he's her boss."

"True."

"Okay. Anybody else I need to worry about?"

"His father."

"What do you know about him?"

"Not much. I've never met him. Never had reason to investigate him until I found out the truth, and before we went to Paris, Julien took my laptop and smartphone away. So I couldn't get more information about him. Before that, even when I was looking into the arms dealer involved in the Cairo bombing, nothing pointed to him."

"About that. You said your article led to that guy's arrest and conviction, but then you said Julien actually did it."

"Yeah. Julien pointed me to the Spaniard. In retrospect, I think Hector must've planted the documents I found. The Spaniard wasn't convicted of the bombing in Cairo. Most of the evidence I uncovered was related to other deals, not that one. I haven't put all those pieces together, and they don't matter now. The guy was an arms dealer, he just wasn't responsible for that particular deal. I don't know how Julien pinned it on the Spaniard, but it worked out for him. The Spaniard was his biggest competitor."

Brady sat back against the sofa and scrubbed his face in his hands. Her husband was diabolical, using his girlfriend to take out his enemy.

Wait, was Brady really talking about arms dealers in Northern Africa with his high-school sweetheart? The conversation was surreal. The whole situation was more than he could wrap his mind around. How could a little New Hampshire girl have gotten sucked into all this intrigue and international crime? Right, this was Reagan McAdams they were talking about, discoverer of secrets and exposer of lies.

He blew out a long breath. "So what was your plan, Rae? Come here, get your gold, and then disappear again?"

She swallowed and stared at the floor. "I was hoping to talk Gram into joining me. I figured I could keep us hidden, and I couldn't bear to be away from her any longer." When Rae looked up, tears spilled from her eyes. She wiped them with her fingers. "I was so sure I knew where the gold was. I figured I'd get into town, get the gold, grab Gram and her stuff, and take off again."

"To where?"

"South America. Maybe Brazil. I speak a little Portuguese. We can blend in there. I can pass Johnny off as a local, at least half-Brazilian. And I can play the grieving widow."

"Why Brazil?"

She shrugged and nearly smiled. "Worked for the Nazis."

His chuckle felt good after all the drama of the previous few days. "So did you just spin a globe and decide to move to the spot your finger landed on?"

"I didn't want to put too much thought into it. I figured if I chose a place based on logic, then Julien could figure out my logic and follow me. So I thought, Brazil. Why not?"

"Interesting."

"There are some remote villages there. As long as I have

access to the Internet, I can access my money." She sighed. "Well, I could access my money, if I had any."

"And what do you know about living in the jungle?"

"About as much as I knew about living in the African desert surrounded by Muslims. I'm adaptable."

His gaze found the baby, and she smiled. "And he won't know anything else. I'll teach him English, homeschool him, and maybe when he's ready for college, we'll come back. Surely Julien will have quit looking for us by then."

"So eighteen years. That's your plan? To live in the jungle for eighteen years?"

She nodded, and he stood and paced.

"You're insane, you know that?"

He cringed. Bad choice of words, and he expected her to rise to the challenge, but she sank deeper into the soft sofa.

"I don't know what else to do. I thought if Julien believed I'd expose him, he'd leave us alone, but after the bombing yesterday..."

Brady froze. "Expose him? What do you mean?"

"I left him a note telling him that if he followed me, I'd send all this evidence to the authorities. I thought he'd leave me alone rather than risk it. But he called my bluff."

Brady stared at her while the words sank in. "You took evidence? You could expose him?"

Her already light skin paled further. "I can't, Brady. No way I'm taking that chance."

FORTY-THREE

Rae shouldn't have mentioned the evidence, not if she didn't plan to use it. Blame that little slip-up on her exhaustion.

Brady stood beside the sofa and stared at her, hands clenched by his sides.

She sipped her soda again and set it on the coffee table. Keeping her voice low so she wouldn't wake the baby, she said, "I can't turn the files over."

"Why not?"

She lifted her eyebrows at his raised voice.

"Sorry." His voice was a near-whisper now, and somehow more vehement. "If you didn't intend to give it to the authorities, why take it?"

"Like I said, to get him to leave us alone."

"And you thought that would work?"

She ignored the incredulity in his voice. "Julien would definitely have come after us otherwise. It seemed like our only chance."

"So why not turn it over?"

"It's not enough to put him away. It might get an investigation started, but—"

"Then why not gather more? That's your specialty, right? I mean, you had time—"

"I couldn't." She sighed, too tired to explain. "I just told you, Julien took my computer and—"

"Why would you let him do that?"

"I was really sick, Brady. I'd been ordered to bedrest. Julien said he wanted me to relax, and how could I argue that having an Internet connection was more important than the health of our child?"

He sat beside her. "It was that bad?"

"They talked about taking the baby early to protect my health, but I promised to be good, to do what they told me." She swallowed and looked away. "And honestly, I was afraid Julien knew I'd gone through his files. I spent weeks worried that right after the baby was born, he might just kill me. But he was so kind, so..." She caught a glimpse of Brady's hard expression. "Anyway, I don't think he knew."

"But you don't have enough information, and now Julien has even more incentive to find you, fast."

She massaged her temples with her fingertips before meeting his eyes again. "He already had all the incentive he needed. I took his son."

Brady quieted, sighed. "How did you find out about his first wife."

"His only wife." She thought back, remembered the moment she'd realized what all those papers meant, remembered the sting of betrayal. "We were in Paris. He has an office there too. I'd already made copies of everything in Tunis. The Paris office was just more of the same. Except the file about Martine." At the memory, her eyes stung. "I found his marriage license. I searched for divorce papers, but there were none. There were a few letters between them that convinced me they were still married. No mention of children. Seemed an amiable relationship. There were photographs of her and their home in France. A vineyard."

Brady's phone vibrated, and he slipped it from his pocket and tapped on the screen.

"Everything okay?" Rae asked.

"Just a text." He read another one as it came in, glanced at Rae, then put his phone away.

"Do you have to go?"

Brady shook his head. "So as far as you know, Johnny's his only child."

"I'm sure of it. Johnny is his only heir. He mentioned so many times what it meant to him to finally have a son to pass everything down to."

"So he had the kid to take over his business someday."

"He loves Johnny. Julien didn't do any *women's work*, as he'd have called it. But he played with Johnny, held him whenever he could. The look in his eyes when he held his son..."

Rae was so stupid to feel as if she were betraying Julien after everything he'd done. Yet being here with Brady, talking about Julien, it all felt so wrong. How had her life spiraled so quickly out of control? Three months before, she'd been a giddy woman in love with her husband and expecting her first child. She'd been part of a family, a group of friends. She'd had a career and a future.

How many more times would life as she knew it crumble to dust? Her father's death. Her mother's insanity, imprisonment, and suicide. Now Gram was gone too. Rae had thought she'd lived through the worst of her life's tragedies. Apparently not. Would she ever finish paying for her mistakes, or would her entire life be one big payback for the stupidity she'd exhibited at eleven years old?

"So you believe Johnny's not in physical danger," Brady said.

She forced her thoughts back to the moment. "Julien won't hurt him."

"But you fear he'll kill you."

She stood, too antsy to keep her chair. "I have no idea. I thought he loved me, too, so what do I know?" She checked the clock on the oven in the kitchen. Nearly five. She wanted something to eat, but not that soup they'd brought from her house. Maybe she could talk Brady into making eggs again.

And maybe she just wanted out of this conversation.

"Rae, what happens if you don't find your father's gold?"

She stared out the back window at the twilight beyond. "I have no idea."

Brady was just about to respond when Johnny cried.

Rae picked him up. Even through his pajamas, she could feel the heat radiating from his skin. "Would you get his medicine?"

Brady'd already headed for the kitchen. He returned with a medicine dropper a moment later. "Tip his head back."

Once Johnny had been medicated, Brady fixed his bottle while Rae tried to comfort him. With the fever back, his little whimpers were sadder than usual. Her heart nearly broke as she rocked him and cooed until Brady returned with the bottle. Johnny took less than half before he nodded off again.

Rae tried to wake him, but he wasn't having it. She looked at Brady. "Why won't he eat?"

"Do you eat when you're sick?"

Made sense, but it still scared her. Funny how she and Brady had traded roles again. Now she was the worrywart and he the sensible one. They'd always made a good team.

She changed Johnny's diaper, hoping the activity would wake him up, but he slept through it. Defeated, she returned him to the middle of the king-sized bed. Maybe when the medicine kicked in, he'd want to eat again.

Brady seemed antsy when she returned, his feet bouncing like it was all he could do to stay seated. "Would you at least consider taking your evidence to the FBI?"

The very thought of it set her heart beating faster. She carried the half-empty bottle into the kitchen and rinsed it out. When she was finished, she sat on the sofa and braced herself for the fight that was surely coming. "I don't think they can protect me."

"They could put you in witness protection."

"No one can protect us, not from Julien. He has too many friends in government—in Tunisia, in Europe, and in America. I have a list of their names, people in law enforcement, one guy in the justice department. No way I'm going to trust them to take care of my son and me. With my luck, they'd throw me in prison for kidnapping."

Brady stood and paced. Finally he faced her, eyes blazing, jaw set. "So you're just going to run away again? Like you did after that stupid party? Like you did after college, running away to Europe instead of coming home to your grandmother? Why don't you try facing a problem head-on for a change?"

She bolted to her feet. "For a change? Do you remember what happened the last time I faced a problem head-on? My mother's dead, Brady."

His features softened. "That wasn't your fault."

"Of course it was my fault."

"She kidnapped a baby. You did the right thing."

"Sending Mom to prison was the *right thing*?" Old, familiar tears trickled down her cheeks. "I should've taken the baby to your house, left him on your doorstep. Your mother would've called the police, and nobody would ever have known..."

"Your mother's insanity wasn't your fault."

Rae looked out the back window. Dusk had settled, and the trees between the cabin and the water were murky silhouettes against the graying sky. No matter how bright the day had been, darkness always lurked over the horizon. "Mom was fine until she had me. It all started with postpartum."

"Your mother was bipolar. That's not caused by pregnancy."

"What do you know?"

Brady closed the distance between them and wrapped his arms around her. Angry as she was, she couldn't force herself to pull away. He kissed the top of her head. "You shouldn't have had to deal with that. Your grandmother never forgave herself for going away that weekend. She felt if she'd been here, none of it would have happened."

Rae sniffed. "It wasn't Gram's fault."

"It wasn't your fault, either."

"She's dead, Brady. Dead because she couldn't handle life in prison. Dead because she made a knife out of a piece of plastic she'd found who knows where and slit her wrist."

"Rae."

She pulled away and crossed her arms. "The authorities never should have put her in prison. The DA should have argued for a mental hospital. The judge should have insisted. But she'd kidnapped a congressman's kid, so who cared about her? Who cared if they did the wrong thing, as long as they looked good doing it? Sticking a crazy woman in the general population, that was their mistake. My mistake was trusting them. I won't do it again."

FORTY-FOUR

A SOFT KNOCK issued from the front door. Rae whipped her head toward it, backed up a step. "Who is that?"

Brady took out his gun and pointed it at the floor. "I think I know." He nodded toward the gun. "Just to be safe." He inched his way forward and looked out the living room window, then turned to her. "Don't be mad."

She crossed her arms. "Don't do anything to tick me off."

His lips twitched. "That's a long list. Not sure I can promise."

He swung the door open, and Samantha stood on the doorstep. She looked from Rae to Brady. "Didn't you tell her I was coming?"

"Rae loves surprises."

Rae swiveled to face Brady. "Are you insane? What is she doing here?"

Samantha lifted a laptop in one hand, a sack in the other. "I brought information and dinner."

Brady bumped Rae's shoulder. "Dinner, Rae. I could hear your stomach growling from the other room."

"That's not the point." She turned to Sam. "I'm glad to see

you, but it's not safe for you to be around me. The last thing I want is people knowing we've been together."

Sam smiled and stepped inside. She was dressed in slacks and a pretty gray sweater. A teal scarf completed the look, and Rae was again struck by how much Samantha had changed over the years. "It's dark. Nobody saw me. And I do own this cabin."

"Right. All the more reason for you to keep your distance—"

"I'm here now," Sam said.

"Yeah, but—"

"And I parked the Trooper in front of the cabin two doors down. If anybody from town happens by and notices it, they'll assume I'm cleaning for a renter. I'm out here all the time."

Rae was starving, but that's not what had her waffling. "What kind of information?"

Samantha passed her and headed for the small kitchen table, setting her laptop bag on the counter on her way by. "Dinner first. McNeal's had their fish and chips on special, so I got two platters. I also grabbed three cups of potato soup, because theirs is the best in the world. And just to be safe, I grabbed a Reuben. I remember you used to like those, Rae."

Real corned beef from a real Irish restaurant. Her mouth was already watering.

Sam set the sack on the kitchen table. "Brady, the drinks are in the car. Would you mind? I left it unlocked."

"I'm on it." He stepped outside.

Rae grabbed plates and silverware while Sam pulled containers of food from the sack. "I really appreciate your help, Sam, but if anything happens to you because of me, I won't be able to live with myself."

Sam paused, a Styrofoam container in her hand. "You think I want something to happen to you? I have to help if I can."

"But this is my fault," Rae said. "It's not your problem."

"How is it your fault you fell in love with a criminal?"

"Well—"

"And even if you were somehow to blame," Sam continued, "I'd still help."

Brady came through the front door. The screen slammed behind him as he carried a drink holder stuffed with three giant cups and set it on the kitchen table before returning to the door to lock it.

"Iced tea," Samantha said. "Unsweetened. But I grabbed some sugar and sweetener, if you want."

Rae grabbed a cup and added a packet of sugar. She looked at Sam and smiled. "Thanks for bringing dinner. How much do I owe you?"

Brady said, "It's on me." He turned to Samantha. "You had them put it on my tab, right?"

Samantha grabbed her tea. "Decided against that."

Brady's eyebrows lifted. "Since when do you turn down a free meal?"

She laughed. "I told Bonnie I was taking dinner to my brother and sister-in-law." She turned to Rae. "Andrea's second baby is two months old, so it made sense." She turned back to Brady. "If I'd told them it was for you, then there'd be questions. And since Rae is in town, people might assume that I was getting the food for the three of us. And I think it's safer if I keep my distance from Rae. Everybody thinks she hates me..." She looked at Rae and winked. "Frankly, I'm okay with that. I know too much about Julien and his minions. I don't want to be on their radar."

Brady nodded. "A very good point. I didn't think of that.'"

Samantha and Brady shared a look.

Rae sighed. "What?"

Samantha looked away. "He wants you to stay, and he's not afraid of Julien. Me? I'm smarter than he is."

Rae nodded. "Obviously."

They sat, and Rae took a few bites of the fish and chips. The platters were big enough to feed a small Tunisian village. Best she'd ever had. She cut the Reuben in fourths and ate one portion. And she devoured her soup. Rae enjoyed the meal more than any she'd had since the last time the three of them had been together. It was as if nothing had changed. If only.

She set down her spoon. "I was hungrier than I thought."

Brady dipped a french fry in ketchup. "You haven't eaten all day. And you were up half the night."

Rae nodded to Samantha. "Thank you. This was perfect."

"Glad to do it."

"Now, tell us what information you brought."

Samantha wiped her fingers on her napkin. "Not a whole lot, but it's a start." She set up her laptop on the kitchen table. "I'm sure I haven't learned much you didn't already know. Brady told me you'd found Moreau's files, so I doubt any of this will be a shock to you." Samantha outlined what she'd learned about Alejandro's organization and even mentioned a few of the arms deals Julien himself had been involved in. "I can't prove any of these," she said, "but with the contacts, the timing... I think maybe Julien had a hand in them."

Reagan forced her jaw closed. "How in the world...?"

Samantha shrugged. "I made some calls, dug around on the Internet..."

"Don't even ask about that," Brady said. "Seems our little Samantha has a skill for hacking."

"This information was all obtained legally," she said, a twinkle in her eyes. "As far as you know."

He glared at her. "I am an officer of the law."

Samantha glared right back. "And Rae's life is in danger."

Rae couldn't help but smile. It was high school all over again. Brady and Samantha were often at odds, and apparently nothing had changed. Samantha had been Rae's partner in crime—like Nancy Drew and Bess Marvin, though they never settled which was Nancy and which her sidekick. They'd spent their childhood snooping out mysteries that were none of their business. Not that they'd ever fed Nutfield's very active gossip mill. Rather, they'd enjoyed knowing the truth where others only guessed.

Rae'd thought she'd taken it to the next level, becoming an investigative journalist. Seemed Samantha had too. Maybe her friend had never left Nutfield, but with the ability to hack into private servers... Oh, what the two of them could discover together.

If only Rae could stay. She pushed the thought away and watched her friends in their latest showdown.

Brady blinked first. "Go on."

Samantha's lip twitched, fighting the satisfied smile Rae'd seen so often. She turned to Rae. "Am I right about these arms deals?"

"As rain."

That smile came out now. "Thought so. Your husband's a dangerous man."

"You have no idea."

Her smile faded. "I'm sorry. That stinks."

The understatement of the century.

Sam continued. "He's here, in the States. Flew over on Sunday."

Rae's heart dropped to the floor. Of course he was here. Of course he was looking for her. Still, to have it confirmed.

"He flew to San Diego first," Sam said. "Any idea why?"

"There's where I told him I was from."

"That makes sense, then. Anyway, he traveled with two people." She clicked the mouse. "Let's see. Hector del Bosque and Farah—"

"Hanachi." Rae met Brady's eyes and shrugged. "So much for friendship." She looked back at Sam. "Nobody else?"

"Those three tickets were purchased together. First class." Samantha cleared her throat. "He left San Diego on Monday and flew to New York."

So they'd been to Columbia. He already knew too much. "He's too close. If he finds me, it's not like I can fight him."

"We could, together." Brady pushed his food to the center of the table and leaned toward her. "We could try."

Could they? Was there any chance the three of them could defeat Julien and Hector? And then what? Rae would stay in Nutfield. She could live in Gram's house, restart her career, raise her child. She and Samantha could be friends again. And she and Brady... They could be a family.

But the only way to defeat Julien would be to kill him. And Hector. And what about Farah? What would become of her? And could Rae be involved in killing Johnny's father? And what if it didn't work? What if Brady or Samantha or somebody else in town got hurt? Rae had caused her mother's death. Inadvertently, but still. She could never live through Brady's or Samantha's, especially not if it were her fault.

And in the end, what would happen? Even if they eliminated Julien and Hector and dealt with Farah, it wouldn't matter. Julien's father would never allow her to live. Bad enough she had evidence against him, but if she killed Alejandro's son...

The familiar sting of tears blurred her vision. She reached across the table and took Brady's hand. "There's nothing I'd like more than to stay here. But I gave up the chance to come home again the day I met Julien. Johnny and I have to go."

Brady squeezed her hand. "Okay, then. We go together."

"This is your home. You'd give up everything if you went with me. Your parents, your sisters, your job. I couldn't ask that of you."

"You're not asking."

Rae allowed herself to consider it. She thought about the little shack she been picturing since she'd known she'd have to disappear. What if Brady were in that picture? Her husband, her protector? But if Julien found them, he'd kill Brady too. It wasn't worth the risk.

She had to stop his line of thinking. And there was only one way to do it.

She pulled her hand away. "I'm sorry. This has been nice, getting to know you again. I'm so glad we worked things out. But—"

"Nice?" His eyebrows rose. "It's been *nice?*"

"And I always wondered, you know, about you and me. If we could have made it work. If what we had was more than just adolescent hormones on overdrive."

Color drained from his face, and he leaned against the back of his chair.

It took all her self-control not to take the words back.

"It's just...this situation is clouding our judgment. My life is in danger, and you're a protector by nature. I needed you, and I think you like to be needed. But beyond that..." She let her words trail off, not sure if she could force more lies from her throat.

He jerked forward and grabbed her hand. "You're lying."

"I'm sorry."

"I don't believe you."

She inhaled a deep breath, pushed it out, and made herself say the words. "I. Don't. Want. You."

Brady snatched his hand away, pushed back from the table, and stormed into the living room, where he paced across the floor.

Rae stared at the table until Samantha cleared her throat.

"I understand," Samantha whispered.

Rae nodded but couldn't seem to form any words.

The baby cried, and she pushed back from the table.

Brady said, "I'll get him." A moment later, the whimpering stopped. Brady carried the baby into the living room.

"Does he feel warm?"

"Nothing to worry about."

She started toward them, but Brady glared at her. "He's safe with me." He disappeared into the second bedroom and closed the door.

That look on his face just before the door had closed, the hurt, the pain. How could being near her son help him? And how could she rip Johnny from his arms? She returned to her spot at the kitchen table and dropped her head into her hands.

"It's better this way," Rae said.

"He loves you. And you love him. Maybe you could—"

"No. And you can never tell him the truth. It'll only hurt him. Okay?"

Sam nodded. "Do you have a plan? Do you know where you're going?"

Rae forced her thoughts to shift away from Brady. "Nothing concrete."

"Maybe I could help—"

Rae looked up and shook her head. "The less you know, the safer we'll both be."

"Brady told me Johnny has RSV. My nephew had that. It was really serious, and he wasn't nearly as young as Johnny. I'm surprised they didn't hospitalize him."

"My first lucky break. But we have to go soon."

"I'll pray for him. Poor baby. And you have everything you need?" Samantha asked. "If we found out he was on your trail tonight, you could pack up and be gone?"

She nodded. "Except I'd be broke." She quickly explained about her father's gold. "I really thought I could find it. So now...

It would be hard enough to disappear with the cash. I thought, if we had some money stored away, I could live on it, and I wouldn't have to work." She sighed. "Maybe I could teach English. I wanted to be a hermit, keep to ourselves. Better chance he'd never find us that way. I fear I'll be more exposed if I have to work."

Samantha nodded. "You could sell your house."

"How, though, without risking somebody's life? Whoever I asked to take care of the details for me would become a target for Julien. I'm not willing to put anybody else in danger."

Samantha closed her laptop. "We need to find that gold. Seems that'd be the best bet."

"I've looked everywhere. I have no more ideas."

"Well, maybe a fresh set of eyes—"

"Absolutely not. If you're at the house and Julien shows up…"

Samantha nodded slowly. "Right. Okay, then. I have some money I can give you."

"I'm not taking your money."

Sam shook her head slowly. "It's only money, Rae. It's not nearly as important to me as you are."

FORTY-FIVE

Brady paced the cabin's tiny bedroom. He figured he'd better get used to not having Rae around, since she seemed determined to leave him behind. Again.

Had he read her wrong? When they'd kissed, he'd thought she had feelings for him. Was it really nothing more than nostalgia? Or was she lying to him now? He knew she was worried something would happen to him. She'd never recovered from her mother's death, because she'd never stopped blaming herself. But nothing was going to happen to Brady that could be worse than losing her again. Did she think it was any easier for him to send her off to God only knew where, alone and unprotected, with an infant?

He snuggled the baby tighter and paced between the twin beds. As long as he kept moving, Johnny kept sleeping. He should try again to lay him down, but he really didn't want to give the little guy up.

Rae was worried about Brady, but what about his worry for her? For this child? Didn't she understand that?

No way he was letting her go. Wherever she went, he'd be right beside her.

The gold would've helped them disappear. But they didn't have any more time to search for it now. Brady had some money saved, which he'd intended to use as a down payment on his own home. That money would be a start.

But he couldn't do anything right now. He maneuvered the baby over his shoulder and grabbed the remote off the nightstand between the beds. He flipped on the TV and was about to switch to ESPN to find out the score of the football game when he saw the *Special Report* graphic.

The news reader reported a bombing. In America.

At Columbia.

His stomach filled with acid as he stared at the images from the scene. One killed so far, multiple wounded. Too soon to tell how many. No idea yet the motive for the bombing. But maybe it didn't matter, because maybe the true motive was another message for Rae. He watched just long enough to discover that the reporter didn't have any more real information. Then he stepped into the living room.

Rae and Samantha were still at the kitchen table, laughing, a beautiful sound he remembered from their childhood. They could giggle about the stupidest things. He'd always loved it. And he was about to end it.

Rae heard him and looked up. Her smile faltered. "Is Johnny—?"

"He's asleep. You need to see something."

The light in her eyes dimmed. "What happened?"

Brady kneeled beside her and stroked her hair.

She batted his hand away.

He forced a deep breath. "I was watching the news. There's been another bombing. I don't know if it's related."

"Where."

"At a coffee shop. On the campus at Columbia."

He watched her face as it registered shock, then horror.

"Oh, my God. He wouldn't..." She shook her head. "I can't believe... I thought, the first time... I didn't think he'd do it again. How could he?"

She seemed to be looking for answers on Brady's face, then Samantha's. "Was anybody killed?"

"One so far."

She wrapped her arms around her stomach. "My fault. All my fault."

He started to wrap his free arm around her, but she stood and pushed past him.

She turned on the TV in the living room, then stared at the images on the screen.

"You really think it was Moreau?" Samantha whispered.

"Pretty big coincidence if it's not," he said.

"Did anybody take credit for it?" Sam asked.

"Not yet."

They rounded the island and stood beside Rae.

"I don't believe it," Rae said.

Brady rubbed her back. "I know, it's—"

"Don't." She ducked away from him and glared. She must've seen hurt in his eyes, because she softened her expression. "Sorry. I'm just... I mean I don't think it was Julien."

He stepped back and studied her face. She seemed sincere. A wave of anger swept over him. He marched into Rae's room, gently laid Johnny in the middle of the bed, and returned to the living room, closing the door behind him. "Why not? You believe he killed those Tunisians. Why not Americans?"

She must've heard the anger, because she turned her gaze to him. "I just—"

"Maybe you think your *husband* is just too nice a guy to kill Americans. What? Are they more valuable than Tunisians?"

"Not one bit, and don't look at me like that."

He crossed his arms and glared.

"He's a monster," Rae said. "I know that. But I also know—"

"He's just such a sweet guy."

"Brady," Samantha said, "why don't you let her explain?"

Brady glanced at Sam, glared at Rae. "Explain."

"You're going to think this sounds stupid, but Julien loves America."

"Yup. Sounds pretty stupid."

"Brady." Samantha stared hard at him, then nodded at Rae. "Go on."

Rae turned to Samantha. "Whenever I would talk about America, he would get this look on his face, almost awe. He always referred to America as my home, and when I corrected him and told him I was home, right there in Tunis, he'd shake his head like he couldn't understand me. Once, I asked him to explain his fascination with America.

"'The land of the free,' he said. 'The land of opportunity, where you can be anything, do anything.' I didn't understand at the time. He owned this business, made millions of dollars, went anywhere he wanted. He was helping people, bringing jobs to some of the poorest people in the world. He seemed as free as anyone I'd ever met. But of course, that was all a front for his real work. And maybe…"

Rae's voice trailed off, and she stared at the window behind Brady. He resisted the urge to yell. A moment later, she met his eyes.

"I know he's a bad guy. A murderer. I know that. But can't you see that he probably never had any other options? He is who his father created him to be. Did he ever have the choice to walk away from his father's business?" She looked at Samantha. "Can't you see that, deep inside, maybe he doesn't feel free at all? Maybe he never has."

Samantha nodded as if she understood.

Brady didn't understand one bit. Nobody'd forced Moreau

to become an arms dealer. The man could've walked away from his father, from the business, and faced the consequences. Didn't matter who asked him to, Brady would never do the things Julien had done. No self-respecting man would.

Julien was a bigamist, a murderer, and worse. All Rae could think about was how unfortunate the guy had been.

What was he supposed to say? *Sure, your not-quite-husband seems like a real winner. Let's invite him for dinner and talk about that random bombing at Columbia that he couldn't possibly have instigated because of his great love for the red, white, and blue.*

Couldn't say that. Couldn't walk away, either.

He looked at the television set. "So how do you explain that?"

FORTY-SIX

IN THE OTHER ROOM, Johnny wailed. Rae left her friends and picked Johnny up. She pressed her fingertips to his forehead and felt the heat. Not too bad, thank heavens, because it wasn't time for more medicine. She returned to the living room.

"Think he'll eat?" Brady asked.

"Can't hurt to try. Sam, would you hold him for me?"

Sam took the baby while Rae refused to acknowledge the hurt in Brady's eyes.

She went to the kitchen to fix a bottle.

She didn't believe Julien had instigated that bombing, but she also wasn't stupid enough to think it had nothing to do with her. By now, Julien would know that much of what she'd told him about her past was a lie. Samantha confirmed that he'd flown to San Diego, so he'd probably been to the real Rachel Adams's home. Surely he'd discovered that she looked very little like her. Had he found her? Her family? Had he frightened them or hurt them? She doubted it. Julien was smart enough to realize the real Adamses knew nothing about her. And the actual Rachel Adams had never known Rae's real name.

Unfortunately, Julien knew that Reagan had graduated

from Columbia. That part of her story was true, and now that he was in New York, he could confirm it very quickly. That's where her path collided with Rachel Adams's past. So that's where he would go.

Rae glanced at the TV, at the footage running on a loop, and remembered that cafe. It was a popular hangout for students. If it had been an academic building or a bus stop or something else, she might have been able to convince herself it was just a coincidence, but a cafe, like the one where they'd met, the one where a bomb had exploded in Tunis.

Too many coincidences.

What did it mean? If Julien hadn't set off that bomb, who had?

She took Johnny from Sam's arms and worked the bottle into his mouth. He sucked hungrily.

Rae resumed pacing while she fed him, feeling Brady's and Samantha's stares.

Hector. He wouldn't have any trouble killing innocent people. But he also wouldn't act outside of Julien's orders. He was like a trained dog. He needed a master.

She peered down at Johnny. He'd fallen asleep with the nipple in his mouth. She set the bottle on the coffee table and cradled her child closer.

If Hector were responsible for that bombing, and Julien didn't tell him to do it, then who did? She froze when it came to her. The answer sent a shudder down her spine.

Julien's father was behind this, and in that case, Rae was in more danger than she'd believed.

Brady touched her arm. "What are you thinking?"

She stepped away. He needed to stop touching her, or her resolve would melt. "His father's involved." She nodded to the TV. "If Julien didn't do that, then Alejandro did."

"Does that make a difference?"

Johnny stirred. She shifted him over her shoulder, felt his warmth on her neck. "Julien might've had mercy on me. He's a killer, but he cared for me. That wasn't a lie. And he loves his son. I had a chance with Julien. Johnny would be safe with him. But Alejandro? He's a cold-hearted killer. He has no affection for me, no connection to me. He wouldn't show me any mercy."

"You never thought Julien would show you mercy," Brady said.

"I never said it, but I hoped. Not that I want to go back with him. But if I could've been with Johnny—"

"You'd have gone back?" Brady swallowed hard and glared. "You'd have been the wife...no, the mistress of a murderer?"

"I'd have been with my son. But if Alejandro's involved..."

Samantha said, "He'll kill you."

"Yes." Rae looked back at the screen. "People are dead because of me."

Sam stroked her back. "You're trying to save—"

"And how many more will die?" She didn't expect an answer and wasn't surprised when neither said a word. "I can't do it."

Brady started to reach for her, then dropped his hand.

The tiny move nearly made her weep. Or maybe it was the truth she was being forced to face. "It's wrong, Brady. You're right. I can't run away from this. I have to deal with it."

He stood straighter, his eyes brightening. "We can fight him. You can take the evidence to the FBI and..." He trailed off when she shook her head. He stepped back. "What's your plan?"

"I don't know. Maybe the FBI is the answer. Just let me think."

Rae turned to Samantha. "You should go. If Julien is on my trail, I don't want you here when he shows up."

Brady said, "How is he going to find you here? Nobody knows where you are."

Samantha stood. "I'd like to stay."

"I need you to go." Rae turned to Brady. "You, too."

He crossed his arms. "I'm not leaving."

"I need to be alone, to think."

"Think all you want. I won't get in your way."

Rae turned back to Samantha and smiled. "I'm glad you came over tonight." She stepped forward and gave her friend an awkward hug, the baby between them. "I won't leave without saying goodbye, not if I can help it."

"Okay."

Rae squeezed her hand. "I'm sure I'll see you tomorrow." She turned to Brady. "Just until morning, okay?"

"I'm not leaving."

"You said it before, Brady. If he knew where I was, why would he bomb a building in New York?"

"Still—"

"We'll be okay until morning. I promise."

FORTY-SEVEN

Brady stormed outside. Rae wanted him to leave? Fine.

He yanked open the door of his pickup and climbed into the cold cab. He started it up, turned on the heat, then frowned at the cabin.

What was she up to? He'd seen that look before. Determination. Resolve. But to do what? To take off without telling him goodbye? To leave him again, forever this time?

Or was she planning something else?

Whatever it was, she didn't want him around to witness it. Seemed she wanted Brady gone enough to risk what might happen if Julien showed up.

Maybe that's what she wanted, though. Maybe Brady had misread the entire situation, and deep down, Rae was simply looking for an excuse to stay with the monster. She'd all but admitted she'd go back to him, if that's what it took to protect Johnny.

The truth hit him like a mortar blast.

Rae was in love with Julien. Nothing else accounted for this. She said she'd only go back to protect Johnny. But now, refusing Brady's help, refusing to get law enforcement involved? No, there was something else going on. Rae'd stolen evidence that might be able to topple Julien's enterprise, but when it came down to it, she wasn't willing to use it. She couldn't seem to bring herself to hurt the man she'd called her husband. The man she loved.

Brady saw one slat of the blinds lift. She was watching.

He reversed out of the driveway and turned down the narrow road that circled the lake. A hundred yards down the road, he pulled over.

What was he doing? He couldn't leave. She might not love him, but he loved her with an intensity he'd never known. He'd stay, he'd watch what happened. If that meant he had to witness her happy reunion with the man of her dreams, so be it. More likely, he'd witness her stealing out of town in the middle of the night like a criminal.

Brady turned his truck around, drove back to the cabin, and stopped just before the driveway. The trees should hide him from her view. Not too far, though. He needed to be able to see the front door.

He'd stay to see what happened. Maybe he was wrong and Rae wasn't planning on leaving tonight. On the other hand, maybe Julien and his minions were on their way right now. Rae seemed to think Julien might have mercy on her, but Brady wasn't that stupid. He'd be here to protect her, whether she wanted it or not.

FORTY-EIGHT

Julien stared at the television as horror dripped down his spine. Bodies, broken and charred, were carried from the building. Other victims stood on the sidewalk, their faces covered with blood, soot, and ash. The expressions of the onlookers who hadn't run displayed their dread. More than once he saw people look up as if waiting for a plane to crash nearby. It wasn't the scale of September eleventh, but it was a terrible reminder. Terrorists strike New York, again.

Only this time, the terrorists had bombed a cafe near Columbia. Rae's alma mater.

And this time, the terrorist was Julien.

Nausea twisted in his stomach, and he nearly didn't make it to the bathroom before his dinner came up. He rinsed his mouth and washed his hands. Then he stared in the mirror at the man he'd become.

Looking back was a man he'd never acknowledged. The man he'd always been. Maybe he'd never had a choice about how he spent his life. Did violence and evil pass in the DNA? Maybe somewhere along the way, he might have taken a different path.

Maybe it didn't matter. He was who he was, and there was no redemption now. He'd made his choices. All his fantasies about being an architect had been just that—fantasies. The life he lived, the money, the status, the power. The fear he saw in his underlings' eyes. No, he wouldn't trade it for anything.

The image in the mirror smiled. There was freedom in the truth.

He returned to his spot in front of the TV.

No way Hector had done this on his own. No way he could have. The bombing in Tunis, maybe. The man had enough contacts there. But New York? Hector had never been to New York before. To pull off a stunt like this, he'd have needed help.

Hector wasn't working alone. The truth was clear now. Hector had betrayed Julien to his father. And Alejandro was pulling the strings.

So much for friendship and loyalty.

He turned to find Boyle staring at him. The man had long since quit struggling with the ropes that bound him. He seemed to have lost the energy. "You really will stop at nothing to find her."

"Shut up."

"Was your friend right? Or do you approve of his methods?"

"I don't approve of my wife stealing my child." He turned his attention back to the news.

"Why are you doing this?" Boyle asked.

Julien didn't respond.

"Rae loved you."

It was the first time the reporter acknowledged that he'd recognized him. Julien glanced at him, surveyed the man's injuries, his resolve to do the right thing.

"You should have heard the way she talked about you," Boyle said. "She respected you. She admired you, and that's saying something. Rae doesn't admire just anybody."

Was the man speaking truth? Had Rae truly loved him? All his theories that their marriage had been nothing but a ruse to bring him to justice or work with his enemies—was none of that true?

"I'm surprised you were able to fool her so thoroughly," Boyle said. "You must've really charmed her. She thought you were a saint."

Julien wanted to silence the man. Not because he didn't want to hear the words. More because he wanted them so badly to be true. Those words flowed over his scarred and broken places like a healing salve. Had she ever really felt anything for him, though? Or were these just more lies.

Boyle continued. "I guess she figured out you're not the Boy Scout she thought you were. I guess she figured out you're really just a two-bit terrorist."

Julien lifted the gun from the nightstand and pointed it at Boyle. "Be quiet."

"You aren't going to hurt me. That's what you pay Hector for, right?"

He shrugged and lowered the gun. "I prefer not to get blood on my hands."

Boyle nodded toward the television set. "You have plenty of blood on your hands, Julien Moreau."

Julien glared at him, then turned away. He studied the ropes that bound Boyle to the bed. The way he'd winced when Hector had moved him, Julien suspected a few broken ribs, if not more. The man was no threat. Julien tossed the gun back on the bed and glanced at the door.

"What are you going to do when you find her?" Boyle asked.

"Are you going to tell me where she is?"

The man started to shake his head, then stopped abruptly and closed his eyes. Julien could just imagine the headache pounding after Hector's many blows. Boyle swallowed hard. "You keep killing people, she'll find you."

He glanced at the carnage on the TV, then back at the reporter. "Do you have feelings for my wife?"

Boyle met his eyes. "Do you?"

Julien nearly smiled. "You wouldn't understand."

"I guess not."

A moment passed before Julien said, "I'm trying to protect her."

"I'm not going to tell you where she is, so there's no point in lying."

"I'm not lying." He turned off the television. "If my father gets the opportunity, he'll kill her. Mine is not a family one runs from. I don't want to hurt her. I hope she doesn't force me to."

"You could just let her go."

"A death sentence. My father will never let her go."

"And you would?"

Julien pondered the question. If given the option, would he? No. Never. She belonged to him.

He reclined on the other bed and stared at the ceiling. Boyle didn't say another word, and the seconds ticked until finally, the door opened. Hector stepped in first—the man hadn't an ounce of basic manners. Farah followed, small and nervous. And of course she would be—she knew what he'd done.

Julien pointed at the black TV screen. "This is your idea of a plan, Hector? Kill people all over the world."

Another of Hector's rare grins filled his face. "You said to find her using—"

"Yes, yes. Surely you could have found a better way. At least you could have bombed a building that wasn't occupied."

"She needs to be motivated."

"And how many people are looking for you right now?"

Hector shrugged. "I paid a fall guy who'll take credit. By the time the man tells them the truth, we'll be out of the country. Besides"—Hector nodded toward Boyle—"he needs to be motivated."

The reporter's eyes widened.

Julien looked back at Hector. "What is your plan?"

Hector's face shone with excitement.

FORTY-NINE

Rae watched at the window until their cars disappeared.

Why had she sent them away? What she wanted most was to be with them, her best friend and the love of her life.

But she knew the answer before she'd finished locking the cabin door. Now that she was back in Nutfield, she never wanted to leave again. Being with Brady and Sam was just making it harder. And if Brady got any inkling of her plan before she was ready to implement it, he'd talk her out of it. She'd gladly let him. And then what would happen?

The cabin's living room seemed foreign, almost surreal. How had she gotten here? She'd changed her name in college for what had seemed a perfectly logical reason. Who wouldn't tire of being famous—infamous to some—for sending her mother to prison? She'd been the girl who'd rescued the congressman's infant from the crazy woman, dogged and hounded by the media until she couldn't take it anymore. Changing her name had enabled her to avoid Brady and Samantha, a nice bonus when she was so angry with them. Seemed ridiculous now. Childish even.

The news frenzy had finally died down as the media turned

its attention to something new. Rae had grown up, looked different, and suddenly wasn't recognized anymore. She'd planned to go to Cornell until that reporter had shown up at Brady's house graduation night. She'd been working on some sort of *where are they now* stories about child celebrities. As if Rae had ever wanted to be a celebrity. She'd turned the woman down for interview after interview, so when she'd seen her at Brady's house that night, Rae had been furious.

She'd made a scene. Thank God the reporter had left already, encouraged by Brady's father when he saw Rae's shock. Maybe Rae had been justified in her anger after Brady's mother's accusation. "I told you, she's just like her mother."

But that was nothing compared with Brady's silence. He'd had two choices that night, defend her or join her accusers. He'd chosen the second.

Somewhere through the years, Rae realized Brady's mother had been fearful. Her son had fallen in love with the daughter of a crazy woman, and Mrs. Thomas didn't want that kind of wife for her son. She didn't want those genes passed along to her grandchildren.

And Brady—well, Rae probably had seemed insane to him. He'd been an eighteen-year-old kid. He'd had no idea how to fix it—and Brady had always been a fixer.

And maybe, for a moment, Rae had been as crazy as Mom.

Rae looked down at little Johnny. No, she was sane. She'd talked to a psychiatrist about her fears once, and after explaining the life she'd had, the trials she'd gone through, the shrink had patted her arm reassuringly. "If you were prone to the disease, I believe it would have shown itself by now. All that stress..."

Little Johnny was just two generations removed from Rae's mother's illness, but Rae refused to worry about it. He would be sane and healthy. She had to believe that.

Whatever Brady's mother's fears had been, they didn't

matter. One more safe place had been ripped from Rae's life. As she walked back through her childhood, she asked herself—had she ever felt secure? Even before she'd reported her mother for kidnapping, the kids and teachers had always known Rae's secrets. The town itself was no better. She'd felt their stares, their hate. Maybe that's why she'd always been so bent on exposing everyone else's secrets. To level the playing field.

Rae rocked Johnny and considered that. Had it been hate in the eyes she'd seen back then? Had she been wrong? She'd always felt they blamed her for the town's notoriety. Reporters filling the few restaurants, their news vans lined along the once-quiet streets. In retrospect, that didn't really make sense. She'd been put in a position no eleven-year-old should find herself. Had Rae read into the townspeople's looks something that wasn't there? Had that condemnation simply been her own guilt mirrored back to her?

Was it possible those looks had been filled with compassion?

Rae shook her head and paced again. What did it matter now?

New York City had been the perfect hiding place, Columbia instead of Cornell. Meeting Rachel Adams had seemed a gift from heaven. A girl her age, also about to begin at Columbia but who instead wanted to disappear. Rachel had been a drug addict, and from what Rae could determine, she'd been abused by her stepfather for years. The girl just wanted to get away, to hide where he could never find her. Rae was more than happy to give her money in exchange for her identity. With Dad's life insurance policy, she'd had plenty of cash.

When the real Rachel Adams's folks had shown up searching for her, Reagan had been summoned to the bursar's office. She'd met them, acted like their identical names had been an odd coincidence, and told them she had no idea where their daughter was. A clerical snafu, the woman in the office said.

And just like that, Rae was a new person. Nobody recognized her from those old news reports. And Brady and Samantha had never found her.

The light from the TV flickered. What was the point of this bombing? If the first had been designed to smoke her out, to get her to call Nate, then it had worked. If it had been a warning, was this another one? Was Julien trying to scare her? To get her to surrender? To show her what he was capable of?

And was it even Julien? She couldn't imagine the man she'd loved would be capable of such a thing, but how well did she know him?

A car drove by on the gravelly street. She lifted one of the slats on the wood blinds and peered into the dark night. Headlights headed toward the main road reflected off something shiny. Tall and shiny.

Brady's truck.

She laid Johnny on his blanket, grabbed her phone from the kitchen counter, and returned to the window. Definitely Brady out there. Brady thought he could take on Julien, and maybe he could. But Hector too? She wasn't willing to take that chance.

The 9-1-1 operator answered right away.

"I need to report a suspicious vehicle."

After she gave the dispatcher her name and the address of the cabin, she leaned against the window.

All her ruminating about that bombing wasn't going to make a bit of difference. Fact was, she couldn't let people die in order to save herself. Not even to save her son.

But she couldn't sacrifice Johnny. Julien wouldn't hurt his child, not physically. But he would raise him to take over the family business. Hadn't he been thrilled Johnny was a boy so he could do just that? "An heir to inherit all I've built."

Julien would turn their child into a killer, just like his dad had done to him.

Rae wouldn't have it.

A few minutes later, she peeked through the blinds again and watched a black-and-white cruiser stop on the street in front of the cabin. A uniformed police officer approached the driver's side window. A moment later, Brady stepped out and stood at the end of the short gravel driveway, hands on his hips, facing her.

She dropped the blinds and stepped away from the window.

Rae was packing when Johnny woke again. The child needed sleep, but he'd barely slept more than an hour at a time all day. She managed to get some food into his belly before he rejected it with a cry, then she rocked him until he drifted off again.

She settled him in the middle of the bed. While she packed, she formulated her plan. Wrestled with it, more like. When she came to her decision, she put it out of her mind. She'd never be able to function otherwise.

Another attempt at contacting Nate. He hadn't been answering her calls, but she was confident he'd gotten her messages. Still, she'd feel better if she spoke to him.

No answer.

She should have expected that, but her heartbeat kicked into high gear. If anything happened to Nate, she'd never forgive herself. Trembling now, she dialed the phone again. Nothing.

She ended the call, then typed a text. *Please call me. I fear you're in danger.*

She set the phone down and waited, willing it to ring. A moment later, it did. "What do you want?" Nate's voice sounded tight, angry. Strained.

"Thank God you're all right."

A short pause. "What did you mean in your text? What danger?"

He was irritated, obviously. "Did I catch you in the middle of something?"

"You could say that."

"You haven't had any questions about me?"

A short pause. "I told you I'd call."

"Nothing suspicious, unusual?"

"I'm having a really bad day. What do you want?"

"Look, I'm afraid I've put you in danger. It's a long story, and it doesn't matter, because it's almost over. Would you consider coming home for a couple days? Or just get out of the city, a vacation, or maybe you can go somewhere to investigate a story."

This time, the pause was longer before he said, "What happens after a couple of days? Does it all go away?"

"It doesn't matter. I'm going to fix this, but I'll need three days. Can you go somewhere? Please?"

"Fix it how?"

"I don't have time to explain. Come home, and I'll tell you everything."

He blew out a long breath. "Maybe." The word sounded... Resigned. Good.

"Promise me you'll think about it. Please?"

"Rae, you need to..." There was a muffled sound, and then he hung up.

Need to what? Explain, probably, and Nate deserved an explanation. Maybe he'd call back, and she'd give him one. She glanced at the clock. He'd probably been on the subway or something. He'd sounded strange. And he was angry with her, that much was evident. But he was considering getting out of New York. If she could put her plan into place, she should be able to keep him safe. She should be able to keep them all safe.

FIFTY

THE ECHO of Rae's voice hung in the room.

Hector's knife still rested against Boyle's neck. A trickle of blood dripped from its tip, a result of Hector's warning a moment earlier. Hector's breathing was loud and fast, his eyes bright, anticipating what he thought would come next.

Julien said, "Let him go."

Hector frowned, though the knife stayed put. "Why?"

"Now." Julien kept his expression impassive. He couldn't let Hector see the effect Rae's voice had had on him.

Hector lowered the knife, and Boyle's head sagged. He sobbed silently, the emotions of a defeated man.

Julien was glad Farah wasn't there. He'd sent her to grab some snacks from the vending machine before they'd had Boyle call Rae back. They'd ignored other calls from that number. It was the word *danger* that had them dialing. If the person who answered hadn't been Rae, they'd have hung up.

But Julien would know Rae's voice anywhere.

He looked at Boyle. "I assumed you two met at Columbia."

The man looked up and met his eyes. "You know what they say happens when you assume." The words were bold, the tone, resigned. The man had given so much to protect Rachel only to have her expose herself. He'd almost warned her too. Thank goodness Hector had hung up.

Julien felt sorry for the guy. "No, what do they say?"

"It makes an ass out of you—"

Hector backhanded him. Boyle's head sagged as Hector reared back to hit him again.

Julien stepped forward. "Stop."

Hector lowered his arm, though that seemed to take more effort than the blow had.

"We have what we need," Julien said. "There's no point in hurting him further."

"He shouldn't talk to you that way."

"I think it was an expression," Julien said. "And my feelings are quite unharmed."

Hector stepped into the restroom to wash the blood from his hands.

Now that they had the means to find Rae, Julien couldn't let Hector alert his father. He had to keep him busy. He stepped to the open bathroom door. "Bring a glass of water."

Hector dried his hand, filled a glass, and carried it toward Julien.

"Give him a drink."

Hector glared at Boyle, seemed to be wondering why. But he lifted the glass to the man's lips. Liquid dripped down his chin, thanks to Hector's inability to do even that one thing right. He was good at hurting, not helping.

Julien grabbed his cell and pretended to fumble it. It flew over the bed and crashed against the radiator on the far side of the room, then landed on the floor between the bed and the window. Julien circled the bed and, just before he reached down to grab the phone, stepped on it, hard. Then he lifted it up and swore in French.

Hector set the glass on the bureau. "What's wrong?"

He lifted the phone so Hector could see the cracked screen. "I broke it."

"How did that happen?"

"It hit the radiator." He tossed the ruined phone on the bed. "Give me yours."

Hector stared at him a moment, then reached into his pocket. "What do you need? I can—"

"You need to put Boyle in the car."

"Why not just kill him and leave him here?"

"Our fingerprints are all over this place. I don't feel like wiping it down, do you?"

The man shrugged his giant shoulders.

"Give me your phone and move him to the trunk." He could feel Boyle's gaze. "We'll dump him on the way."

"Where are we going?"

"Give me your phone, and I'll figure it out."

Hector reluctantly handed the phone over, then untied and lifted Boyle.

Julien pressed the button on the phone to bring the screen to life. A passcode. Of course. "What's the code?"

Hector froze, Boyle slung over his shoulder like a sack of wheat. He started to put the man down.

"Just tell me," Julien said. "I'm not going to read your love letters."

Hector forced a smile and gave him the code.

Julien keyed it in, committing the digits to memory while the phone unlocked. He navigated to the Internet and typed in *Nathan Walter Boyle*. Julien scrolled to a Wikipedia entry. He clicked on it and read until he discovered Boyle's hometown.

Nutfield, New Hampshire.

Julien lowered the phone and let the answer roll over him. He'd caught Rae's scent. By tomorrow, he'd have her back. He clicked on the town, hit the map, and saw the directions. Four-hour drive. But first they had to make a pit stop. He entered the location and waited for a new map to fill his screen.

Hector returned to the room, Farah on his heels.

Julien shut off the screen and slid the phone into his pocket. "Grab everything and get in the car. I'm driving."

FIFTY-ONE

Julien exited the highway. The sun had set, and the temperature had dropped in the two hours since they'd left the hotel. He glanced at Farah beside him. She sat straight, despite the hours they'd spent in the car. Julien checked the rearview to see Hector stretched out in the backseat, eyes closed. The drive had been silent. Hector had asked once where they were going, but Julien had only told them about this first stop.

Since Hector had no cell phone and Farah didn't know what Rae had revealed about living in Boyle's hometown, neither of them should know their final destination. They didn't have an easy relationship, Hector and Farah. He was too brutal, she too gentle. They worked together because Julien required it. He didn't think Hector would enlist Farah's help. In any event, Julien didn't intend to give either of them the opportunity to update his father.

The passenger in the trunk had kept quiet. Boyle's hands and feet were bound tight, so he shouldn't be able to maneuver the trunk open or push out a taillight. Nor did he have the strength to do either, not after Hector's beating. Had he bled to death, or was he unconscious?

Julien pulled into the vast parking lot and parked. He turned to Farah. "I assume you'd like to use the restroom?"

"Oui, if there's time."

"Of course." He met Hector's gaze in the rearview mirror. "Stay with the car. We'll be right back."

He noted the slightly narrowed eyes when Hector nodded. The man was dying to get his phone back, but Julien wouldn't offer it. And Hector didn't dare ask. Did Hector know Julien had figured him out? If he did, then this could be a very dangerous game. A fatal game.

Julien offered a smile. "We'll be right back, and then we'll find a place for you to use the facilities. I don't want your face recorded on the many cameras inside, in case you were seen this afternoon in New York."

Hector nodded again. "Okay."

Julien and Farah walked into the Foxwoods Casino in Connecticut. Here, he could find what he needed.

He left Farah at the restroom. "Wait for me here. I need to talk to you before we rejoin Hector."

"Oui, monsieur."

He rushed to get what he needed, feigning patience as he waited in line with the Friday night crowd for the cashier's cage. Funny how people went about their business as if everything were normal. He overheard one couple talking about the bombing that day in New York, heard another group of guys boasting about what they'd do if they ever caught the guy. But mostly, it seemed people at the casino wanted to pretend it hadn't happened. Pretend they were safe, that terrorists weren't on their soil right now. In these people's case, the terrorist was standing beside them in line.

He wasn't used to thinking of himself as a terrorist. The bombing had been Hector's doing. His father's doing. He would never have killed those people.

Though he admitted that, by his inaction, he'd allowed it. But it was Rae's fault, not his. She'd brought him to this.

Finally, he got what he needed and returned to the restrooms, where Farah stood near the wall. In Tunis, she always wore an abaya and hajib, but in Paris and here, she donned Western clothing. Right now, she wore black slacks and a silky red blouse. Her hair was up, though as the day wore on, more little strands fell, softening her features. She really was striking. Pale skin, silky black hair, and the biggest, most innocent eyes he'd ever seen.

The area teemed with people, but nobody paid Farah or him any notice as he maneuvered through the crowd and approached. He stopped near her, and the scent of her perfume reminded him of long, sensual nights. There was a reason why he rarely got this close to her. He stood like he had when he'd taken her as a lover. After he'd parted from Martine and before he'd found Rae.

Farah kept her gaze on the floor, as had always been her custom. Her father and her late husband had taught her that obedience, and after all her years in his employ, she still practiced it. Her subservience was alluring, and he found himself stepping closer until they nearly touched. He held her chin between his thumb and forefinger and lifted her face to look in her eyes.

"You have been with me a very long time."

She blinked twice, her mouth forming a little O. Finally she forced a "Yes."

"You have remained loyal. And even after we returned to this...business relationship, you stayed with me."

"Of course, monsieur."

"You used to call me Julien."

She shook her head slightly. "It wouldn't be right."

True. But he needed to know.

"We are alone now. Just once, for me, say my name."

She swallowed, lifted the corners of her mouth in a slight smile, and said, "Julien."

He closed his eyes and let the word roll over him. No, he'd never loved Farah, but he did adore her adoration. She loved him, always had. He knew it. And he had to use it.

He stared down at her. "Are you on my side, Farah?"

Her smile vanished. "What do you mean? Of course."

"When you left with Hector, did he make any calls?"

"Um..." Her mind seemed to race to catch up with his. "Yes. He walked away, though, and told me not to follow."

"And you obeyed?"

"Of course. It wouldn't be right to—"

"Yes, yes. Do you know who he called?"

"I thought he called you."

"Why?"

She blinked, looked past him a moment, then returned her gaze to his face. "I could see that he was talking to someone he respected. He stood straight and tall. You know how he nods when you tell him to do something? He did that two or three times."

Hector'd been talking to Julien's father.

He glared at her, hardened his voice. "You're telling me the truth?"

Tears pooled in the corners of her eyes. He'd hurt her with the accusation. "I would never betray you. You are my life."

The right answer. He believed her, and he needed to keep her loyalty. It mattered more now than ever. He rested his hands on the wall behind her, trapping her in place. "If only things could have been different. My father..." He shook his head and whispered in her ear. "He would not allow us to be together. I loved you, but Papa would have taken you away from me. Maybe even hurt you. I couldn't let that happen." The lies sounded so pretty. He leaned back to study her face again. "Do you understand?"

Emotions played across her features. The love. The joy. Yes, Farah was on his side. He could trust her. He wrapped one arm around her back and used the other hand to brush a stray lock of her hair behind her ear. Then he wove his fingers into her hair as she slid her hands over his shoulders and around his neck. He felt her trembling just as he kissed her.

If only he could pretend it was Rae in his arms, not this substitute. After just enough time, he ended the kiss.

Tears streamed down her cheeks.

"I'm sorry." He wiped her tears. "I shouldn't have done that. I have worked so hard to keep my distance. I don't want to hurt you again."

She trailed her fingers along the back of his neck. His body responded in ways it should not, not in Farah's arms. But he didn't pull away.

She smiled through her tears. "As long as I can be at your side, I am happy. I will always be here for you. Always."

He stepped back. "I cannot tell you how it soothes me to know that. I couldn't do this without you."

She nodded and looked at the floor.

"Hector is working against me."

Her gaze snapped up.

"I have a plan," he said. "Can I count on you to help me?"

"Of course. Whatever you need."

Satisfied, he led her to the car.

After a quick stop for gas, they were back on the road. Julien returned to the interstate in silence while Farah cast him knowing glances and Hector glared from the backseat. No one spoke.

Less than an hour later, he pulled off the highway near Warwick, Rhode Island, and found a cheap hotel. He passed the parking lot, scanned for video cameras, and saw none. He stopped in the Denny's lot next door.

"Are we stopping for the night?" Hector asked.

"No. You two get a fresh car and meet me. I'll find a place and send you the location."

"Is it wise to switch cars?" Hector asked.

"I believe so, yes. The cars in this lot won't be discovered missing until morning, but this car has most likely been reported stolen by now. And the New York plates draw attention."

He watched Hector in the rearview mirror as he nodded once to Farah. "Let's go."

Hector stepped out of the car and Farah followed, meeting Julien's eyes before they walked away. Julien left to search for the perfect place.

It didn't take long to find a quiet street in an industrial park. He parked on the edge of an empty parking lot on the far side of a large dumpster and next to the thick woods. He sent his location to Farah's cell. If they left now, it would take them twenty minutes to get there. He should have time. Farah knew to keep the phone away from Hector. Of course he could take it from her forcibly, but not without showing his hand. This plan should work.

Julien pulled his gun from the glove box and, after he stepped from the car, shoved it in his waistband at the small of his back.

Boyle didn't move when Julien opened the trunk. He reached in, touched the man's neck, felt the pulse just as the man stirred.

"Do you need to stretch?"

Boyle nodded. The gag Hector had shoved in his mouth prevented him from speaking. Julien felt the gun, ensured it was handy if he needed it, and said, "If you scream or make any noise, I'll kill you. You understand?"

Boyle nodded again, and Julien removed his gag. "Where are we?" His voice was tired and rough.

"We're switching cars." He pulled Boyle's bound legs out of the trunk, untied them while Boyle sat awkwardly in the trunk, and shoved the rope in his back pocket.

"Why haven't you let your friend kill me yet?"

Julien helped him stand. "I haven't found her yet. I need you alive."

Boyle's eyebrows lifted. It was too dark to see his eyes, but Julien imagined a spark of hope there. "So you're going to let me go?"

Not likely, but there was no reason to tell him that. If for some reason Rae couldn't be found, Boyle might still prove useful. Seemed they'd grown up together, so maybe if she wasn't at her home, Boyle could help them locate her.

Julien looked into the forest. Such dark, thick woods. This would work.

He grabbed the man's upper arm. "Come." He led Boyle into the trees, where branches snapped underfoot. The scent of fallen leaves reminded him of his childhood years, when he and Hector would play in the forest on the edge of the school grounds.

Julien pushed the memories away and supported Boyle over knobby roots until Julien found a sturdy trunk far enough back. "Sit."

Boyle slid to the ground, and Julien turned to look at the car. From here, Boyle would be able to see everything. Did Julien care?

He didn't have time to worry about it.

He tied Boyle to the tree. "I don't know what's going to happen next. Just be quiet." He crouched down and met his eyes. "I'm your only hope. Hector will kill you as an afterthought. Farah will do as I say. Or as Hector says. So be silent."

"What are you going to do?"

Julien ignored the question and returned to the car. He slammed the trunk closed and kept the gun in his waistband as he slid into the driver's seat. Two minutes later, he saw the headlights. A nondescript dark-colored sedan. Perfect.

Hector parked behind Julien, and Hector and Farah stepped out. Julien did, too, and met them at the back of his car.

"Well done, my friend."

Hector nodded. "There weren't many to choose from. The newer ones are harder to hot-wire."

"Yes, yes, but you managed, like you always do. *Merci.*"

Hector blinked at the second compliment, then nodded toward the trunk. "We kill him and leave him here?"

"Seems a good place."

Hector looked around at the grounds, at the light poles which were placed sporadically around the parking lot but not close enough to illuminate them.

Julien stepped away from the car. "Go ahead."

As Hector lifted the trunk, Julien pulled the revolver out. He gripped it in both hands and aimed it at his best friend just as Hector's gaze snapped up from the empty trunk to meet his. It fell quickly to the gun in Julien's hands.

Julien told himself to fire, but his finger wouldn't cooperate. His oldest friend, his best friend. His only friend. Was this the right decision?

Hector reached into the pocket where he kept his gun.

Julien had no choice. He pulled the trigger, felt a sharp pain in his shoulder as he watched his friend stagger backwards one step, then two. Hector covered the wound in his chest with his hands, trying to stem the blood. It dripped between his fingers and down his arm.

He sat heavily on the asphalt and looked at Julien.

Julien kept the gun raised.

Slowly, Hector lay down, and Julien stepped closer.

"You shot me," Hector said, his voice weak.

"You're working with my father."

"Yes."

The single word, and Julien exhaled a breath. For a moment, he'd worried he'd been wrong, but to hear it from Hector's mouth, after all they'd been through…"How could you betray me?"

Hector pulled in a rattling breath. "Always worked for your father."

Julien blinked. "What do you mean?"

His friend forced another breath. "You're going to let me die?"

"Tell me what you mean."

"When we were school children, your father paid my tuition. Not the first year, but after that." He struggled through another breath, and blood trickled from his mouth with his exhale. "My loyalty was always with your father."

Julien raised the gun and shot Hector between the eyes.

He turned to see Farah staring, mouth agape.

"Did you know?"

She shook her head quickly, her gaze darting from him to Hector and back. "I swear—"

"Get in the car."

"But monsieur, you're hurt."

The adrenaline must've kept the initial pain away, but Farah's reminder brought it back. Julien touched the wound on his shoulder, felt the hot sticky blood on his fingers, and swore under his breath.

Farah approached. "Let me look."

"How did he do it? He never even pulled his gun out."

"He fired through his pocket."

Sure enough, when Julien bent to investigate, he saw Hector's jacket had a hole in it. Quick thinking. Julien grabbed Hector's gun and stuck it in his own pocket. Then he pulled out a poker chip and handed it to Farah. "Wipe that off and stick it in Hector's pocket."

Her jaw dropped, but she did as she was told, approaching the corpse cautiously as if Hector might wake up and grab her.

Julien leaned against the car, paused to let a wave of dizziness pass, and said, "Drag Hector's body into the woods. Make sure he's well hidden."

Farah heaved the bodyguard's dead weight into the woods. He could hear the strain in her occasional grunts, which sounded loud over the drag of the body on the ground. He forced himself not to scold her for taking so long.

Finally, she returned, breathing hard and sweating in the cool night air.

"Walk into the woods about twenty feet." Julien nodded in the right direction. "You'll find the reporter. Bring him back."

Even in the dim light, he could see the terror in her eyes. She looked into the woods, then back at him. "But you didn't kill him?"

"I still need him."

She swallowed hard.

"I'm not going to shoot you, Farah. Unless you've betrayed me."

She shook her head vehemently.

"And the reporter's not going to hurt you, either." He raised his voice and said, "Right, Boyle?"

The man's reply was soft and pained. "I promise."

"If you try anything," Julien started.

"I can hardly move," Boyle said. "What do you think I'm going to do?"

Farah obeyed Julien, as he'd known she would. A moment later, she returned from the woods supporting Boyle, who hobbled beside her. She approached the trunk, but Julien shook his head.

"Back seat." He looked at the man. "You're going to behave, right?"

The man bowed, stood straight, and then cringed. "I can barely walk. I'm sure as heck not going to run."

They settled in the car, he and Boyle in the backseat. While Farah pulled out of the parking lot, Julien glanced back at where the body of his only friend lay in the darkness.

He faced forward. Time to find his wife.

FIFTY-TWO

It was the longest night in history. Johnny only slept in snatches. Rae managed to pack during one of his naps, then tried to grab some sleep herself. After the events of the day, it proved impossible to silence the voices in her head. The next time Johnny woke, this time with a diaper full of the only gift he had to give, she gave up on sleep altogether.

If she were at the house, she'd use the time to search for the gold, but she couldn't go back there. Not ever. She wished she'd thought of that when she'd grabbed her things the day before. She'd never get to see the place again.

She rocked Johnny. "What was the point in all of this?"

He scrunched up his eyes and wailed. She knew exactly how he felt.

She'd come back to Nutfield to see her grandmother and get the gold.

Her grandmother had already passed away, and the gold was gone.

Coming home had all been for nothing.

She thought about Brady and Samantha and the time they'd spent together. No, her time here hadn't been for nothing. She'd repaired her relationship with Sam, at least. She and Brady...well, he might never forgive her for rejecting him. Still, she wouldn't trade the time spent with him for anything.

She set Johnny in his bouncy seat and ignored his cries just long enough to grab another cup of coffee.

Rae's plan would only work if she set it in motion long before Julien found her. With Nate's assurance that he hadn't heard from Julien, she knew she had some time.

She looked at the baby's red cheeks. He was still sick, but he'd be well cared for. And she couldn't think about that, not now.

Rae'd never thought to ask Samantha for her phone number. Fortunately, she'd been with Brady when he'd stopped at Sam's condo for the key to the cabin.

The sun hadn't risen above the trees when Rae snapped Johnny into the car seat, ignoring his cries, and climbed behind the wheel. She hadn't driven with him enough to know if this would put him to sleep, but other parents swore by it. She backed out of the driveway and turned toward the main road.

A police cruiser was parked about ten feet from her driveway. Brady was more stubborn than she, and that was saying something. But the driver wasn't Brady. Rae waved as she passed, and the man followed.

She had to admit, she felt safer with the police car behind her, and very thankful it wasn't Brady. She couldn't see him yet.

At Samantha's condo, Rae pulled into an empty spot and climbed out. Johnny had fallen asleep, so she grabbed his seat and crossed to the door just as the police car parked across the street. She rang the bell.

Samantha answered a few seconds later. She was dressed in gray yoga pants and a navy top and carrying an oversize coffee mug. Rae was happy she was awake.

"Rae?" Sam peered behind her at the police car, then back into her eyes. "What'd you do?"

"Brady has somebody watching me. Protection, I suppose."

"That's good."

"May I come in?"

Samantha stepped out of the way, and Rae entered the condo.

She let her gaze roam the space. It had looked small from the outside, but the great room she stepped into was spacious and bright, decorated in earth tones and cream. She'd expected the place to look like Samantha's parents' house. Rae was clearly stuck a decade in the past. Instead of the country decor Samantha's mother had favored, Samantha had chosen a sleek, uncluttered look. It was...cosmopolitan. It took Rae a moment to reconcile the girl she'd known with the sophistication here.

"It's beautiful."

"What's going on, Rae?"

Rae indicated a chair. "Mind if I sit? Johnny kept me up all night."

"Be my guest. Did something happen?"

Rae set the car seat on the floor. Johnny was still sleeping, thank God. "I didn't have your phone number." She yawned hugely. "I need your help."

"Let me get you some coffee."

After Samantha handed her a steaming cup, Rae sipped and tried to figure out how to ask for what she needed. The direct approach might be the easiest.

"I need to fake Johnny's death."

Samantha's eyebrows asked the question for her.

"If Julien thinks he's dead, he'll quit looking for him."

"Do you think he'll quit looking for you too?"

"I have a plan. But first, I have to make sure Johnny will be safe."

"And you'll be...?"

Rae attempted a smile. "If my son is safe, then I'll be fine, no matter what."

Sam reached across the table and took Rae's hands. "I'll do whatever I can to help. So what's your plan? You'll run with Johnny, but somehow get word to Julien that he died?"

Rae blinked back the tears. She couldn't think too much, or she'd lose her courage. "I think Brady's fallen in love with him." When Samantha nodded, she continued. "He'll take him. He lost a son, and I have one who needs a home. Brady will be a great father."

"No." Tears filled Sam's eyes. "Oh, Rae."

"You understand, right? I would never leave my son if I had a choice."

"Of course. But there must be another—"

"Don't." She pulled her hand away and squared her shoulders. "I need it to look real. Can you do it?"

Samantha nodded slowly. "I can print a death certificate."

"Can you hack into...wherever one would hack to make it look official?"

"I think so."

"If you get caught, will you get into a lot of trouble?"

Samantha shook her head. "My life isn't on the line, Rae. It doesn't matter if I get fired. Or prosecuted."

"I don't want you to get into trouble."

"I'll cover my tracks. I think I can do it without anybody knowing. It's worth the risk. To save Johnny."

"To save Johnny."

Samantha wiped her eyes, then sipped her coffee. She studied Rae over the rim of her cup. "Brady doesn't want to lose you. Why can't you two just run away, take Johnny with you?"

"And let Julien and his father keep killing people?"

She nodded slowly. "Right. So you're going to hand over the evidence to the FBI?"

"Something like that." Rae couldn't think about her next move, not yet. She tapped her fingers against the table. "Do you know anything about how Brady can get legal custody? I'm afraid if I do anything official..."

"Julien will figure it out."

"Yeah."

Samantha stared out the sliding glass door. Rae followed her gaze to a playground and beyond that, to the condominiums on the far side of a green field. Trees dotted the area, their leaves fluttering in the wind, hanging onto that last thread of hope before autumn.

Samantha said, "Let me do some research. When do you need this done?"

"Soon. Today."

"I need to get started. I'll have to do some of it from the office."

"It's Saturday. Will that be a problem?"

"I have a key." She pulled Rae up and hugged her tight. "I love you."

"I love you."

Samantha squeezed harder, and Rae held onto her friend for another moment before she forced herself to pull away.

"I have to get back to the cabin."

"I know." Samantha squeezed her hand. "I'll call you when it's done."

FIFTY-THREE

Rae must've checked the time a hundred times that morning. Johnny fussed, finally ate a little around noon, then fussed an hour after lunch. Rae didn't mind. All she wanted was to stare into those beautiful eyes and memorize them.

If only he'd smile at her once before she abandoned him.

Instead, he cried. The sound was precious.

She'd called Samantha a few times, nestling Johnny in her left arm so she wouldn't have to put him down. Samantha had the death certificate and had even forged a doctor's name. "I made the signature illegible," she said. "I pray your husband will trust the document. But won't he want to bury his son?"

"Probably." Rae had no idea how she would get around that, but she couldn't think about it. Not yet.

Samantha hadn't been able to hack the hospital's website or the state's yet. So Rae waited and rocked her son and dreaded the moment she knew was coming.

Johnny finally fell asleep. Much as she wanted him awake, he needed his rest. She laid him on the bed, then loaded the car with her suitcase. When she was finished, she set her phone to vibrate, lay in bed beside her perfect little boy, and cried herself to sleep.

Her phone vibrated an hour later. The text from Sam simply read, *It's done. Shall I come there?*

She typed, *No. Can you send Brady's address?* She considered her next move as she slipped from the bed and made her way into the living room.

Sam answered. *Just saw him at the station.*

The station. Right next to the bank. It was all too easy.

Except that Rae had to go out. The bank hadn't been open earlier when she'd visited Sam, but it would be open now, and she needed the evidence from her safe deposit box.

But sweet Johnny needed his sleep. It was hard enough considering leaving him, but leaving him ill?

So, what could she do?

The answer seemed suddenly obvious. She dialed Caro's cell phone. The girl answered on the second ring.

"Hey, Rae. What's up?"

Rae could hear the sounds of what sounded like a party behind Caro's voice. "Sounds like you're busy."

"Nah. Just hanging out at Zio's with Finn and Trent."

Apparently the boys had cleared up their little misunderstanding. If only all problems were so easily solved. "Could you watch Johnny for a little while? Maybe an hour. He's sound asleep. The only problem is, I can't pick you up. You'd need to get a ride."

"Omigosh, I'd love to babysit! Hey, Finn. Finn!" There was a pause before Caro continued, speaking to her boyfriend. "Hey, can you take me to Rae's house, like, right now?"

"Actually," Rae said, "I'm in a cabin by the lake."

"Seriously? I wondered when I stopped by last night. I got a part, by the way."

"Oh, good." A part in a play Rae would never get to see. It

was the least of her worries, but the thought still made her tear up. "Anyway, if I send you the address—"

"Yeah, Finn said it's no problem. He's just telling Trent where we're going."

"Great. See you soon."

Rae hung up and texted the cabin's address to Caro. The last thing she wanted to do was leave the baby, but at least she knew he'd be safe here. Just Brady, Sam, and now two teens knew where she was, and in just a short time, it wasn't going to matter anyway.

Caro showed up a few minutes later, waving to Finn as he drove away. She stepped inside as she told Rae about the part she got in the play—the queen. Apparently it wasn't the lead role, but it was a good one.

"I have more lines than the princess and the prince," Caro said. "I know, 'cause I counted. But don't tell anyone, 'cause that makes me seem sorta petty, right?"

"Just excited." Rae imagined Brady sitting in the auditorium, watching the play, her sweet Johnny in his arms.

No, she wouldn't think about that.

Caro looked around the cabin. "Awesome place. How's Johnny?"

"He's better. Thanks for doing this."

"Sure. Did you know there's a police car out there?"

"I saw it earlier."

"It's not the quarterback," Caro said.

Rae almost smiled. "I don't think he likes to be called that."

"I don't know why. Who's cooler than Tom Brady?"

Rae fought to keep her tone light. "I know, right?"

"So why are the cops stalking you. You break the law or something?"

She shook her head. "Brady's just paranoid. Everything's fine."

Caro smirked and looked away. "I wish that were true."

Great. Teenager angst. She didn't have time, but Caro looked so distressed. "What's going on?"

"Remember the other night when Finn was fighting with Trent? At the school?"

Seemed like years ago, not days. She nodded.

Caro settled in a barstool beside the island. "Well, he'd been acting weird anyway, even before that. I tried to find out what that conversation was about, but he wouldn't tell me. It wasn't nothing, though. You know? 'Cause I heard Finn threaten to go to the cops, and Trent said he wouldn't dare. And with my sister and my parents... I just can't get pulled into anything illegal. I've been trying so hard not to end up like my parents, and I thought I found a nice church kid, but maybe I was wrong." She rubbed her eyes and continued. "So today, he told me everything was fine and not to worry. We met Trent at Zio's, and they seemed okay, but there's something going on with Trent. I don't like him."

Rae was too tired to follow the girl's rambling. "Going on? Like?"

"No clue. But it scares me, you know? What could Finn be doing?"

All sorts of terrible things, but Rae didn't voice that thought. She grabbed her purse and her keys from the kitchen island.

Caro's cell binged, and she looked at it. "Oh, Finn's brother is coming home." She read the text. "*Nate just texted. He's coming home for the weekend, and I have to go with my parents to Manchester. So I can't pick you up later.*"

Rae paused at the door. "Nate Boyle?"

"Uh-huh."

That was the best news Rae'd heard all day. He should be safe here.

"You know Nate, right?" Caro walked to the door with her. "Finn said you guys went to high school together."

"Long time ago."

"So I guess I need a ride home later."

"No problem." She imagined Brady could take the girl home when he picked up Johnny.

Tears stung her eyes, and she blinked them back. She couldn't think about that. Not until it was done. "You have my number. Johnny should sleep until I get back. If he wakes up, call me, then you can rock him. Can you do that?"

The girl's eyes were wide as saucers. "I won't let you down."

"And no company."

Caro smiled. "No parties. Got it."

Rae tried to return the grin but figured she'd failed when Caro said, "I'm just kidding. I promise to take good care of him."

Rae squeezed the girl's arm. "I know you will."

After she pulled out of the driveway, she stopped beside the police car on the street. Before she could get out of her car, a young uniformed officer approached her window. She lowered it. "Good morning, Officer."

"Ma'am."

"I left my infant inside with a babysitter."

"Detective Thomas thought there might be trouble."

"There still might be," she said. "So please stay here and keep an eye on them. Okay?"

He looked at the house, then back at her. "I'll have to call the detective."

"While you're at it, tell him I'm on my way to see him."

FIFTY-FOUR

BIENVENUE. If Julien were less groggy, in less pain, and less eager to get where he was going, he might find irony in the fact that the sign marking the New Hampshire state line welcomed them in French.

As it was, he had just enough energy to point and mumble, "Why French?" to Boyle.

The man's answer was a grunted, "Canadians."

That made sense, if nothing else did.

Even after all that sleep, he was too groggy to respond. He leaned against the backseat door and willed the pain away.

After they'd left Hector's body the night before, he'd told Farah to drive to New Hampshire. Just a few hours away from his Rachel, and he couldn't wait any longer.

But Farah had defied him.

He still couldn't believe it.

She pulled off the interstate just a few exits down and stopped at a pharmacy. "I'm going to get something to wrap your wound."

She returned with a full sack and started on her way again.

"I thought you were going to wrap this."

"When we get where we're going."

"We're going to find Rachel."

She'd ignored him. Ignored him! If his shoulder hadn't been throbbing, he might have broken his own rule about hitting women. As it was, he barely had the energy to keep from resting his head in the reporter's lap.

Julien had sat in the backseat to make sure Boyle wouldn't try to escape or alert another car. Julien had considered putting him back in the trunk, but he needed the reporter alive, and he feared Boyle might bleed to death or suffocate if he spent too many hours in the confined space. Fortunately, Boyle seemed too tired and wounded to try anything.

A few minutes later, Farah put on her blinker, and Julien looked at her destination.

"We don't need a hotel room for you to bandage me."

"I hate to tell you this," Boyle said, "but you should probably do what she says."

He shot a look at the man beside him. "You keep your mouth closed, unless you want to ride in the trunk."

Boyle shrugged. "You're about to bleed to death." He looked at the back of Farah's head. "Will you let me go, once he's dead?"

She maneuvered to a parking spot far from the street lights and met Julien's eyes in the rearview mirror. "I'm sorry, monsieur, but he is right."

"You need a hospital," Boyle said.

"No." Farah twisted to face him. "American doctors are required to notify the police when somebody has been shot. Is that not true?"

Boyle shrugged, then winced. "Better arrested than dead."

Julien wanted to yell at them both to shut up, but it hurt to talk. The best he could muster was, "We need to get back on the road."

"Oui, monsieur. Soon."

"But Rae—"

"You will not find her if you are dead. The reporter is right." She took the keys from the ignition, grabbed her purse, and stepped out of the car. She bent and looked at him. "I will be right back. Don't go anywhere." Then she slammed the door.

She'd never defied him before. His wound must look bad.

Didn't feel all that great. Throbbed, and he could still feel blood trickling down his chest.

"A few inches south, and you'd already be a goner," Boyle said.

Julien didn't want to think about that. Didn't want to think about the fact that he'd shot his best friend. The only real friend he'd ever had, on his father's payroll since grammar school.

He and the reporter remained silent until Farah returned. She drove around the building. "I asked for a first floor room. This one should be private enough. Mr. Boyle, do you think you can help me—?"

"I can walk," Julien said. "And don't think you're going to get away with this defiance, Farah."

"I pray you'll be well enough to punish me tomorrow."

Boyle chuckled. If Julien's shoulder weren't throbbing, he might've punched the guy.

Julien led the way into the room. He feared he might collapse if he paused even to let Farah precede him. He sat on the closer of the two double beds while Boyle hobbled in, Farah behind him, Hector's gun in one hand.

"Please sit over there," she said.

Boyle collapsed on the bed farther from the door. The man was white as a sheet. Julien wondered if he looked that bad.

Judging by the expression in Farah's eyes when she turned

to him, he did, perhaps worse. She handed the gun to Julien, stripped him of his shirt, and looked at the wounds—entrance and exit. At least the bullet wasn't still in there. She poured some astringent on the bullet holes to clean them. Julien barely kept himself from crying out at the pain. Then she dressed both wounds.

When she was finished, he insisted it was time to go.

"No, monsieur." She shook two pills out of a bottle and handed them to him with a glass of water. "They will help."

He swallowed them while Farah nodded to Boyle. "His turn."

The man was half asleep on the bed. Julien pointed the gun. "Sit up. I don't feel like arguing with her."

Boyle obeyed.

But she didn't dress his wounds right away. Instead, she worked on tying him to the headboard.

"What are you doing?" Julien asked.

"Better to be safe."

Boyle sighed loudly but didn't argue. He seemed resigned to it. Maybe he believed Julien would let him go if he behaved himself.

Julien would keep the man alive until they found his wife, and then perhaps use him to teach her a lesson.

When Boyle was tied to the bedpost, Farah grabbed the alcohol and cotton balls, and Julien dropped his gun and laid his head on the pillow. He figured he may as well rest while he had the chance.

He awakened covered with a thick blanket. Sunshine streamed through the glass.

He sat up, nearly passed out with the wave of dizziness, and lay back down. Farah, who had been lying beside him, sat upright. "Please, try to move slowly, monsieur." She stood and walked around to his side of the bed as Boyle stirred.

Julien looked at the man. Farah had bandaged his head wound. He was still tied to the bed.

He glanced at the clock, and his heart nearly stopped. "It's almost noon."

"We were all tired." She remained calm despite his anger.

"There's no way I could have slept that long. What did you give me?"

"Tylenol."

"What kind of Tylenol?"

Farah ignored the question as she shifted the blanket and checked his wounds. The bandages were bright red.

"Still bleeding," she said.

And throbbing, but he didn't say that. "If Rae is gone by the time I get there, you will pay."

She met his eyes, nodded, and grabbed fresh gauze. "If you had died, I would never have forgiven myself."

Twenty minutes later, Farah navigated back onto the highway while Julien checked Boyle's phone. The boy, Finn, had texted multiple times that morning and continued to text. Julien just wanted to shut the kid up.

Flying home today, he typed. *Should arrive in an hour.*

The kid replied, but Julien didn't have the energy to converse with a teenaged boy with girl troubles. He finally responded. *Can't talk. On the plane.*

That ought to shut him up.

One more text came, a promise to meet his flight in Manchester. Julien tossed the phone to the floor. "Your brother is persistent."

"It's a family characteristic."

By the time they exited the interstate, it was almost three

o'clock. Despite the long night's sleep, Julien could barely keep his eyes open.

"You're almost home," he said to Boyle.

"Not exactly how I pictured my next homecoming, accompanied by terrorists."

"I am not a terrorist."

The man shrugged. "Whatever helps you sleep at night."

Julien was regretting having let him live this long.

"So, how much did Rae know about your real life when she married you?"

Julien ignored the question.

"Because if I know Rae, and I do—"

"I think you should shut up." Julien sat taller and peered into the forest surrounding the interstate. "Lots of places around here to hide a body."

"You're going to have to kill me, Julien. I don't know why you haven't yet."

"I still have use for you."

Boyle blew out a short breath. "So, what do I have to lose?" After a short pause, he started again. "Rae can't have known what you really did for a living. How did she find out?"

Julien rested against the seat and closed his eyes, letting the latest wave of pain pass. When it did, he sighed. "I told her not to go through my files. Apparently, she did."

Boyle actually laughed. It died quickly. "You told her not to? And you thought she'd stay away?"

He glared at the man.

"You know nothing about Reagan."

"Reagan?"

Boyle chuckled and shook his head. "Geez, you don't even know her real name."

"Reagan Adams?"

Boyle opened his mouth, then closed it. Then he smiled. "I

mean, telling her there are secret files is like giving a bloodhound a scent. Her favorite thing is ferreting out secrets."

That information had come about thirteen months too late.

A few minutes passed before Boyle said, "You killed your friend."

"He was not my friend."

"Aren't you going to have to tell your father where Rae is? How can you protect her?"

"You know nothing."

"I've done my homework since Rae called."

Yes, she had called him. Hector's plan had worked. Papa's plan, more likely. They'd located her, and it had only cost a handful of lives. He'd been angry with Hector for the bombings, but if he were honest, he'd admit he'd take ten times more lives, a hundred, if that's what it took to locate her.

"How is your father going to accept this?" Boyle said. "Seems to me he's pretty ticked off already, and now you've killed his man."

"He's never going to know. That's what the poker chip was for."

"What poker chip?"

He shook his head. "Never mind."

"You've gotten yourself into quite a pickle," Boyle said. "I can't see a way out. The best thing you could do is leave Rae alone."

"That is not an option."

"Save your own skin. As long as you're safe."

Julien pulled the gun from his jacket pocket and pointed it at Boyle's head. "Tell me Rae's last name."

The man cringed, swallowed, and squeezed his eyes shut. Then they opened, filled with resolve. "No."

Julien pressed the gun against the reporter's temple. "First, I will kill your brother, Finn. Then your parents. How many more will have to die in order to protect her? I don't have to stop at your family. I'm sure there are plenty of lovely people in Nutfield. Will they be as willing to die as you are?"

The man blinked, as Julien had known he would.

"McAdams." Boyle exhaled a long breath. "Reagan McAdams."

"Her address?"

"She lives near the center of town. I'll show you."

He pushed the gun against Boyle's temple, and Boyle leaned away until his head was pressed against the far window.

"Address," Julien repeated.

Boyle rattled it off, his eyes filling with tears. Fear, or grief that he'd betrayed his friend? Yes, Boyle cared for Rae. Too much. Had they been more than friends? The thought of Rae in this man's arms made him tremble with rage.

It would be so easy to pull the trigger.

Boyle spoke again, his resolve back. Or maybe he was simply resigned to his own death. "What's one more, compared to the lives you've already taken?"

He pushed the gun harder, until Boyle's face was mashed against the window. Just one squeeze, and this friend of Rae's would never taunt him again.

Her friend.

He pictured his wife, imagined her face whenever she spoke of Margot, another friend. The friend whose death he'd had a part in. The friend whose death had been the reason he and Rae had met in the first place.

Was that what this was about? He thought of the files he'd stored in Tunis. Could it be that simple? Had she discovered that he'd sold the explosives that killed her friend?

Was he willing to kill another?

"What are you waiting for?" Boyle's remark was bold, his voice, tremulous.

Julien lowered the weapon and returned it to his pocket. He remembered how Rae had cried for her friend, how she'd grieved her. Had all of this been about that woman, Margot? One random woman, inconsequential in the scheme of things, killed by munitions he'd sold.

Had it all come down to that?

FIFTY-FIVE

Brady hung up the phone in the squad room. Rae was on her way. He'd already known Rae was still in town, just like she'd promised. When she'd run him off the night before, he'd called the chief and told him about the threat. Not everything, just enough to get the man to agree she needed someone to keep an eye on her.

He paced across the squad room. He wanted to fix this for Rae, to make it all okay. But he had no idea how, and even if he could come up with a plan, she seemed determined to leave without him.

Again.

Well, they had to have a way to communicate. Two untraceable cell phones. That might work. Maybe he could follow her later. Maybe eventually she'd realize she wanted him around. Maybe someday she'd realize she needed Brady as much as he needed her.

He tried to focus on the work that had piled up since he'd been preoccupied with Rae. He didn't usually work on Saturdays, but what else did he have to do? She'd made it clear she wanted him to stay away.

He'd visited with Laurie Nolan that morning, Caro's older sister. She swore she'd had no idea the guy she'd met that night was a dealer. Brady warned her that he'd be keeping an eye on her, and she seemed grateful there were no more repercussions than that.

Maybe he'd been able to keep one Nutfield citizen safe. If only he could protect Rae too.

His gaze found the door about ten thousand times. What was taking her so long?

Maybe she'd changed her mind. Donny, the police officer assigned to her house, had told Brady Rae'd left Johnny with a teenager who'd been dropped off earlier. Had to be Caro. Why would she leave the baby at home? Didn't she know Brady would have come if she'd called?

He looked again at the entrance, but a moment later, Rae and Samantha stepped in from the town offices on the opposite side of the room. Sam pulled Rae into a hug. He couldn't hear their whispered conversation, but he saw the strength of that embrace.

Seemed Rae was saying goodbye.

Samantha met his eyes, shook her head, and returned the way she'd come.

Rae approached his desk. She carried a manila envelope in her right hand. Her keys stuck out from her jeans' pocket. "Hey."

He pointed to his chair. "Want to sit?"

She looked around the room. "Can we go someplace private?"

"Sure. Follow me." He led her to a small room beside the chief's office, which served as everything from the interrogation room to the break room. "The baby's with Caro?"

She nodded and sat on the far side of the long laminate table.

He closed the door, sat beside her.

She wiped the tears dripping from her eyes. Her fingers were trembling.

"What happened?"

"I need you to do me a..." She twisted her hands together and lowered her gaze. Her shoulders shook a moment before she looked at him again. The tears were dripping off her chin now.

He snatched a stack of McDonald's napkins from the table that held the coffee maker and handed her one.

"Thanks." She wiped her eyes, sniffed, and squared her shoulders. "I have a plan."

"I know. You're going to—"

"Just listen, okay?"

He nodded once, and she continued.

"It doesn't matter if Julien or his father is behind these bombings. Either way, I have no reason to believe they'll stop. He'll kill innocent people until he finds me. I can't let that happen."

"You're ready to go to the FBI?"

"I don't have enough evidence."

"Why don't you let me look at it. It's worth—"

"The risks are too great."

"There's always witness protection."

She shook her head. "Maybe it would work. Maybe it wouldn't. But I won't raise my son to live in fear of his father. And what happens while the feds build a case? Julien keeps blowing up buildings, killing people to find me?"

Brady had no answer for that. "So what's your plan?"

She traced her finger around the edges of the envelope she'd set on her lap. "Will you...?" She met his eyes and swallowed. "Will you take Johnny for me?"

"Yes." He nearly strained his neck nodding. "That's a great

idea. We'll split up, throw Moreau off. Just tell me where to meet you."

He ignored her shaking head. This was the perfect plan.

"Rio's a huge city," he said. "We can find a place there. Isn't there some famous church or something? We could meet. Maybe two weeks. Both take different routes—"

"Brady—"

"Then we'll disappear. Rae, we could do this."

She covered her face and sobbed. It was a moment before he heard her whisper, "I wish we could."

"We can—"

"And let him keep killing people?"

There was that.

Her eyes were so sad. "We couldn't live with ourselves."

"We have to bring him down. We have to—"

"Please let me talk."

He crossed his arms. Ignored the stupid prickling in his eyes.

"I need you to raise Johnny for me. I need you to change his name. Adopt him. I don't know how it'll work legally. He'll have to be like...like an abandoned kid." Her words faltered. She sniffed and continued. "Promise me you'll never let him end up in foster care."

Brady couldn't keep up. Take her son? "What are you talking about?"

"You're so good with him. You'll be a great father."

He fell against the back of his chair. "Father," he whispered. He looked at the table and let her words sink in. She wanted him to be Johnny's father. He'd imagined that, God help him. How many times since he'd seen the baby had he wished Johnny were his? How many times had he imagined the two of them playing ball or wrestling. He'd pictured teaching the boy to hunt and fish. Holding him and feeding him and raising him.

Trouble was, in those fantasies, Rae'd always been in the picture.

He looked up. "You're going to run alone? Just leave your son and take off? You think that'll work? You're the one who just said Julien wouldn't quit killing people until he found you. He'll figure out who Nate is, and once he makes the connection—"

"He's not going to have to find me, Brady. I'm going back."

FIFTY-SIX

Farah drove past the house slowly, and Julien surveyed the property. No cars in the driveway. Looked older. It stood fifty meters from the street, further from the neighboring homes. Two-story, white, with a nice porch on the front. A barn stood to its side. The property was ringed in tall trees whose leaves were just beginning to change.

Farah continued down the street, past the next house and around a bend.

"Stop here."

She pulled over, and he stepped out. It was a lovely day. Blue skies, mild air. Birds high in the pines chirped a melody. He pulled in the scent of fallen leaves and moist soil and flashed back to Hector's body in the woods the night before.

Served him right.

Julien's shoulder throbbed, but the pain seemed to have lessened. He pulled his gun from his pocket and opened Farah's door, ignoring the fresh jab of pain.

She stepped out and stretched.

"Open the trunk," he said.

She did so.

"You have Hector's gun?"

"Yes." She pulled the pistol from her pocket.

"Point it at Boyle. If he tries anything, shoot him."

She nodded, confident with the pistol. Before these last two days, he'd never seen her hold one before. She seemed to have experience she'd left off her resume. Interesting.

They circled the car and opened the back door. Julien pointed the gun at Boyle. "Get out."

"Is this where you kill me?" Boyle stepped out, wincing with every move.

Julien looked around, then up at the canopy of maples. "A nice place for a grave, I think, but I still might need you alive." He nodded to the trunk. "Get in."

Boyle sighed. "I think I'd rather you killed me."

"Don't tempt me."

Boyle climbed in, and Julien slammed the trunk closed.

They climbed back in the car. Farah drove nearer to the house and parked about a hundred meters from the driveway.

"Stay here."

He walked, his shoulder throbbing with every step, into the woods, then picked his way over the tree roots and bracken parallel to the road and out of sight until he reached Rae's house.

There was a car in the driveway now. It had been empty just a few minutes before. His wife?

Julien's pulse quickened, and he willed it to slow down. No need to push blood out of that wound any faster. He watched the house for signs of life, then noticed a man standing by the barn door.

Julien crept closer, right to the edge of the house's grassy front yard. He stopped behind a tree and watched.

The man looked over his shoulder, first the right, then the left, before he pulled a key ring from his pocket.

It wasn't a man at all, but a nervous teenage boy.

Julien pointed his gun at the ground and stepped into the clearing.

"Turn around."

The boy jumped about a foot, dropped the keys in the gravelly dirt, and spun. His eyes were wide, his jaw slack.

"Who are you?" the boy said.

"I'm the man with the gun. Who are you?"

The kid looked at Julien, then at the gun.

"I'm...I'm just...I thought, because I know the lady who lives here, right? And she, uh... She like asked me to like—"

"If you're going to be a criminal, you're going to have to learn to lie better than that."

The boy nodded, then shook his head and swallowed. "No. I just—"

"What is your name?"

"Trent."

"Are you alone, Trent?"

"Yes."

Julien walked slowly closer. "I know you told me the truth, because it didn't take you any time to think. See, that's the problem when you lie—the time it takes to create the story. And all the tells. You'd make a terrible poker player."

The kid nodded like he agreed.

"Are you supposed to be here?"

Trent closed his lips tight.

"I see." Julien stepped close enough to see the sheen of sweat on the kid's face. "Does anybody know you're here?"

He shook his head.

"Where are the people who live here?"

"Um...I don't know exactly, but somewhere by the lake."

"You know them?"

"Like, not really, but like, I've seen her, you know. And the kid."

Her. The kid.

Julien was so close.

"I see," he said slowly. "By her, you mean Ms. McAdams, right? Reagan McAdams?"

The kid nodded, and the relief Julien felt almost had him sitting down. The adrenaline from the hunt was seeping out, and he feared he might swoon like a fairy tale princess if he didn't lean on something. He stepped to the edge of the barn and fell against it, then took two long breaths.

It all led here.

"You're hurt," the kid said.

"Are you a doctor?"

"No."

"If you tell me where Rae and the baby are, I won't call the police. I won't tell them I caught you trying to break into her house. Deal?"

The kid was nodding before Julien finished speaking. But then he stopped. "Who are you?"

"I'm her husband."

"Oh. That's okay then. But I don't know exactly where they are."

Julien worked to stay upright. "I think you'd better find out, then, hadn't you?" He waved the gun in the boy's direction. "And do it quickly. And I'm trying to surprise her, so don't tell."

Trent nodded again, then reached in his pocket.

Julien lifted the gun. "What are you doing?"

"Getting my phone," Trent said. "So I can call."

The kid retrieved his phone and dialed. For all Julien knew, Trent was calling the cops.

The kid spoke into the mouthpiece. "Where are you?"

He waited, then said, "I wanted to talk to you. I wanna tell you what's been going on. Finn's gonna tell you anyway, and..."

Trent paused, watching Julien and the gun. Finally he said, "I'll be there for like two seconds. I won't even come inside. You won't get in trouble, okay? I promise."

Thirty seconds later, he hung up. "She's gonna text me the address."

"Who is 'she'?"

"My friend, the kid's babysitter."

FIFTY-SEVEN

Going back to him.

The words, their terrible meaning, filled his mind. Brady pushed back from the conference table and stood, nearly toppling the chair in the process.

"You're going back?"

"I have no choice."

"He'll kill you. He'll... You think he's just going to let me keep his son? He'll come after Johnny. Have you lost your mind?"

Rae fought with the metal clasp of the manila envelope, her shaking fingers finally managing to get it open. She slid out a piece of paper and held it out to him.

He didn't want to take it. Because she was way ahead of him, and he wouldn't be able to catch up in time to stop her.

The paper hung between them.

Her gaze held his. "Please?"

He took the paper and read.

Certificate of Death.

Beneath those fancy-scrolled words, he saw the name

printed. *Jean-Louis Moreau*. And the date of death. Yesterday's date.

This is what Samantha'd been doing all morning, helping Rae fake her son's death—and plan her own.

The rest of the certificate blurred. He turned toward the wall and lifted his gaze to the ceiling. He needed to think. To focus.

He tried to formulate a good argument. This was a terrible idea. It wouldn't work. There had to be a flaw, but he only found one. Because if Rae went through with this, chances were good Johnny would be safe. But Rae...

He turned to face her. "What about you?"

"I'll be with him again. His..." She faltered and cleared her throat. "I'll gather more evidence. Enough to put him away. Maybe enough to bring down his father. The whole organization."

"You could do that, Rae? Live with him? Sleep with him? Be the killer's mistress?"

"What choice do I have?"

"If you go back, you won't have any choices, because he'll kill you."

She shrugged. "Maybe. I know it's hard to believe, but I think he loved me."

His face must've registered his opinion, because her eyebrows lifted. "That's so unimaginable?"

"That someone could fall in love with you, Rae? No. I did that fifteen years ago, and I haven't gotten over it yet."

She blinked. Fresh tears filled her eyes.

"But this monster? This man who lied to you about his wife, about his business, about his family? This man who kills innocent people? Is he capable of love?"

"In his way, I think."

"And when he doesn't get *his way*? Then what? When you

tell him that after you stole his son and ran away, his baby got sick and died... Will that monster forgive you?"

She reached out and took the certificate out of his hand. She slid it back into the envelope with trembling fingers. "As long as Johnny's safe, it doesn't matter."

"It matters to Johnny. It matters to me."

She closed the metal clasp and rested the envelope on her lap. "You'll manage."

He stared at her, at those red-rimmed eyes. Her hair, nearly her natural color, her skin paler than usual, the few freckles over the bridge of her nose more pronounced. Her lower lip trembled, giving away her fear. And determination.

He knelt beside her chair and took her hands. "All those years you were gone, I never stopped thinking about you. There were other women. I got married. And I loved her. I loved a lot of them, to a degree. I decided to love them. I wanted to love them. But all those years, no matter how much effort I put into it, no matter how many women I met, I could never stop loving you. I think it's the reason I spent so much time with your grandmother. To be near someone who was near you. Knowing you were alive and well, it's kept me going. Even though you weren't here." He lifted her hands, kissed her fingers. "I can't imagine a world without you in it."

She gently tugged one hand away and trailed a finger beside his eye, along his jawline. She leaned forward slightly, and he closed the distance between them. This kiss wasn't filled with passion but sadness. She tasted of tears.

When he felt her pulling away, it took all his strength to let her.

He rested his forehead against hers. Her breath warmed his cheek.

"I love you, Brady."

He couldn't stop these tears, and he couldn't force himself to turn away to hide them.

Her cell phone rang.

"Don't answer," he said.

"It could be Caro." She pushed the chair back, stood, and pulled the phone from her back pocket. "Hello?"

Her eyes widened. "Julien."

FIFTY-EIGHT

"It's lovely to hear your voice, *ma cheri*."

Rae scanned the dingy conference room of the police department. Julien's voice didn't belong here. Julien and his French accent dripping with charm and lies belonged far away, in Paris or Tunis, not here. Not in her safe place. "What have you done?"

"Your babysitter is here, and she's safe for now. You need to come home."

"You're at the cabin?"

"Your house. It's quite charming."

"How did you find me?"

"I don't think Boyle ever would have told us where you were. It was so thoughtful of you to call him."

Come home, she'd said. She'd given herself away.

She squeezed her eyes closed, an image of Nate flitting through her mind. He'd been a loyal friend to her for a decade. And she'd probably gotten him killed.

"Hurry home," Julien said. "And I'd prefer you come alone."

"I'm coming. Just don't... Please don't hurt anybody."

A moment of silence passed. "I'll be waiting."

The line went dead.

FIFTY-NINE

BRADY WATCHED as Rae's face lost what little color it had left. She stumbled toward the door of the police station conference room.

Brady grabbed her elbow. "What happened?"

"I have to go."

"Rae, what happened?"

"Get out of my way!"

Brady gripped Rae's upper arms, trying not to hurt her as she struggled to free herself.

"You have to listen to me," he said.

Her eyes were wild. "You don't understand." Her voice rose in pitch and volume. "Julien's there."

He held her tight. "Don't panic."

"He's got Johnny. I have to go."

Brady shook her gently and tried again. "Listen to me. We have to think."

"There's nothing to think—"

"Reagan, listen to me."

She blinked. Sheer terror in her eyes.

"I love Johnny too." His admission silenced Reagan if only

for a moment. It threw him off-balance. He'd already lost one son. There was no way he was going to lose another. "I'm going to do everything I can to protect him."

"But—"

"You can't fight Moreau. You told me that yourself."

"He has my son."

"You told me he wouldn't hurt him."

"But Caro—what about her?"

Caro was a problem. Not that it changed anything. "How will surrendering yourself to Julien help Caro? Why wouldn't he just kill her as soon as he has what he wants?"

She started to protest, but Brady continued. "Johnny needs you alive, Rae. He needs his mother alive and thinking clearly."

"But what if Julien takes off? What if he leaves with Johnny, and I never see him again?"

"We'll get officers there to watch the cabin. They won't let him leave. What did he tell you?"

"He told me to come to him. He's at my house. Not at the cabin."

"Okay." He opened the door. "Eric, get in here."

Rae continued. "Julien might not kill them, but he can hurt them." Her shoulders slumped, and Brady pulled her into his arms. Her weeping broke his heart, but he needed to focus.

He stepped back. "Sit down."

She opened her mouth to speak, but he shook his head and pointed at the chair. "Trust me."

Eric stepped into the room.

If Julien had Johnny and Caro, that meant he'd somehow gotten past the police officer Brady had stationed at her cabin. "Get Donny on the line."

"He was supposed to check in a few minutes ago. I've been trying, but I can't reach him."

Brady swore, imagining his young officer hurt—or worse.

"Get someone out there to check on him, and send two radio cars to the McAdams place immediately. I want one in the front, one in the neighborhood behind. We have a hostage situation."

Eric's jaw dropped. "A hostage—"

"Call the chief and tell him, but ask him to keep it quiet. I need to think this through."

Eric ran back to his desk and grabbed his phone, and Brady turned to Rae. The look in her eyes held such despair that he nearly looked away. "You with me?"

"What are we going to do? We have to get him back." Her gaze found the manila envelope. "Julien knows now. My plan—"

"Listen to me."

She looked at him and sniffed.

"The evidence. Where is it?"

"In the safe deposit box."

"Good. Moreau needs that evidence. It might not be enough to put him away, but I bet it'd be a good start."

That seemed to register. "True."

"So he can't leave with Johnny, and he can't kill you, not until he gets it."

"But what about Caro?"

His hostage. Leverage. "He has no reason to hurt her."

"He has no reason not to."

"Is he a monster, or isn't he?"

Rae shook her head. "I have no idea."

Eric stepped in the room. "I'd already sent Sanders to the cabin. He just called. Donny's unconscious, but he's alive. Looks like he took a blow to the head."

"Ambulance on the way?"

"Yes. Collins and Murphy are headed toward the McAdams house."

"Let me know when they're on the scene."

Eric nodded. "One more thing. Gordon Boyle's here and insists on speaking with you." Eric stepped aside, and Gordon Boyle stepped into the doorway. His wife, Ellen, and their son, Finn, stood behind him.

"Gordon, I'm sorry, but we've got a situation here."

"It's about Nate. He said he was flying to Manchester, but he didn't get off the flight."

Rae stood. "It's my fault." She focused on Brady. "Julien has Nate. He told me."

Gordon looked at Rae. "What does this have to do with you?"

Rae explained the situation through her tears.

Gordon and Ellen sat heavily in the chairs while she related her story. Finn paced between the coffee maker and the window.

"After I called Nate," Rae continued, "I realized Julien could track me down through him."

Brady turned to Gordon. "It looks like her husband and his thugs grabbed him."

"This Moreau," Gordon said. "What do you know about him?"

"He's a terrorist," Brady said.

Gordon went from pale to ashen. He wrapped his arm around Ellen. She was dry-eyed, shocked. Gordon reached past Ellen and tried to grab Finn as he passed by, but the boy angled out of his grasp.

"So you're saying he's here, her terrorist husband?" Finn pointed at Rae, then looked at Brady. "If you know he's here, why don't you go get him?"

Brady met Rae's eyes and shook his head to tell her to keep quiet, but she obviously didn't get his message.

"He's at my house with the baby and—"

"Caro." Finn's jaw dropped. "She was babysitting. I took her to the cabin. He found it. How did he...?" He looked at Rae. "So you put both my brother and my girlfriend in danger?"

"I'm going back." Rae stood, sniffed, and wiped her eyes on a napkin. "If I surrender, he'll let Caro go."

Brady waited until he could speak calmly. "Absolutely not."

Rae grabbed her bag and hefted it over her shoulder before she turned back to Brady. "I can't be responsible for any more deaths. Don't you understand? If I die... Well, that's what happens when you marry a killer. But Caro? Johnny? Nate?"

"It's out of your hands."

Eric stepped inside. "The chief's on his way. He called the state. And I called in the rest of the guys."

"Good." Brady turned to Rae. "Sit down. You're not going anywhere. You need to let us handle this."

"But—"

"Rae, you have to trust me." His gaze held hers until she nodded once and sat. He looked at the Boyles, at Finn, who seemed to be trying to light a fire on the carpet with his pacing, then at Rae. "We're going to formulate a plan. You guys hang tight, and we'll—"

"Are you going to try to get into her house?" Finn stopped pacing.

"All those windows," Brady said. "I don't know how—"

"I do." Finn walked around the table and stopped in front of Brady.

Things were clicking in place. "Want to explain that, son?"

Finn sighed and turned to Rae. "I was going to tell you everything, anyway." He stopped, swallowed, and turned back to Brady. "Me and... No. I'm the one who's been breaking into the house."

"Oh, Finn, you didn't," Gordon said.

Brady looked at the older man. "Please let him talk."

Gordon nodded and tightened his grip on his wife.

"Go on, son," Brady said.

"I overheard Dad telling Mom that Miss McAdams's father"—he glanced at Rae—"hid a bunch of gold in the house a long time ago, and he didn't know what happened to it. I've been looking for it." He looked at Rae. "I'm sorry I scared you last week. I just…"

"There was somebody else with you that night," she said.

He shrugged and turned back to Brady. "I can tell you how to get in the house."

SIXTY

Rae never thought she'd be thankful for prowlers. But as Finn took his seat at the far end of the table, a tiny flutter of hope rose. Maybe she could still rescue her son from his father. Maybe.

Brady took the seat beside him. "You know how to get in the house?"

"It's sort of a long story. See, years ago—"

"We don't have time for the whole story," Brady said. "If you cooperate, that'll help when you go in front of a judge."

Finn swallowed hard. Seemed to be processing those words, *a judge*.

"How do we get into the house?" Brady asked.

"There's a passage. It leads from the barn to the pantry."

"The pantry?" Rae shook her head. "There's no passageway in the pantry."

Finn turned to her. "The shelves at the back. They're hinged. There's a latch under the bottom shelf, a little slide-thingie you can access from either side. You slide it back, then you just pull, and the door opens into the passageway."

Rae said, "It's crazy, though. What about the basement..."

Her words trailed off as she thought of it. The pantry had been added onto the house. It stuck out on that side, so there would be no basement beneath it. "I can't believe this. All these years..."

"Where's the opening?"

Finn looked back at Brady. "The floor in the barn. Under that old rug."

The ruined rug. "But how did you get into the barn?" Rae asked.

He pulled out his keys, sifted through them until he found the one he was looking for. He showed it to her.

"Where did you get this?" Rae asked.

His face turned red. "Your grandmother kept the key to the barn in that junk drawer. I went over there sometimes to help her move stuff, so I knew where it was."

Brady shook his head. "But how did you find the passage without Dorothy seeing you?"

"Thursday nights. She never missed a cribbage game."

Gordon shook his head. "Son, I can't believe..."

"Good," Brady said. "Give me that."

Finn slid it off his key ring with shaking hands. He handed it over.

"How long is the tunnel?"

"Maybe twenty-five feet."

Rae pictured the space. The rug was on the side of the barn nearest the house. The pantry was on that outside wall in the kitchen. It wouldn't be very far.

Brady asked, "Can we stand and walk through it, or—?"

"Yeah," Finn said. "We figured it'd be a crawl space or something, but no. It's as tall as me. You might have to bend, but—"

"Wide enough for one person, or more than one?"

"Barely one."

Brady looked past the kid, seemed to be considering that.

He looked at Finn again. "So how long would you figure from the time we get to the barn until we get into the house?"

"Uh..." Finn glanced at his dad, then back at Brady. "Maybe two minutes?"

"Anything else you think I should know?"

"The hinge creaks. We greased it awhile ago, but I noticed a little creak coming back."

Rae imagined those boys breaking into her house, greasing that hinge so it wouldn't make any noise. Very industrious. Imagine if they used those powers for good.

Actually, right now, Finn was.

Brady nodded. "You might have just saved the day." He met Gordon's eyes, then Rae's. "Stay here. I'm going to figure out what to do next."

Gordon said, "You'll find Nate?"

"We won't know anything until we question Moreau. We'll do whatever we can."

Gordon nodded while Brady left the room, closing the door behind him.

Rae stood to follow him.

"Miss McAdams," Finn said. "I'm sorry. I shouldn't have... I didn't think Gram knew about the gold, and you never came home."

"Thank you for being honest."

"I'm sorry I scared you the other night."

That prank seemed pretty unimportant in light of the current situation. Still..."The next time I went in the barn, the rug was right where it was supposed to be. Did you go back?"

He turned red all over again. "Early the next morning. I put everything back the way it was supposed to be, so you wouldn't know. I'd been trying to tell..." He glanced at his dad. "I'd decided not to go back again."

"But your friend didn't want to give up the hunt."

He stared at her a minute, then at the table. As if it mattered.

"Did you tell Julien how to find the cabin?"

"No! I would never..." Finn swallowed again.

"Your friend then? Did he drive to the cabin with you two?"

"He was with us when you called Caro."

One more possible hostage. Just what they needed.

She was itching to find out what was going on. She needed to tell Brady about the other possible hostage, not that she'd interrupt their planning to do that. She forced herself to stay seated.

"So." She looked at Finn. "Did you find it?"

Finn's head snapped up. He met her eyes, shook his head. "I swear, we didn't take anything."

"It's not in the passageway?"

"As far as we can tell, it's not anywhere."

All of this for a handful of gold coins. Coins that were probably gone for good.

Gordon lifted his head, glanced at Rae, at Finn, then around the room. His eyes were red-rimmed and brimming with fear. Both his son and hers were in danger. And on both counts, it was her fault.

Ellen held her husband's hand. Her eyes were closed, probably praying. Ellen and Gordon had been going to church with Gram for years. Gram would be praying, if she were here.

If only Gram were here.

A sob formed deep in Rae's chest. She couldn't just sit there. She stood and rushed out of the room before any of them could stop her.

She halted right outside the door. At least ten people filled the squad room. Two women, the rest men. All fit and ready. Some wore uniforms, others plain clothes. Two wore different kinds of uniforms. State police, probably, but she couldn't tell from the back.

They were all looking at a white board. Brady stood beside it, taller than everyone else, marker in hand. He'd drawn an outline of her property. On the edge of the white board, he'd drawn a very rough layout of the main floor of her house.

"So the entrance to the tunnel is here," he said, tapping the board.

"We can't just storm the house, though," a man said.

"I know," Brady said. "First, we're going to try to talk him out. If that doesn't work, we use that as a distraction to get into place."

"How much time will we need?" one cop asked.

"Five minutes, at least," Brady said. "Time to get into the barn, open the trap door, and make it through the tunnel."

"You think this'll work?" A curly-haired, uniformed guy asked.

Brady leveled his gaze across the crowd. "We're not going to do anything we don't believe will work. We'll call the house, try to talk him out. He'll be watching the windows. The front windows are out of the line of sight of the kitchen, so we should be able to get in."

"But how do we get others in place? We are assuming he's armed, right? And how do we know there isn't someone in the kitchen who'll hear us. How do we—?"

"All good questions," Brady said. "Truth is—"

"I can do it." Rae stepped forward as the crowd turned in her direction. "I'll go. I'll talk to him. I'll get him away from the kitchen, somehow."

Brady glared at her over the sea of faces. "No."

"It's the best chance," Rae said. "You said yourself he can't hurt me until he gets the evidence I took."

"Assuming he's rational, assuming he's thinking ahead. But

people don't always behave rationally. Especially when they're surrounded by the police and staring down a lifetime in prison. We can't count on him to keep his head."

"You're right," Rae said. "So even though I believe, on a normal day, he would never hurt his son, he could. Or Caro. Which is why I have to do this."

"Forget it."

The cops turned back to Brady.

"I'm open to suggestions. Maybe we have a presence in front, someplace for him to focus..."

The police officers continued. Their plan was decent, but not foolproof. And though she didn't have a foolproof plan, either, there was no way she was going to sit here while those guys put Johnny and Caro, maybe Nate and the other teen—not to mention themselves—in danger.

She patted her jeans' pocket, felt her keys, and slipped out the door that linked the police department and the town offices. The space was empty and dark.

Two minutes later, she was on her way to the house. She would rescue Caro and her son from Julien, or she would die trying.

SIXTY-ONE

Rae pulled over in front of the closest neighbor's house, a good fifty yards down the road. Two cops were sitting in two cruisers, blocking the drive. That was a problem, but one she could solve.

She was going to have to get past them. And maybe there was some elegant way to do it. Brady'd probably swing through the trees or belly crawl through the woods. Forget elegance. She needed speed.

She closed her eyes and pictured the front yard. Yes, it could work.

But first she needed to figure out what in the world she was doing. She could get inside, and maybe she could reason with Julien. But if Hector were in there? There was no reasoning with him. What would he do to her?

She shuddered, then forced the thought away. Julien had always held Hector on a short leash. He wouldn't let the man hurt their son, and if Rae got hurt? Too bad. She only cared that Johnny and Caro were safe. And Nate. She squeezed her eyes shut and thought of all Nate must have endured. If only...

No time for regrets.

All Rae needed to do was to get inside and then find a way to tell Caro to get into the kitchen with the baby. The only door to the outside that was in the kitchen was visible from the living room, and the only window was over the sink. Not an easy place to escape, so why would they worry if she sent Caro in there? If Rae could get Caro and the baby through the passageway, Brady would take it from there. Maybe Nate could escape too. And then whatever happened to her wouldn't matter.

If she couldn't do that, maybe she could make sure Julien and Hector were in the living room. Then the police could get inside.

And then what? Would there be shooting? Would Julien be killed? Would a stray bullet kill Caro or Nate? Or Johnny?

No. She wouldn't let that happen. And maybe, just maybe, she could reason with Julien, get him to surrender. Because, regardless of all he'd done to her, all the lies and deception, he was still the father of her child. She didn't want to be the cause of his death. She didn't love him, probably never had, not like she loved Brady. But he'd given her the greatest gift she could have imagined. She didn't wish him dead.

Rae thought about Brady, imagined what he'd do if he knew where she was right now. He wouldn't let her do this, no way. But not because it wasn't a good idea. The problem with Brady was that he wanted to protect her as much as he wanted to protect her son, Caro, and Nate. Whereas Rae only cared about the others. She couldn't think about Brady. If she did, she might never get the courage to go through with this.

Rae took a deep breath, blew it out, and pressed down on the accelerator. Not too fast—she didn't want to alert the cop. She smiled at him as she passed, then hit the gas and squealed into a turn. She raced into the yard and bumped down into a slight depression. For one horrible second, the wheels spun in the moist dirt before they made purchase. The car lurched forward across the grassy space. She slammed on the brake, jammed the car into park inches from the porch, and bolted out.

She was halfway up the porch steps when one of the cops screamed, "Stop!"

She ran to the front door and let herself in.

SIXTY-TWO

Brady stared at the white board and tried to figure out what could go wrong. Any number of things, of course, and he couldn't account for all of them. Moreau could start firing as soon as they pulled up. He could kill Nate, kill Caro, kill his child, kill himself. He could light the place on fire. A million things could happen. But despite what he'd told Rae, in Brady's experience even criminals behaved rationally, and Julien Moreau wasn't some two-bit home invader. He was educated, sophisticated, and clever. He might've made a mistake by showing up at Rae's house, but from what Brady could surmise, the man wasn't suicidal. And if Rae were to be believed, he wasn't homicidal, either, not unless there was a payday in it for him.

The plan should work.

He turned back to the crowd around him and met Will Jamison's eyes. He'd expected the chief to take command, but when Brady'd tried to hand over the floor and the white board marker, the chief had shaken his head. "This is your party."

Next time Brady had a party, he wanted balloons, not firearms.

The chief nodded. "It's a good plan."

As the officers prepared to leave for the McAdams house, Brady checked the back of the room for Rae. Seemed she'd gotten bored, or frustrated more likely, and returned to the conference room. He stepped inside to find the Boyles seated at the table. "Where's Rae?"

Gordon frowned. "She left. I assumed..."

He wheeled around. Even as he let his gaze roam the room, scanning the police officers as they checked their weapons, he knew what she'd done.

He should've handcuffed her to the chair.

"Eric!"

The officer turned around, eyes wide. "What is it?"

"Get Sanders on the line." He yelled over the murmuring of the officers' voices. "Tell him Rae's on her way there, and he absolutely cannot let her into that house."

Before he'd finished speaking, Eric was calling.

Brady grabbed his gun from his desk drawer and yanked his keys from his pocket. He was halfway to the door when Eric grabbed his arm.

He knew from the expression on Eric's face. It was too late. Rae was inside.

"I'm sorry," Eric said. "We didn't notice."

"Not your fault." He kept moving for the door.

"We're not in place," Eric said. "You need to wait."

Brady yanked his arm away. "She's inside with that madman. I have to go."

Eric stepped in front of him. "The plan you just came up with, it's a good one. Now we have one more hostage. I think the plan remains the same. It'll be easier now, with Rae inside."

Brady opened his mouth, then snapped it shut. The thought of what Rae had walked into...what Julien and Hector might do to her.

But Eric was right. Brady nodded and turned around. Seemed everybody was ready. Their eyes focused on him.

He forced a deep breath. "Slight change of plans," he said. "There's another hostage. Reagan McAdams went in on her own."

SIXTY-THREE

Rae closed the front door behind her, turned, and leaned her forehead against it. What was she doing?

"I knew you'd come."

At her husband's familiar voice, she pulled in a deep breath and turned. Julien stood just a few feet away, their child snuggled on his shoulder. The sight of Johnny brought tears to her eyes.

Julien's eyebrows lifted infinitesimally. "Surely you knew I wouldn't hurt our son."

She nodded. "You would never hurt him."

"And yet."

She swallowed. The tears dripped down her cheeks, but she couldn't make her hands move to wipe them away. "And yet."

He sighed. "I'd invite you in, *ma cheri*, but alas, it is your home." He turned and walked into the kitchen.

Why the kitchen?

She followed, peeking into the living room along the way, searching for Caro or Nate.

Oh, Nate. What had Julien done to him?

Julien sat at the table in what was usually Brady's chair. Back to the wall.

Right next to the pantry door.

"I'm sure you have a few questions for me," he said. "I have a few questions for you as well."

She slid into the chair across from him. "Where is Caro?"

"Charming girl, but quite young to watch our child, don't you think?" He kept his voice quiet, his tone conversational. "I'd have thought you'd be more careful."

"Jean-Louis was asleep, and I only planned to be gone a little while."

"As you can see, plans change."

Indeed.

"And your grandmother? I was certain I'd meet her today."

Tears prickled, as if she had time for grief right now. "Gram passed away the day Jean-Louis was born."

His expression softened, filled suddenly with the compassion she remembered too well. "I'm sorry."

She shrugged.

"So you came for her funeral?"

Not exactly, but why bother to explain. "Something like that."

Johnny shifted slightly. His mouth opened, then closed again, and he settled into his father's arms.

"He is ill, no?" Julien said. "He feels as if he has a fever."

She nodded. "A respiratory virus. I took him to the doctor. He's on the mend."

"'On the mend,'" he repeated. "Such a funny phrase. It means he's getting better?" She nodded, and he continued. "I see. Do you think he picked it up when you were fleeing from me?"

She considered denying it, then shrugged. "Probably."

"You've taken a lot of risks with our son."

"I think the biggest risk I took was to marry a murderer."

His lips flattened. "I am a businessman."

"And my friend, Margot, you had nothing to do with that? Or maybe that wasn't her body I identified in the morgue that day. Because it sure looked liked her."

That steely look remained. "I didn't kill your friend."

"You sold the explosives—"

"Yes, yes," he said, his voice nearly a whisper. "Let's not wake the baby. He was quite frantic earlier. It took me some time to get him to sleep."

She wasn't surprised. Johnny had rarely liked being held by his father. Funny how quickly the baby had taken to Brady, though. Maybe her son already had better instincts than she.

Rae took a deep breath and lowered her voice. "You might as well have killed her."

"In this country, people can buy handguns on every corner. Do you blame the people who sell those guns for all the violence?"

"It's not the same, and you know it. Legitimate businessmen here don't sell explosives to terrorists, but you—"

"The people I sold those explosives to might not have had the best intentions. I don't ask them what they're going to do with the merchandise I sell. I still didn't kill your friend. Terrorists did that."

"Children, Julien. Those terrorists, they were teenagers. Stupid, young, ignorant—"

"They had the money."

"You have no shame."

"A trifle I cannot afford in my line of work."

Her temper boiled over. "That's it?" She wanted to scream at him, to beat him. She glanced at her son and lowered her voice. "What kind of man—?"

"I am not like you." His jaw was set, his teeth gritted shut. She'd seen this Julien, just a time or two, and he'd frightened her then. He terrified her now. "I'm not *good*. I've never been good. I come from killers. I was raised to take over a business that transports illegal drugs, gets people addicted. A business that steals young girls and sells them for profit. I refused to do those things." He swallowed and looked at Johnny. A moment later, he looked back up. "Yes, I sell arms. And yes, maybe some of my clients wouldn't pass an American background check. But it could be worse. I could be worse."

She shook her head. "You're unbelievable."

His face paled slightly, and she noticed the dark circles beneath his eyes, the yellow pallor to his skin. Searching for them had taken a lot out of him.

He blew out a breath. "I took the money I made from deals like the one that led to your friend's death, and I invested it. My father created a corporation to launder money, but I built it into something bigger. Something real. My company brings jobs to people who might otherwise starve. My business is good for the community. It's good for Africa."

"You think it's good for Africa to have buildings explode in downtown Cairo? In Tunis, your own home?"

His gaze turned to their son. He held the boy closer. "That wouldn't have happened if you hadn't run."

"Because killing innocent people is the logical reaction when your wife leaves you."

"Those people weren't important to you. I knew the owner of the cafe. Did you know that? That his son was killed, all because you decided to run away, run around New Hampshire doing God knows what while you leave my child with a mere child."

She turned and looked around again, as if the answer might

be right behind her. She turned back to Julien. "Where is Caro?"

He sighed. "You have so little regard for me. Do you think I would hurt that girl?"

"I don't know you."

"And I know you, Rachel Adams? Or is it Reagan McAdams? Or is this all a lie too?"

"That was..."

The house phone rang.

His eyebrows lifted. "I would like to hear the story, but it seems your friends want to talk to me. Are they about to burst in the door?"

It rang again. "I don't think they'd call first," she said, "if that were the plan."

Another ring. "And what is the plan?"

"I have no idea. I left before..." The phone rang again. "Where is Caro?"

He sighed, waited through another ring, and said, "She's upstairs. She's with a friend."

Rae imagined poor, sweet Caro stuck with Hector. Her fear must've shown on her face, because Julien said, "She's unharmed."

She wanted to ask about Nate, but her courage failed her. Julien was possessive, and any regard she might show for her ex-boyfriend could backfire. She'd figure out what happened to Nate after she got Johnny and Caro to safety.

The phone quit ringing. "Your promises mean a lot to me. Ever since we stood before your friends and took vows."

His mouth slid into that charming smile she'd fallen for. "Perhaps, we're not legally married."

"So you're a murderer and a liar."

The smile remained. "When I told you I loved you, that was

not a lie. I've never known a woman like you. I never felt for anybody what I felt for you."

"Lying to me? Is that how you showed me your love?"

"You lied to me too."

"That was different. I changed my name and my story long before I met you. If you'd just proposed and given me some time, I'd have told you the truth before the wedding. But then, just like that"—she snapped her fingers—"we were married."

"You could have said no."

If only she could live the moment again. Her life was one long string of if-onlys. "I should have."

"But you didn't."

She shrugged.

"Because you loved me."

She met his eyes. "I loved who I thought you were, Julien. I loved a fantasy."

"Did I love a fantasy, too, *Rachel*?"

She bristled at the name. "I am who I am. I didn't lie to you about that. About what mattered to me. About what I believed. And I planned to tell you about my past. I just could never—"

"Could never quite figure out the right time? And telling you I was an arms dealer, you think there was a *right time* for that?"

"What about telling me you were already married?"

He nodded, that stupid smile back in place. "Yes, yes. A good point."

"And you knew, you had to know, that if I found out you killed Margot, I'd hate you. You knew if I found out about your wife, I'd hate you. You knew how I felt. And still—"

"I fell in love with you."

"Right."

He shifted the baby and cringed, his face paling further as he settled into a new position.

"Are you all right?" The question popped out before she

could stop it.

"Do you care?"

She shrugged.

"Ah." He nodded slightly. "I think I'll take that as a yes."

"Take it however you want."

"So what's your story, Rachel? Or should I call you Reagan?"

"Rae works either way."

The phone rang. She said nothing, and neither did he. It rang five times before it stopped.

Julien tipped his head toward her, and she said, "Reagan Elizabeth McAdams. I was named after Ronald Reagan. My father was a big fan."

"Charming," he said. "Reagan McAdams. Your name is familiar, yes?"

Even he'd heard of her. He'd been in America in college when the scandal had broken, so perhaps it wasn't that big a shock. Still. "You've heard my name for the same reason I changed it." She told him about her father's death, her mother's madness, and her part in returning that kidnapped baby boy to his parents. "I knew they'd return the baby to his mother. I never thought they'd throw my mother in prison."

He chuckled darkly. "You turned in your own mother. You and I never had a chance."

"No relationship built on lies can last."

Julien stared beyond her for a moment, seemed to be reining in emotion. Finally his gaze flicked back to her. "So you changed your name because you were famous?"

"Infamous. College was a time for me to reinvent myself. I

no longer wanted to be known as the girl who'd rescued a congressman's kid and sent her mother to prison. I wanted to be invisible, not famous."

"I cannot imagine how difficult that must have been for you," he said. "To lose your father when you were so young, to have all that media attention. And then to lose your mother too. I wish you'd told me."

She didn't need his compassion right now. His words were just lies, anyway.

He stroked his son's cheek. "I hope he has your courage." He looked back at her and smiled. "I hope he has more courage than I did."

"What does that mean?"

He swallowed, and she saw a flicker of uncertainty in his features.

"Did I ever tell you I wanted to be an architect?"

An architect? "You always liked to look at buildings."

"Ever since I was a kid, I've loved buildings. Old ones, new ones. Big ones. Houses like this one. So many things flit away from generation to generation, but the architecture stands as a testament to the past. To be able to contribute to that..."

"So why didn't you?"

"Do you believe that when I was a small child playing with my blocks that I thought, I want to be an arms dealer when I grow up?"

"You could have walked away."

He shook his head. "I never had the courage to stand up to my father. If I had—"

"Would you have given it all up?"

"We can never know." He looked around and smiled. "This is where you grew up?" She nodded, and he continued. "Imagine if I could have stood up to my father. I wouldn't have married Martine."

"She was your father's idea?"

"Her father was a rival. A criminal, like Papa. They formed an alliance. He arranged my marriage to Martine. We'd known each other for many years, and she was beautiful, a little older. I was in awe of her when I was young. Even when I got to know her and grew out of that awe, I liked her. I thought, why not? I had never been in love, so I didn't know to wait for it. It wasn't as though she expected me to be faithful."

"Was she faithful to you?"

His eyes darkened. "Once, she was not. Her lover met with an unfortunate accident."

"So you are a killer."

He glared at her, and she swallowed.

"I didn't do it," he said. "I would never have. I didn't love her, and she didn't love me. When we discovered she wouldn't be able to have children—"

"That was so important?"

He glanced at Johnny. "My brother is attempting to usurp my position in the family. Between his wife and his mistresses, he has many sons. With nobody to take over after me and the fact that my brother will do anything for money, my position was tenuous."

"But now you have Johnny."

"I planned to legitimize more of the business when I took over."

She noted the past tense. What did that mean?

"Once Papa died, I planned to end our involvement in the drug trade and the sex trade and focus on my corporation. But my brother, he likes the lifestyle, the easy cash. He is like Papa—he has no morals."

"And you do?"

He ignored her. "Martine and I decided to give up the

charade and live separate lives. We were happy with the arrangement."

"Why not divorce?"

He leveled his gaze at her, and the look said more than the words. "One doesn't walk away from my family."

That's just what she'd tried to do. Failed to do, because here he was. Her heartbeat raced, and she forced herself to take a deep breath. She couldn't help but think about the man Martine had been with. And Brady's kiss. If anything happened to him, she'd never forgive herself. "You say you didn't hurt the man she was with, but somehow he ended up dead."

He nodded. "She has never forgiven me."

"But it wasn't you."

He blew out a breath, then looked out the window. She followed his gaze. The blinds were tilted up, so they could just make out the tops of the trees.

"New Hampshire is quite beautiful."

"Different from Africa."

"But lovely. You belong here. I'm sure you have family here. Friends? A community? You seemed so starved for that when I met you. Perhaps because you missed this one?"

Had she been so transparent that her desperation to belong showed to the world? Or did Julien just know her better than she'd realized? She started to tell him that no, she didn't have those things here, but then she thought of the week she'd spent here. Of Samantha and Gordon and Finn and the police that were rallying around her even now. She thought of Brady. Yes, she had people here. If only she'd known it sooner.

When she didn't answer, Julien continued. "I visited once, when I was at Harvard. Some friends and I rented a car and went skiing." He tilted his head to the side, then shook it. "Perhaps that was Vermont."

"Was it fun?"

He shrugged. "A little pathetic, compared with the Alps, but the town was charming. Like you. Down to earth. Homey. No pretense or sophistication."

"Gee, thanks."

He smiled his genuine smile. "I don't mean it that way. Just that you never tried to be what you weren't, despite your name change. You were always just...you." He tapped on the old kitchen table. "Like this place, you don't need to put on airs to be charming. You just are. You belong right here."

She looked around the kitchen with its sunny yellow walls and forever-old cabinetry, at the wood planks on the floor, well-worn in the high-traffic spots. She did belong here. Right here, in this house, in this town, in this state. And not with this man. She pictured Brady, knew he'd be coming soon. Her gaze was drawn to the pantry door beside Julien. If she could get him to move into the other room...

The phone rang again.

Julien sighed. "I suppose we should answer."

"Shall I?"

"Would you tell them I'd like a few more minutes with you?"

She grabbed the receiver of the wall-mounted phone. "It's Rae."

"This is Chief Jamison. Are you all right?"

"I'm fine. Johnny..." She looked at Julien, whose eyebrows rose. "I mean, Jean-Louis is fine. I haven't seen Caro, but Julien tells me she's fine too. She's upstairs with somebody. I don't know who."

"Somebody dangerous?"

"Probably."

"Is Julien listening in?"

"No. He's holding the baby."

"Okay. So the baby is his shield. That's good to know."

Rae looked at the man she'd loved for more than a year, the way he was holding their child. No, Julien wasn't using Johnny as a shield. He wouldn't hurt their son.

The chief said, "Are you in imminent danger?"

"I don't think so."

"The baby? Caro?"

"We're okay right now," she said, meeting Julien's eyes.

"Besides the girl and whoever she's with," the chief said, "is anybody else in the house?"

"I don't know."

"Where are you?"

"In the kitchen."

Julien's eyebrows rose. "Am I going to see one of those red laser dots on my chest, Rae?"

"Was that him?" the chief asked. "Can you put him on the phone?"

She said to Julien, "He wants to talk to you."

"Tell him I need ten more minutes."

She did, then hung up and sat down. "What happens in ten minutes?"

He shrugged. "It will all be over."

SIXTY-FOUR

BRADY SURVEYED the scene at Rae's house. Another month and the leaves would be off the trees. The three police cars, the ambulance, and the fire truck would have been visible through the forest. As it was, he'd had the fire truck parked a hundred yards down the road, just in case. But these woods were dense, and Rae's house was set off the road. He didn't think Moreau would be able to see them.

More police cars had been stationed in the neighborhood behind her house. Four cops had crept through the woods, past the big rock that had served as home base for a thousand games of tag. They'd taken up position in the back of the property to ensure Julien and his goons didn't escape that way.

By all reports, there was no activity in the house. Sanders had seen Rae go inside. No movement since.

The chief slid his phone into his pocket. "Rae answered."

"He let her answer?" Brady asked, looking toward the house again. What was Moreau thinking? "That's unusual."

"She's fine and said the baby is too. She didn't see the girl, but Moreau assured her Caro's unharmed, upstairs with somebody. She and Moreau are in the kitchen."

"Great. So there are at least two bad guys in there, and she and Moreau are sitting in the room we need." He glanced at the upstairs windows. Wished he had more information. "Did you talk to him?"

He shook his head. "He told Rae he needed ten minutes."

"For what?"

"No way to know."

There was no time to waste trying to figure it out. Brady turned to Eric. "Ready?"

"Let's do it."

Brady led the way through the woods to the side of the barn. Because the barn blocked the view of the west side of the house, unless one of Julien's men were outside, Brady and Eric wouldn't be seen. The toughest part would be getting in the door. They'd chosen the front because they felt it more likely that a bad guy might step out back. Julien had to know there were cops out front.

And to ensure nobody stepped outside, Brady signaled the chief when he and Eric were ready, and Chief Jamison drove a radio car into the driveway.

As soon as they saw the black-and-white, he and Eric bolted into the open space in front of the barn. While Eric watched the front door, gun drawn, Brady slid the key Finn had given him into the lock. They slipped inside.

Eric closed the door behind them, and Brady crossed to the rug Finn had mentioned. Beneath it they found the same wood planks that made up the rest of the floor. If he hadn't known there was a trapdoor there, he'd have missed it. There was a slightly larger gap in the floor around a misshapen, roughly three-foot by four-foot space.

Brady'd have to ask Finn how he and his friend had found it. Those boys might be good at police work one day, assuming they could keep from breaking into old ladies' houses.

Brady pulled a small pry bar from his jacket pocket and silently thanked Finn for the heads' up. He slid it between the planks and pressed down. The door lifted, and he and Eric quietly rested it on the floor to the side.

Brady grabbed his flashlight, clicked it on, and met Eric's eyes.

He nodded, and Brady climbed down the steps into the tunnel.

The air was moist and smelled like earth. The walls were hard-packed dirt, more like clay. Not the kind of soil common in this part of New Hampshire, so someone must've brought it in and packed this space. For what purpose he couldn't imagine. As far as he knew, New Hampshire had never been a hotbed for any sort of military engagement. Maybe during the Revolution, but this house wasn't that old.

He reached the bottom of the steps, crouched down, and headed toward the house while Eric descended the stairs behind him.

This tunnel was crazy. Why in the world...? On the other hand, in the cold, winter months when snow was measured by the foot instead of by the inch, a tunnel from the house to the barn would have been quite convenient. Maybe it was that simple. Somebody who wanted to feed the animals without having to step outside.

Well, whatever the purpose, this tunnel, God willing, could save the day. Brady looked up at the dirt ceiling. He wasn't much of a praying man, but he couldn't help but think, *thank you, God, for this*. Then he added, *please protect them. If You're there, we need You now*.

No answer, but he didn't need one. His answer would come when he held Rae and Johnny in his arms.

He reached the other end of the tunnel and shined his flashlight on the stairs. His foot hit the first step, and he froze.

He could hear a man's voice.

Brady crept up. The man's accent reminded him of Pepe Le Pew. Though Julien was more a snake than a skunk.

He shook off the thought and pulled the can of WD-40 from his jacket pocket. He found the hinges with the flashlight and waited. He could barely make out the words. He waited until it sounded like Moreau was on a roll, then he sprayed the hinges and hoped the sound wouldn't travel.

No change in the voice inside.

Now if only the hinges wouldn't squeak.

When Eric was standing behind him, Brady slid the latch and pulled on the door. It stuck at first, then gave way to reveal the darkened pantry. Had the door scraping across the linoleum floor alerted Moreau? Brady waited and listened. Nothing had changed, except now he could hear Rae's voice. They were obviously right there, in the kitchen, just like she'd said.

He turned and met Eric's eyes. Eric had a question there. Brady wished he had an answer. With Rae and Julien in the kitchen, there was nothing they could do but wait.

SIXTY-FIVE

The sound of a car pulling into the driveway had Rae and Julien peering toward the front of the house. Rae expected him to rise, to see what was going on, since they couldn't see the front door from where they sat. If she could get him out of the kitchen, maybe he'd stay out. But without knowing where Caro was, how could Rae escape, even if she could grab Johnny? Julien might take out his anger on the girl.

The point was moot, because Julien settled deeper in the chair.

"I'm sure whoever that is, they're here for you." He shifted the baby, reached into his jacket, and pulled out a pistol.

She gasped, and he set the pistol on the table.

She swallowed, tried to think of something to say. Tried to force her voice to work. All she could do was stare at the gun.

"It's almost over now," he said.

She tore her gaze from the gun to look at their child. His breathing was normal, deep and clear. No wheezing, no screaming. She willed him to stay asleep. Whatever happened, she didn't want her baby to witness it.

She wasn't going to think about that gun. Julien wouldn't

hurt their child, and as long as Caro, Johnny, and Brady were safe, she didn't care what happened to her.

That's what she told herself, but tears filled her eyes. She wasn't ready for it to end here.

Dear God, she thought, then stopped. What did they call that? A foxhole conversion? She'd always snickered at the idea, but it wasn't so funny now. If she'd paid more attention in church, she might know what to say. As it was, she couldn't think of anything but *help*.

Julien shifted, and when he did, he winced.

"Are you sick?" she asked, mostly to fill the silence. "Maybe you picked up something on the plane too."

He chuckled. "I definitely picked up something."

"Can I get you some ibuprofen? A glass of water?"

He glanced at the back windows, then at the kitchen cabinets. "How very gracious of you."

She stood and found the pills in the cabinet. While she was filling the water glass, she said, "We can go in the living room, if you like. You might be more comfortable."

"I'm comfortable here," he said, though he looked anything but.

She handed him the pills and held the water glass. The gun was just inches away. She considered reaching for it. If she could just grab it... What could she do, with Johnny in his arms? She could run, but not without her son. She could point it at Julien, force him to put the baby down. Yell for Brady. Was he right behind that pantry door? What could she do?

She could do something besides just stand there.

He cleared his throat. "Have you decided yet?"

She turned to him, and he smiled.

"Would you shoot me, Rae?"

"Aren't you going to shoot me?"

He frowned and looked away. "I would never have hurt you."

If you hadn't left.

She set the glass on the table in front of him and took her seat.

With his free hand, he popped the pills in his mouth, then swallowed them with a sip of water. He sipped more water before he set the glass back on the table.

He looked so weary, she feared he might drop the baby. "You want me to take Johnny?"

Anger flashed in his eyes. "You've stolen enough time from me, don't you think?"

She swallowed and nodded.

"And his name isn't Johnny. When did you come up with something so ridiculous?"

"I like it," she said. "And Jean-Louis doesn't fit in New Hampshire."

"So this was your plan, to stay here?"

"Not exactly."

"Of course not. You were too easy to find."

He was right, of course. She'd been foolish to come here, more foolish to stay as long as she had. She should have left on Sunday, the day after she discovered Gram had died, instead of searching for some nonexistent treasure. But if she had, she would never have realized all she'd left behind in her hometown. Her love for Brady and Samantha. The community she'd thought never cared for her. Perhaps it would have been better that way.

Of course, no matter where in the world she was, she could never have stayed hidden, not as long as Julien was willing to kill innocent people until he found her.

The question was, had he stopped killing people, or was she next on his list?

SIXTY-SIX

Pain pulsed in Julien's shoulder. His blood was seeping out, warming the baby's blanket. It took all his energy, all his acting skills, to remain still and placid. Yet he wasn't ready for it to be over.

Rae's gaze flicked from Jean-Louis to the gun and back. He'd never seen such fear in her eyes. This had been the plan, and yet he hated himself for putting the fear there. When she'd fled, she'd left him few choices. The journey she'd begun in Paris just eight days before had led right to this spot, and as he looked at the sunny yellow kitchen, he wondered if this had been their fate all along.

All he'd wanted was to take her home. And keep her forever. Was that so much to ask from his wife? And it didn't matter that they weren't legally married. She was his wife—he'd never thought of her as anything less.

How many had already lost their lives in his quest to bring her home? How many families had he destroyed?

And he wasn't finished.

Rae blinked away fresh tears. "Whatever happens, just promise me Jean-Louis will be safe."

At least she'd used their son's proper name. And the promise seemed the least he could do. "I think we've already established I would never hurt him."

"And Caro?"

"If all goes according to plan, the girl will remain unharmed."

"Trent. The boy. Is he here?"

"I sent him away. He thought I was here to surprise you."

"Some surprise." Her focus moved to Jean-Louis. "What are you going to do?"

"May I ask you a question?"

She nodded.

"Do you feel anything for me?"

Her gaze snapped back to him. She blinked twice.

"Anything good," he clarified.

"I loved you."

His eyebrows rose. "But no longer?"

"When I found out what you were... Why did you do it, Julien? Knowing I made a living out of exposing criminals and corruption, knowing how strongly I believe people like you need to be brought to justice. Why did you marry me?"

"As I have already explained, I fell in love with you."

She opened her mouth, then closed it. "But... Still. You had to know this wouldn't end well."

He should have known. Ever since the day he'd shot his dog, he should have known. The truth bubbled up, and like the blood still trickling from his bullet wound, there seemed no way to stop it. "I fell in love with you, Rae. You were...you are beautiful. Strong and good. You are everything I could never be."

She leaned a tiny bit toward him, and the small gesture gave him the courage to continue.

"I thought, if you could love me, too, then perhaps that meant I was worthy of it."

"But I didn't know you. You hid your real self from me."

"The night we married, when I held you in my arms, that was me."

Her cheeks filled with a beautiful rosy blush. Yes, she remembered.

"When we were alone, just the two of us... You knew my charm, and you loved me not because of it, but despite it. Or so I thought."

"I did, but when I found out the truth..."

He snapped his fingers. "So much for love."

"You weren't who I thought you were."

"It was the fantasy you loved. The businessman with the connections and the money and—"

"I don't care about money or connections. I do care about doing the right thing. I care about justice."

Justice. Is that what she thought this was? "I know you hate what I do."

Her gaze faltered.

"But fleeing from me, stealing our son from me?"

"Would you have let me go?"

"Never."

She opened her mouth, then snapped it shut. Her unspoken words hung in the air. Perhaps she felt she'd had no choice, but she was wrong. She should have stood by him, as Maman always stood by Papa. Perhaps Maman didn't approve of Papa's business. But she'd been loyal. Rae should have loved Julien in spite of it.

Julien kissed the top of his sleeping child's head, reveled in his warmth, the only thing alleviating the pain in his shoulder. "If you were to raise our son, and if you felt you raised him well...if you were to do all the things necessary to teach him right from wrong, and if he still turned out to be more like my side of the family than yours, if he made poor decisions, perhaps broke the law... Would you stop loving him too?"

She frowned. "I..." She blinked twice, and he wondered for a moment if she would defend their child as if nothing but innocence could ever come from him. As if Julien hadn't started out exactly the same way.

Then she chuckled. "If he doesn't end up like your family, maybe he'll end up like mine. My father was a womanizer, and my mother was insane."

He joined her in the laugh, and the moment felt right. Yes, this was why he'd fallen in love with her.

And for all his talk, he knew little Jean-Louis would not be a criminal or insane. Womanizer? Perhaps he had bad genes on both sides of the family where that was concerned. But if anybody could steer him on the right path, Rae could.

Her laugh died. "If I get the chance to raise him, I will love him, no matter what."

"I'm not going to hurt you, Rae."

"Then why the gun?"

"Insurance."

"Which one of us is your insurance policy? You already promised not to hurt Caro and Jean-Louis." She inhaled sharply. "Nate. Is he still...?"

Her look of hope infuriated him.

"You want to know if I spared your lover's life?"

"We're only friends."

"Always?"

She swallowed hard and looked away. "Since before I met you."

"Funny how you didn't mention that when you introduced us."

She looked behind her, as if the man might walk right in. Had Julien done the right thing regarding Rae's friend?

She returned her gaze to him. "Is he still alive?"

"I need a favor."

She blinked and narrowed her eyes. "What favor?"

"Farah has been loyal to me—"

"Speaking of former lovers."

"I..." He tripped over his next words, stuttered, and started over. So unlike him. "How did you know?"

"I'm observant, Julien. The way she talks about you. The way she looks at you."

"Could just be a crush."

"I always wondered, but your reaction proves it."

"That ended long before I met you."

"So I should have told you about Nate, but you—"

"Yes, yes, it's a double standard, but that is what I expected. In fact, I'd have preferred if no man had ever touched you. Were there others?"

Her gaze flicked to the door on his right.

Did she keep her former lovers in the cupboard?

"Nate was the only man I was intimate with before you."

He heard what she hadn't said. "But did you ever love another man?"

Again, her gaze found the closet door.

He looked. "What's in there?"

"It's a pantry. I'm just thinking."

"Is it such a difficult question?"

There was somebody. Unfortunately he didn't have the time to find out who, and even if he did, what could he do about it, in his condition? Still, adrenaline filled his veins, jealousy pumping faster than the blood dripping from his wound.

"So what about Farah?" she asked.

He sighed and forced his dark thoughts away. "She has done everything I asked and more. I need you to vouch for her. Tell them I coerced her. Whatever you have to say to keep her out of prison."

"She helped you find me?"

"Of course. I couldn't have done it without her. So you owe her too."

"Right. Because this is a dream come true. Remind me to send her a thank-you note."

"You do owe her your thanks." Could Rae still not understand the danger she was in? Surely she was not that naive. "If my father had found you first, you'd already be dead."

She whipped around, though no noise could have startled her. "Where is Hector?"

"Promise me you'll keep Farah out of prison."

"What are you going to do?"

"Do I have your promise?"

"I'll protect her, if that's what you want, but you have to tell me your plan. Surely you don't intend to leave me here? And even if you wanted to, how do you plan to get away?"

He ignored her inquisition. "There's a poker chip in my pocket. It's very important..." He pulled in a breath. It was getting harder to breathe. To think.

"Important...?"

"That it stay there. And my identification."

"What are you—?"

"If you would be quiet and listen, please." The words were getting more difficult, the pain fading—but perhaps more than just the pain.

Julien noted the question in Rae's eyes. The concern for him. He would hold onto that. "You will need to find a way to transport me back to Rhode Island." He paused for another deep breath, then coughed and tasted blood. "South of Warwick." He gave her the address of the industrial complex and described its location.

"Why...?"

He held up his hand to stop her question, found he hardly had the energy for that, and let it drop.

"Julien, are you all right?"

"This gun needs to stay with me. There is another one in my jacket pocket. It needs to be with Hector."

She lifted her eyebrows, and he continued.

"They will find Hector's body soon, I think."

She gasped.

"He was working for my father." A pause to catch his breath. "He was never loyal to me."

"What happened?"

"I had no choice. I used his cell to text my father that we were following your trail. Bangkok, I told him."

He watched her reaction. For once, she seemed speechless.

"Papa could spend years looking for you there."

"But why?"

"I know you don't believe me, sweet Rae, but I really do love you. If Papa had never learned of your disappearance..." He hadn't the energy to explain. "Hector told him. I had to stop him."

"Your father wants to kill me?"

"If you are wise, and you are, he will never find you."

"And you're willing to turn yourself in?"

He shook his head, stared at the gun. "I cannot. Papa would find me. I could never stand up to him. I am not nearly as strong as your friend Nate."

"So what are you going to do?"

He wanted to explain the whole plan to her. Desperately needed her to know all he'd done to get them to this point. But he wouldn't last long enough. "There's a flash drive in my pocket." After every phrase, he paused to breathe. "Tell them to say it was sewn into the lining of my jacket. It must be hidden."

"Julien, what's going on? You're sick or hurt or... What can I do?"

"Take the baby."

She stood, but he held his child closer for one moment. His eyes stung as he lifted the baby and settled him on his lap, nearly dropping him. Julien stared into that tiny, innocent face. He'd lost that innocence as a child. But Jean-Louis still had a chance. He leaned forward and kissed his son's cheeks, then his forehead, then his tiny, puckered mouth.

"What did you do to him?"

Julien's gaze found Rae, whose eyes were wide and horrified. He looked back at the child and only then saw what she must have noticed from the start.

"It's not his blood," Julien said.

She snatched the child from him, laid him gently on the kitchen table, and peered beneath his clothes to check for wounds. Jean-Louis's eyes opened, and he scrunched up his face as if to cry.

"It's okay, baby."

His tiny eyes blinked, then closed again. How did Rae do that? It had taken him an hour to get the baby to stop crying.

Seemingly satisfied that Jean-Louis was all right, Rae picked him up and soothed him. "What happened?"

"Hector."

"You need a doctor. I'm calling help."

He lifted the gun. It took all his effort. "Sit down."

She looked at the gun, then at his wound. "You'll bleed to death."

"Sit."

She settled in the chair.

He rested his hand on the table but didn't lay the gun down. She had to hear all of this before it was too late.

"The flash drive contains evidence." Now that Jean-Louis

was gone from his arms, he felt his life dripping away. He shivered. "It will implicate Papa and Geoffrey." A thin breath. "The poker chip will make Papa think Aziz..."

She blinked, shaking her head slightly. Of course she had no idea what he was talking about. He couldn't explain it all.

"He'll think Geoffrey was behind my death. That will make them enemies. With the evidence, when they're not united..." He set the gun on the table and pressed his hand against the wound. He wasn't finished yet.

She started to rise, but he stopped her with a glare.

"Send it to Interpol."

"Why would you bring down your own family."

He was so cold. "Geoffrey betrayed me. Papa... They don't care about you or Jean-Louis. Only money."

"Please let me get you a doctor." Tears pooled in her eyes, the most beautiful thing he'd ever seen. "We'll figure out a way to make it work. You don't have to die."

Yes, she loved him.

That made it worthwhile.

She slipped to the floor at his feet and took his hand with her free one. The baby, held against her shoulder with her other hand, whimpered.

"I don't know what to say," she said.

"Did you ever love me?"

"I did. You, but not..."

Not what he did. "Just protect Farah, and raise our son well."

She nodded. Tears dripped from her cheeks onto their joined hands.

His eyes were drifting closed when he saw movement at the door. He blinked them open, then pushed Rae to the floor as the figure stepped into the room and raised a gun.

SIXTY-SEVEN

Rae cradled Johnny as she tumbled to the floor. She rolled, barely managing to keep the baby's head from hitting the hardwood. She scrambled to a sitting position and turned to confront Julien.

His attention was directed toward the door. Though his face remained placid, she saw a spark of fear in his eyes that terrified her.

From where she'd landed, the table blocked her view of whatever had drawn Julien's attention. Surely Brady and the other policemen wouldn't just walk in like that. But someone was there.

"Farah," Julien said. His focus was on the opening to the living room.

"I will not allow you to do this." Farah spoke in French, and Rae scrambled to translate. The woman's voice, always so kind and gentle before, was filled with vehemence and desperation. "You will not die for her."

"Put the gun down," Julien said.

"You aren't going to shoot me, Julien. You love me, and I you."

Rae couldn't see, but Julien must've pointed his gun at her. He'd killed Hector, his best friend. Would he shoot Farah?

"It's too late for me." Julien responded in English, his voice raspy. "But Rae will make sure you're safe."

"You think I want help from your American whore?"

"Remember your place, *ma cheri*." His words were gentle, his tone commanding.

"You need help. If she loved you, she'd insist on saving you. But she does not love you. Not like I do. Once she's gone, you and I will escape. I'll get you a doctor to tend that wound, and we'll raise Jean-Louis together. We don't need her."

Johnny whimpered, working up to a full cry.

Rae shushed him and peeked beneath the table. She saw Farah's legs as the woman slowly skirted the edge. Another two feet, maybe just one, and Farah would have a clean shot. Rae wrapped her arms around the baby and shifted to shield him from Farah's bullets.

Was Brady listening on the other side of the pantry door? Should Rae call him? Should she push herself further under the table? But then she'd be trapped. At least here, she could try to escape through the kitchen and out the front door. If she could yank open the pantry door...but there wouldn't be enough time.

If she called Brady and he came through that door, Farah might fire at him. Could Rae risk Brady's life in order to save her own?

She patted Johnny's back, willing him to stop crying. This wasn't about saving herself. It was about saving her son.

Julien chuckled, but Rae could hear the strain, the pain in it. "You think I want to be with you? If I'd wanted you, we'd be together."

Farah's feet quit moving. "You told me you cared for me. I know you care for me."

"Don't be stupid," Julien said. "I took what I wanted from you, and then I discarded you."

"No." The woman's voice trembled.

"I kept you around because I knew you'd stay loyal to me."

"You're lying. You love me. You said."

Julien's laugh turned into a cough, then a groan. "How else could I find out if I could trust you?"

"No!" The pitch in Farah's voice rose. "You're lying. You love me, not that whore. You tracked her down to find your son."

"I came for them both,"

"Liar!" Her scream pierced the small room.

Farah lunged around the table.

Rae cradled the baby and waited for the bullet.

Julien threw himself on top of Rae and Johnny. His body was heavy, and it took all her effort not to crush Johnny beneath them both.

A gunshot.

The pantry door slammed open. Another gunshot.

Rae fought to get out from beneath Julien to see what was happening. She was trapped.

Heavy footsteps.

"She's down." Brady's voice. Thank God.

Then someone pulled Julien off her.

"He's hurt." Another voice.

Rae pushed herself to a sitting position, still holding Johnny.

Farah was lying a few feet away. Blood seeped from her forehead. Her eyes stared unseeing at the ceiling.

Nausea rose in Rae's throat.

Someone was screaming. It took her a moment to realize it was Johnny. Rae rocked him. "It's okay, baby. Shh..." She pushed the chair aside to see Julien, who was lying a few feet away surrounded by uniformed men.

In the gap between the people, she saw bright red blood covering the floor beneath her husband. A new wound.

Brady kneeled on the floor beside her. His face was filled with concern. He scanned her shirt, and his eyes widened. "Are you hit?"

"I'm okay."

Brady looked past her, fear in his eyes.

Rae felt a person crouch behind her. She turned to see another uniformed man. The one she'd seen at the police department. He touched her back in a few places before she heard, "No wounds."

"Johnny?" Brady said.

"He's fine. Julien—"

"Bullets can penetrate. Are you sure you're not hit?"

"I'm all right." She looked at the baby, who was screaming, but unharmed. "We're all right. How's Julien?"

Brady turned his attention to her husband, and Rae scrambled around him to see. His eyes were open, and he blinked. He wheezed in a breath, let it out. Blood seeped from his abdomen, bubbled from his lips.

Brady turned to the other cop. "We need an ambulance."

Julien grasped Rae's free hand. "No."

Rae squeezed. "But you're—"

"It's the only way." He wheezed again and looked at Brady. "You can still save them."

Brady looked at Rae. "What's he talking about?"

Julien answered. "Papa will..." A thin breath. "Find her... She'll tell you. Please." His eyes closed, his breathing paused.

Brady leaned closer. "What do you want me to do?" He looked at Rae. "Do you know?"

She rocked her baby and wept. "He doesn't want us to save him."

Brady looked at her, looked at little Johnny, still screaming in her arms. Then he turned his attention back to Julien.

She watched through a haze of tears as Brady checked his pulse, then met Rae's eyes. "I'm sorry."

SIXTY-EIGHT

Police filled the space. Too many. Brady left Rae on the floor beside her husband and found the chief in the living room. "We have to keep this quiet."

The man regarded Brady with narrowed eyes. "We have so far."

Brady studied the cops already in Rae's house, then looked out the open front door at the police cars in the driveway. "We have to make sure nobody talks about what happened here."

They both watched as an ambulance wheeled into the driveway.

Brady turned back to the chief. "Seems our terrorist had a plan. He wanted to protect her. I haven't got the details yet, but I'm sure it'll be better if we don't make it public knowledge that he died here. Not if we want to keep his father from finding Rae."

The chief ran a hand over his nearly bald head, then spoke into his radio. "I need everybody in the front yard, now."

"Don't tell them to keep it quiet," Brady said. "Just give them a story. Prowlers. Kids. Something like that."

The chief nodded. "Okay. I'll tell them we were wrong about it being Moreau, and we're still getting information."

"Thank you." Brady returned to the kitchen and crouched beside Rae, who seemed to be guarding Julien's body. "Can I take the baby?"

She shook her head and held Johnny tighter.

"Okay. Can I help you up? Let's go into the living room."

She looked at him, unsure. Her face had paled, and she looked confused. A moment later, she leaned over her husband's body and kissed his forehead. Brady looked away while she said goodbye. Finally, she leaned back, and he helped her stand.

They walked into the living room as the paramedics entered the kitchen. He eased her onto the sofa, grabbed a blanket, and wrapped it around her.

"Stay here until the paramedics can check on you."

"He didn't hurt me," she said. "He's trying to protect me."

Was, but Brady didn't correct her. "You're in shock. Stay here, okay?"

She rocked Johnny. They both cried.

"Brady, I found something."

He followed the sound to the stairs. Eric was on his way down. "They were tied up in one of the bedrooms."

Nate Boyle and Caro Nolan were behind Eric.

Brady met Nate's eyes. "Thank God."

He nodded to Eric as he passed, then clasped Nate on the shoulder. The man winced.

"Sorry. Are you hurt?" Stupid question. The man's face was more black and blue than not.

Nate turned to Caro, who seemed untouched, then back to Brady. "We survived. How's Rae?"

"She and the baby are fine."

Nate nodded but couldn't seem to speak past the emotion. Brady looked away to give him a minute to rein it in.

Caro reached the landing. Silent tears fell from her eyes, but otherwise she seemed fine. Brady pulled her into a hug and held her tight. After a moment, she pulled away and wiped her tears. "Are my grandparents here?"

"I'll have someone take you to them. Are you hurt?"

She shook her head. "They never touched me."

Brady regarded the girl, her bright red hair and wide eyes. "I'm so glad. You were very brave."

"Not even. I almost peed my pants when that lady walked in."

Lady? Brady would get the whole story soon enough. "But you didn't?"

"Just barely."

"That's better than a lot could have done." He spoke into his radio. "Eric, come back."

The door opened a moment later. Brady asked him to take care of Caro, and the two walked out the front door. Brady turned his attention back to Nate. One of his eyes was swollen shut. His lip was swollen to match. Brady figured there were a lot more wounds beneath the clothes. "You need a paramedic."

Nate shook his head and headed into the living room. He crouched beside Rae.

She looked up from the baby, met Nate's eyes, then leaned onto his shoulder. She didn't speak a word, but she didn't need to.

Nate wrapped his arms around her while Brady propped against the door jamb, arms crossed, and watched. They'd been together, Nate and Rae. Nate had known about Rae's new name. Known all this time where she'd been and what she'd been doing.

On the other hand, Nate had been a friend to her. As jealous as Brady was, he wouldn't begrudge her that friendship. She'd needed it, and God knew she hadn't wanted it from him.

He tuned into their conversation, though he probably should have walked away.

"I'm so sorry," she said. "I never meant to put you in danger."

"You didn't know."

"I shouldn't have called you. I made you a target."

He released her and sat back on his haunches. "I was his only connection to your former life. Whether you called me or not, I was in their crosshairs. There's nothing you could have done."

"I should have known."

"There was no way you could have, Rae." He smoothed her hair. "You fell in love with the wrong guy. I don't blame you."

She looked at Johnny, then back at Nate. "You've always been too good to me."

He shrugged and glanced at Brady.

Brady shifted his gaze away until he heard Nate talking to Rae again. "I need to tell Brady what I know. You okay?"

"I will be." She grabbed his hand. "Thank you, Nate. I owe you."

"Nothing." He stood and returned to Brady. "Let's go outside."

"All right." He looked at Rae. "Wait for the paramedics, okay?"

She nodded, and Brady led Nate out the front door. They passed the police officers, who were crowded around the chief. Caro was sitting on a stretcher, talking on the phone, smiling through her tears. Brady led Nate halfway down the driveway, where they could speak privately. He pulled his cell phone from his pocket.

"First, call your father."

"You need to hear what I know."

"Just tell him you're alive, okay? And nothing else."

Nate grabbed the phone, dialed his father, and walked away. Brady stared at the scene in front of Rae's house and remembered that awful day the police had come to reclaim the kidnapped baby so many years before. He'd held Rae's hand while the chief—Officer Jamison back then—had handcuffed her mother and settled her into the backseat of the cruiser.

And now this. He prayed this house had seen the end of its place in crime drama.

Nate returned, eyes red, and handed Brady the phone. "They snatched me Friday morning right outside my house."

Brady listened to the story with horror and respect for this man who'd risked everything to protect Reagan.

"But when they blew up that coffee shop in New York," Nate said, "I saw the lengths Hector was willing to go to find her. It was one thing for me to get hurt, but I was already thinking I was going to have to tell them where she was. Rae wouldn't want those people to die to protect her."

"Hector? Not Julien?"

"Julien lost his lunch when he saw it on the news. He had no idea what Hector'd been planning. He knew it was bad, though. He had the chance to stop it and chose not to. I think he'd have done anything to get Rae back."

Brady watched the paramedics as they carried Julien's body from the house. "The bombing—that was the last straw for Rae too. She was planning to go back to him."

"Thank God she didn't. I don't know everything, but I'm pretty sure Julien's father would have killed her."

"If Julien didn't first," Brady said.

Nate shook his head. "Julien wouldn't have hurt her." He looked around at the display of police cars, ambulances, and fire trucks. "He wanted her to survive."

Brady let that nugget of information settle in. In his own

demented way, the man had loved Rae. What did that mean for them?

"So I heard a little of what he told Rae, but why don't you tell me what you know of his plan?" Brady asked. "How do I protect her from Alejandro Moreau?"

"First, you need to come up with a plausible story. You need to keep Julien's name out of the news and far from here."

"We're working on that."

"Moreau has an enemy, a terrorist working mostly in Northern Africa. Name's Aziz. Apparently, whenever that guy assassinates someone, he leaves a poker chip on the body. It's his calling card. Julien knew he was going to die. At some point today, he seemed to stop trying to figure out how to get her home. I think he decided he'd just let himself die. After he sent Farah after Caro and the baby, he told me the plan, because he wanted me to make sure someone would do it. He'd left a poker chip on Hector's body, and he has one in his pocket. He wanted his father to believe Aziz killed him."

"And that takes the pressure off Rae how?"

"Julien used Hector's phone to text his father, throw him off her track. Hector had been checking in often. Alejandro will be looking for her in Asia."

"So why the poker chip?"

"Because Julien's brother was working with this Aziz guy, so their father will think it was Geoffrey, his brother, who was behind Julien's murder. That'll pit father against son. Divide the empire."

Brady considered that. "So if the father and brother are working against each other, maybe the evidence Rae brought—"

"Coupled with the flash drive Julien has, Interpol should be able to mount a case against them. And if they're working against each other..."

"They could bring down the entire empire."

"Bingo."

Brady stared off into the trees, nodding slowly. "Wow. This is..." Bringing down an international crime family. That ought to land him the chief's job.

Funny. He didn't really care. As long as Rae was safe, Brady would take whatever job the department had for him. Heck, he'd wait tables in the diner as long as Rae was safe.

He looked back at Nate. "What about the woman? Farah?"

"She seemed so sweet. That other cop told me she shot Julien."

The memory came before Brady was able to stop it.

He'd been listening behind the pantry door. Much of it had been muffled at the end, but from what he could piece together, it had seemed like they weren't going to have to rescue Rae after all. Julien was going to let himself die, and it seemed he wanted her to survive. As Brady had breathed a sigh of relief, a new voice joined the conversation. He could barely make out her words, especially over the baby's crying, but he clearly heard Julien's when he'd said, "Put the gun down."

Brady had turned the knob then. The woman's scream had him through the door an instant too late. If Julien hadn't thrown himself on top of Rae, Farah's bullet would have hit her. Maybe killed her. Or Johnny.

Brady had been too late to stop Farah's bullet, but not too late to stop the woman for good.

He'd fired off the shot before she could fire a second. If he hadn't been there, would Farah have slaughtered them all?

He never thought he'd owe Julien Moreau a debt of gratitude, but the man had saved Rae's life.

"I couldn't hear what Farah was saying through the door," Brady said. "Do you know?"

"What door?"

Brady shook his head. "Never mind. Do you know what she was doing?"

"No idea. I just know she left us tied to Rae's grandmother's bed, and I assume she crept downstairs to hear what was going on. And then we heard gunshots."

Maybe Rae could shed some light, though at this point, it didn't really matter. The official report couldn't have any of these details. "Anything else I need to know?"

"I'm sure I'll think of something."

"Thank you. For protecting her."

Nate nodded once. "Did she tell you about her and me?"

He swallowed hard, kept his voice even. "She did."

"It was a long time ago, after you two broke up."

"I know."

"I cared for her."

Brady said nothing. What was there to say?

"But her heart always belonged to you." Nate lifted the eyebrow over the only eye he could open. "You two are back together?"

"Does that bother you?"

Nate chuckled, then winced. "I think I've had just about as much of Reagan McAdams as I can handle in this lifetime."

Brady felt the first real smile since the whole thing had begun. "She can be a little high-maintenance."

"You said it."

"When we found out Julien had you, we thought you were a goner."

"You and me both."

Brady nodded toward the ambulance. "Let the paramedics take a look at you." He held out his hand, and Nate shook it. "Thank you."

Nate looked around. "Biggest story of my life, and I can't report it."

"You sorry about that?"

"Not a bit." He walked toward the ambulance, where a paramedic situated him on a gurney. Brady figured Nate might've argued if he hadn't been so tired he was about to drop.

He turned to see the chief waiting on the porch for him. Brady approached and filled him in on Moreau's plan.

"Okay," the chief said. "I'll contact the FBI. I'm sure they'll be happy to take over if we turn over all the evidence."

"So much for my big collar," Brady said.

The chief clasped him on the shoulder. "It might not be official, but I know about it."

"They're safe. That's all I care about."

Jamison squeezed his shoulder. "Go on in and check on them. We'll figure the rest out later."

SIXTY-NINE

Brady passed Rae's house on his way to work Friday morning. Less than a week had passed since Julien's death. Brady'd spent most of that time battling between the FBI and Interpol, debriefing, and trying to protect Rae from some of it. They'd grilled her more than he liked. Seemed Interpol was confident that between the files Rae gave them and the evidence Julien supplied, they would be able to bring down the entire operation. Still, Brady's primary concern was keeping Rae safe.

So far, the truth about what happened that day at her house hadn't leaked. Most of the townspeople believed the story Brady'd given the reporter at the local paper that a couple of kids looking for trouble happened upon the McAdams house. They'd invaded, taking Caro and the baby hostage. The police had snuck in and arrested the perpetrators. The story was that the intruders were under eighteen, so he'd refused to release their names or the details about who they were. The reporter from the *Gazette* was, of course, skeptical, but everybody involved was toeing the line. Trent, the kid who'd given Moreau Rae's location, and Finn had agreed to keep the story quiet in exchange for community service. If either of them leaked it, felony charges would be filed. Nearly a week had passed, and the story was already fading away. And with it, Brady hoped, the truth about what had really happened that day.

Unfortunately, other things about the situation were also fading away. And though Brady was glad Rae was safe, he wasn't sure what that meant for him. For them.

Would there be a *them*?

He turned into the parking lot of the police department.

His feelings for Rae hadn't changed in fifteen years. But her feelings for him? Brady had no idea where he stood. He could picture the way she'd clung to her husband's body, kissed him goodbye. She'd loved the man, and now she was grieving for him.

Where did that leave Brady?

He'd just stepped into the squad room when he heard Chief Jamison's voice. "In here, Thomas."

He beelined for the chief's office and paused in the doorway. "You need something?"

"Have a seat."

Brady sat in the worn leather chair across from the chief's desk and regarded the older man. His head was bent over paperwork on his desk. His buzz cut looked fresh, and Brady could see the sunburn on his scalp. He made a mental note to buy the chief a fishing hat.

Finally, Jamison looked up. "You back today, or are you meeting the feds again?"

"They're done with me for now."

"Good to hear." The chief tapped his pencil on the desk, and Brady braced himself. "So we need to talk about that Farah Hanachi woman."

Brady forced his face to remain impassive but lowered his hands to his lap. No need to let the chief see the tremble that came back whenever he thought of that moment. "Feds managed her too. Officially, she was found with Moreau and his goon. They even got another poker chip to make it look authentic."

Jamison ran his hand over his scalp. "You've never killed anybody in the line of duty before."

Brady sat back in his chair and swallowed. "Not as a cop. But when I was in the service—"

The chief waved that away. "It's different."

He shrugged, but he disagreed. It was the same. Both were terrible.

"You doing all right?"

"I saw the shrink."

"You going back?"

"Have to until he releases me." And needed to, but he didn't say that. Because maybe he hadn't had a choice about killing her. Maybe Farah Hanachi hadn't left him one, but it was still hard to come to grips with sending another human to meet her maker.

"A woman," the chief said.

"Yeah."

"But you did it, Brady. I wasn't sure you had it in you."

"It was her or Reagan. Didn't have much of a choice."

The chief's eyebrows lifted. "Still..."

"I'm handling it." He hadn't meant to sound so frustrated.

Jamison regarded him a moment, then nodded once. "Good. Let me know if you want to talk about it."

"Sure."

"Aside from the situation with the feds," Jamison continued, "it's been a quiet week."

"I talked with Finn and Trent. They know nothing about the other break-ins, so it looks like they're not connected to the burglaries by the lake. I think we need to talk with the folks who live on the lake year-round, see if they can get a neighborhood watch going. And increase police presence. If we can't catch them, maybe we can at least get them to move into someone else's jurisdiction."

Jamison smiled. "Spoken like a true chief."

Chief? His face must've registered his surprise, because the man laughed.

"Talked to the town council, and they're on board with offering you the position."

Looked like he'd be getting the job he wanted after all. At one point, it had been all he'd wanted. Now, he could barely muster a smile.

"I'll stay on 'til after the holidays," Jamison said. "You and I can spend the next few months getting you up to speed. Then come January first, I'm retiring."

"I won't let you down."

The chief stood. "See that you don't." He looked beyond Brady, then met his eyes. "Keep it quiet for now. We'll announce it in a few weeks. Let all this die down first."

"Works for me."

"Why don't you take the rest of the day off? You could use the rest."

Brady thought of the many messages on his phone and shook his head. "I'll rest next week. Today, I need to finish this stuff up."

The chief shrugged. "Suit yourself." He came around the desk and shook Brady's hand. "The town's a better place since you came back. Congratulations on the new job."

Brady swallowed an unexpected lump of emotion. "Thank you for trusting me with it."

SEVENTY

Rae held Johnny and stood beside her car, staring at McNeal's. It was one of those crisp New Hampshire days. Deep blue sky, a cold breeze carrying the scent of ripe apples and a faraway wood fire. It was too bright outside to see inside the windows. What kind of reception would she get when she walked in? She hadn't been into McNeal's since she was a kid, and back then she'd felt like such an outsider she couldn't wait to leave. The stares, the snickers. Even Gram had understood. After her mother's arrest, they'd never gone back.

But this was where her friends were congregating, and she'd been invited. Samantha had called and said everybody wanted her to come. Who was *everybody*, and why did they care? They'd never cared about her before.

Or had they, and she just hadn't understood?

She shouldn't be so nervous. But it wasn't just facing the townspeople of Nutfield that had her standing there, quivering in her boots. The Boyles were in there. This would be the first time she'd seen them since she'd almost gotten Nate killed.

She heard tires and turned to see a white Isuzu Trooper park behind her Accord. Rae'd spent a lot of time with her best friend in the week since the incident. Samantha'd arrived at the house before the police left that day, offering her support. When Rae hadn't been able to talk for the emotion, Samantha'd sat beside her silently. Probably praying. She seemed to do a lot of that. Rae certainly wasn't going to complain. Here she was, alive and well. Maybe there was something to it.

Samantha had listened to Rae's stories, held her when she'd cried for her late husband, and understood. Julien hadn't been the saint Rae had first thought, nor was he the monster she'd come to imagine. He'd somehow been both—and neither. Maybe she'd never truly known the man who was the father of her son. The man who'd died to protect her and Johnny.

Samantha joined her on the sidewalk. "I took care of the death certificate."

"Oh. Thank you. I didn't think of that."

"No problem." She scanned the cars lining the street. "I don't see Brady's truck. Is he here?"

"No idea. He's been busy."

"You two still haven't talked?"

Rae shrugged and stared toward the police station.

"He's giving you space," Sam said.

"I don't need space."

Samantha shook her head. "Julien was your husband, Rae. Maybe not on paper, but still..."

"What does that have to do with Brady?"

"Don't you think he wonders where your heart is now?"

Rae started to protest, then stopped herself. Did Brady doubt her devotion? "Maybe you're right."

"Where is your heart?"

Rae smiled and kissed Johnny's little head. "It's right here."

Samantha nodded toward the door. "Good. Then let's go. I'm starved." She led the way across the street, pushed open the door like it was no big deal, and stepped inside.

A few heads turned. People smiled. Gordon's wife, Ellen, crossed the space to meet them at the door. She gave Sam a quick hug, then turned to Rae. "We're so glad you came." She grabbed Johnny's little fist. "He's adorable. Can I hold him?"

Rae handed Ellen the baby as Gordon approached. He peered at the infant, then turned to Rae. "Glad you made it."

Rae'd been practicing her speech for hours. She looked around to make sure nobody could overhear. Then she swallowed hard and took a deep breath. "I'm so sorry for everything I put you through. I put Nate in danger when I introduced him to Julien. I made him a target. And though I didn't do any of it on purpose, it still hurt him, and you. I hope you can forgive me."

Gordon's smile vanished, and he shook his head. "There's nothing to forgive."

"There is. If I had just been honest..."

"We love you, Rae." Ellen shifted the baby to her shoulder and patted his back. "Nate is safe. You're safe. We're just glad to have you home."

"But—"

"I told you she'd blame herself." Nate hobbled across the small entry, smiling at her.

Ellen stepped aside so he could join their small circle. The swelling in his face had gone down, and his bruises had faded to a brownish-yellow. He walked stiffly, thanks to the broken ribs. But he was standing upright.

"You have to stop, Reagan." Gordon's voice was commanding, like her own father's would have been, if he'd been here. "Your father's death, your mother's choices, Julien's lifestyle. None of those things are your fault."

"Well, no."

"You don't have nearly as much power as you think."

She started to protest. Then she looked at Samantha, Nate, Ellen, and Gordon, saw their smiles and their concern. Four people who'd always stood by her, and always would. "That's a good way to look at it."

"The only way," Gordon said. "My only complaint is that you still haven't come by to talk about your grandmother's estate. Can I pencil you in for Monday?"

"I'll be there."

"Good. Now I'm starved. Come on. We've got the big booth in the back. Great view of the TV." He turned as if the conversation were settled. And perhaps it was.

She and Samantha followed the Boyles. The restaurant was not the dive she remembered from her youth. It was larger, for one thing. They must've bought out the place next door and expanded. The old wood paneling had been torn out, the walls painted a sage green and decorated with sports paraphernalia—mostly professional teams, but a few photographs of the Nutfield Squirrels teams joined the rest. The bar was still there, its dark stain brighter than before. Booths lined the walls, and round tables filled the center of the room. It was cheerful and packed with people.

Gordon weaved among the tables toward the back. They passed one, and Rae smiled at the picture there. Caro and Finn were sitting side by side, perhaps a little too close, deep in conversation. Caro pushed her bright red hair behind her ear, and Rae caught the blush on her cheeks.

A young woman sipped a soda beside Caro. The girls looked so much alike, this had to be Laurie, her sister. She whispered something in Caro's ear, and the younger girl tore her attention away from Finn, followed her sister's gaze, and giggled.

An older couple filled the other two seats at the round table. Must be Caro's grandparents. The woman looked uncomfortable, but the man was having an animated conversation with an older gentleman sitting at a booth across the aisle. Oh, it was Mr. Young, the janitor from the high school. Though *young* didn't quite describe him anymore. The white-haired Mrs. Young, Rae's former English teacher, sat beside him chatting with a woman Rae didn't recognize and sipping from a bottle of beer.

There was a picture you didn't see every day.

Eric, the police officer Brady worked with, was standing beside another man behind the Youngs' table, watching the Patriots on the TV mounted over the bar. More people were watching the game, talking. Every seat in the place seemed taken. Some turned when she walked by. Some stood to greet her with a hug, others just waved hello as if she'd never left. Rae greeted neighbors she'd known since forever and friends from school she hadn't seen in years. People she'd never met but who acted like friends already. They welcomed her as if she were one of them.

After everything, could she be one of them? All the ambitions she'd had when she lived here, and now all she wanted was to stay and make a home.

They reached the large, circular booth, but Rae couldn't sit down. Too overwhelmed or overjoyed or something. The Boyles slid in, but Samantha caught her eye. "We can stand, if you want."

"That'd be good." She caught Ellen's eye. "Want me to take Johnny?"

"Not a chance, sister."

Rae laughed. "Just let me know."

Samantha leaned in. "You'll be lucky to get your baby back at all today."

Rae started to join the laughter, then froze.

Chief Jamison walked in the door. Brady was right behind him. He saw her, said something to the chief, and then maneuvered through the packed room to meet her. "How you doing?"

He was close enough to touch, and she almost did. "I didn't see your truck."

"I parked it at the station."

She stepped closer. "I'm glad to see you."

"Yeah?" He looked...hopeful. All her anxiety melted away. Silly man.

She turned to the table, saw that Johnny seemed content in Ellen's arms, and turned back to Brady. "Can we talk?"

"Sure." He looked around, then led the way through the crowd and out the door onto the sidewalk.

The trees towered over the street, their leaves just starting to turn. Another couple of weeks and they'd explode in color. And she'd be there to see it. The thought made her eyes sting with tears. She walked down the sidewalk slowly, taking in the view of this town she'd always refused to love. But she could now.

The Patriots must've done something right, because a roar came from the restaurant. She smiled and headed for a bench in front of a T-shirt shop. She leaned against the back of it, and Brady stood across from her.

"Where've you been?" she asked.

"Trying to work out all the details."

"And?"

"Officially, they found all three bodies in Rhode Island, all with poker chips. The FBI's gotten Interpol involved. They'll inform Alejandro tomorrow."

"And the evidence?"

"Turned it over to the FBI. They're working with Interpol. I'm sure there're all sorts of jurisdictional issues, squabbling over who gets credit, but from what I saw, it looks like it could indeed take down the whole enterprise."

"Wow."

Julien hadn't been able to do much good in life, though their son was the exception. But he had accomplished plenty in death, not just saving her but helping to put an end to his father's criminal activity. Someone else would step in and take over. She'd investigated enough criminals to know there was always someone new waiting in the wings. But to bring down one operation, there was satisfaction there.

"You were right about Julien," Brady said. "Nate said he was horrified at the bombings."

"I wasn't right about him. He was a terrorist, a killer. The man I knew though—the man he showed himself to be..." She pictured his smile, remembered his easy laughter. "I'd hate to think I'm that bad a judge of character."

Brady nodded and stared beyond her.

"Doesn't change anything," she said.

He glanced at her, and she saw pain in his eyes.

She took his hand. "Brady?"

He looked at their joined hands, then at her. "You don't have to..." He swallowed and looked away. "We said some things. You were under a lot of pressure. You thought he was going to kill you. You thought you were going to have to disappear forever. It's hard to think straight under those circumstances. And maybe you didn't mean..." He met her eyes, though it seemed to take considerable effort. "That day when I offered to go with you, you said you didn't want me, but I didn't believe you. I should have. And now that you're safe, you're probably going to go back to...wherever."

She took his other hand. "I'm not going anywhere."

His eyebrows lifted. "No?"

"Not unless you are."

He smiled slowly. "Nutfield is my home, Rae. I'd prefer to stay."

"It's my home too. I didn't realize it until a few days ago. This is where I belong." She quieted, listened to the voices coming through the restaurant door, and smiled. "All these years, I thought I had to do it alone. That I couldn't count on anybody. That nobody was on my side. But then you, and all the police, and the whole town—you saved me. This is my home." She tipped her head toward the restaurant. "Those are my people."

He squeezed her hands. "I'm glad you finally figured that out. You belong here. But you and me... I wasn't sure. I mean, your husband just died."

"I am grieving. I'm grieving his death, and I'm grieving the man he could have been. But even before I discovered that Julien and I weren't legally married, I'd quit thinking of him as my husband. I hadn't loved him in a long time."

Brady let go of her hands and wrapped his arms around her waist. He pulled her close, rested his cheek against her temple, and whispered, "That's good, because I've been thinking of you the way a man ought not to think of another man's wife."

The husky promise in his words made her shiver. She shifted, and he met her lips with his own. The kiss tasted like forever.

EPILOGUE

Rae read the story one last time. It wasn't the deep, investigative journalism she'd become accustomed to, but she'd managed to make the local Thanksgiving Day parade sound pretty amazing. She hit send, and a moment later received a reply from the editor at the *Nutfield Gazette*.

Great job. Enjoy the rest of your day.

She smiled and closed her laptop, then headed into the kitchen. The scent of the roasting turkey brought memories of so many holidays in this house. She could imagine Gram basting the bird, then sprinkling more salt and pepper, rosemary and thyme. She pushed away the tears. Her grandmother wouldn't want her to spend this Thanksgiving grieving.

Brady stood from the kitchen table. "Finish your story?"

"Just now."

He opened the oven door, and she gave him a look that had him closing it again.

"Gram always said you need to leave it alone or else it'll dry out."

Brady pulled her into his arms. "I just wanted a nibble."

"You'll have to wait until dinner."

He brushed her hair aside and kissed her neck. "How about I nibble the cook instead?"

She tingled down to her toes. "Hmm...that seems like a fair compromise."

A clearing throat had them stepping apart, and Rae giggled. "I guess you'll have to wait on that too."

Brady growled as Caro stepped into the room, Johnny on her hip. The baby saw Rae and broke into his joyful smile.

She'd never seen anything so beautiful.

She reached for Johnny, but Caro held him closer. "Not yet. Once Nana gets here, she won't put him down."

Rae needed to set the table, anyway. "Can you change his clothes? I left that new outfit on his changing table."

"Sure!" She disappeared toward the stairs, and Rae turned back to Brady.

"Can you get the dishes out of the breakfront for me?"

"How many?"

"Let's see." She tapped her finger against her chin and counted. "You, me, Caro and her grandparents. Sam, Gordon, Ellen, Finn, and Nate."

"Ten?" He looked seriously concerned. "I hope we have enough turkey."

"There'll be plenty."

His eyebrows lifted, skeptical.

"Ellen's bringing another one."

"Oh, thank God."

She swatted his arm. "Start setting the table, mister."

He did as he was told while she pulled the potatoes from the pantry. She'd explored the tunnel that led to the barn, amazed that she'd never discovered it in all her years in the house. She'd have to find out how Finn and his friend had done it. Now that they were off the hook for breaking into her house, maybe Finn would tell her what else they'd found. She'd ply him with pie, see if that did it.

But there was no rush. She had the rest of her life to figure out all of her house's secrets. She could still hear her father's voice, the stories he used to tell about this place. She'd figured they were all make-believe until she saw that tunnel to the barn. Now, she wasn't so sure.

Dad had told her stories of secret passageways and hidden compartments, the inventions of one of his ancestors, cobbled together to fill the time and feed his imagination. If only Dad were here now to help her find them all.

Caro was coming down the stairs, and Rae froze when the third step from the bottom creaked.

"No way," she said.

Brady paused, his hand in the silverware drawer, and looked at her. "What?"

"Could it be that simple?"

He closed the drawer. "What are we talking about?"

She set the potatoes on the counter and walked to the staircase, wiping her hands on her apron.

Caro, halfway to the living room, turned to see. "What's going on?"

Brady answered. "Rae's lost her mind, I think."

"It was just a matter of time," Caro said.

Rae kneeled on the first step and studied the third. She could remember the conversation she'd had with her father all those years ago. She could see the shining gold pieces as he showed them to her, the box they'd sat in.

They'd been standing right here.

She placed her fingers under the third step and pulled up. She felt the nails slip just enough to confirm her suspicions.

"Rae," Brady said, "what are you—?"

"I need to get this up."

"Let me help. You're going to ruin your ring."

She glanced at the solitaire diamond Brady had given her a month before. It was perfect. Simple. Just what she'd always wanted from the man she'd always loved.

She sat back. "Get me a pry bar or something."

He kneeled beside her. "What is it?"

"Can you lift this? I think we need a crowbar or..."

Her words trailed off as Brady pulled the step up. The nails creaked against the wood and filled the silent space. Even Johnny was quiet as they watched.

The wood lifted, and Brady set it aside.

There, in the hollow space, was her father's box.

Rae pulled it out and wiped the thick layer of dust from the top.

"Is that what I think it is?" Brady asked.

She lifted the lid, and there inside lay perfect rows of gold coins. Rae pulled one out, removed it from its plastic sleeve, and laid it on her palm.

"Holy cow," Caro said.

Her father's final gift had been there all along. Funny that she couldn't care less about the money now. Maybe it would fund Johnny's education. Or maybe they'd find another use for it. But it wasn't about the money.

Brady closed her fingers over the gold coin. "How did you figure it out?"

She shrugged. "I don't know. I was thinking about Daddy, and then Caro made the step creak, and it just came to me."

He grinned at her. "Another secret exposed."

She looked at Caro and Johnny, then at Brady. "Imagine if I'd found it before? I'd have left."

His frown told her what he thought of that. "And now?"

"Now, there's no place I'd rather be than right here. With you."

He leaned in and kissed her. "Welcome home."

The End

If you liked Rae and Brady's story, you won't want to miss the adventure their friend Nate and his beautiful old friend, Marisa, get into in *Twisted Lies*.

She thought they'd never find her...
Marisa Vega's life as an adoptive mom in a tiny Mexican village isn't what she'd dreamed while growing up in New York, but as the target of a man who's convinced she stole millions from him, hiding is her only way to stay alive. When her daughter Ana is snatched and held for ransom, Marisa must discover who really stole the money in order to rescue her.

He swore he'd never play the hero again.
Months after being kidnapped, tortured, and left with PTSD, Nate Boyle is ready to live a quiet life in rural New Hampshire. When the source of his breakout newspaper article—and the woman who haunts his dreams—begs for help, he gets pulled into a riddle that's proved unsolvable for nearly a decade.

Can Nate and Marisa unravel the years-old mystery and bring her daughter home?

Download *Twisted Lies* today.

ALSO BY ROBIN PATCHEN

The Coventry Saga

Glimmer in the Darkness: Part of the Dangerous Deceptions Boxset

The Nutfield Saga

Convenient Lies

Twisted Lies

Generous Lies

Innocent Lies

Beauty in Flight

Beauty in Hiding

Beauty in Battle

Legacy Rejected

Legacy Restored

Legacy Reclaimed

Legacy Redeemed

Amanda Series

Chasing Amanda

Finding Amanda

Standalone Novellas

A Package Deal

One Christmas Eve

Faith House

ABOUT THE AUTHOR

Aside from her family and her Savior, Robin Patchen has two loves—writing and traveling. If she could combine them, she'd spend a lot of time sitting in front of her laptop at sidewalk cafes and ski lodges and beachside burger joints. She'd visit every place in the entire world—twice, if possible—and craft stories and tell people about her Savior. Alas, time is too short and money is too scarce for Robin to traipse all over the globe, even if her husband and kids wanted to go with her. So she stays home, shares the Good News when she can, and writes to illustrate the unending grace of God through the power and magic of story.

Copyright © 2016 by Robin Patchen

All rights reserved.

No part of this book may be reproduced in any form or by any electronic or mechanical means, including information storage and retrieval systems, without written permission from the author, except for the use of brief quotations in a book review.

Seedlings Design.